of

L PHENOMENA

A *New York Times Book Review* Notable Book of the Year
*Washington Post* Bestseller
NPR Bestseller
A #1 Indie Next Pick
A Barnes & Noble Discover Great New Writers Pick
A *Christian Science Monitor* Best Book of the Year
An Amazon.com Best Book of the Year
A *Publishers Weekly* Top 10 Book of the Year
A *Kirkus Reviews* Best Book of the Year
A *Library Journal* Top 10 Book of the Year

"A flash in the heavens that makes you look up and believe in miracles.... Here, in fresh, graceful prose, is a profound story that dares to be as tender as it is ghastly, a story about desperate lives in a remote land that will quickly seem impossibly close and important.... I haven't been so overwhelmed by a novel in years. At the risk of raising your expectations too high, I have to say you simply must read this book."

—Ron Charles, *Washington Post*

"Over and over again, this is an examination of the ways in which many broken pieces come together to make a new whole. In exquisite imagery, Marra tends carefully to the twisted strands of grace and tragedy.... Everything in *A Constellation of Vital Phenomena*...is dignified with a hoping, aching heartbeat."

—Ramona Ausubel, *San Francisco Chronicle*

"Marra is a brisk and able storyteller, and he moves deftly between a number of characters who are drawn into contact by the war.... The writing is vivid throughout."

—*The New Yorker*

"A powerful tale . . . rivals anything Michael Ondaatje has written in its emotional force. . . . There are many reasons to read *A Constellation of Vital Phenomena* . . . to marvel at the lack of fear in a writer so young. To read a book that can bring tears to your eyes and force laughter from your lungs. . . . But the one I kept returning to, the best reason to read this novel, is that this story reminds us how senseless killing often wrenches kindness through extreme circumstances."

—John Freeman, *Boston Globe*

"Many people can write beautifully, but few manage to create a whole that is more valuable than the sum of its parts. Marra does this in spades. It is a brilliant book."

—Ann Patchett, *New York Times* bestselling author of *State of Wonder*

"Remarkable . . . Comparisons to Tea Obreht's *The Tiger's Wife*, set in the Balkans, are inevitable. While Marra shares Obreht's belief in the power of story to temper suffering, he's more focused on exploring how the trauma of war bares a person's character, for better or worse."

—*Plain Dealer*

"The most moving book I've read in years . . . A timeless tragedy about the victims of war."

—*Washingtonian*

"Marra is not looking to explain the inexplicable. He's not laying out politics, his book does not run on fear or horror. He is, in capturing the experiences that form lives, telling what feels like a very real story set in Chechnya."

—*Denver Post*

"With remarkable pathos and a surprising amount of humor, Marra keeps the focus on the relationships, struggles, and tiny triumphs of an unforgettable group of characters. . . . Marra creates a specific and riveting world around his characters, expertly revealing the unexpected connections among them. . . . This novel, full of humanity and hope, ultimately leaves you uplifted. *Constellation* deserves to be on the short list for every major award. It's an absolute masterpiece."

—Sarah Jessica Parker for *Entertainment Weekly*

"Excellent . . . [A] grave, complex, elegant exploration of how war and occupation warp the human psyche."

—*New York* magazine

"Marra is trying to capture some essence of the lives of men and women caught in the pincers of a brutal, decade-long war, and at this he succeeds beautifully. . . . His storytelling impulses are fed by wellsprings of generosity. . . . [The] ending is almost certain to leave you choked up and, briefly at least, transformed by tenderness."

—Sam Sacks, *Wall Street Journal*

"A book of violence and beauty, and the undisputed arrival of a major new literary talent."

—*Globe and Mail*

"Powerful, convincing, beautifully realized—it's hard to believe that *A Constellation of Vital Phenomena* is a first novel. Anthony Marra is a writer to watch and savor."

—T. C. Boyle, *New York Times* bestselling author of *When the Killing's Done* and *The Women*

"Both devastating and transcendent. The story of eight people (and a nation) navigating two brutal wars, it's a novel of loyalty and sacrifice and enduring love. You'll finish it transformed."

—Maile Meloy, author of *Both Ways Is the Only Way I Want It*

"Anthony Marra's fine debut novel reaches tenderly, unflinchingly, into the center of the Chechen conflict of the late 1990s. This tale has its roots in shocking brutality, and its beauty in the human redemption that can come from unaccountable human kindness. . . . A richly layered and deeply beautiful journey."

—Vincent Lam, author of *The Headmaster's Wager*

# A
# CONSTELLATION
## *of* VITAL
# PHENOMENA

# A
# CONSTELLATION
## of VITAL
# PHENOMENA

A NOVEL

ANTHONY MARRA

HOGARTH

LONDON   NEW YORK

Copyright © 2013 by Anthony Marra
Reader's Guide and Author Q&A copyright © 2014 by Random House LLC

All rights reserved.
Published in the United States by Hogarth, an imprint of the Crown Publishing Group,
a division of Random House LLC, a Penguin Random House Company, New York.
www.crownpublishing.com

HOGARTH and the H colophon are trademarks of Random House LLC.
"Extra Libris" and the accompanying colophon are trademarks of Random House LLC.

Originally published in hardcover in the United States by Hogarth,
an imprint of the Crown Publishing Group,
a division of Random House LLC, New York, in 2013.

Library of Congress Cataloging-in-Publication Data

Marra, Anthony.
A constellation of vital phenomena : a novel / Anthony Marra.
        p.       cm.
1. Chechnia (Russia)—History—Civil War, 1994—Fiction. 2. Women physicians—
Fiction. 3. Hospitals—Russia—Fiction. I. Title.
PS3613.A768726C66    2013
813'.6—dc23
2012017444

ISBN 978-0-7704-3642-1
eBook ISBN 978-0-7704-3641-4

Printed in the United States of America

Book design by Maria Elias
Cover design by Christopher Brand
Cover photographs: Peter Starman/Photodisc/Getty Images (suitcase),
Lynn James/Photonica/Getty Images (snow), Jan Fassbender/Gallery Stock (trees)

7   9   10   8

First Paperback Edition

*To my parents and sister*

It was of this death that I was reminded by the crushed
thistle in the midst of the plowed field.

—Leo Tolstoy, *Hadji Murád*

# A
# CONSTELLATION
## of VITAL
# PHENOMENA

# THE FIRST AND SECOND DAYS

CHAPTER

I

ON THE MORNING after the Feds burned down her house and took her father, Havaa woke from dreams of sea anemones. While the girl dressed, Akhmed, who hadn't slept at all, paced outside the bedroom door, watching the sky brighten on the other side of the window glass; the rising sun had never before made him feel late. When she emerged from the bedroom, looking older than her eight years, he took her suitcase and she followed him out the front door. He had led the girl to the middle of the street before he raised his eyes to what had been her house. "Havaa, we should go," he said, but neither moved.

The snow softened around their boots as they stared across the street to the wide patch of flattened ash. A few orange embers hissed in pools of gray snow, but all else was char. Not seven years earlier, Akhmed had helped Dokka build an addition so the girl would have a room of her own. He had drawn the blueprints and chopped the hardwood and cut it into boards and turned them into a room; and when Dokka had promised to help him build an addition to his own house, should he ever have a child, Akhmed had thanked his friend and walked home, the knot in his throat unraveling into a sob when the door closed behind him. Carrying that lumber the forty meters from the forest had left his knuckles blistered, his underarms sopping, but now a few hours of flames had lifted what had taken him months to design, weeks to carry, days to build, all but the nails and rivets, all but the hinges and bolts, all into the sky. And too were carried the small treasures that had made Dokka's house his own. There was the hand-carved chess set on a round side-table; when moved, the squat white king wobbled from side to side, like a man just sober enough to stand, and Dokka had named his majesty Boris Yeltsin. There was the porcelain vase adorned with Persian arabesques, and beside that a cassette deck–radio with an antenna long enough to scrape the ceiling when propped up on a telephone book, yet too short to reach anything but static. There was the eighty-five-year-old Qur'an, the purple cover writhing with calligraphy, that Dokka's grandfather had purchased in Mecca. There were these things and the flames ate these things, and since fire doesn't distinguish between the word of God and the word of the Soviet Communications Registry Bureau, both Qur'an and telephone directory returned to His mouth in the same inhalation of smoke.

The girl's fingers braceleted his wrist. He wanted to throw her over his shoulder and sprint northward until the forest swallowed the village, but standing before the blackened timbers, he couldn't summon the strength to bring a consoling word to his lips, to hold the girl's hand in his own, to move his feet in the direction he wanted them to go.

"That's my house." Her voice broke their silence and he heard it as he would the only sound in an empty corridor.

"Don't think of it like that," he said.

"Like what?"

"Like it's still yours."

He wound her bright orange scarf around her neck and frowned at the sooty fingerprint on her cheek. He had been awake in bed the previous night when the Feds came. First the murmur of a diesel engine, a low rumble he'd come to fear more than gunfire, then Russian voices. He had gone to the living room and pulled back the blackout curtain as far as he dared. Through the triangle of glass, headlights parted the night. Four soldiers, stocky, well fed, emerged from the truck. One drank from a vodka bottle and cursed the snow each time he stumbled. This soldier's grandfather had told him, the morning the soldier reported to the Vladivostok conscription center, that he would have perished in Stalingrad if not for the numbing grace of vodka; the soldier, whose cheeks were divoted from years of applying toothpaste to his adolescent acne, believed Chechnya to be a worse war than Stalingrad, and rationed his vodka accordingly. From his living room Akhmed wanted to shout, beat a drum, set off a flare. But across the street, they had already reached Dokka's door and he didn't even look to the phone that was without a pulse for ten years now. They knocked on the door once, twice, then kicked it down. Through the doorway, Akhmed watched torchlight move across the walls. So passed the longest two minutes of Akhmed's life until the soldiers reappeared in the doorway with Dokka. The duct tape strip across his mouth wrinkled with his muted screams. They pulled a black hood over his head. Where was Havaa? Sweat formed on Akhmed's forehead. His hands felt impossibly heavy. When the soldiers grabbed Dokka by the shoulders and belt, tumbling him into the back of the truck and slamming the door, the relief falling over Akhmed was quickly peeled back by self-loathing, because he was alive, safe in his living room, while in the truck across the street, not twenty meters away, Dokka was a dead man. The designation **02** was stenciled above the truck bumper in white paint, meaning it belonged to the Interior Ministry, meaning there would be no record of the arrest, meaning Dokka had never officially been taken, meaning he

would never come back. "Where's the girl?" the soldiers asked one another. "She's not here." "What if she's hiding beneath the floorboards?"
"She's not." "Take care of it just in case." The drunken soldier uncapped
a petrol jug and stumbled into Dokka's house; when he returned to the
threshold, he tossed a match behind him and closed the door. Flames
clawed their way up the front curtains. The glass panes puddled on the
sill. Where was Havaa? When the truck finally left, the fire had spread
to the walls and roof. Akhmed waited until the taillights had shrunk
to the size of cherries before crossing the street. Running a wide circle
around the flames, he entered the forest behind the house. His boots
broke the frigid undergrowth and he could have counted the rings of
tree stumps by the firelight. Behind the house, hiding among the trees,
the girl's face flickered. Streaks of pale skin began under her eyes, striping the ash on her cheeks. "Havaa," he called out. She sat on a suitcase
and didn't respond to her name. He held her like a bundle of loose sticks
in his arms, carried her to his house and with a damp towel wiped the
ash from her forehead. He tucked her in bed beside his invalid wife
and didn't know what to do next. He could have gone back outside and
thrown snowballs at the burning house, or lain in bed so the girl would
feel the warmth of two grown bodies, or performed his ablutions and
prostrated himself, but he had completed the *isha'a* hours earlier and if
five daily prayers hadn't spared Dokka's house, a sixth wouldn't put out
the flames. Instead he went to the living room window, drew open the
blackout curtains, and watched the house he had helped build disappear
into light. And now, in the morning, as he tightened the orange scarf
around her neck, he found a fingerprint on the girl's cheek, and, because
it could have been Dokka's, he left it.

"Where are we going?" she asked. She stood in the frozen furrow of the previous night's tire tracks. The snow stretched on either
side. Akhmed hadn't prepared for this. He couldn't imagine why the
Feds would want Dokka, much less the girl. She stood no taller than
his stomach and weighed no more than a basket of firewood, but to

Akhmed she seemed an immense and overwhelming creature whom he was destined to fail.

"We're going to the city hospital," he said, with what he hoped was an assertive tone.

"Why?"

"Because the hospital is safe. It's where people go when they need help. And I know someone there, another doctor," he said, though all he knew of her was her name. "She'll help."

"How?"

"I'm going to ask if you can stay with her." What was he saying? Like most of his plans, this one seemed so robust in his mind but fell like a flightless bird when released to the air. The girl frowned.

"He's not coming back, is he?" she asked. She focused on the blue leather suitcase that sat on the street between them. Eight months earlier, her father had asked her to prepare the suitcase and leave it in the closet, where it had remained until the previous night, when he thrust it into her hands and pushed her out the back door as the Feds broke through the front.

"I don't think so."

"But you don't know?" It wasn't an accusation, but he took it as one. Was he so incompetent a physician that she hesitated to trust him with her father's life even in speculation? "We should be safe," he said. "It's safer to think he won't come back."

"But what if he does?"

The longing knotted into such a simple question was more than he could contemplate. What if she cried? It suddenly seemed like a terrifying possibility. How would he stop her? He had to keep her calm, keep himself calm; panic, he knew, could spread between two people more quickly than any virus. He fiddled with her scarf. Somehow it had survived the fire as orange as the day it was pulled from the dye. "How about this: if he comes back, I'll tell him where you are. Is that a good idea?"

"My father is a good idea."

"Yes, he is," Akhmed said, relieved they had this to agree on.

They plodded along the Eldár Forest Service Road, the village's main thoroughfare, and their footprints began where the tire tracks ended. On either side he saw houses by surname rather than address. A face appeared and vanished in an unboarded window.

"Pull your headscarf tighter," he instructed. But for his years at medical school, he had spent his whole life in Eldár and no longer trusted the traditional clan system of *teips* that had survived a century of Tsarist rule, then a century of Soviet rule, only to dissolve in a war of national independence. Reincarnated in 1999, after a truce too lawless to be called peace, the war had frayed the village *teip* into lesser units of loyalty until all but the fidelity of a parent for a child wore thin enough to break. Logging, the village's sole stable industry, had ceased soon after the first bombs fell, and without viable prospects those who couldn't emigrate ran guns for the rebels or informed for the Feds to survive.

He wrapped his arm around Havaa's shoulder as they walked. The girl had always been strong and stoic, but this resignation, this passivity, was something else. She clomped along, kicking snow with each footstep, and in an attempt to cheer her Akhmed whispered a joke about a blind imam and a deaf prostitute, a joke that really wasn't appropriate for an eight-year-old, but was the only one Akhmed could remember. She didn't smile, but was listening. She zipped her puffy jacket over a sweatshirt that in Manchester, England, had warmed the shoulders of five brothers before the sixth, a staunchly philanthropic six-year-old, had given it to his school's Red Cross clothing drive so his mother would have to buy him a new one.

At the end of the village, where the forest narrowed on the road, they passed a meter-tall portrait nailed to a tree trunk. Two years earlier, after forty-one of the villagers had disappeared in a single day, Akhmed had drawn their forty-one portraits on forty-one plywood boards, weatherproofed them, and hung them throughout the village. This one was of a beautiful, self-admiring woman whose second daughter he had delivered. Despite his hounding her for years, she never had paid him for the delivery. After she was abducted, he had decided to draw on her portrait a single hair curling from her left nostril. He had grinned at the vain woman's ghost and then made peace with it. She looked like a beheaded giantess staring from the trunk. Soon she was no more than two eyes, a nose, and a mouth fading between the trees.

The forest rose around them, tall skeletal birches, gray coils of bark unraveling from the trunks. They walked on the side of the road, where frozen undergrowth expanded across the gravel. Here, beyond the trails of tank treads, the chances of stepping on a land mine diminished. Still he watched for rises in the frost. He walked a few meters ahead of the girl, just in case. He remembered another joke, this one about a lovesick commissar, but decided not to tell it. When she began straggling, he led her five minutes into the woods to a felled log unseen from the road. As they sat down, she asked for her blue suitcase. He gave it to her and she opened it, taking a silent inventory of its contents.

"What's in there?" he asked.

"My souvenirs," she said, but he didn't know what she meant. He unwrapped a hunk of dry black bread from a white handkerchief, split it in two uneven pieces, and gave her the larger one. She ate quickly. Hunger was a sensation so long situated in his abdomen he felt it as he would an inflamed organ. He took his time, tonguing the pulp into a little oval and resting it against his cheek like a lozenge. If the bread wouldn't fill his stomach, it might at least fill his mouth. The girl had finished half of hers before he took a second bite.

"You shouldn't rush," he said. "There are no taste buds in your stomach."

She paused to consider his reasoning, then took another bite. "There's no hunger in your tongue," she mumbled between chews. Her cupped hand caught the crumbs and tossed them back in her mouth.

"I used to hate black bread," he said. When he was a child he would only eat black bread if it was slathered in a spoonful of honey. Over the course of a year, his mother weaned him from it by slicing larger pieces, until his breakfast consisted of a small, sad oasis of honey on a desert of black bread.

"Can I have yours, then?"

"I said used to," he said, and imagined a brimming jar of honey, standing on a counter without a breadboard in sight.

She dropped to her knees and examined the underside of the log. "Will Ula be all right alone?" she asked.

His wife wasn't all right alone, with him, with anyone. He believed she had, in technical terms, lupus coupled with early-onset dementia, but in practice her nerves were so crisscrossed that her elbows ached when she spoke and her left foot had more sense than her brain. Before leaving that morning he had told Ula he would be gone for the day. As she gazed at him through her blank daze, he felt himself as one of her many visions, and he held her hand, and described from memory the placid pasture of a Zakharov oil painting, the herb garden and the cottage, until she fell back asleep. When she woke again that morning would she still see him sitting on the bed beside her? Perhaps part of him was still there, sitting on the bed; perhaps he was something she had dreamed up.

"She's an adult," he said at last and without much thought. "You don't need to worry about adults."

Behind the log, Havaa didn't reply.

He had always tried to treat Havaa as a child and she always went along with it, as though childhood and innocence were fantastical creatures that had died long ago, resurrected only in games of make believe. The only times she had been in a schoolhouse were when they went to steal child-sized desks for firewood, but sometimes he imagined they shared what was essentially the same wisdom separated by years and experience. It wasn't true, of course, but he had to believe that she had lived beyond her years, that she could confront what no eight-year-old is capable of confronting. She climbed from the log without looking at him.

"What's that?" he asked. She carefully lifted a yellow shape from her palm.

"A frozen bug," she said, and put it in her coat pocket.

"In case you get hungry later?" he asked.

She smiled for the first time that day.

They trod along the edge of the road and the girl's quickened pace compensated for their stop. With deep breaths he tried to unweave threads of diesel fumes or burning rubber from the air. The daylight provided a degree of safety. They wouldn't be mistaken for wild dogs.

They heard the soldiers before the checkpoint came in sight. Akhmed raised his hand. Wind filled the spaces between his fingers. Once used to transport timber, the Eldár Forest Service Road connected the village to the city of Volchansk. The gaps between the tree trunks provided the only exit points between village and city, and in recent months the Feds had reduced their presence to a single checkpoint. It lay another half kilometer away, at the end of a sharp curve.

"We're going back into the woods."

"To eat again?"

"Just to walk. We need to be quiet."

The girl nodded and raised her index finger to her lips. The entire forest had frozen and fallen to the ground. Crooked branches reached through the snow and scratched their shins from every angle as they walked a wide arc around the checkpoint. Visible through the trees, the checkpoint was no more than a wilted army tarp nailed to a poplar trunk in a failed attempt to lend an air of legitimacy. A handful of soldiers stood by it. Crossing the floor of frigid leaves in silence was impossible, but the soldiers, eight men who between them could share more venereal diseases than Chechen words, seemed no more alert than brainsick bucks, and they returned to the road a quarter kilometer past the checkpoint. The sun shone yolk-yellow between white clouds. Nearly noon. The trees they passed repeated on and on into the woods. None was remarkable when compared to the next, but each was individual in some small regard: the number of limbs, the girth of trunk, the circumference of shed leaves encircling the base. No more than minor particularities, but minor particularities were what transformed two eyes, a nose, and a mouth into a face.

The trees opened to a wide field, bisected by the road.

"Let's walk faster," he said, and the girl's footsteps hastened behind him. They were nearly halfway across when they came upon the severed hindquarters of a wolf. Farther into the field, blood dyed the snow a reddish brown. Nothing had decomposed in the cold. The head and front legs lay exposed on the ground, connected to the wolf's back end by three meters of pulped innards. What was left of the face was frozen in the expression it had died with. The tongue ribboned from its maw.

"It was a careless animal," Akhmed said. He tried to look away, but there was wolf everywhere. "It didn't watch for land mines."

"We're more careful."

"Yes, we'll stay on the road. We won't walk in the fields."

She stood close to him. Her shoulder pressed against his side. This was the farthest she'd ever been from home.

"It wasn't always like this," he said. "Before you were born there were wolves and birds and bugs and goats and bears and sheep and deer."

The heavy snow stretched a hundred meters to the forest. A few dead stalks rose through the brown frost, where the wolf would lie until spring. With heavy breaths they shaped the air. No prophet had augured this end. Neither the sounding of trumpets nor the beating of seraphic wings had heralded this particular field, with this particular girl, holding his particular hand.

"They were here," he said, staring into the field.

"Where did the Feds take them?"

"We should keep walking."

White moths circled a dead lightbulb.

A firm hand on her shoulder lifted her from the dream. Sonja lay on a trauma ward hospital bed, still dressed in her scrubs. Before she looked to the hand that had woken her, before she rose from the imprint her body had made in the weak mattress foam, she reached for her pocket, from instinct rather than want, and shook the amber pill bottle as though its contents had followed her into her dreams and also required waking. The amphetamines rattled in reply. She sat up, conscious, blinking away the moth wings.

"There's someone here to see you," Nurse Deshi announced from behind her, and began stripping the sheets before Sonja stood.

"See me about what?" she asked. She bent to touch her feet, relieved to find them still there.

"Now she thinks I'm a secretary," the old nurse said, shaking her head. "Soon she'll start pinching my rump like that oncologist who chased out four secretaries in a year. A shameful profession. I've never met an oncologist who wasn't a hedonist."

"Deshi, who's here to see me?"

The old nurse looked up, startled. "A man from Eldár."

"About Natasha?"

Deshi tensed her lips. She could have said *no* or *not this time* or *it's time to give up*, but instead shook her head.

The man leaned against the corridor wall. A one-size-too-small navy *pes* with beaded tassels roosted on the back of his head. His jacket hung from his shoulders as if still on the hanger. A girl stood beside him, inspecting the contents of a blue suitcase.

"Sofia Andreyevna Rabina?" he asked.

She hesitated. She hadn't heard or spoken her full name aloud in eight years and only answered to her diminutive. "Call me Sonja," she said.

"My name is Akhmed." A short black beard shrouded his cheeks. Shaving cream was an unaffordable luxury for many; she couldn't tell if the man was a Wahhabi insurgent or just poor.

"Are you a bearded one?" she asked.

He reached for his whiskers in embarrassment. "No, no. Absolutely not. I just haven't shaved recently."

"What do you want?"

He nodded to the girl. She wore an orange scarf, an oversized pink coat, and a sweatshirt advertising Manchester United, likely, Sonja imagined, from the glut of Manchester apparel that had flooded clothing-drive donations after Beckham was traded to Madrid. She had the pale, waxen skin of an unripe pear. When Sonja approached, the girl had raised the lid of the suitcase, slipped her hand inside, and held an object hidden from Sonja's view.

"She needs a place to stay," Akhmed said.

"And I need a plane ticket to the Black Sea."

"She has nowhere to go."

"And I haven't had a tan in years."

"Please," he said.

"This is a hospital, not an orphanage."

"There are no orphanages."

Out of habit she turned to the window, but she saw nothing through the duct-taped panes. The only light came from the fluorescent bulbs overhead, whose blue tint made them all appear hypothermic. Was that a moth circling the fixture? No, she was just seeing things again.

"Her father was taken by the security forces last night. To the Landfill, most likely."

"I'm sorry to hear that."

"He was a good man. He was an arborist in Eldár Forest before the wars. He didn't have fingers. He was very good at chess."

"He *is* very good at chess," the girl snapped, and glared at Akhmed. Grammar was the only place the girl could keep her father alive, and after amending Akhmed's statement, she leaned back against the wall and with small, certain breaths, said *is is is*. Her father was the face of her morning and night, he was everything, so saturating Havaa's world that she could no more describe him than she could the air.

Akhmed summoned the arborist with small declarative memories, and Sonja let him go on longer than she otherwise would because she, too, had tried to resurrect by recitation, had tried to recreate the thing by drawing its shape in cinders, and hoped that by compiling lists of Natasha's favorite foods and songs and annoying habits, her sister might spontaneously materialize under the pressure of the particularities.

"I'm sorry," she repeated.

"The Feds weren't looking for Dokka alone," he said quietly, glancing to the girl.

"What would they want with her?" she asked.

"What do they want with anyone?" His urgent self-importance was familiar; she'd seen it on the faces of so many husbands, and brothers, and fathers, and sons, and was glad she could see it here, on the face of a stranger, and not feel moved. "Please let her stay," he said.

"She can't." It was the right decision, the responsible one. Caring for the dying overwhelmed her. She couldn't be expected to care for the living as well.

The man looked to his feet with a disappointed frown that inexplicably resurrected the memory of *b) electrophilic aromatic substitution*, the answer to the only question on her university organic chemistry exam she'd gotten wrong. "How many doctors are here?" he asked, apparently deciding to try a different tack.

"One."

"To run an entire hospital?"

She shrugged. What did he expect? Those with advanced degrees, personal savings, and the foresight to flee had done so. "Deshi runs it. I just work here."

"I was a GP. Not a surgeon or specialist, but I was licensed." He raised his hand to his beard. A crumb fell out. "The girl will stay with you and I will work here until a home is found for her."

"No one will take her."

"Then I will keep working here. I graduated medical school in the top tenth of my class."

Already this man's habit of converting entreaty to command annoyed her. She had returned from England with her full name eight years earlier and still received the respect that had so surprised her when she first arrived in London to study medicine. It didn't matter that she was both a woman and an ethnic Russian; as the only surgeon in Volchansk, she was revered, honored and cherished in war as she never would be in peace. And this peasant doctor, this man so thin she could have pushed against his stomach and felt his spine, he expected her acquiescence? Even more than his tone of voice she resented the accuracy of his appraisal. As the last of a staff of five hundred, she was engulfed by the burden of care. She lived on amphetamines and sweetened condensed milk, had regular hallucinations, had difficulty empathizing with her patients, and had seen enough cases of secondary traumatic stress disorder to recognize herself among them. At the end of the hall, through the partially opened waiting-room door, she saw the hemline of a black dress, the gray of once-white tennis shoes, and a green hijab that, rather than covering the long black hair, held the broken arm of a young woman who was made of bird bones and calcium deficiency, who believed this to be her twenty-second broken bone, when in fact it was merely her twenty-first.

"The top tenth percent?" Sonja asked with no small amount of skepticism.

Akhmed nodded eagerly. "Ninety-sixth percentile to be precise."

"Then tell me, what would you do with an unresponsive patient?"

"Well, hmm, let's see," Akhmed stammered. "First I would have him fill out a questionnaire to get a sense of his medical history along with any conditions or diseases that might run in his family."

"You would give an unconscious, unresponsive patient a questionnaire?"

"Oh, no. Don't be silly," he said, hesitating. "I would give the questionnaire to the patient's wife instead."

Sonja closed her eyes, hoping that when she opened them, this idiot doctor and his ward would have vanished. No luck. "Do you want to know what I would do?" she asked. "I would check the airway, then check for breathing, then check for a pulse, then stabilize the cervical spine. Nine times out of ten, I'd be concentrating on hemostasis. I'd be cutting off the patient's clothes to inspect the entire body for wounds."

"Well, yes," Akhmed said. "I would do all of that while the patient's wife was filling out the questionnaire."

"Let's try something closer to your level. What is this?" she asked, raising her thumb.

"I believe that is a thumb."

"No," she said. "It is the first digit composed of the metacarpal, the proximal phalange, and the distal phalange."

"That's another way of saying it."

"And this?" she asked, pointing to her left eye. "What can you say about this besides the fact that it is my eye, and it is brown and used for seeing?"

He frowned, uncertain what he could add. "Dilated pupils," he said at last.

"And did they bother teaching the top tenth percent what dilated pupils are symptomatic of?"

"Head injuries, drug use, or sexual arousal."

"Or more likely because the hallway is poorly lit." She tapped a small scar on her temple. No one knew where it had come from. "And this?"

He smiled. "I have no idea what's going on in there."

She bit her lip and nodded. "Okay," she said. "We need someone to wash dirty sheets anyway. She can stay if you work." The girl stood behind Akhmed. In her palm a yellow bug lounged in a pool of melting ice. Sonja already regretted her consent. "What's your name?" she asked in Chechen.

"Havaa," Akhmed said. He gently pushed the girl toward her. The girl leaned against his palm, afraid to venture beyond its reach.

A year earlier, when Natasha had disappeared for the second and final time, Sonja's one- and two-night stays in the trauma ward had lengthened into weeks. After five weeks had passed since she'd last slid the key into the double lock, she had given up on the idea of ever going back. The twelve blocks to her flat might as well have been the Sahara. Waiting for her there was a silence more terrible than anything she heard on the operating table. Years before that, she had posed with her hand pressed against a distant Big Ben, so that in the photograph her fiancé had taken, she appeared to be holding up the clock tower. He had taken it on the eighth of their seventeen-day engagement. The photograph was taped above the desk in her bedroom, but not even its rescue was enough to lure her home. Living in the trauma ward wasn't much of a change. She'd already been spending seventeen of her eighteen waking hours in the ward. She knew the bodies she opened, fixed, and closed more intimately than their spouses or parents did, and that intimacy came as near to creation as the breath of God's first word.

So when she offered to let the girl stay with her, she meant here at the hospital; but the girl already knew that as she followed Sonja to her room.

"This is where we'll sleep, all right?" she said, setting the girl's suitcase by the stacked mattresses. The girl still held the bug. "Is there something in your hand?" Sonja asked tentatively.

"A dead bug," the girl said.

Sonja sighed, grateful, at least, to know she wasn't imagining it. "Why?"

"Because I found it in the forest and brought it with me."

"Again, why?"

"Because it needs to be buried facing Mecca."

She closed her eyes. She couldn't begin with this now. Even as a child she had hated children; she still did. "I'll be back later," she said, and returned to the corridor.

If nothing else, Akhmed was quick to undress. In the time it took her to show the girl to her room, he had changed into white scrubs. She found him preening before the hallway mirror.

"This is a hospital, not a ballroom," she said.

"I've never worn scrubs before." He turned from her, but the mirror held his blush.

"How could you go through a residency without wearing scrubs?"

He closed his eyes and his blush deepened. "My professors didn't have much faith in me. I never had, exactly, what you would call a residency."

"This isn't what I want to hear right after I take you on."

"I just feel privileged to work here." The sleeves showed off his pale biceps. "I always thought these would be looser."

"They're women's scrubs."

"You don't have any for men?"

"No men work here."

"So I'm wearing women's clothes."

"You'll need to wear a hijab, too." His face paled. "I'm kidding," she added. "A headscarf is sufficient."

He nodded, unconvinced. Clearly, she had hired a buffoon, but a buffoon who could wash linens, make beds, and deal with relatives was better than no buffoon at all. "Have you ever been here before?" she asked, disinclined to give more than a brief tour of the hospital.

"Yes."

"When?"

"I was born here."

She took him through the ghost wards: cardiology, internal medicine, endocrinology. A layer of dust and ash recorded their path. "Where is everything?" he asked. The rooms were empty. Mattresses, sheets, hypodermics, disposable gowns, surgical tape, film dressing, thermometers, and IV bags had been moved downstairs. All that remained was bolted to the floor and built into the walls, along with items of no practical use: family portraits, professional awards, and framed diplomas from medical schools in Siberia, Moscow, and Kiev.

"We moved everything to the trauma and maternity wards," she said. "They're all we can keep open."

"Trauma and maternity."

"It's funny, isn't it? Everyone either fucking or dying."

"No, not funny." He stroked his beard, burying his fingers to the first knuckle. His fingers found their way to his beard in moments of trouble or indecision, trawling the thick dark hair but rarely touching upon wisdom. "They are coming and they are leaving and it is happening here."

They climbed a stairwell washed in blue emergency light. On the fourth floor she led him down the corridor to the west side of the building. Without warning him she opened the door to the storage room. Something gleeful and malicious shot through her when he took a step back, afraid of falling. "What happened?" he asked. The floor broke off a meter past the doorframe. No walls or windows, just a cityscape muraled across the winter air.

"A few years back we harbored rebels. The Feds blew off the wall in reply."

"Was anyone hurt?"

"Maali. Deshi's sister."

"Only one person?"

"A benefit of understaffing."

On days when both sides abided by the ceasefire, she came to this doorway and looked across the city and tried to identify the buildings by their ruins. The one that flickered with ten thousand pieces of sunlight had been a sheet-glass office building in which nine hundred and eighteen souls had labored. Beneath that minaret a rotund imam had led the pious in prayer. That was a school, a library, a Young Pioneers' clubhouse, a jail, a grocery store. That was where her mother had warned her never to trust a man who claims to want an intelligent wife; where her father had taught her to ride a bike by imitating the engine growl of a careening municipal bus sure to run her over if she didn't pedal fast enough; where she had solved her first algebra equation for a primary school teacher, a man for whom Sonja's successes were consolation whenever he pitied himself for not having followed his older brother into the more remunerative profession of prison guard; where she had called for help after witnessing one man spear another on the university green, only to learn they were students rehearsing an Aeschylus play. It looked like a city made of shoeboxes and stamped into the ground by a petulant child. She could spend the whole afternoon rebuilding it, repopulating it, until the hallucination became the more believable reality.

"Before, you couldn't see the river from here," she said. "This hospital is the tallest building in the city now."

There had been tall buildings and plans to erect taller ones. After the dissolution of the U.S.S.R., oil reserves had promised prosperity for Chechnya in the coming capitalist century. Yeltsin had told the republics to grab as much sovereignty as they could swallow, and after two thousand years of foreign occupation, it had seemed the republic would finally achieve independence. Her grandparents had moved to Volchansk in 1946 after Stalin added lorry drivers and seamstresses to the expanding list of professions requiring purging, but she felt as buoyantly patriotic as her Chechen classmates who could trace their family trees back to the acorns. That sense of electric optimism was evident in the designs that had been solicited from architects in Riyadh, Melbourne, and Minsk. City officials had made a show of the blueprints, displaying them on billboards and distributing them as leaflets at the bazaar. She'd never seen anything like it. The sketches had suggested that the pinnacle of design no longer consisted of cramming the greatest amount of reinforced concrete into the ugliest rectangle possible. Once she had held a leaflet against the horizon and as the red sun bled through the paper the towers had become part of the skyline.

"Did they really want the girl?" she asked, turning her attention back to Akhmed. It didn't surprise her, but she asked anyway. Disappearances touched down as randomly as lightning. Only those actually guilty of abetting the insurgency—an infinitesimal fraction of those abducted—had the benefit of understanding their fate.

"It doesn't make sense," Akhmed said. Whether he meant the floorless room, the crushed city beyond, or the girl, Sonja didn't know. In the distance, a faint stream of tracers streaked skyward, disappearing into the clouds.

"Payday must be coming," Akhmed said.

She nodded. The Feds were only paid if they used a certain percentage of their ammo. If the soldiers tired of firing blindly into the sky, they might bury their excess rounds, then dig them up a few hours later to claim the bonus given for discovering a rebel arms cache. "Let's go," Sonja said.

They passed the original maternity ward, unused since Maali's death, and descended the stairwell to the new maternity ward. Deshi set down her knitting needles and eyed Akhmed suspiciously as she crossed the room to meet them. After twelve love affairs over the course of her seventy-three years, each beginning with a grander gesture, each ending with a more spectacular heartache, Deshi had learned to distrust men of every size and age, from newborns to great-grandfathers, knowing they all had it in them to break a decent woman's heart. "Will he be joining us?" she asked.

"Provisionally," Sonja said.

"And the girl?"

"Provisionally."

"You're the nurse," Akhmed said, curtly. "We met earlier."

"He speaks out of turn, without being addressed," Deshi observed.

"I just wanted to say hello."

"He continues to speak without being spoken to. And he has an ugly nose."

"I'm standing right here," Akhmed said, frowning.

"He tells us he is standing right here. As if we have been made blind and idiotic."

"What am I doing wrong?" he asked Sonja. "I'm just standing here."

"He seems to believe that his presence might somehow transform the ugliness of his nose, but seeing that nose, right here in front of me, provides irrefutable evidence."

"What am I supposed to say?" He looked desperately to Sonja. She smiled and turned to Deshi.

"Do you see the way he looks at me?" Deshi asked, her voice trembling with indignation. "He is trying to seduce me."

"I'm doing nothing of the sort. I'm just standing here!"

"Denial is the first impulse of a traitor."

"You're quoting Stalin," Akhmed said.

"You see? He's a lecher and a Stalinist."

"Don't be ridiculous."

"He must be an oncologist."

"There are few fields of medicine more important than oncology."

Deshi appeared flabbergasted. "You see!" she shouted. "A lecher, a Stalinist, *and* an oncologist? It is too much. It can't be."

"With respect, I'm thirty-nine and you're old enough to be my mother. I have no desire to have anything but a professional relationship with you."

"No desire? First he leers, then he insults. Mocking an old woman like me, has he no shame?"

"I'm sorry, okay? I'm sorry. I'm just trying to get along with you."

Deshi's lips sharpened into a scowl. "Only a weak man apologizes to a woman."

His eyes were watery by the time Sonja interrupted the exchange. He looked more shocked than he had when she opened the door to the fourth-floor storage room, and through her laughter, she couldn't help feeling guilty for exposing the man to Deshi without warning. "Enough," she said. "Akhmed, this is Deshi. Deshi, Akhmed. Let's work."

"It's a pleasure," Deshi said, and returned to the desk beside the incubator.

"What's wrong with her?" Akhmed asked when the nurse was safely out of earshot.

"And now he thinks there's something wrong with Deshi," Sonja said. A look of horror sank into his face. She assured him she was joking. "She once fell in love with an oncologist. It didn't work out."

A woman with dark greasy hair lay in the first bed with a child suckling her left breast. She pulled the bedsheet past the child's head when she saw them approach.

"It's okay," Sonja said. "He's a doctor too."

"But he's a man," the woman countered.

"This hospital is a madhouse," Akhmed said, as he turned away. The woman glared at his back, unamused by the implication that her three-day-old son was a lunatic, and then edged the bedsheet down her chest to reveal the child's scrunched face fastened to her nipple.

"The baby is hungry," Sonja said.

"He'll get used to it," the woman said, and closed her eyes.

The mother in the next bed slept on her side with her face half swallowed by the pillow. An incubator on a metal cart sat beside her bed. Inside, the infant was underweight and overheated, more like a crushed bird than a human.

"Poor nutrition in utero?" Akhmed asked.

"No nutrition in utero. Since the second war began, we've only had a handful of mothers healthy enough to give birth to healthy children."

"And I imagine their fathers aren't civilians?"

"It's not our policy to ask those questions." She walked to the door. In the corridor she stopped at a darkened lightbulb. "Do you see any moths there?"

"What?"

"Nothing," she said. In five weeks she would find a moth flapping in the canteen, and wouldn't believe it real until its wings crumpled under her palm. "The trauma ward is just down the hall."

# CHAPTER

## 2

WITHIN DAYS AFTER the proposal of the Khasavyurt Peace Accord, Sonja broke up with her Scottish fiancé, resigned from her residency at the University College Hospital, and sat through connecting flights from London to Warsaw to Moscow to Vladikavkaz. The backseat of the gypsy cab she took from the airport had been removed to allow room for luggage, and her single suitcase slid with the curvature of the road, thudding again and again against the back of her seat, as if to reiterate the lesson that despite the illusions she'd entertained while Brendan's chest rose and receded against hers, her life was small enough to fit inside a piece of luggage. Fuck me, she thought, what am I doing back here?

Dark plumes drifted from distant smokestacks, a chain of wind-rounded mountains, the taste of post-Soviet air like a dirty rag in her mouth. When they reached the bus terminal, she waited until her roller suitcase was safely on the ground before paying the driver. The Samsonite, a final gift from Brendan, might as well have been a neon-lit billboard advertising her foreignness as she rolled it past the imperial-era steamer trunks of other travelers. The nationalized bus line no longer ran routes into Chechnya, but after she had waited for an hour in a three-person line, a clerk directed her to a kiosk that sold lesbian porn, Ukrainian cigarettes, Air Supply cassettes, and tickets on a privately owned bus that made a weekly journey from North Ossetia to Chechnya. The next departure wasn't until the following morning. Though tired from travel, she knew she wouldn't sleep. She sat through the night on a wooden bench with one of her shoelaces tied around the suitcase handle to discourage gypsy children from rolling off with it.

"I am driving you all to your graves," the bus driver announced as he walked down the aisle to collect tickets at a quarter past six in the morning. He leaned back as though balancing an invisible shot glass on his round stomach. "If given the opportunity, I will sell you all to the first bandit, kidnapper, or slave trader we come across. Don't say you haven't been warned. I wouldn't have to drive *this* bus to *that* country if you hadn't purchased *these* tickets, and for that I will drive over every pothole and divot to make the ride as miserable for you as it will be for me. And no, we will be making no bathroom breaks, and yes, it is because I know the pain a pothole causes a full bladder."

She dozed for an hour with her head resting against the window. Every bump in the road was transferred through the glass and recorded by her temple. The sharp pitch of brakes, followed by the bullhorn-amplified instructions of a Russian border guard, brought her back to sudden consciousness. The soldiers were all fear and peach fuzz. They ordered the passengers off the bus and demanded each open his or her luggage in a field twenty meters from the road, while they, the waiting soldiers, crouched with their arms wrapped around their legs and their eyes clamped tight, as if jumping into a lake. The poor driver swayed from side to side. Since he was a boy, living on the banks of the Terek, he had dreamed of owning his own tour boat. Six and three-quarter years earlier, just a week before the Berlin Wall fell, the driver had sunk his life's savings into a tour boat, never built, and a contract, never fulfilled, to ferry Party members along the Terek. Now he sat on the ground and rested his back against the tires of the bus, but the land was a swelling and uncertain ocean and he would feel seasick for many years.

The checkpoint left Sonja charged, and as they crossed from Russian-controlled North Ossetia into Chechnya, she stared through the window she had slept on. On the crater-consumed road the driver made good on his pledge. They passed deserted fields. A toppled farmhouse. A plow resting at the end of a furrow, four months past sowing season. A burning oil well. At the horizon the mountains wore skullcaps of snow. It took ten hours to drive the two hundred kilometers to Volchansk. Checkpoints dotted the highway more regularly than the boarded petrol stations. At each one she carried her suitcase twenty meters from the road and opened it as soldiers held their ears in anticipation.

She spoke to the elderly woman sitting beside her, rolling each word in her mouth like an olive pit before spitting it out, and the woman was a wonderful listener, quiet and attentive as Sonja unfastened the latch to what had been her life until two days prior. She cataloged Brendan's shortcomings—his unclipped hangnails, his habit of singing Rodgers and Hammerstein while peeing, his reluctance to correct her grammatical errors—but even as she tried to convince the old woman that Brendan would have made a lousy husband, she missed the way he would write his initials in the pad of her thumb with his hardened hangnails, the way the flush of toilet water accompanied *the hiiiiiiilllllls are aliiiiiiiiive with the sound of muuuuuusiiiiic*, the intentional grammatical mistakes he would make, to see if she would catch them, as they took a sledgehammer to the rules of English and reassembled the pieces into a language only they understood. It was wonderful to unburden herself to a sympathetic ear. An hour passed before the old woman pulled a notepad from her purse, scribbled on it, and passed it to Sonja. *I thought you would have realized*, the old woman had written. *I'm deaf.*

The four-story Volchansk terminal was now a one-story rubble heap. The bus driver held out his hat for tips as they disembarked. "You will all die in this hellscape," he cheerfully announced. "Would you rather your rubles go to your godless murderers, or to me, an honest and pious bus driver, who braves death each week to provide for his family?"

Against her better judgment, Sonja dropped a hyper-inflated thousand-ruble note into the hat, and climbed down before he could curse her. At the next block she caught up with the old woman, who had flagged down a lemon-colored Lada. The old woman had grown up on a lemon orchard and for her first seventeen years she hadn't eaten a meal that wasn't made of lemon. There had been lemon cucumber salad, lemon vinaigrette beans, lemon-glazed chicken, lemon-stuffed trout, lemon lamb kabob, lemon-dill rice, lemon-roasted chicken thighs, lemon-curd dressing, lemon pudding, lemon-apricot cake, lemon marmalade cookies, and on it went. She was still four years and one month away from her seventy-sixth birthday and the miracle of her first lime.

The old woman gestured for her to take the cab, and when Sonja refused, she pulled out her notepad and just below *I'm deaf* wrote *Curfew will begin soon and you are younger and prettier than me.*

What had been a delivery van blocked the road three blocks from the flat. Sonja climbed out, and the lemon-colored Lada sped off before she could close the door. The apartment block on the left had lost its exterior wall and she observed the rooms like a mouse peering into a dollhouse. She turned to the road where pieces of ground went missing at regular intervals. The land was supposed to be flat, no hills or valleys for fifty kilometers, yet here she was, climbing into a canyon, the dirt wet and thick as she descended asphalt and clay, clambering over broken masonry that had fallen through six stories of air and one story of earth, finding her footing on sewage pipes, cursing and kicking the Samsonite when she remembered the instruction booklet's clearly stated direction that the luggage was only suited for paved surfaces, and she was standing at the bottom of the crater when it hit her—*I'm standing at the bottom of a fucking crater!*—and the impact doubled her over, followed immediately by the uppercut of a question—*What am I doing in the bottom of a fucking crater?*—to which the answer was as insubstantial as the word on her lips, three syllables naming the reason for her return—*Natasha*—her sister, haughty, beautiful, and unfathomably comfortable in social situations, whom she had last spoken to on the phone the day the first war began, one year, nine months and three weeks earlier, whom she had last seen the day she left for London, four years, eight months, and one week earlier, whom she had last envied five years and two months earlier, on the day before the day she received news of the London fellowship, and whom she had last loved at some indeterminate point in the past before they had grown into the people they were to be. She wouldn't climb out of bed for her sister, but she had climbed into a crater. She wouldn't cross a room, but she had crossed a continent.

Her apartment block stood past the bakery where, as a child, she had been given tea cakes in exchange for sweeping flour from the floor and repackaging it in brown paper bags. The apartment block windows were blown out and a line of bullet holes leaked light into the doorframe, but it still stood. The front door lay before the threshold like a welcome mat. She climbed to the third floor. Her breaths didn't fill her chest.

Her flat was locked and she knocked on the door and waited, but no pattering footsteps or groaning floorboards answered her. After a fourth quartet of raps led to a fourth silence, she pulled the spare key from her toiletry bag and opened the door. She didn't call out; the thought of her own unheard voice seemed unbelievably sad. Across the room empty window frames held square pieces of twilight. A half-burned candle sat on the dining table, anchored in a shot glass by melted wax. In the past two days she'd slept five hours and an aching exhaustion reverberated through her, tingling her skin. She lit the candle and the small glow fluttered across the egg-white walls. No receipts or envelopes or letters remained, nothing light enough for the wind to carry through the empty frames, nothing on which a good-bye might be written. The furniture was as she remembered: the divan against the right living room wall, still stained where Natasha had dropped an entire pot of borscht; the black-and-white Ekran television set perched on a milking stool; the wooden kitchen table leveled by three matchbooks. This had been her home. This had been her life. That had been her divan. She was returning to it, burying her face in the cushions and weeping into fabric that all these years later still held the scent of beets.

The next morning she went to the doors of the adjacent units. She couldn't recall the names of her neighbors, and judging from her unanswered knocks, they had fled from their flats as from her memory. On the fourth day footsteps came from the hallway. Sonja found a hunched woman wearing a green raincoat even though the sun was shining. The woman carried a dozen plastic shopping bags layered inside each other and tied at the straps.

"Who are you?" the woman asked, with enough suspicion to flatten the question to an accusation. Laina had been on the far side of middle age when Sonja accepted the London fellowship. She had worked the cosmetics counter at the Main Department Store and had gorgeous skin, skin that a thirty-year-old would envy, skin that her supervisor correctly cited as the cosmetic counter's most effective advertisement, skin plied with every moisturizer and emulsion stocked within the glass display case, skin that Sonja and her mother and even her sister had admired, that now looked like the skin of a peach left for many days in the sun.

"I'm Sonja." Laina's fingertips scrutinized her, holding her wrists, bending her ears. "I see," Laina said, at last convinced of Sonja's corporeal form. "You lived here."

"I heard you in the hall," Sonja said a few minutes later, as they drank tea in Laina's flat. "I thought you were someone else."

"You shouldn't open the door when you hear strangers. It's never a good idea."

"It was this once."

"This is the one in a million."

"Then I'm very, very lucky."

"No, you are very, very stupid."

"Why are you wearing a raincoat? There isn't a cloud for kilometers."

Laina went to the empty window frames, through which she could see what was left of the city, a view that stretched sixteen blocks farther than it had two years earlier. "I don't trust God. Who knows what he's planning up there." The bazaar had gradually been repopulated with vendors and sheet-metal kiosks and elderly women like Laina for whom war was no hindrance to a good haggle. She had just bartered a jar of engine oil for sandals that bore the blackened imprints of forty different toes. Once she had had a husband, now dead, whom she could trust not to cheat on her in a brothel. Once she had had a son, now missing, whom she had threatened to marry to Sonja if he misbehaved. Cosmonaut Yuri Gagarin smiled on the face of the clock hanging over the stove, and Sonja studied him as she gathered the breath to dislodge the question that for one and a half years had been wedged in her voice box. When the hour hand fell into the cosmonaut's outstretched palm, she inhaled and asked, "Do you know where Natasha is?" Laina bit her lip and shook her head. "I don't know where anyone is."

No one could answer the question. Days turned to weeks and Sonja accosted the few remaining tenants as they left for work, food, battle or better shelter, but she never received more than a shake of the head, a shrug of the shoulders, an apology. There was no sign of forced entry and the made bed in Natasha's room suggested a deliberate departure. In the bottom dresser drawer Sonja found the burgundy cardigan she'd given Natasha for her eighteenth birthday, the one Natasha had hated and called a babushka's sweater, and never wore, not even once, on a chilly day, to appease Sonja. It was just what Natasha would leave behind.

She held that sweater, wrapping the arms over her shoulders as if in an embrace.

Hospital No. 6 hired her without requesting an application or résumé. When she provided a list of references in London, Deshi crumpled the paper, tossed it under the desk, and told Sonja that Dr. Wastebasket would dutifully contact each recommender. Sonja's former professors had fled to the West, to the countryside, to private practices in places where they could save lives without endangering their own. Unimpeded by a hierarchical bureaucracy or institutional memory, she rose from resident to head surgeon in two months. Land mines didn't obey the Khasavyurt Peace Accord, and within a year she had more trauma surgery experience than the professors she'd studied under. She worked with gratitude for the pain of her patients. In their cries she heard her name as though she were the missing sister, recalled by their gibberish to this place where she amputated limbs and stanched bleeding, where her training was so needed and scarce her patients saw her hovering over the hospital bed as the last prophet of life, whom they pleaded with and praised and spoke to in prayer.

The days were urgent, without pause for reflection beyond the recall of case studies and anatomy lessons. At night she drifted home. If she remembered, she would brush her teeth with baking soda and recite the prayers her mother had taught her. Her tongue fumbled with those awkward and ancient words, and though no one was listening she found a measure of peace in this obsolete language of supplication. After crossing herself, she lay back on the divan and squirted a cool puddle of hand lotion from the bottle she'd brought from London. Invariably she would apply too much, and her hands would be slick and shiny in the candlelight as she asked for another pair with which to share the excess.

The weeks stacked into months that were flipped from the Red Cross calendar hanging behind the waiting-room reception desk; the calendar was from 1993 and would be reused until 2006 and for those thirteen years her birthday would always fall on a Monday. She marked the days, but time didn't march forward; instead it turned from day to night, from hospital to flat, from cries to silence, from claustrophobia to loneliness and back again, like a coin flipping from side to side. Happiness came in moments of unpredictable loveliness. The blind man who played accordion for her as she splinted the broken leg of his guide dog. The boy who narrated his dreams while recovering from meningitis.

Then, one evening, a knock sounded from the door as she prepared for sleep. She considered and disregarded Laina's advice as the doorknob slipped in her greasy grip. When she opened the door she wanted to scream. Natasha stood right there, in front of her, close enough to hold. She did scream, and she embraced Natasha, and later, on the divan, she took Natasha's hands in her own and rubbed until hers were dry.

DESPITE AN ADMITTEDLY unimpressive first day, Akhmed left Hospital No. 6 with his eyes on the stars and a swing in his gait. Sure, Sonja was a cold, domineering woman, whose glare could wither flowers and cause miscarriages, and Deshi was clearly a lunatic, and though there wasn't a sliver of compassion between the two of them and the only fate worse than having those two as caretakers was having them as colleagues, it had been a good day. Havaa was safe. His medical training was put to use, and for the first time in months, Ula wasn't his only patient.

He was the first person from Eldár admitted to medical school, an institution so distant and rarefied his inclusion had been celebrated as a village-wide achievement. There had been feasts in his honor, collections to pay for his textbooks. In 1986, Akhmed became the greatest hero in

village history since an Eldár barber trimmed the beard of the great
Imam Shamil one hundred and forty-one years earlier. There was talk
he would move to Volchansk, or even—they would drop their voices
to a whisper—Grozny. Anywhere farther was too far to dream. Did he
realize the hopes the village had pinned on him? Not really. Despite telling Sonja he had graduated medical school in the top tenth of his class,
he had, in fact, graduated in the bottom tenth, the fourth percentile to
be precise, and he blamed his inability to find a job on prejudice within
the Soviet Medical Bureau rather than on the fact that he had skipped a
full year of pathology to audit studio art classes. Eventually the village
had offered him an abandoned house on the outskirts, haunted, it was
said, by the ghost of a pedophile. He had turned it into a clinic. Even
though the villagers overcame their fear of the pedophilic specter—
though many wouldn't let their children enter—and even though their
lives were undeniably improved by the presence of a clinic, Akhmed
always felt he had let them down, or at least let himself down, by returning to the village that had celebrated his escape. But after applying
to twenty-three different hospital positions, and receiving not one interview, he was, today, finally, a physician at Hospital No. 6. And not only
a physician, but third in command! When put like that, it was a higher
honor than he could have ever imagined. He trekked along the service
road more confidently than he had that morning, and imagined what
those smug search committees would have had to say about it. They
probably wouldn't say anything. They were probably all dead. In this
way the war was an equalizer, the first true Chechen meritocracy. He
was an incompetent doctor but a decent man, he believed, compensat-
ing for his professional limitations with his empathy for the patient, his
understanding of pain. Passing the field where the wolf's frozen carcass
lay in moonlight, he thought of Marx. Perhaps here was where history
had reached its final epoch. A civilization without class, property, state,
or law. Perhaps this was the end.

The final fifty meters through the village were the most dangerous of the eleven-kilometer slog. His footsteps, if overheard, could prove as lethal as land mines. He slowed as he approached the only house without blackout curtains. The light of generator-powered bulbs burned through the windows. Ramzan, sitting inside, picking at a shiny slice of meat, didn't look like an informer or a collaborator, looked no more menacing than a man in the throes of a mighty indigestion. In the next window, Khassan, Ramzan's father, sat reading at his desk. Khassan hadn't spoken to his son in the two years since Ramzan had begun informing, and though Akhmed never blamed the old man for his son's crimes, the electric bulbs bathed both in the same light.

The glow of their house shrank to a glimmer as he reached his own. The doorframe was intact; the door still stood. Opening it, he tensed, waiting for a forceful grip on the shoulder, a rifle butt to the forehead. None came. He lit a kerosene lamp and walked into the bedroom. Ula lay on the bed. She rolled on her side and into the yellow glow.

"Where were you?" she asked. Divorced from tone, the three words still suggested accusation, and he hoped his silence would extinguish her question, as it often did. "Where were you?" she asked again. Her head barely indented the pillow.

"I went to see Dokka," he said. "I helped him shear the sheep."

She smiled wide enough to show the tips of her teeth. Twelve years earlier those incisors were beloved by the city dentist, a young man who plugged his most lascivious thoughts into the open mouths of young women; but the dentist died a virgin when a misaimed mortar shell landed on his practice and carried him to Paradise in an erupting gray cloud. "Dokka is so impatient," she murmured. "If he waited a month, the flock would give more wool."

"Yes," he agreed. "Dokka was always impatient." He sat on the bed and set the lantern next to the bedpan and the broth bowl. Each was half full. An ellipsis of wet footprints followed him to the bed. He unlaced his icy boots, massaged the balls of his feet, and lay beside Ula. Once she would have had to roll over to make room for him, but there was less of her now.

"How is his family?"

"They are well," he said. He turned onto his side and slid his left hand beneath her nightshirt to warm his fingers on her stomach.

"They should eat with us soon," Ula said.

"They will bring corn and cucumbers," he whispered to the tiny translucent hairs standing from Ula's earlobe. "The coals will smolder on the *mangal* and we will grill *shashlyk* and we will eat in the afternoon and the sun will shine. The lamb is already marinating in Dokka's white plastic bucket with tomatoes and onions and sliced lemons and *uksus*. We will invite Dokka's parents and they will come and perhaps Dokka will bring his chessboard, not the one with the fine wooden pieces, but the plastic one that Havaa gave him for his birthday, the one he said he loved though everyone thought a chess player of his skill would never play on a plastic board. But he did. Do you remember? He taught Havaa to play on it and let her win on her sixth birthday. We will invite them to eat someday."

"I'm hungry," she said. "I don't want to wait that long."

He pressed his lips to his wife's forehead and let them linger until the kiss became a conversation between their shared skin. How could his wife's sickness both repulse and bind him to her? His love, pity, and revulsion each claimed her, each occupied and was driven from her, and even now, as he sealed a postage stamp–sized square, he was afraid that in moments, when he broke away, his disgust would overwhelm the imprint of his lips.

"I'm hungry," she repeated. Reluctantly he leaned back. Leaving the lantern beside the bed, he crossed the darkness to the kitchen. After a decade without electricity, his soles knew the way. Eight steps to the living room, a quarter turn, six to the kitchen threshold, two to the stove. He set firewood on the previous night's ashes, aimed a squirt gun of petrol at the white wood, and struck a match. He prepared a pot of rice and a saucer of powdered milk as the firelight lapped against his legs. While waiting for the rice to cook he pulled a stool to the iron stove and leaned toward the light. He wanted to say something consoling to Dokka, and when his words burned in the stove chamber he hoped the sentiment would rise up the chimney pipe, carried by wind or wing to Dokka's ears, but even if Dokka could hear him, he didn't know what he would say, and he said nothing.

When the rice was moist he scooped it into a ceramic bowl and left the spoon slanting against the rim as he carried the bowl and the mug of powdered milk for two steps, six steps, and a quarter turn in blindness. Was this how a child felt in the womb? He had delivered dozens of newborns, but he couldn't imagine those first few moments. A tear in the shroud and suddenly colors, shapes, coldness, a world of hallucinations.

The lantern cast a circle on the floor and he entered it reluctantly to reach her. He sat beside Ula and brought small spoonfuls of rice to her mouth. Sonja's skill and Deshi's experience didn't matter; neither could care for Ula as he could. "Was anyone looking for me today?" he asked. She shook her head. "Are you sure? No knocks at the door? Nothing?"

"I don't think so. I was sleeping."

"But you would remember if Ramzan called from the door?"

"Oh, yes. Ramzan. He's such a nice man. He always asked my opinion," she said, and took a sip from the blue mug. "I think the milk has turned."

He washed the dishes, undressed, and slid beneath the sheets. Her fingers crawled through the covers for his.

"Things are getting worse, aren't they?"

"No," he said. "Nothing is getting worse."

"I don't have much time left, do I?"

These moments were the least bearable, when her meandering trail of questions led to clarity and he couldn't say what was lost to her. Did she really think he'd spent the day shearing sheep sold, slaughtered, and consumed long ago? Had she already forgotten Havaa sleeping beside her, the girl's slender body like a splinter of warmth in the dark room, or was the girl the material of dream itself, burned away by morning light? An equally disturbing thought: what if she consciously participated in these delusions to placate him?

"None of us does," he said, and squeezed her hand.

When her breaths stretched into sleep, he slid his fingers from her loosened grip and contemplated the next day. What would it be like to treat a patient again? Was he capable? Six months had passed since he had last treated patients at the clinic, but he remembered their reluctance as he led them into the examination room, as they realized their bodies had betrayed them once by sickness, and again by forcing them to rely on an incompetent physician. Sometimes he wondered if his own self-loathing manifested itself as harm to his patients, as if some dark part of his heart wanted them to suffer for his failures. And, now, to be confronted with Sonja, a surgeon whose renown had even reached Eldár. She had asked what he would do with an unresponsive patient, and he, in a blundering moment, had taken it to mean *quiet* or *unwilling to talk*, and had thought of the mute village baker, who communicated only through written notes—which had proved problematic the previous winter when the baker suffered from a bout of impotence he was too ashamed to write down, even to Akhmed. Akhmed had resolved the problem—shrewdly, he thought—by giving the mute baker a questionnaire with a hundred potential symptoms, of which the baker checked only one, and so had saved the baker's testicles, marriage and pride. But Sonja didn't know that; he'd been too flustered and embarrassed to explain. She had glared at him, knowing that an imposter like him could never belong to the top tenth. She hadn't asked how he had come by her name, why he'd come to her specifically. He hadn't intended to hide the truth from her, but when she didn't ask, he saw no reason to tell her about the chest stitched together with dental floss.

.   .   .

Sonja had made a bedroom of the office of the former geriatrics director, a man she'd never seen but whose tastes conjured an image so
defined—browline glasses, a wardrobe predominantly tweedy in character, finely sculpted features, dainty hands—she could have identified
his body among the dead. The gerontology department had been closed
in the first war due to a scarcity of resources and the general consensus
that prolonging the lives of the elderly was a peacetime enterprise. But
the director, a bachelor who devoted a healthy portion of his monthly
paycheck to office décor, had the most extravagantly furnished office in
the hospital, so of course Sonja was quick to make it hers. A vermillion
Tajik rug sprawled across the floor. At the end of the desk stood an an-
tique vase swathed in ornate Persian patterning, beneath which she had
found a photograph of a woman framed against the Black Sea, smiling
curiously, undated and unidentified, a ghost of the director's life that
survived him. Here, the director had spent his life loving a woman he
hadn't seen since his twenty-first year, when his father had married her
to a Ukrainian for fear of ruinous scandal; the woman was his half sister,
and the love he felt for her caused him so much confusion he could only
express it as love for the bewildered and incoherent elderly. The desk
was pushed against the wall and on it lay a final payroll still awaiting the
director's signature. Six mattresses stacked three abreast formed Sonja's
bed, where, after Akhmed had left, she found the girl clothed in limp
latex gloves.

"What have you done?" she asked. It was a remarkable sight. The girl
had stapled cream-colored latex gloves to her sweatshirt, to her trousers, had pulled them over her feet, and even wore one on her head like
a five-fingered mohawk. "I repeat, what have you done?"

"See?" the girl asked and stood up. See? See what? She didn't think
she needed another reason to renounce children, but here it was: they
speak in riddles. "I see a tremendous waste of medical supplies and I
very much wish I wasn't seeing it."

"See what I am?" the girl asked.

"A nuisance?"

"No, a sea anemone."

The girl spun in circles. It seemed she was hoping that the gloves would inflate and reach out like tentacles, but those gloves would barely open when Sonja jammed her fingers in them, and they just flailed limply against the girl's chest, back, and legs. The whole production seemed so sad that Sonja couldn't muster the anger this profligacy deserved.

"Sea anemones don't talk. Now change into your other clothes." Sonja nodded to the blue suitcase, still standing beside the mattress where she had left it six hours earlier.

"No. It's my just-in-case suitcase."

"Just in case what?"

"In case there is an emergency. So I'll have the things that are important to me."

"There was an emergency," Sonja said. She sighed. The child was as dense as a block of aged cheese. "That's why you're here."

"There might be another one."

"I'll make a deal with you," Sonja said, rubbing her eyes. "Change out of this ridiculous thing and you won't sleep in the parking lot."

The girl, who, the previous night, had watched her father's abduction, feared many things, but this ornery and exhausted doctor wasn't among them. She glanced down to the drooping latex gloves; her father would have found her performance enchanting, would have scooped her up in his arms and called her his sea anemone. His approval sparked magic into the blandest day, could layer her in the self-confidence and security she otherwise might lack; and without it, without him, she felt small, and helpless, and the idea of sleeping in a parking lot suddenly seemed very real. "I'll change," she told Sonja with a defeated sag of her shoulders. "Only if I don't have to unpack."

"I insist you don't," Sonja said, turning as the girl undressed. "It's my greatest wish that you and your suitcase will have vanished into the sea by morning. What's so important in there that you can't unpack?"

"My clothes and souvenirs."

"Souvenirs? Where have you been?"

"Nowhere." This was the first night she'd ever spent away from the village. "The souvenirs are from people who've stayed at my house."

When the girl finished changing, Sonja said, "You have a dirty fingerprint on your cheek. No, not that cheek. The other cheek. No, that's your forehead." Sonja licked her thumb and rubbed the sooty fingerprint from the girl's cheek. "Your face is filthy. It's important to stay clean in a hospital."

"It's not clean to wipe spit on another person's face," Havaa said defiantly, and Sonja smiled. Perhaps the girl wasn't as dense as she had assumed.

They ate in the canteen at the end of the trauma ward, where Sonja flaunted the hospital's most sophisticated piece of technology, an industrial ice machine that inhaled much of the generator power but provided filtered water. The girl was more impressed by her warped reflection on the back of her spoon. "It's December. The whole world is an ice machine."

"Now you're practical," Sonja said.

The girl made a face at the spoon. "Can fingers ever grow back?" the girl asked, setting down the spoon.

"No. Why do you ask?"

The girl thought of her father's missing fingers. "I don't know."

"How do you know what a sea anemone is, anyway? The nearest sea is a few countries over."

"My father told me. He's an arborist. He knows everything about trees. I'm still a minimalist."

"Do you know what that is?"

Havaa nodded, expecting the question. "It's a nicer way to say you have nothing."

"Did your father tell you that?"

Again, she nodded, staring down to the spoon head that held her buckled reflection. Her father was as smart as the dictionary sitting on his desk. Every word she knew came from him. They couldn't take what he had taught her, and this made the big, important words he'd had her memorize, recite, and define feel for the first time big and important. "He told me about minimalists and arborists and marine biologists and scientists and social scientists and economists and communists and obstructionists and terrorists and jihadists. I told him about sea anemonists."

"It sounds like you know a lot of big words."

"It's important to know big words," the girl said, repeating her father's maxim. "No one can take what's inside your head once it's there."

"You sound like a solipsist."

"I don't want to learn new words from you."

Sonja dunked the dishes in a tub of tepid water. Behind her the girl was quiet. "So your father is an arborist," she said as she scrubbed their spoons with a gray sponge. It was neither a question nor a statement, but a bridge in the silence. The girl didn't respond.

Back in the geriatrics office she gave the girl a blond-haired Barbie doll from the lost and found. It had belonged to the daughter of a devout Warsaw Catholic who believed the makers of department-store toys were conspiring to turn his ten-year-old girl into a heathen, and so he had boxed up all but her Nativity figurines and, filled with the spirit of Christian charity, sent them to a heathen country where they could do no harm to the souls of children already beyond salvation. The doll, dressed in ballroom gown and tiara, appeared surprisingly chipper given her emaciated waistline. The girl inspected the doll, distrustful of this vision of humanity.

"Why is she smiling?" the girl asked.

"She probably found that tiara on the ground and plans to sell it for a plane ticket to London."

"Or maybe she killed a Russian."

Sonja laughed. "Sure, maybe. She could be a *shahidka*."

"Yes, she's a Black Widow," the girl said, pleased with the interpretation. "She snuck into a Moscow theater and took everyone hostage. That's why she's wearing a dress and jewelry."

"But where are her hostages? I don't see any. Why else might she be smiling?"

The girl concentrated on the doll's unnaturally white teeth. "Maybe she's starving and just ate a pastry."

"What about a cookie?" Sonja asked, as the idea came to her.

"She'd probably smile if she ate a cookie."

"Would you?"

The shadow of the girl's head still bobbed on the wall when Sonja found a chocolate-flavored energy bar in the upper left desk drawer, a new addition to the humanitarian aid drops, designed for marathon runners. The girl chewed the thick rubber and grimaced. "What is this?"

"It's a cookie."

She shook her head with wide-eyed betrayal. "This is *not* a cookie."

"It's like a cookie. Cookie-flavored."

"How can something be flavored like a cookie and not be a cookie?"

"Scientists and doctors can make one type of food taste like another."

"Can you do that?"

If only she could. "I'm not that type of doctor."

The girl took another bite, then crinkled the foil around the remnant and slipped it under her pillow.

"It's not that bad," Sonja said, annoyed by the girl's finicky palate.

"I'm saving it."

"For what?"

"Just in case."

The girl lurched against the blankets, but still fell asleep first. Sonja tightened her eyelids and pressed into the pillow but couldn't push herself into oblivion. She only knew how to sleep alone. Since she had returned from London eight years earlier, her casual affairs had never been serious enough to warrant an overnight bag. She sighed. When Deshi woke her that morning, she could have never imagined the day would end like this, with her trying to fall asleep beside this bizarre little thing. Even so, she was glad for Akhmed's help. She needed another set of hands, no matter how fumbling and uncertain they might be. Not that she'd admit it to him. She had to harden him, to teach him that saving a life and nurturing a life are different processes, and that to succeed in the former one must dispense with the pathos of the latter.

The pull of sheets transmitted the girl's shape, her indentation in the mattress, that slight heat burning off her skin. Sonja didn't want her here, couldn't imagine what the girl had seen, or knew, or was blind to or ignorant of that had put her in the Feds' crosshairs. Somewhere a colonel tossed in bed, wanting to find Havaa as much as Sonja wanted her gone, and she would happily trade the girl for Natasha, or her parents, or a plane ticket to London, or a decent night's rest. The girl had lost her father and she had lost her sister and though their shared experience might lead to shared commiseration, she felt cheated. Moths had fluttered on the edge of her vision as she floated into the hallway that afternoon, hoping the man brought news. Her sister had taken the Samsonite when she vanished the previous December. There was no note or explanation, not even under the divan, where Sonja had crawled with a broomstick and the vain hope that the breeze had hidden Natasha's good-bye. It was as if she'd opened the door to the fourth-floor storage closet and fallen off the earth. Poof and gone. But there were no arrest reports, no border-crossing records, no body, and the absence of evidence was enough to allow Sonja to go on hoping that the next patient funneled through the waiting room, through the swinging doors of the trauma ward would be Natasha. But there had to be a quota. An upper limit to the number of miracles one is privileged to in a lifetime. How many times can a beloved reappear?

The night-light coated the girl in a green film. Those smooth, spit-cleaned cheeks gave no indication of the dreams crowding her skull. Should she make it to adulthood, the girl would arrive with two hundred and six bones. Two and a half million sweat glands. Ninety-six thousand kilometers of blood vessels. Forty-six chromosomes. Seven meters of small intestines. Six hundred and six discrete muscles. One hundred billion cerebral neurons. Two kidneys. A liver. A heart. A hundred trillion cells that died and were replaced, again and again. But no matter how many ways she dismembered and quantified the body lying beside her, she couldn't say how many years the girl would wait before she married, if at all, or how many children she would have, if any; and between the creation of this body and its end lay the mystery the girl would spend her life solving. For now, she slept.

1994  1995  1996  1997  1998  1999  2000  2001  2002  2003  **2004**

A SHADOW APPEARED against the white horizon, filling the sleeves of a familiar navy overcoat. Two mornings earlier, Akhmed would have waved and walked to greet his friend. He would have walked until the shade dissolved from Khassan's face and then walked farther, to raise his voice, without fear or hesitation, had this been two mornings earlier. But these were afterthoughts as he ran into the forest and hid behind a gray trunk only half his width. He crouched at the base of the trunk and gulped the dawn air and hoped Khassan, a sharpshooter in the Great Patriotic War, hadn't seen him flee. He cradled his jaw in his palms. Was this how he would live now? Fleeing into the forest at the slightest rustle?

Three taps sounded on the birch trunk. "Is anyone home?" the old man asked. Akhmed stood and turned ruefully. His footprints led right to the tree trunk. From the wrong ends of binoculars, Khassan could have tracked him here.

"It's cold to be out so early," Akhmed said. He couldn't raise his gaze above Khassan's shoulders as they walked back to the service road. The old man's frame still filled his overcoat and he held a two-kilogram weight in each hand. At the age of seventy-nine—a full twenty years past the life expectancy of the average Russian man, as he often pointed out—Khassan maintained the exercise regimen he had begun in the army a half century earlier. Fifty squats, sit-ups and push-ups, plus a five-kilometer run that had slowed to a saunter over the decades.

"My balls have frozen in Poland and in Nazi Germany and in Kazakhstan. They have frozen in nine different time zones. But now?" He sighed and gazed sorrowfully at his crotch. "Now I'm too old to need them, so why should I care if they freeze?"

As a child and an adult, Akhmed had been captivated by stories of Khassan's sixteen-year odyssey. To a man who had never even been to Grozny, Khassan's travels rose to the realm of legend. In 1941, the Red Army gave him five bullets and an order to find a gun among the dead. With a rifle pried from frozen fingers in Stalingrad, he shot a path through Ukraine, Poland, and Germany. He pulled two bullets from his left thigh, lost three friends to hypothermia, killed twenty-seven Nazis by bullet, four by knife, three by hand, fought under five generals, liberated two concentration camps, heard the voices of innumerable angels in the ringing of an exploded mortar, and took a shit in one Reichstag commode, a moment that would forever commemorate the war's victorious conclusion. After his years of service he returned to a Chechnya without Chechens. While he had fought and killed and shat for the U.S.S.R., the entire Chechen population had been deported to Kazakhstan and Siberia under Stalin's accusations of ethnic collaboration with the fascist enemy. His commanding officer, a man whose life Khassan had twice saved, was to spend the next thirty-eight years working as a train porter in Liski, where the sight of train rails skewering the sun to the horizon served as a daily reminder of the disgraceful morning he shipped Khassan, the single greatest soldier he'd ever had the pleasure of spitting orders at, to Kazakhstan on a train packed with Russian physicians, German POWs, Polish Home Army soldiers, and Jews. Khassan's parents hadn't survived the resettlement, and in 1956, when—after the death of Stalin three years earlier—Khrushchev allowed Chechen repatriation, Khassan disinterred their remains and carried them home in their brown suitcase.

"From what you told me," Akhmed said, "they weren't cold from disuse."

Khassan smiled. "Thank goodness the borders are closed. Who knows how many frauleins might otherwise track me down for dowries?"

Violet light veined the clouds. Akhmed searched for something to say, a sentence flung to pull them from the sinkhole of Dokka's disappearance. "How's the book?"

Khassan winced. Not the right sentence. "I'm giving up on that," he said.

"It's not writing itself?"

"History writes itself. It doesn't need my assistance."

"But it's your life's work."

"Your life's work could be scrubbing piss from a toilet bowl. Work isn't meaningful just because you spend your life doing it."

For four decades Khassan had drafted and redrafted his six-volume, thirty-three-hundred-page historical survey of the Chechen lands. Akhmed was a child when he had first seen the pages. After cancer had put his mother in the ground, he and his father had received weekly invitations to dine with Khassan in the three-room house built by Khassan's father in a time when men were expected to grow their own corn, raise their own sheep, and build their own homes. A partial draft, kept in eight boxes beneath Khassan's desk, was written in the careful cursive of a condolence letter. Akhmed found it one afternoon while his father and Khassan sat outside, gossiping like married ladies beneath a June sun.

Each afternoon, while Khassan taught at the city university, Akhmed snuck into the living room and stole a single page. He read it at night, after completing his homework, and exchanged it the next afternoon for the following page. Khassan had begun his history in the time before humanity, when the flora and fauna of Chechnya had existed in classless egalitarianism. In a twenty-page account of Caucasian geology, Khassan proved that rock and soil adhered to the same patterns of dialectical materialism proffered by Marx. A seven-page explanation of natural selection compared kulaks to a species that failed to adapt to environmental changes. Akhmed read seventy-three pages in total, only reaching the Neolithic period before Khassan realized pages had gone missing: the three Akhmed had lost, the two he had turned into paper airplanes, and the one, a description of Eldár Forest before man invented chainsaws, that had been too beautiful for him to return. Believing the culprit to be a secret police informant, Khassan had burned the pages in his wood stove.

"But you need to finish it," Akhmed urged, unsure if Khassan was serious. The Khassan obsessed with a history book that, even if published, no one would read was the only Khassan he knew. Khassan could renounce his legs and sound no more ridiculous.

"You're right," Khassan said. His parted lips revealed a row of teeth the color of cooking oil. That city dentist had been so in love with the teeth of his young women patients, he couldn't look inside the mouth of an old man for more than a few moments without feeling a wash of revulsion and betrayal; he had never told Khassan to floss. "And I'm sorry, Akhmed. For Dokka."

"Was he taken to the Landfill?"

Khassan's shoulders sloped in a shrug. They both knew the answer but that didn't make it any easier to admit. "I don't know. I don't know anything."

"Can you ask Ramzan . . ." Ask him what? Ramzan had no answers;

the blindness he walked through was a shade darker than theirs. "Can you ask him to let the girl be? She's gone."

"Ramzan hasn't heard my voice in the one year, eleven months and three days since he began informing. I've counted every day of silence. It's stupid, I know, but silence is the only authority I have left."

Each looked past the other, into the woods stretching on either side of the road, uncomfortable and ashamed. "I'm a pariah. The father of an informer," Khassan continued. "You and my son are the only people in the village willing to speak to me, and I can't speak to him. In one year, eleven months and three days the only conversations I've had have been with you. You still speak to me. Why?"

Akhmed focused on the trees. He didn't know. He didn't know that when Khassan returned home that morning he would write down what he remembered of their conversation in a shorthand his son couldn't decipher, or that later Khassan would read it quietly, without speaking a single word aloud, and even on the page their exchange would lift that blanketing silence like tent poles. What he did know was that Khassan was his friend, a decent man, and that was as rare as snowfall in May.

"You ran away from me just now," Khassan said, before Akhmed could answer. "I understand. My son is weak and cruel. That's fine. You know, I've been thinking of the Festival of the Sacrifice recently. In the resettlement camps we celebrated in secret, slaughtering a wild dog in place of a lamb. I wonder if Ibrahim's palms were damp as he walked his son to the summit. Did he tell him they were going on a hike? Did he take water? I think he must have glared at the knife until his reflection was part of the blade. I think relief must have replaced his horror when he unsheathed his knife and recognized his face. He must have known that what he was to do was of such significance it had already become who he was, and so he offered both his son and himself to the *kinzhal*'s edge."

Hunched over, Khassan pressed his bare hands into the snow. He sank them to his forearms and left them there in what a stranger might take to be a demonstration of endurance, but what was, Akhmed knew, a private ritual of contrition. His face was broken in a way Akhmed couldn't look at, let alone understand, let alone mend. "Walk on both sides of the service road so my footprints can't be followed," Akhmed said. "I'll be gone all day. Make sure no one knows where I'm going. Do that."

Khassan's head bobbed. He scooped two palmfuls of snow and pressed them to his eyes. Melting rivulets circled his wrists. "Ibrahim's willingness to sacrifice his son isn't hard to believe. His son was an innocent. It's so much harder when you know what your son would do to you if he survived. When you know just what would happen if an angel was to grab the knife from your hand."


*Distal phalange, proximal phalange, metatarsus, medial cuneiform, navicular, talus, calcaneus.* Akhmed recited the bones composing the big toe and followed the Latin north to the ankle as he walked to the hospital. Before leaving that morning he had torn a half dozen diagrams from his old anatomy textbook and he studied them as he hiked, glancing up every few seconds to check for land mines. He'd be ready for any more of Sonja's quizzes. The sun had fully risen when he entered the hospital and the guard, whose left arm ended at the elbow, stopped him.

"Here?" he asked, exasperated. "I've walked nearly to Turkey avoiding checkpoints."

The cuff of the guard's left jacket sleeve was sewn to his shoulder. The slender beard descending from his chin looked like the tail of a squirrel hibernating in his mouth. "You need to pull the glass shards from your boots," the guard instructed.

"Don't worry," Akhmed said. "I'm the doctor."

"No, Sonja is the doctor," the one-armed guard corrected. "You are the idiot with glass shards in his boot soles. Now have a seat on that bench and take those pliers and pull out the glass if you want to enter the hospital."

No one could walk through the city without lodging a full pane of glass shards in his shoe soles, and the guard, who had for eighteen arduous months fought with the rebels and had witnessed and participated in all manner of horrors, was afraid of Sonja and what she would do if she found glass shards tracked into the hospital. He watched Akhmed pry out fourteen shards and deposit them in an ashtray.

Akhmed sighed, crestfallen. His first day as a hospital doctor wasn't beginning well. "Tell me," he asked, nodding to the guard's missing arm. "Do they pay you half rate?"

The guard, thirty-one years old, had never received a paycheck, and wouldn't have known what to do with one if he had; in three years, when the hospital issued paychecks again, beginning with a whopping nine years of back pay, the guard would frame his in glass and hang it on his wall without ever depositing it. For the rest of his life, he wouldn't trust the numbers people put on paper. "They should pay me more than they pay you," the guard said, smiling. "Even I know better than to give an unresponsive patient a questionnaire."

Akhmed's flush hadn't faded when he pushed open the double doors. The cannonball of Havaa's head crashed into his stomach.

"You came back!" she exclaimed, breathless from her sprint across the room. He raked his fingers through her almond-brown hair, a shade shared by the back of his hand. He had been so concerned with Latin nomenclature he'd forgotten about her, and as her arms formed a tourniquet around his waist, the tight press slowed his breaths. She hadn't forgotten him for a moment.

"Of course I came back. Where else would I go?"

"Has he——" she began, and he squeezed her shoulder as consolingly as he was able.

"We'll both be here a little longer, okay?"

"I guess," she said. She loosened her embrace and stepped back as the enthusiasm of the prior moment drained from her face. Her blue suitcase stood by the folding chair where she had been sitting.

"Planning on going somewhere?"

"In case we were going home," she said. Again Akhmed squeezed her shoulder, but the gesture was small and futile, and reasserted the helplessness she seemed to foist upon him.

"How was your night?" he asked, hoping to cheer her up. "Did Sonja turn into a bat after the sun went down?"

She shook her head.

"Are you sure?"

"Yes," Havaa said, dropping her voice to a whisper. "She just became boring. She wouldn't stop talking about her ice machine. And she called me a solipsist."

Akhmed followed her across the waiting room to the perimeter of paint-chipped folding chairs and sat down beside her. She lifted the blue suitcase to her lap and wrapped her arms around it. "Do you want me to carry that back to your room?" he offered. She gave a slow, dejected shake of her head, raised the suitcase on its side, and hugged it. "You know what you should do," he said, turning to her. "You should teach the guard downstairs to juggle."

"But he only has one arm."

"But he really wants to learn. He's embarrassed by his arm so he'll refuse at first. But you need to be persistent."

"I can be persistent," she said.

"Yeah?"

"My father says persistence is a polite way of being annoying."

"You're good at that, aren't you?"

With a slight smile, she acknowledged her considerable expertise. But the smile he had worked for wilted when the trauma doors swung open and Sonja walked in. Each step produced a rattle from her bleached-white scrubs. Pink veins cobwebbed her eyes. "You're late,"

Sonja snapped, completely oblivious to the important work happening there, on the waiting-room chairs, between them.

He raised his eyebrows to Havaa and then followed Sonja into a corridor cloaked in curtains of pungent ammonia. She turned into the staff canteen, where, in the corner, the notorious ice machine brooded. Sheets and towels draped from clotheslines and silver instruments shifted in pots of boiling water. Duct tape covered the windowpanes and the overhead emergency lights cast a dull blue glow across the walls. Even in war conditions he had expected Hospital No. 6 to be more glamorous than this.

"Was everything all right with Havaa last night?" he asked.

Sonja didn't turn to him. "Let's say she's an inexperienced house-guest," she said, and felt the hanging sheets for moisture. She handed him scrub tops from the farthest clothesline. Still damp.

"What about the ones I wore yesterday?" he asked. "I left them in a cupboard down the corridor."

"No, they need to be clean. And just as important, they need to be white."

"Why white?"

She leaned against the wall and slid her hands into the cavernous pockets of her scrub bottoms. He concentrated on her face as if preparing to draw her portrait—the angles, ratios and proportions of her features—all so he wouldn't have to meet her eyes.

"Our appearance is as important as anything we do. Our patients need to believe we operate no differently from a hospital in Omsk," she said, and, elbow deep, pulled a cigarette from her pocket.

"So the perception of professionalism is more important than being professional?" It was an idea he could stand behind.

She raised her chin and blew a line of smoke at the ceiling. "We're three people running a hospital that requires a staff of five hundred. We need to appear to be consummate professionals because it's the only way we'll fool anyone into thinking we are."

"So, right now, because you're smoking a cigarette and I'm not, I'm the more professional of us two?"

Her laughter rang more pleasantly now that it wasn't at his expense, and he watched with satisfaction as she dipped the ember into a puddle collecting beneath the clothesline, and flicked the butt into the wastebasket. "You're walking two steps ahead of your shadow."

"About that, I was thinking that since this is my first day, it might be better if I didn't begin working one-on-one with patients immediately."

"That might be the best idea you've ever had," she said, and handed him the rest of the scrubs. When he began to undress, she took her time looking away.

Patients funneled into the trauma ward—a young man with a deep tubercular cough, an elderly woman whose hair had caught on fire, two teenagers who had beaten away half their faces as they negotiated the ownership of a supposedly lucky rooster's claw—and Akhmed, thankful, attended to none of them. It might feel good to be back between the earpieces of a stethoscope, but it felt much better to be in the canteen, where no calamity greater than a cross word from Deshi befell him. He spent the morning following her, nodding politely as she denounced the Russians for various earthly ills, and a few—volcanoes, winter, her arthritic hips—that fell within God's jurisdiction.

"If we could, we'd blame constipation on the Russians," he said.

"I already do. Roughage is so rare." She picked a pair of brown trousers from the pile on the floor and emptied its pockets on the counter. A scatter of folded paper, loose change, keys, plastic cards, and lint fell out. She slid all but the identity card and loose change into the trash.

"Anything good in this one?" he asked. It was the fourteenth pair of trousers Deshi had laid on the counter that morning, the fourteenth she had searched for money, cigarettes, whatever else the dead man hadn't thought to use before he went on his way. "Maybe a plane ticket?"

"A plane ticket." She waved her hand to dismiss the very breath that carried so stupid a question. "Where would he go, anyway?"

"I don't know. Grozny."

"Grozny?" She gaped at him. Every Saturday from 1976 through 1978 Deshi had met the seventh of her twelve great loves, an oil geologist, in the suite of the Grozny Intourist Hotel, until the Saturday night she walked in to find him occupied with another nurse; she would never forgive the city for harboring that man. "Is he serious?"

"I've never been to Grozny," Akhmed said.

"If he could go anywhere, he'd choose Grozny?"

"I've never been there before," he said softly. In the decade and a half since he'd left medical school, he'd forgotten just how wide the world stretched beyond his village, just how provincial and unremarkable his little life was when compared with nearly anything. Deshi, who, judging from her tone of disapproval, would be impressed with nothing short of a circumnavigation of the globe, was quick to remind him.

"Unbelievable," she sighed, and turned her back to him. She glanced at the identity card to see if the trousers belonged to an acquaintance, then tossed it into a shoebox filled with several dozen others. It was a simple gesture, no more than a flick of her fingers, performed without malice or contempt, but with complete disinterest, and it cut through Akhmed like a fin through water. In her indifference he saw the truth of a world he didn't want to believe in, one in which a human being could be discarded as easily as pocket lint. But Deshi was no longer paying attention to him. "Grozny," she muttered. "Small-minded and an idiot doctor. He'd probably prescribe *kalina* berries for pneumonia. And that gargoyle squatting where his nose should be. Long enough to keep the tips of his toes dry in a rain shower."

She turned the trouser legs inside out and spread them on the counter; a pouch protruded from the inseam, just below the knee, where it was sewn in with black thread. She ran a razor blade across the stitching, and removed a few crumpled bills and a folded sheet of notepaper. Akhmed's stomach clenched as she reached toward the trash can with the note. "Wait," he said. He knew what was written on it, knew the time had passed to provide for any final request, but asked anyway. "What does the note say?"

Deshi frowned. " '*90 October the 25th Road, Shali*,' " she read. " '*Return me for burial.*' Too late, my friend. You should have stitched your note to the outside of your trousers."

"Where is the body?"

"Already in the clouds. It's sacrilege, I know, but they burn nearly every body that isn't claimed. Can't come by a body bag these days. The Feds requisition them to make field *banyas* while on patrol. The strangest thing I've ever seen, three hundred soldiers, naked as the day they were born, huddled within black plastic bags that trapped the steam of cold water poured over stone fires. Only a Russian could find pleasure inside a body bag."

As she refolded the note and dropped it into the trash can, he wanted to reach out, to snatch the tumbling rectangle before it landed and was lost among the last words of two dozen others who died far from their villages, who were pitched by strangers into furnaces, who were buried in cloud cover and wouldn't return home until the next snowfall. Akhmed's own address was written on a slip of folded paper and stitched into his left trouser leg, where with every step it chafed against his leg, awaiting the decent soul that would one day carry him, should he die away from home.

"What's his name?" he asked. That man had a sister in Shali who would have given her travel agency—now no more than a once prestigious name—her parents-in-law, and nine-tenths of her immortal soul to hold that note now lying at the bottom of the trash can, if only to hold the final wish of the brother she regretted giving so little for in life.

In the shoebox the identity cards were layered eight deep. She held a card to the light and set it back down. "He's one of these," she said.

.    .    .

While Sonja spent her afternoon in surgery, Akhmed spent his in the canteen, folding bedsheets into rectangles that soon filled the wicker laundry baskets. At first he had protested, complaining it was the duty of a maid, until Sonja reminded him that those were the only duties he was qualified to perform. While folding he imagined his wife lying on a grayer bedsheet, her head propped on her favorite of their two pillows, the thick foam one that cramped his neck on those nights when they fell asleep sharing it. If she had the energy, she might lift one of his art books from the stack beside the bed. Those hard clothbound covers held worlds of marble statues, woodblock prints, lily pads, bouquets, long-dead generals, and placid landscapes where aristocrats in funny hats pranced around. At night he narrated the scenes to her as if he knew what he was talking about, inventing biographies for every portrait, intrigues for each glance within a frame. Since he had first started skipping first-year pathology to audit still-life drawing classes, he had maintained an abiding interest in art, and for a man who had never been to Grozny, he had amassed a respectable collection of art books. Each morning he reordered the stack so that the first book she reached for was new to her.

He folded the sheet and set it beside the others. How long since he'd last changed Ula's sheets? Ten days, at least. She rarely rolled from her side of the bed, and when he carried her to the living room divan and stripped the linens from the mattress, he found her tawny silhouette sweated into the fabric. That musky darkening was so particularly, irrevocably Ula that he would hesitate to wash it. But then, scolding himself for being sentimental, he would fill the basin with soapy water and submerge her outline and watch her disappear. He was losing her incrementally. It might be a few stray brown hairs listless on the pillow, or the crescents of bitten fingernails tossed behind the headboard, or a dark shape dissolving in soap. As a web is no more than holes woven together, they were bonded by what was no longer there. The dishes no longer prepared or eaten, no more than the four- and five-ingredient recipe cards stacked above the stove. The walks no longer walked, the summer woods, the undergrowth unparted by their shins. The arguments no longer argued; no stakes, nothing either wanted or could lose. The love no longer made, desired, imagined, or mourned. The illness had restored to Ula an innocence he was unwilling to pollute, and the warmth of her flesh cocooning his was a shard of their life dislodged from both their memories.

It had begun in late spring 2002, a year after the *zachistka* that claimed the lives of forty-one villagers, on the morning she slept through breakfast. "I feel sick," she mumbled, and he carried her tea to the nightstand. Had he known the cup was the first of hundreds he would take to her bedside, he would have made a more bitter brew. He took her temperature, pulse, and blood pressure: all normal. Her eyes were clear, her skin colored. When asked she couldn't provide a coherent description of her pain. It was like a loose marble tumbling around her insides, migrating from her ankle to her knee to her hip, and back down. Some days her toes contained all her hurt. Or her fingers. Or elbows. Or kidneys. Eventually it settled somewhere between her chest and stomach, only leaking into her legs on Mondays. Pain is symptomatic rather than causal, even he knew that, and the only reasonable conclusion was that the sickness was seated in her mind. But while he didn't believe she was physically sick, he couldn't deny the reality of her suffering. A year earlier the *zachistka* had leveled a third of the village. Angels descended. Prophets spoke. Truth was only one among many hallucinations.

For the first few weeks he had resisted taking her to Hospital No. 6. He may have graduated in the bottom tenth of his class, but he was still a licensed doctor, and a decent one, even if he didn't always know what he was doing. What would people say if they knew he couldn't diagnose his own wife? Already his patients rarely paid their bills; if news of his ineptitude spread, they would starve. But a month passed without decline or recovery and this static state, this purgatorial non-progression, finally convinced him that his wife's illness exceeded his abilities. He tried to take her to the hospital. Three times they ventured to Volchansk in Ramzan's red pickup, but army cordons blocked all roads into the city. He dreamed up and in his notebook drew ways of conveying her: a sedan chair, a tunnel, a kite large enough to lift her bed. After the fourth attempt, when an unspooled shell casing popped Ramzan's tire ten meters past the house, he gave up. What would the hospital doctors say anyway? With so many real injuries to tend to, they would dismiss Ula and her phantom sickness. The thought of her forced to defend her pain made his fingers curl into fists.

For eight and a half months he cared for her with paternal devotion. But each morning as he set the teacup on the nightstand, he wondered if physical deprivation might revive her ailing mind, and so, ten days before Dokka lost his fingers, Akhmed left her teacup in the kitchen. As the day wore on she called his name in cries more confused and desperate with each iteration, until his name was no longer his but a word of absolute anguish. Unable to stand the call of his name, he stayed with Dokka's wife and daughter for three nights. On the fourth morning he returned and found her on the bedroom floor. The beginnings of bedsores reddened her shoulder blades. In that moment he came to understand that he would spend the rest of his life atoning for the past three days, and that the rest of his life wouldn't be long enough. He lifted her from the floor and set her beneath the sheets. He took her a glass of water from the kitchen, then five more. "You never have to get up again," he promised her. He laid his head on her chest and her heart pattered against his temple. "Akhmed," she said. "Akhmed." His name was now a lullaby.

He never again tried to coerce Ula into health. It would end. Everything did. But when he emptied the bedpan in the backyard, or brushed her teeth despite her protestations, the afterglow of resentment still smoldered. She was gone but still there, the phantom of the wife the war had amputated from him, and unable to properly mourn or love her, he cared for and begrudged her. And so the previous day, when he had offered to work at the hospital until other accommodations could be found for Havaa, he had hoped Sonja would agree for his sake as much as the girl's. That morning, when he left Ula alone with four glasses of water and a bowl of lukewarm rice on the nightstand, he double-locked the door and entered the dawn chill with the confidence that Havaa's future meant more than his wife's, and he trudged eleven kilometers through a broken obligation that only a child's life could justify.

When he folded the last sheet he ducked beneath the clotheslines and opened the cupboard. His trousers lay folded on the bottom shelf. Along the left leg inseam he found a familiar bulge in the stitching. If he were to die away from home, he hoped a kinder soul than Deshi would find him.

"Tomorrow we'll go to Grozny," Sonja announced as she strode through the canteen doorway, stopping at the counter to inspect the scalpels he'd boiled.

"Did Deshi tell you that?" he asked, unable to mask the panic building behind his eyes. "I was only kidding. Of course I'd use the plane ticket to go somewhere else. Tbilisi, even Istanbul."

"You boiled these for ten minutes?"

"You're joking, right?"

She gestured toward him with the scalpel blade, a little too casually for Akhmed's comfort. "About ten minutes in boiling water? I've never been more serious."

"No, about Grozny."

"Did you or did you not boil these for ten minutes?"

"Yes, but are we going to Grozny?"

She frowned, seeming to think *he* was the one talking in circles.

"You don't get to ask any more questions," she said. "A question mark in your mouth is a dangerous weapon."

"So are we?"

She gave a defeated sigh. "Yes."

"Why?"

She pulled a cigarette lighter from her pocket. "Do you smoke?"

"I am an excellent cigarette smoker." It had been seven weeks since his most recent cigarette, and two months more since the one before that, and technically those had been *papirosi*, capped with a filterless cardboard tube and jammed with coarse tobacco that left him violently nauseous for the rest of the day.

Perhaps inspired by his earlier display of professionalism, she waited until they reached the parking lot before lighting up. She passed him the square pack. He knew the Latin alphabet, but hadn't used it in years. "Duh . . ."

"Dunhill," she said.

He selected one from the two erect rows and leaned it into Sonja's lighter. The first drag slid into his lungs without the paint-scraper harshness of his two most recent cigarettes, and he stared at the slowly burning ember, admiring the quality of the tobacco and the quality of the flame, pleasantly surprised that he didn't feel ill. "Where did you get these?" he asked.

"Grozny."

"We're going there to get cigarettes?"

She smiled. "I can't believe you'd really use that plane ticket to go there."

"I've never been."

"It's something else."

"So why are we going?"

Farther down the street the side of a building had crushed all the cars in a parking lot. He was thirty-nine years old and had hoped to own a car by this age.

"I go once a month to pick up supplies," Sonja said. "Not just cigarettes. About everything in the hospital comes through a man I know in Grozny with connections to the outside. I also call a friend of mine who lives in London and updates me on what's been going on in the world."

"What's happening out there?" he asked. By now the wider world was no more than a rumor, a mirage beginning at the borders. Thirty-two years earlier, in the rancid air of his primary school—built on a block bookended by a sewage treatment facility and a lumberjack brothel—his geography teacher had expected him to believe that the world was the same shape as a soccer ball. He had been the first of his classmates to accept it, not because he knew anything about gravity, but because the air was more nauseating than usual that afternoon, and he wanted to leave. For the rest of her career that geography teacher would pride herself on being the first to recognize Akhmed's aptitude for the sciences.

"Last month he told me that George Bush had been reelected," Sonja said.

"Who's that?"

"The American president," Sonja said, looking away.

"I thought Ronald McDonald was president."

"You can't be serious." There it was again, condescension thick enough to spread with a butter knife. His mother was the only other woman to have spoken to him like that, and only when he was a child— and only when he wouldn't eat his cucumbers.

"Wasn't it Ronald McDonald who told Gorbachev to tear down the wall?"

"You're thinking of Ronald Reagan."

"English names all sound the same."

"That was fifteen years ago."

"So? Brezhnev was General Secretary for eighteen."

"It doesn't work like that over there," she explained. "They have elections every few years. If the president doesn't win, someone else becomes president."

"That's ridiculous." The wind lifted the ash from his cigarette and scattered it across the empty parking lot.

"And you can only be president for ten years," she added.

"And then what? You become prime minister for a bit and then run for president again?"

"I think you just step down."

"You mean Ronald just stepped down after ten years?" he asked. She had to be putting him on.

"He just stepped down and George Bush became president."

"And then George Bush shot Ronald Reagan to prevent him seizing power?"

"No," she said. "I think they were friends."

"Friends?" he asked. "It makes me wonder how we lost the Cold War."

"Good point."

"And so George Bush has been president since Ronald Reagan?"

"There was another guy in there. Clinton."

"The philanderer. I remember him," he said, pleased. "And then George Bush became president again?"

"No, the George Bush who is president now is the first George Bush's son."

"Ah, so that's why they don't shoot the previous president. They're all related. Like the Romanovs."

"Something like that," she said distractedly.

"Then who is Ronald McDonald?"

"You know, Akhmed," she said, looking to him for the first time in several minutes. "I'm beginning to like you."

"I'm not an idiot."

"You used the word, not me."

A blast rippled from the east, a long wave breaking across the sky.

"A land mine," she said, as if it were no more than a cough. "We should get going."

He dropped his cigarette without finishing it, the first time he'd done so in six years, and was careful to avoid the glass shards as he followed her back to the entranceway.

"Sew the pockets of your trousers before you come in tomorrow," she advised. "We'll pass a dozen checkpoints to reach Grozny and with that beard you look like a fundamentalist. I don't want the soldiers to plant anything on you."

Akhmed looked to the clouds before following her into the corridor. It wouldn't matter even if he had found a plane ticket. Ten and a half years had passed since he had last seen commercial aircraft in the sky.

The man dragged into the waiting room wasn't the first land-mine victim Akhmed had ever seen, not the first he'd seen accompanied by an incomprehensible woman, not even the first he'd seen dragged on a tarpaulin along a slick scarlet trail; he wasn't the first man Akhmed had seen writhing like a lone noodle in a pot of boiling water, not the first he'd seen with half his shin hanging by a hinge of sinew. But when Akhmed saw this man it was like seeing the first man for the first time: he couldn't think, couldn't act, could only stand in shock as the air where the man's leg should have been filled the floor and the room and his open mouth. The woman tugging at the corner of the tarpaulin spoke a language of shouts and gasps and looked at him as if he could possibly understand her. What a volume her chest produced. The true color of her dress was indistinguishable for the blood. When he finally remembered how to use his feet, he walked right past the woman and the writhing man, to the corner chair, where he draped a white lab coat over Havaa's head.

Then the man's pulse was a haphazard exertion against his finger.

The woman was asking one question after the next. Her dress was showing the curves of her legs. Her breath was on his left cheek. An artery was severed. His face was pale yellow. Sonja was there. She was strapping a rubber tourniquet below the knee. She was rolling him on a gurney and into the hall. The gurney was turning into the operating theater and Deshi was taking the man's blood pressure. "Sixty over forty," she was calling out. The blood pressure meter was velcroed to the young man's arm. The bulb was swinging above the gurney wheel. The wound was wet with saline.

With swift, well-rehearsed movements, Sonja inserted IVs of glucose and Polyglukin into the man's arms. She pulled a surgical saw from the cabinet and disinfected the blade as Deshi called out blood-pressure readings. At seventy over fifty, she injected Lidocaine just above the tourniquet. Deshi anticipated her requests, and the clamps he'd boiled were in her reach before she asked. She worked without looking at the man's face or hearing his cries as though her patient were no more than his most grievous wound. Blood reached her elbows but her scrubs remained white. The man, and he was a man, it was so easy to forget that with all his insides leaking out, had graduated from architecture school and had been searching for employment when the first bombs fell. When the land mine took his leg, he had already spent nine years searching for his first architectural commission. Another six and three-quarter years would pass before he got that first commission, at the age of thirty-eight. With only twenty percent of the city still standing, he would never be without work again.

"Come here," Sonja called. Akhmed looked over his shoulder to summon a more capable ghost from the Brezhnev-beige wall. "Akhmed, come here," she repeated. He stepped forward, wiggling his toes in his boots. One step and then the next, with an immense gratitude for each. The skin was peeled back toward the knee. The calf muscle, cut away. The bone wasn't wider than a chair leg.

She gestured with her scalpel. "For a below-the-knee amputation, you want to keep in mind that stumps close to the knee joint will be difficult to fit for a prosthesis. Long stumps are also difficult to fit and can lead to circulation issues. First, you'll need to make a fish-mouth incision superior to the point of amputation. You want a posterior flap long enough to cover the padded stump and to ensure a tensionless closure when sutured." She described how to isolate the anterior, lateral, and posterior muscular compartments in dissection. She showed him how she had ligated the tibial, peroneal, and saphenous veins, and noted that the blood pressure always rose after the peroneal artery was tied off. She transected the sural nerve above the amputation line and let it retract into the soft-tissue bed to reduce the phantom limb sensation. With a clean scalpel she incised the dense periosteum. She gave directions in the flat, bored tone of a carpenter teaching a child to measure and cut wood, and Akhmed heard her without listening. All her Latin words and surgical jargon couldn't mitigate the helplessness he felt while watching her finish what the land mine had begun.

"Leg amputations are normal business here," she said, and handed him the saw. He held it, expecting her to ask for it back. She looked to it and nodded. No, she couldn't be serious. She didn't expect him to do *that*, did she? She barely trusted him to fold bedsheets properly. "You should get comfortable with this procedure as soon as possible."

He gazed from the blade to the bone. The bone was a disconcerting shade of reddish gray; he'd expected it to be white. He had been six years old when he first realized that the drumstick he slurped the grease from was, in principle, the same as the bone that allowed him to walk, run, and win after-school soccer matches. He hadn't eaten meat again for two years, so great and implacable was his fear that another carnivore would consume his own leg in reprisal. "I'm not qualified for this," he stammered.

"This is the deal," she said calmly. She reached for his hand. That grip held more of her compassion than the past two days combined, and then it was gone, replaced by hard pragmatism, and her fingers wrapped his around the foam grip. "This is what we do. This is what it means for you to work here."

His hands shook and hers steadied them. The last leg surgery he had performed had been after the *zachistka*, on a boy named Akim. He had tried his best, he really had, but he couldn't be faulted for his lack of supplies and experience, for the lack of blood in the boy's body and the great abundance drenching the floor, for the bullet he didn't shoot, or for the war he had no say in; if anyone had bothered to ask his opinion, he would have happily told them that war was, generally speaking, a bad thing, to be avoided, and he would have advised them against it, because had he known that not one but two wars were coming, he would have dropped out of medical school in his first year, his reputation be damned, and gone to art school instead; had he known a domineering, cold-hearted Russian surgeon would one day ask him to cut off this poor man's leg, he would have studied still-life portraiture, landscape oil painting, sculpture and ceramics, he would have sacrificed his brief celebrity within the village, if only to safeguard himself from this man's leg.

"There's only one amputation now, but what about next time?" Sonja said. "There could be five, ten."

He exhaled. Sweat pasted his surgical mask to his cheeks. Sonja pushed his hand forward. The blade grated against the bone. The vibration of each thrust ran up the blade, through the handle, to his hand, and into his bones. The name of the bone was *tibia* and it was connected to *fibula* and *patella*. He had studied the names that morning, but what he knew wouldn't push the saw.

"Press harder," she instructed, steadying the bone for him. "This isn't a delicate operation."

Halfway through, the blade unexpectedly went red with marrow. He stopped sawing.

"What's wrong?" Sonja asked.

He could have answered that question several different ways, but he shook his head, and kept sawing. "I didn't know human bone marrow is red. I thought it would be golden. Like a cow's."

"The marrow of a living bone is filled with red blood cells. If we were to shake a little salt and pepper on this bone and roast it in the oven, the marrow would turn golden in about fifteen minutes," she said.

He feared he might vomit.

"Fine work," she said, as he sliced through the tibia. "Just one more bone to go."

He set the blade on the fibula and his quick hard saw-strokes spat into the air a fine white bone dust that drifted toward him, drawn by his breath, eventually dissolving into his damp surgical mask. Sonja's dark eyes leered at him in his periphery, and he pushed the saw harder, faster, wanting Sonja to see in him more than his helplessness, wanting to finish before he fainted. A dozen strokes later the foot dropped to the table. He held the remnant by the ankle, and without pause or consideration, he flipped it on its end, and blood and marrow coated his fingers as he counted six shards of glass glinting in what was left of the man's sole.

"Set that aside," she said. "We'll wrap it in plastic and give it to the family for burial." She showed him how to round off the amputated bone and pad it with muscle. She pulled the posterior flap over the muscle-padded stump, trimmed the excess skin, and sutured it with black surgical thread.

When they finished, he peeled off his latex gloves and massaged the pink soreness of his right palm, where the skin between his thumb and forefinger had swollen from the handle's pinch. Sonja noticed, smiled, and when she raised her right hand he wanted to be back in bed with Ula, where he could pull the covers over their heads and in the humidity of their stale breaths hold the one person who believed he was knowing, capable, and strong.

Calluses covered Sonja's palm.

CHAPTER

5

1994 1995 1996 1997 1998 1999 2000 2001 2002 2003 **2004**

KHASSAN GESHILOV COMPLETED the first draft of his Chechen history on the one day in January 1963 when it didn't snow. The manuscript was 3,302 pages. When he submitted it to the city publisher in Volchansk he was told he needed to send it to the state publisher in Grozny, and when he submitted it to the state publisher in Grozny he was told he needed to send it to the national publisher in Moscow; and when he submitted it there he was told he needed to send *three* typed copies. Tears leaked from the corners of his eyes as he looked at his poor, battered fingers. But he purchased the postage, paper, typewriter ribbons, and cigarettes such a monumentally monotonous activity required, and eighteen months later he received a phone call from the head editor of the history section, Kirill Ivanovich Kaputzh.

"We're launching a thrilling new series called 'Prehistories of Soviet

Autonomous Republics' and we would like to publish your book as our lead title," Kirill Ivanovich said. Even in his surprise and excitement, Khassan asked what the publisher meant by prehistory; the book he had written ended in 1962. "Prehistory," Kirill Ivanovich explained, "is the time before the cultural and political presence of the Russian state."

"But for Chechnya that would mean 1547."

"Indeed."

"But that's just the first chapter of my book."

"You must be delirious in your excitement, Citizen Geshilov. That is your entire book."

"No, that is the first two hundred twenty-eight pages. Some three thousand follow it," Khassan insisted. He had never imagined that the joy of being published at all and the despair of being published poorly could be tied together like opposite ends of a shoelace.

"Yes, in your joy and astonishment you have become confused. Go and celebrate your achievement, Citizen Geshilov. Accept my congratulations and best wishes. Not everyone has the opportunity to publish a two-hundred-twenty-eight-page book."

And so *Origins of Chechen Civilization: Prehistory to Fall of the Mongol Empire* appeared the next year with little fanfare. The sole review, written for the university newspaper by one of his students, called the book "more interesting than the average reference book." No one wanted to read pre-Russian history books, which was precisely why Moscow was so eager to publish them. By the time Khassan reworked the remaining three thousand pages into a lopsided companion piece—burning a partial draft after pages began disappearing—Khrushchev had been deposed; in response to murky shifts of politics, Kirill Ivanovich Kaputzh, receding farther into the safety of the past, decided to publish only pre-human geological surveys. They were heady days for Khassan's earth-science colleagues.

Then Brezhnev grabbed the wheel of power and captained the country with the exploratory heart of a municipal bus driver. Each passing year the publisher waded farther into the morass of human history, first allowing histories of the Sumerians, then the Ancient Egyptians, and by 1972, the year Ramzan was born, publishing books on the Hellenic age. Sensing the border of 1547 might be crossed within the decade, Khassan revised his tome under the title *Chechen Civilization and Culture Under Russian Patronage*. He wrote as the voice of appeasement, justifying, glossing over, but never forgiving the four centuries of Russian depredations, believing all the while that he might slip three thousand pages of subtext past censors so sensitive to insinuation they would expurgate rain clouds from an International Workers' Day weather forecast. In a knee-height cradle, Ramzan, skull-capped and swaddled, dozed while Khassan wrote. He would never feel closer to his son than he did then, when the rustle of Ramzan's sleep accompanied the scratching of his pencil, and with one hand on the page and the other dipping into the crib he was the wire connecting this halved legacy; much later, he would remember those months when he and his boy could spend the whole day in the same room and mean nothing by the silence.

In 1974 Kirill Ivanovich provisionally accepted the book for publication, with the stipulation that two thousand pages be cut, before he was fired and briefly imprisoned for being too conservative with his edits, too vocal with his own opinions, and too Polish; eight months later, on hard labor duty some four thousand kilometers east of Poland, Kirill Ivanovich would stumble upon the artifacts of an ancient settlement while digging the foundation for a prison latrine, and would remember his assistant, a young man for whom he harbored the pangs of love that time and captivity hadn't blunted, a young man whom Kirill Ivanovich had listened to, as he read aloud passages from Khassan Geshilov's history of early civilization, passages Kirill Ivanovich kept intact in his memory, like jars to hold and preserve the beautiful voice of his assistant. Kirill Ivanovich's successor, an editor whose aquiline nose pointed toward the prevailing political winds, decided the book required more radical revision to conform to the tedium of the era. And so began a decade of rewrites that mirrored the plummeting Brezhnev reign. The new editor stressed that the book didn't need to be more concise—if anything it should be longer, the editor said, so reviewers would dismiss its shortcomings as the price of ambition—and Khassan reupholstered the paragraphs he'd stripped under Kirill Ivanovich's guidance. He wrote tracts on nineteenth-century threshing techniques, the history of Chechen meteorology. The new editor would respond with changes so vague and inconsistent it took weeks to divine a politically safe interpretation. "Rewrite chapter twelve as though you were not a person but a people," one letter said. "If you write on the fatherland, your words will face the heavens," said another.

No longer did he write in his son's company. Ramzan had learned to speak, though Khassan wished he hadn't. The boy used his voice like a rubber mallet; *can I* was the only question that escaped his mouth, never *what* or *how* or *why*. Ramzan wasn't clever or kind or imaginative, or even overly obedient or cruel or dull, and Khassan built his aversion upon the empty cellar of what his son was not. In the historical sources there were kings and princes whose distaste for their progeny took more sadistic forms than Khassan's indifference; compared to Ivan the Terrible, he was a paradigm of good parenting. You can choose your son no more than you can choose your father, but you can choose how you will treat him, and Khassan chose to treat his as if he wasn't there. He chose to write when he should have spoken, to speak when he should have listened. He chose to read his books when he should have watched his son, to watch when he should have approached. One day when Ramzan was eight he entered Khassan's office and asked his father to teach him to ride a bicycle. "You'll fall," Khassan said, without looking up from the page. The moment would haunt him later. What if he had looked up?

Brezhnev appeared to be on his deathbed ten years before he finally passed, but on November 10, 1982, the country's beloved grandfather smoked his last white-filtered Novost cigarette. Brezhnev was buried in his marshal's uniform along with the two hundred medals—everything from Hero of the Soviet Union to the Lenin Prize for Literature—he had accrued in his eighteen-year tenure as General Secretary. Watching the mournful proceedings with his family (they all searched for Galina Brezhneva among the mourners to see if she would cause scandal even at her father's funeral), Khassan finally accepted the futility of his endeavor. He had traveled farther than Herodotus but had written no *Histories*, had witnessed more combat than Thucydides but had written no *History of the Peloponnesian War*. His son sat on one side, his wife on the other, and they watched the tributes paid to a man whose tepid mediocrity encapsulated the era. For years he had relegated history to the past, where it was time-dulled and safe and ever-receding, but history was right there, in that moment, on the television screen, where balding and bejowled politicians paid their respects before determining the shape of the empire, where the flat, embalmed face of the beloved grandfather went translucent under the spotlights, and where finally they caught a glimpse of the daughter of the departed, her dress a scandalous pink.

Yuri Andropov replaced Brezhnev, only to die fifteen months later, and Konstantin Chernenko replaced Andropov only to die thirteen months after that. Again Khassan watched the funerals with his family; state funerals were the only times they came together. He couldn't have known this would be the final televised funeral of a General Secretary, but later, when remembering the gloomy cavalcade, he would imagine that the entire Soviet state was buried in Chernenko's casket. Gorbachev at least looked like he might live more than a year on the job, and soon after his ascension to General Secretary, Khassan received a call from a new, reform-minded editor, who had deposed Khassan's previous editor. The reform-minded editor had found Khassan's original manuscript from 1963 and thought it a more accurate and readable document than any of his subsequent revisions. "All that's left is honing and updating," the editor said. "Now is the time. A few years ago you would have been sent to Siberia. Today you'll be lauded."

Even the renewed fervor of his revisions couldn't keep pace with the deluge of declassified information released by state agencies. For a quarter century his book hadn't been published because it was too accurate. Now it wouldn't be published because it wasn't, and couldn't be, accurate enough. A three-thousand-page draft took years to write. He couldn't possibly analyze and incorporate the disclosures that, on a daily basis, changed the way a Soviet historian was allowed to interpret his material. Even so, he finished a draft he was reasonably pleased with in the late summer of 1989. A few months later, when the Berlin Wall fell, not even a news agency as reliably incompetent as Pravda failed to speculate on its consequences. The reform-minded editor loved the new draft and wanted to schedule publication for the following year, but Khassan demurred. The morning headlines made the previous day's work obsolete; publishing the book now would be like building nine-tenths of a roof. The rind of buffer states diminished as republics peeled away. All of central Europe had shrugged off communist leadership, and now the Baltic states, the Black Sea states, even Moldova was discussing secession. For the first time in two millennia Chechnya had a chance at sovereignty. Everything was changing. It had to go into his book.

Everything did change, faster than his fingers could type. What he had been too cautious to hope for was pulled from his dreams and made real on the television screen. At that momentous hour on December 26, 1991, as he watched the red flag of the Union of Soviet Socialist Republics—the empire extending eleven times zones, from the Sea of Japan to the Baltic coast, encompassing more than a hundred ethnicities and two hundred languages; the collective whose security demanded the sacrifice of millions, whose Slavic stupidity had demanded the deportation of Khassan's entire homeland; that utopian mirage cooked up by cruel young men who gave their mustaches more care than their morality; that whole horrid system that told him what he could be and do and think and say and believe and love and desire and hate, the system captained by Lenin and Zinoviev and Stalin and Malenkov and Beria and Molotov and Khrushchev and Kosygin and Mikoyan and Podgorny and

Brezhnev and Andropov and Chernenko and Gorbachev, all of whom but Gorbachev he hated with a scorn no author should have for his subject, a scorn genetically encoded in his blood, inherited from his ancestors with their black hair and dark skin—as he watched that flag slink down the Kremlin flagpole for the final time, left limp by the windless sky, as if even the weather wanted to impart on communism this final disgrace, he looped his arms around his wife and son and he held them as the state that had denied him his life quietly died.

In the following years he lost his publisher, then his university job, then his wife, who one Tuesday morning passed away as meekly as she had lived; he didn't notice until eleven hours after her final breath. The chain saws went silent and the forest grew back, and one war came and then another, and Khassan had his son and his book, and the prospect of finding fulfillment in either seemed as unlikely as the prospect of either surviving the decade. But Khassan still had them, and at a time when all belief dissolved, the act of possession was more important than what was possessed. The things in his life that caused him the most sorrow were the things he'd lived with the longest, and now that everything was falling they became the pillars that held him; had he a thirty-two-year-old toothache rather than a thirty-two-year-old son, he would have treasured it the same. But that, too, had its time. The unseasonably warm afternoon one year, eleven months and three days earlier, when Dokka and Ramzan returned from the Landfill—Dokka missing all ten fingers, Ramzan missing only his *pes*—was the last day Khassan had spoken to his son.

First Ramzan feigned indifference, then shouted, then pleaded for his father's conversation. How could Ramzan have known he would miss his father's monosyllabic disapproval? How could he have known that he lived in reaction to his father's expectations, needed them to know precisely the person he had failed to become?

"I'm doing this for you as much as for me," Ramzan had said with the desperate logic of the unconvinced. "We have a generator, electric lights, food on the table. Is it such a crime to give you insulin? To have clean drinking water?"

But Khassan, a career apologist, was fluent in the rhetoric of justification and accustomed to ignoring his son. By the fifth month his son's anger burned away, and a dense depression descended. Ramzan's footsteps filled the night. Soon painkillers and sleeping pills joined the hypodermic needles, cotton balls, alcohol swabs, and insulin brought back from the military supplier. The ovular green pills left Ramzan comatose for sixteen hours, and in these spells, when the house exhaled and the floorboards went silent, Khassan entered his son's room.

On earlier excursions, he had explored the drawers, closet, and shelves. In the upper left bureau drawer, he found the thirty-centimeter blade of the *kinzhal* he'd given Ramzan on his sixteenth birthday, a knife his father had given him, and his grandfather his father. Within the pages of an algebra textbook a list bore the names of those Ramzan had helped disappear. The list contained three names when he first found it neatly folded between pages 146 and 147, farther into the textbook than his son had ever ventured in school. The last time he checked, a few weeks before Dokka's was to be added, twelve names were listed. But most mornings, like this one, the second morning after Dokka disappeared, Khassan had no need or desire for further incrimination. Instead he sat on the bed, and held Ramzan's hand, and spoke to him.

"I saw Akhmed this morning and he ran away from me," Khassan said. "He ran into the forest and hid behind a tree because I am your father."

In these moments when his son lay encased beneath the surface of a chemically sustained slumber, when his words were extinguished like sparks released into a vacuum, Khassan spoke freely. He told stories from his youth, begged clemency for certain villagers, and once suggested Ramzan drink peppermint tea for his cough. What else could he do when honor-bound to shun his son, when disavowal was his last vestige of paternal authority? The one-sided conversations were long treks across bridges leading nowhere, but he knew no other way to span the divide; he enjoyed the spoils of the collaboration he condemned, disavowed his son for lacking the compassion he had never taught him. "Let Akhmed be," he whispered. "Let the girl be. Forget their names. They are gone."

In the bureau he found the *kinzhal* sheathed unceremoniously in an undershirt. Three paces away, Ramzan's Adam's apple nodded like a bobber on the tide. One slice was all it would take. He had told Akhmed as much a few hours earlier. He could have taken one step, then the next, and the third. He could have lodged the butt of the handle against his breastplate and fallen forward and so taken gravity as his accomplice. There would have been blood, but he could have stomached it; a Chechen, he knew, had more blood in him than a Russian, but far less than a German. He could have, as he could have other times; but he pulled a green apple from his pocket and sliced through that instead. The core sat in two blocks of pale flesh and with the undershirt he wiped the juice from the blade and wished he had the fortitude to make the juice blood. What father fantasizes about killing his son? Even murderers, rapists, and politicians deserve fathers who separate love from repudiation, but Khassan couldn't manage that; like dye poured into water, what he felt for Ramzan was a singular, inseparable opacity. Uncomfortable with only three paces between the *kinzhal* and the neck, Khassan carried the apple outside. He sat on the shoveled back steps and whistled three times.

He surveyed the yard while waiting for the dogs to emerge from the woods. The slate grave markers and stone perimeter of the herb garden were no more than dips and rises in the snow. The garden had been his wife's suggestion, one of the few he acted on in their twenty-three years of marriage. Sharik, a pup then, had followed his nose around the yard as though pushing an invisible ball, and Khassan had planted seeds in rows marked with bent wire hangers. The dishes his wife had cooked for years soon tasted new, as though prepared by another woman, and Khassan had imagined that other woman when he made love to his wife five times that spring. Now she lay buried at the far end of the garden, beside the brown suitcase containing the bones of his parents, commemorated by a slight depression in the snow and a frozen dog turd.

Feral and matted, whittled by deprivation, the dogs loped toward the back steps. They had belonged to the neighbors his son had disappeared, and even in this state he knew them by name. They trotted through the hole he'd clipped in the fence and gathered before him in a tight semicircle, jostling and snapping at the thin slivers of apple falling from the *kinzhal* blade. He held out his hands and they licked the juice from his fingers. Like them, he was unwelcome at the homes of his neighbors and avoided on the street. Like them, he was a pariah. He nuzzled the snout of a brown mutt, reaching from the dog's muzzle to her ears, and before he knew what was happening, he was holding her as he hadn't held a human in years. The mutt—which had been a husband's tenth-anniversary gift to his wife, who had been expecting something smaller, inanimate, and in a box—licked the grease from his hair.

"You think I'm wonderful, don't you? You think I'm the kindest, bravest, most generous man ever given a pair of feet to step into the world," he said, and the dog kept licking his hair in reply. "That's because you're a stupid dog."

He went to the kitchen, returned with the meat of two chickens and a lamb shank, and laid it in the snow, his hair sticky with saliva, the king and benefactor of their open maws. He would never forget his son's face the morning after Ramzan's fifth trip to the military supplier, when Ramzan opened the refrigerator and found nothing but condiment jars basking in the thirty-watt glow. Ramzan had stormed to the backyard, where the dogs lay on the ground, swollen stomachs pointed skyward, unable to roll, let alone stand, let alone run, and Khassan lay right there among them, his own navel aimed at the clouds, turning the dead grass into confetti, such a lovely and peculiar carelessness known only to elderly men who have napped with feral dogs. Ramzan screamed at him, picking up a thigh bone gnawed clean, pulling the gristle from the slack jaws of a blind wolfhound, and a distant happiness returned to Khassan like a word he could define but not remember. From that day, a year and a half earlier, his disapproval had expanded from silence to sabotage. If Ramzan used food to justify the disappearances, Khassan made sure it all went to the dogs. Canine affection and his son's exasperation became his only sources of pleasure. In response, Ramzan began stashing food around the house, but he soon realized that even processed meat spoiled. Then he bought a fancy refrigerator lock invented for fat Westerners without self-control; each morning he set aside enough for Khassan to eat that day, and locked up. But Khassan would give his three meals to the dogs and go hungry himself, and when he lost enough weight, Ramzan abandoned the tactic. Next Ramzan only brought foods to which dogs are allergic: chocolate, raisins, and walnuts. But Ramzan's teeth began aching, his shit began looking like fancy Swiss candy bars, and with one glance to the insulin bottle Khassan reminded him that a diabetic couldn't live on sweets. They were wonderful days; how he enjoyed terrorizing his son. In the end his boy surrendered. Couldn't outwit his father. For the past year they had communicated by the glares of a resentful truce. Khassan fed the dogs as his only family, and always left enough for Ramzan, though no more than the average villager could hope to survive on in these difficult days.

Khassan stood and smiled at the six dogs, muzzles to the ground, tails wagging languidly. One was bald, another blind. From time to time a dog would race toward the fence, chasing invisible rodents; in the vaporous insanity that had fallen across the land, even dogs hallucinated. A white shepherd dog stood at the back. He tossed him the finest cut.

"Sharik," he said, but the dog didn't recognize his name. Three years earlier, before his son's treachery allowed them food to spare, he had let the dog go. His claws had danced frantically on the floorboards, and Khassan had had to kick twice before he scampered out the open door. For three days the dog had paced the fence, head hung, waiting for Khassan to call him back. Khassan hadn't left the house until Sharik finally had disappeared into the forest. When Ramzan had arrived with the first cardboard boxes of food, he had tried to entice the dog home, but whatever trust had existed between them was dead. Only by caring for the pack could Khassan care for his dog. That was the gift Sharik had given, and Khassan thanked him every morning with the finest cuts.

The dogs followed him around the side of the house, through weeds winter couldn't kill, to the tire tracks furrowed in the road. They clambered behind him, trusting him as people did not, and when he unclenched his fists and wiggled his fingers, he felt cold wet noses and the warmth of their tongues.

"Did I ever tell you the story of the cobbler and his son?" he asked the brown mutt. "Yes, you've already heard it. Sharik tells it best."

He walked to the gap in the block where Dokka's house had stood. The dogs wouldn't follow him onto the frozen charcoal. He found the corner where Dokka's bookcase had stood, and there he bent down and scooped a handful of ash into his coat pocket. The dark dust dissolved into his palm. "A bunch of big tough wild dogs," he said to the pack, which waited for him on the banks of the frozen debris. "But too afraid to follow me . . ." To follow him where? Where was he?

Across the street the curtained windows were two black eyes on the face of Akhmed's house. If Akhmed had left at dawn, and said he would be gone all day, who was looking in on Ula? The most painful revelations were the quietest, those moments when the map opened on the meandering path that had led him here. An ailing woman would spend the day alone; he hadn't envisioned that.

"I could call on her, see if she is all right, if she needs anything," he said, glancing to the dogs for approval. They were all ripples on the same pond. "If I'm looking after a bunch of dogs, the least I can do is look after her. Don't take that tone with me. I am not breaking in. I have the key right here." He displayed the spare key Akhmed had given him with a grin, nine years earlier, on the day the bank that owned four-fifths of Akhmed's house was bombed into oblivion. The dogs cocked their heads, unconvinced. "No, I haven't been called for, but that's beside the point. Are you sure you want to discuss etiquette? I have a lot to say about ass-sniffing as a way to say hello."

Two paces toward the house a burgeoning worry spread through him. What if the dogs thought he was leaving them for human company? Well, he was, but he had to break it to them gently. They were sensitive souls, even if they occasionally dug up and ate newly buried bodies. He dropped to one knee and opened his arms. All but Sharik licked the aftertaste of oats from his breath, and he told them how much he loved them, how much he needed them, how he would never leave them. Then the bald dog sniffed his ass.

His highly critical canine audience observed as he knocked at the front door. "See?" he said to them. "I have no choice but to use the key."

He pushed open the door and crossed the thick mustiness to the bedroom. A pair of slender legs, no more than sheet creases, shifted beneath the covers. For three minutes he watched her from the threshold, a second slice of his day spent watching a second addled mind at rest; then she rolled over. He looked into her eyes and they took their time looking back.

"You've gotten old, Akhmed," she said, and he couldn't suppress his smile. Like a child, this one.

"I'm not Akhmed," he said. Akhmed had been eight days old when they first met in the living room of Akhmed's parents in 1965. He had held the infant in his arms and a relief profound as any he would ever feel had seeped right through him. Akhmed's eight-day-old eyes had held the reflection of ten thousand possible lives. Khassan wasn't an emotive or superstitious man, and nothing like it had ever happened again, but he had found, layered in the infant's half-lidded eyes, innumerable, wanting faces, none of which he had recognized.

"I'm sorry," Ula murmured. "My head isn't right."

He sat on the bed beside the bone of her hip. "Don't apologize. I spent the morning talking to dogs."

"If you're not Akhmed, then why are you here?"

"I wanted to see if you needed anything. If you wanted someone to talk to. Akhmed won't be back for a while."

"He won't be back?" she seemed to ask, but he wasn't sure. She had but two notes in her, and on the wire stretching between them her questions and answers warbled the same.

"Not for a little while," he said. Three full water glasses and a bowl of hardened rice sat on the nightstand.

Sensing his uncertainty, she again asked, "Why are you here?"

"I miss speaking to people," he said. When he admitted it aloud he wanted to laugh. It was that simple. He was that lonely. He had come to an invalid woman to offer the help he needed. "I miss being able to speak. For nearly two years Akhmed has been the only person I've had a conversation with."

"You said you spent the morning talking to dogs."

He smiled and nodded. "I didn't think you'd remember that. He must be the only person you've talked with in that time, too."

"Who?"

"Do you know my name?" he asked. She strained but came back with nothing. "That's okay," he said. "That's just fine."

"Tell me a story," she said.

"A story?"

"There were the stories of paintings. All true."

He frowned. He didn't know the stories of any paintings. "I only know one story," he said. "I can say it happened, but I can't say if it's true. Did you ever meet Akhmed's mother?" He took her empty stare for a no. "I'm glad you remember that because you couldn't have met her. Cancer took her when Akhmed was seven. Her name was Mirza."

She nodded because she was expected to.

"If I tell you this story, do you promise you will forget it?"

"I can't promise anything," she said distantly. He held her wrist, felt its plodding pulse. *A mind too feeble to tell the time of day can still get the right blood to the right places,* he thought. He'd never told anyone about her. "I will tell you about Mirza."

He heard about the mass deportation nearly two years after it occurred, he told Ula, only after he himself had been deported to Kazakhstan. On February 23, 1944, Red Army Day, a day when Khassan had been shooting Nazis in eastern Poland, the Soviet NKVD rounded up Chechens in their town squares and forced them into Lend-Lease Studebaker trucks. Those who resisted or whom the NKVD deemed unfit for transport were shot. Packed into a coal wagon, Khassan's parents and sister slept on maize sacks and ate dry maize meal as the trains slowly steamed eastward. Local soldiers cut their hair and dusted them with delousing powder when they arrived on the Kazakh steppe. Khassan never knew what happened to his sister, only that she had been seen climbing into the coal wagon in Grozny but hadn't been seen climbing out. His parents slept in a *kolkhozniki* dormitory cellar, on a bed of dry mattress straw, and when hungry they made a flour of the mattress straw and fried thin powdery slabs that left them feverish but full. When they ran out of straw, they slept on the stone floor and made soup from grains picked from horse manure. By the time Khassan reached Kazakhstan in autumn 1945, conditions had improved but his parents had already perished, and he pieced together the story of their last year from the memories of their neighbors and friends, and from Mirza.

Mirza had been a child when Khassan left for war, and in 1947, when he came upon her straining water through cheesecloth, he didn't recognize her as the girl who, at the age of eight, had been brought up on criminal charges for drawing a charcoal mustache on her lip and goose-stepping around the barnyard, ordering livestock to become more active builders of communism. "Let me have some," he said, thirsty after his long way. "Go fuck yourself," she said simply. It was their first conversation. She would become the love of his life, but he couldn't have known that as he turned and stepped into dung so deep it reached the knot in his laces. He couldn't have known it as he pried the pail from Mirza's fingers and washed his boot in her clean water.

A year later the schoolmaster died and Khassan replaced him. He was without qualification or experience, but after the war, the squabbles of children approximated peace, and he was happy. Among his pupils was Mirza's youngest sister, a quick-witted girl, with fingernails bitten so short she couldn't lift a kopek coin from a counter, who once set a tack on the chair of the commissar's chubby son to see if he would explode. Though he saved the commissar's son from the tack—and thus Mirza's sister from a bullet—he recognized that thread of recklessness running through her family just asking to be snipped short.

For May Day 1950, Khassan organized a children's parade. Adults lined the stone-marked road to cheer their children and avoid the penalty of ten years' hard labor for nonattendance. Twenty-three of the ninety-six children marching that day wouldn't live to see their native Chechnya. The commissar's son would be among them because the cholera ward, without respect for political class, was the nearest to an egalitarian society that most of them would ever come. Mirza's youngest sister was one of the four who held on a raised pallet the plaster bust of Stalin. Mirza glared from across the street, her hands at her sides, the only pair there not brought together in applause. Her contempt passed through him as light through vapor. The following afternoon she confronted him in the schoolhouse with a look that would have severed weaker necks. "You are a coward," she said, and with that one word wrote a denunciation, a biography, and a prophecy. It was their second conversation.

In 1956, three years after Stalin's death, the Chechen ethnicity was rehabilitated by the pen stroke of a distant bureaucrat. On the evening of the day the first trains arrived to transport them home, Khassan followed the pale stone road to the pale stone cemetery, carrying with him a spade and the brown suitcase his parents had last packed twelve years earlier. The earth was hard and dry, and it took several hours to reach them. His mother's index finger pointed at him through the dirt. The burial shroud had replaced their skin. They were lighter than he had expected, their muscles hard in desiccation. He folded their arms, pulled on their legs until the tendons snapped; he was as reverent as possible. He packed them tenderly within the discolored suitcase lining. Their bones lay bowed and prostrate. He performed no ablutions, and the brown of earth and decay had rusted his hands, but God would forgive him these lesser blasphemies. They had given him as good a life as they could. He wished he could have given them a better death. He decided, then, that he would write a history of his parents, of his people, of this sliver of humanity the world seemed determined to forget. Standing in the mounded dirt the spade was a slender tombstone. He wasn't alone. Hundreds of others had come to raise and return their dead, and the dust reddened the night.

When he reached his cabin, a small shack within a perimeter of pale stone, he wanted to wash his hands. He didn't. Instead he folded the shirts he'd won in cards from Red Army guards, the long underwear he'd stripped from a corpse, the marmot coat a Kazakh widow had traded for the promise that her departed husband's name would remain on his tongue for nine years of nightly prayers. The brown suitcase stood at the door. He had inherited no other, nothing in which to pack the clothes so neatly folded on the floor. For eleven years he had dreamed of leaving behind his folded clothes for whatever Soviet ethnicity next fell from official favor, leaving behind all but his parents' remains, and the following morning, when a locomotive whistle seared through his sleep, he awoke to that dream.

The cattle cars were filled by the time he reached the tracks. The refugees watched uncertainly as trains glided into the pale grasses of the steppe, becoming the only measure of scale. Balancing on a tie, beneath an exhaust cloud that rose like a locust swarm returning to God's mouth, he found Mirza. "You're still here," she said. "I am," he said. She lifted his brown suitcase. "It's light," she said. "It's my parents," he said. It was their third conversation.

The refugees camped along the tracks, afraid of missing the next transport, but Khassan, trusting the sky to convey the clatter of approaching trains, walked into the empty village beside Mirza. Trails of clothing, furniture, and dishware flowed from the open doors of cabins and huts. The commissar and his entourage were the first to flee, and the Party headquarters, the most architecturally sound building for many kilometers, was abandoned. They passed through meeting rooms papered with bulletins announcing the repatriation, and into the commissar's office. Three upholstered chairs encircled a coffee table where a golden fountain pen stood at attention in its reservoir. Behind them, hanging over the doorframe, the plaster bust of Stalin observed them coolly. Khassan lifted it from its perch—two taps to Stalin's forehead echoed in the hollow cranium—and wrapped it in a burgundy drape. Mirza's face was unrecognizable in its approval.

Khassan carried the bust to the steppe and when he set it down the tall grasses radiated around the dead dictator's face. Mirza dropped her heel through Stalin's temple—and what could he do, when she looked at him like that, but become her accomplice? He crushed the big brown mustache, and she joined in, stamping out the left eye; their feet engaged in this fourth conversation until their boots were white with plaster dust, and they had finally committed the treason for which they had been sentenced twelve years earlier. They shrieked and whooped until their voices were hoarse and their lungs ached and the wind was carrying off the dust and it was all celebration. Finally, he spread the burgundy drape across the grass. She reached for his cheek and he reached for her shoulder. On her stomach, to the left of her navel, an oval birthmark spread like a tipped inkwell. He placed his mouth on it.

.   .   .

Ula had closed her eyes, but in the quiet he felt the relief of confession like a current carrying him after he stopped kicking. It felt wonderful to be heard and forgotten. He wanted more. He wanted to erase the past he had spent his life recording. Later, in his study, he gathered his notes, rough drafts, red-line edits, everything, and set them in a bedsheet and carried them into the woods. It would take many trips, many tied bedsheets, but he would erase every word he had ever written. The dogs accompanied him, and behind them followed the memory of Mirza's accusation, now stronger, fortified by the testimony of four decades spent as a Soviet apologist. And after the fire had read his pages, and the dogs basked in the warmth, and the ashes grayed the snow, what would he write? Not a history of a nation that had destroyed history and nationhood. Something smaller. A letter to Havaa. His recollections of Dokka. He would begin with his favorite memory of Dokka, then go back to the first time he had met him, and end with Havaa's birth. It would be the first true thing he had ever written.

1994 1995 1996 1997 1998 1999 2000 2001 2002 2003 **2004**

AT THAT MOMENT, Havaa hated the hospital. She hated the chemi-
cals that sharpened the air and burned her throat just like the bleach
her mother used to launder sheets, when there had been bleach, and
sheets, and her mother. She hated the patients, who were bruised, who
were broken, who took so, so, so long to die. She hated Deshi. The
nurse was old, the nurse was boring, and if she were the face of life, no
wonder so many patients chose death. She frowned at the stupid yellow
linoleum; what was Akhmed doing? She hated him, too. He'd thrown
a lab coat over her and left her to sit by herself in the waiting room
while the man hauled in on the tarpaulin filled the air with screaming
and the floor with bleeding. Through the thin fabric of the lab coat,
she'd watched the frantic shadows thrash about on the floor, straining

to stopper everything that was pouring from that sad man. When they finished, they disappeared down the corridor, and left her there like a coat stand.

And now Akhmed had gone home, had left her again. Would he return tomorrow? Yes, he had to. She couldn't entertain other possibilities. Yes, Akhmed would return tomorrow; he would return tomorrow and he would go to Grozny, a place they always talked about going to *together*, and he would go with Sonja instead, whom he clearly liked more than her, because she was older and had breasts, and they would probably be doing something only the two of them would find fun, like inventing a way to scratch a phantom limb, and tomorrow, when he returned, she would hate him, and until then she would miss him.

A phantom limb. She still hadn't taught the one-armed guard to juggle, as she had promised Akhmed, and she hated that she wanted to impress Akhmed even when he wasn't with her. She found the guard at the hospital entrance, asleep on the bench. He wore the faded olive uniform of the rebels. She pressed her index finger into his stomach as far as it would go, which wasn't very far, because he didn't have much stomach to him. He woke with a grunt. "What do you want?"

"To juggle."

He closed his eyes. "You don't need my permission. Go forth. Juggle."

"No, I'm here to teach you to juggle."

"You must be kidding." He hadn't opened his eyes again.

"You aren't a one-armed freak that everyone feels sorry for," Havaa said, as comfortingly as she could. When Akhmed had taught her to juggle six months earlier, he had used small rectangles of gauze that flapped and turned in the breeze like a shoal of starving white fish. They had stood in the middle of the street, the gusting headwind the nearest thing to traffic, the gauze strips slithering in it, and Akhmed hooting as she chased them. It had taken her all afternoon to learn to juggle one. The next day they had moved indoors. Juggling is more in your mind than your hands, Akhmed had told her; in the still air she had learned in minutes. "Juggling is more in your mind than your hand," she told the one-armed guard.

"I died in my sleep, didn't I? This is Hell, isn't it?"

"You begin by throwing a handkerchief up in the air," she said, and demonstrated in an exaggerated flourish.

The one-armed guard began praying. "Deliver me, Allah, from this cesspool of wickedness."

"You want to make sure you cross the handkerchief, like you're pinning it to the shoulder of an invisible partner. Like a phantom partner; that should be familiar to you!"

"Jesus Christ, hear my plea," the one-armed guard chanted, in case the infidel god was more receptive.

"Then you repeat the same movement with your other hand."

"She thinks I have another hand."

"See how well I can do it?" she said, all three handkerchiefs aloft.

"My phantom hand is slapping you in the face."

"I can't feel it," she said, proudly.

"Neither can I," he said, glumly.

"You seem a little grumpy. Maybe you should take another nap."

As she left the one-armed guard she hated Akhmed even more; if she couldn't tell him, it was as if she hadn't taught the one-armed guard to juggle at all. He had left her, just like her father had, and her mother, and she bandaged that wound with all the stubborn sullenness she could muster, so it would be hidden, well insulated, and so no one could see how in just three hours she had learned to miss him with the same incredible longing she reserved for her parents. She should have known Akhmed would forget her as quickly as he had her mother.

She didn't hate Sonja, not as much as Akhmed. Sure, Sonja was curt and short-tempered, a humorlessist incapable of finding in an hour the fun Akhmed could conjure in a minute. But that was okay because Sonja was different. Sonja was the boss of this place, ordering everyone around, and even Akhmed went pale when she spoke. Not only was Sonja a doctor, she was the head of the entire hospital. Women weren't supposed to be doctors; they weren't capable of the work, the schooling, the time and commitment, not when they had houses to clean, and children to care for, and dinners to prepare, and husbands to please. But Sonja was more freakish, more wondrously confounding than the one-armed guard; rather than limbs she had, somehow, amputated expectations. She *didn't* have a husband, or children, or a house to clean and care for. She *was* capable of the work, school, time, commitment, and everything else it took to run a hospital. So even if Sonja was curt and short-tempered, Havaa could forgive her these shortcomings, which were shortcomings only in that they were the opposite of what a woman was supposed to be. The thick, stern shell hid the defiance that was Sonja's life. Havaa liked that.

And so she wandered along the corridor, wondering what she might be like if she lived like Sonja. Maybe she could be an arborist, like her father. She hadn't thought that women were allowed to be scientists, but if Sonja could be a surgeon and hospital head, why couldn't she be an arborist? Or a sea anemonist? She slowed to peek into the room where the legless man slept. Blood dried darkly on his bandages. His stump poked from the edge of the white bedsheet like a rotten log through snow cover. He slept. Somewhere in that hazy, heroin-induced slumber, he was already designing in dreams the monument to war dead he would, in twenty-three years, make of steel and concrete. He was the only person in the hospital right now she didn't hate.

"I thought I told her to find something to do," Deshi said, entering the room with her customary frown.

"I was."

" 'I was,' she says. Was what?"

"Thinking," Havaa shot out, like a pebble cast toward the nurse's flat face.

"Find something more useful to do," Deshi said. She knitted as she leaned against the wall. The yarn ball slowly rolled in her pocket.

"Does Sonja order you around like this?"

"Why would she say that?"

"Because Sonja runs the hospital."

"Unbelievable," Deshi said with a sigh. "I've been working here since before Sonja was a kick in her mother's stomach, was already retired when I hired her, and she gets the credit for making this place run. They'll take everything from you, even the respect of an orphan girl with too many questions in her mouth."

"Why is the hospital run by women? What happened to all the men?"

"They ran away."

"But they're the brave ones."

"No, they're the ones that break your heart and leave you for a younger woman."

"So you're saying that sometimes women are braver than men. And better doctors."

"I'm saying that if you want to keep a man, you better hide his shoes every night so he can't walk out on you."

"I don't understand."

Deshi shook her head. Her romantic advice was worth a foreigner's ransom, and here she was, giving it freely to a girl who couldn't appreciate the hard-earned wisdom. "Just stay away from oncologists, okay?" she said, and led the girl to the waiting room. "If you just remember that, you'll spare yourself the worst of it. Now, why don't you get your notebook out and draw something?"

"Like what?"

"I don't know. Where would you most want to be right now?"

"My home," she said. She thought the word meant only the four walls and roof that held her, but it spread out, filled in, Akhmed, the village, her parents, the forest, everything that wasn't here. "A week ago."

"And I'd rather be right here forty years ago, when they first offered me the job. I'd wag my finger right in the head nurse's face and say, no, no, you won't trick me, and I'd walk right out those doors."

"It's stupid. There are maps to show you how to get to the place where you want to be but no maps that show you how to get to the time when you want to be."

"Why don't you draw that map?"

"Only if you let me play on the fourth floor."

"Child, if there was such a map, there would still be a fourth floor. Start drawing."

The sharp, chemical-curtained corridor swallowed Deshi's footsteps and Havaa was alone again. The notebook tilting on her legs, she thought of her father. She didn't hate him. Thinking that, realizing it, feeling it crackle through her arm bones, her finger bones, feeling her arms wrapping around her chest, her fingers clasping her shoulders, this trembling inside her that was only the beat of her heart. Each night he would tell her tales about an alien green-bodied race whose faces consisted of a singular orifice through which they saw, ate, smelled, heard, thought, and spoke. Each night he told her a new chapter, and so many nights had gone by, so many chapters had been told, that they referred to it as *chapters* rather than *story*, because stories had endings and theirs had none. According to her father, the green-bodied aliens had destroyed their planet in an interstellar civil war and had migrated to the Moon to begin again. Each night, as civilization collapsed around them, he told her of a new one being built on the lunar surface. She hoped her father was there, among them, up on the Moon.

Sonja strode through the door, reeking of cigarette smoke, her eyelids puffy and her fingers jittering. "You're here," Sonja said, surprised.

"Yes," Havaa agreed. "I'm here. This is the waiting room."

Sonja glanced down to the floor, to the chairs, puzzling over this and then nodding. "You're right. This is the waiting room," she said, and sat in the folding chair beside Havaa.

"How was your day?" Havaa asked.

Sonja shrugged, sparked her cigarette lighter, and stared vacantly toward the wall. "It was an okay day. You?"

"It was okay."

Sonja sighed, closed her eyes, and sparked her lighter in a slow, senseless rhythm.

"Are the Feds going to take me, too?" To ask the question was to acknowledge that it could happen, and in Havaa's experience, any horror that could happen eventually did. Better to armor yourself with the unreal. Better to turn inward, hide in the dark waters among the sea anemones, down deep where the sharks can't see you.

Sonja's hand found hers between the chairs.

"Will the Feds take me to my father?" she asked, while knowing the question had no answer she wanted to hear. Her father was her door to the world; he was the singular opening through which she saw, heard, and felt. Without him she didn't know what she saw, or what she heard, and what she felt; all she felt, was him gone.

"Let's go to bed," Sonja said. Still holding Havaa's hand, she stood. "We close our eyes and there they are, right where we left them, in their own waiting room, waiting for us."

CHAPTER

7

FOR EIGHTEEN DAYS Natasha slept as if her lidded dreamland were her true home, to which she was repatriated for fifteen hours a day. So what, then, could Sonja do? Natasha was here, safe, alive, and real enough to begin resenting. In the flat white light of morning she entered her sister's bedroom, a cup of hot tea in her hand, and inspected her sister's body as she might a corpse, or a comatose patient, or someone whom she had, once, long ago, envied. Her gaze crawled the curves of Natasha's hips, the odd angle of elbows she could unhinge and bend at will, the bitten rims of fingernails, her legs, still long, still lithe, and the little brown hairs on her forearms, which, when they had first appeared in puberty, Sonja had used as evidence to convince Natasha she was turning into a boy. Natasha's skin said what she wouldn't. The scars of habitual heroin use webbed her toes. A buckshot of cigarette burns stippled her left shoulder. If Sonja found these scars on a patient in the hospital, she wouldn't feel pity, but in Natasha's bedroom, she felt it all over. For eighteen days she went to wake Natasha and turned back, afraid of the dreams her sister would rise from, leaving no alarm louder than a cup of tea cooling on the nightstand.

But Natasha wasn't right. On the eighteenth evening, standing at the cutting board, chopping two onions and a potato, Sonja broached the subject. "I think you should talk to a psychiatrist or someone."

From the look her sister gave her, she might have announced they'd be eating the cutting board for dinner.

"I just think it would be good for you to talk with someone. About what happened in Italy. About what it's like being home," Sonja said.

"Talking doesn't do anything."

"It might do one or two things." Sonja punctuated her sentence with a chop.

"All the words in the world won't put those onion halves back together."

"The human mind is a little more complex than a yellow onion."

Natasha held back her hair as she lit a cigarette from the hot plate her father had, twelve years earlier, purchased secondhand from a woman who would never find a flame that cooked an egg quite as well. "Some of us would be lucky to have something as large as a yellow onion between our ears."

Sonja could see her sister backing away from her, from the subject, from whatever had happened in Italy. "Think of the mind as a muscle or bone instead," she said, looking down to address the more respectful audience of cubed potatoes. "Emotional and mental trauma doesn't heal itself any more than a broken bone left unset."

Natasha nodded to the cutting board. "You talk those potatoes and onions into jumping in that frying pan and I'll talk with a psychiatrist."

Despite its monumental aggravation, Natasha's resistance was a good sign, wasn't it? The obstinacy was a pillar running alongside her spine that would support her when not lodged firmly in Sonja's hindquarters. And while she might yearn for a little civility to grease the rusty gears of their relationship, she gladly endured the backtalk and eye-rolls to know that Natasha hadn't lost the ability to drive her fucking crazy. Her sister was a snarky chain-smoking hermit crab that emerged from her shell in the safety of Sonja's presence. When Natasha believed she was alone—those days when Sonja slammed the front door and stayed to spy on her—she searched for thicker shells. It was awful, watching Natasha through the keyhole as she divided her room into smaller increments of shelter. She moved the desk, bed, and bureau like a child arranging the furniture into a make-believe castle, even encircling the structure with a moat of water glasses. On the keyhole's far side, Sonja prayed it would keep the dragons at bay; her heart, as if drawn on a piece of paper in her chest, crumpled every time. When she returned in the evening, the fortress was disassembled and the pieces of furniture had returned to their white rectangles of wall space. She never mentioned what she'd seen, holding it as a reminder to be gentle and patient as she prepared dinner. She whispered sweet nothings to the potatoes and onions, but the little fuckers were as stubborn as her sister, the great big fucker.

Natasha relented when Sonja pointed out that compared with her inexhaustible exhortations, a chat with a psychiatrist would be as pleasant as a summer picnic. She admitted to having spoken with a psychiatrist at the women's shelter in Rome—the one that had provided the six-month supply of Ribavirin, which Sonja found in the bathroom, which was generally used to treat hepatitis, which Natasha refused to admit she had, which Sonja thought was total bullshit.

"She spoke Russian in this ridiculous Italian accent," Natasha said. "I was always afraid she'd start singing an opera."

"I never make promises to my patients, but I promise that whoever I find won't speak a word of Italian."

And she tried. She combed through her contacts only to find that every psychiatrist in the city was dead, exiled, or missing. The ranks of the hospital staff didn't contain a single mental-health professional. She fumed one afternoon in the hospital parking lot, wanting to punch the clouds from the sky but instead venting on a closer object, the hood of an '83 Volga so decrepit she felt the sickening thrill of beating a wounded animal to reiterate its pain. How had she got to this point? She was fluent in four languages and yet her fists against the rusted hood were the fullest articulation of her defeat. In the months before the repatriation her heart had hardened around her sister's absence, letting her love Natasha in memory as she could never love her in reality. The fact was that her exile had prompted Natasha's. The fact was that she had left Chechnya first. The fact was that she had escaped the war Natasha had endured alone. It only made sense that her sister would attempt the same transaction with the only currency she possessed: her body. But now she was home and needed medical care Sonja couldn't provide. Being a bad sister was one thing; being a bad doctor was the more serious sin. Deshi found her out in the parking lot, beating the rust off the Volga hood. Her tears turned brown when she wiped them with her knuckles. "Do you want to talk about it?" Deshi asked. "Go to hell," she replied.

At dinner Natasha took the news with typical smugness. "It's just as well," she said. "Head doctors are a decadence unsuited to a country like ours. They are the bidets of the medical profession."

"You could talk to me," Sonja offered with enough snarl in her voice to ensure that Natasha would demur. Which she did. In seven years and three weeks, when Natasha disappeared for a second time, Sonja would orbit that moment, circling every angle without ever touching down: what if she had tried harder, been kinder, gentler?

As the street noise filled the gap in the conversation, Sonja gave up. If the world was determined to drown her, she'd stop swimming. She lengthened her hours at work, then lengthened her commute. At the bazaar, vendors sold everything that could be lifted and carted away:

emergency rations, grain sacks, spools of uncut cloth, raw wool, floor-boards, industrial kitchen appliances, abandoned Red Army munitions, traffic lights, and oil-refining machinery. She wandered past racks of used shoes that had clocked more kilometers than the average Federal fighter jet, past blocks with more craters than her sister's left shoulder blade, past exoskeletal scaffolding, workmen hoisting wheelbarrows of masonry, all the way to Hospital No. 6.

And as eighteen days turned to twenty, forty, sixty, the trauma ward became the capital of the reconstructed republic. Each day patients arrived with heart attacks and kidney stones, the lesser emergencies of peacetime. When a man limped in with a soccer injury she kissed his cheek; that man and his wife would create the plaque honoring the hospital staff of the war years, which was to be set into the sidewalk eleven years later to little official fanfare. The war was over; no one knew it was only the first. Still, the scarcity of medical supplies remained a constant problem.

She contacted the brother of a man with a mustache made of dead spider legs whose life she'd saved when a land mine had lodged eight ball bearings, four screws, and three ten-kopek coins in his left leg. The brother met her in the backseat of a Mercedes that drove in tight circles on a tennis court–sized slab of asphalt just outside his Volchansk garage, the only unbroken stretch of road worthy of such a fine Western automobile. He pinched a Marlboro filter between his manicured fingernails. She didn't need to look past his first knuckle to verify his access to the smuggling routes snaking through the southern mountains.

"You saved Alu's life," the brother said, setting the cigarette between his delicate lips, moisturized nightly with aloe balm. "For that I owe you a favor. A small one, because of my six brothers, I like Alu the least."

She handed him a list limited to easily procurable medical supplies: absorbent compress dressings, adhesive bandages, antiseptic ointment, breathing barriers, latex gloves, gauze rolls, thermometers, scissors, scalpels, aspirin, antibiotics, surgical saw blades, and painkillers. "It's basic stuff. Any medical distributor will have it. You can find most of it in an average first-aid kit. I just need a lot of it."

"Alu spoke highly of you," the brother lamented. "I should have known you would be a bore. Anything else?"

"I thought I only had one favor?"

"Let me tell you a story," the brother said, holding his cigarette like a conductor's baton. "When I was a child I had a pet turtle, whom I named after Alu because they shared a certain—how can I put it—bestial idiocy. Once I went to Grozny with my father and five of my brothers for the funeral of my father's uncle, and we left so quickly I hadn't the time to provide food for Alu the Turtle. My brother, Alu the Idiot, had a fever and stayed home with my mother. In a moment so taxing on that little intellect that steam surely shot from his ears, Alu the Idiot remembered to feed my turtle. He caught grubs and crickets, likely tasting them before he gave them to my beloved crustacean. Since then Alu the Idiot has grown into a Gibraltar-sized hemorrhoid, but when he was a child he used the one good idea this life has allotted him to feed my turtle, and because of it, you get a second favor."

"Turtles aren't crustaceans," she said.

"Excuse me, half crustacean."

"They're full-blooded reptiles."

The brother gaped at her. "You should hear yourself. You sound ridiculous."

"A turtle is one hundred percent reptile," she said. "I imagine even Alu knows that."

"Don't insult me. Everyone knows a turtle is crustacean on its mother's side."

"Explain that to me," she said, shifting in the seat as the car spun in circles.

"A lizard fucks a crab and nine months later a turtle pops out. It's called evolution."

"I hope your biology teacher was sent to the gulag," she said. She caught the driver's eyes in the rearview mirror. The driver had grown up in a mountain hamlet where more people believed in trolls than in automobiles. The first war had catapulted him from the back of a mule to the inside of a Mercedes, and he would look back at that war as the one stroke of good fortune in a life otherwise riddled with disappointments.

"I can't believe you're allowed to operate on people with such an incomplete understanding of nature," the brother said.

"Any other animals come about this way?"

The brother pursed his lips. "A whale."

"Let me guess. A fish fucks a hippo?"

"Close, an elephant," the brother said, laughing.

"Of course," Sonja said. "How could I forget about the herds of elephants roaming the open ocean."

"I would never dishonor my mother, but someone less noble might suggest that Alu is half monkey. So shall I include Darwin as your second favor?"

She wrote several titles on the list and passed it back.

"My god," he said. "You're worse than I could have ever imagined. No wonder you and Alu got on famously. *Modes of Modern Psychological Inquiry. Post-Traumatic Stress Disorder: Causes, Symptoms, and Treatment. From Victim to Survivor: Overcoming Rape.* This is what you want? I was thinking cocaine and a prostitute or something."

"Do I look like someone in need of a prostitute?"

The brother was all grins. "I've never met someone in greater need," he said.

"Can you get them or not?"

"We'll see. Guns, drugs, uranium, whores, hostages, no problem. But I've never been asked to find books or medical supplies. These will be a challenge."

The Mercedes drove in dizzying circles. She wanted out of this spinning, nauseating contraption. What was wrong with Alu, anyway?

Compared to this ridiculous man, who spoke as if he lived in a genie's lamp, Alu was a model citizen. But what could she do? Those who have the bullets also have the bandages.

"Can you get them or not?"

"Don't insult me," he said. "I can steal the spots off a snow leopard."

"Then thank you."

"That's it? Nothing else? Once you leave this car you'll never see me again."

Could she ask for it? Transport to Georgia? A plane ticket from Tbilisi to London? A visa stamp in the passport she still carried with her, in the money belt around her waist, each time she left her house?

"Yes," she said. The air hummed. The yellow clouds watched indifferently. "I'll have one of your cigarettes."

She took that cigarette and smoked it while walking to the bazaar, where several days later, on a trip in search of fabrics, she stumbled upon an industrial ice machine at the stand of a Wahhabi arms dealer. It was a great gray piece of machinery with a plastic interior the color of potato broth and fretwork ventilation at its back end. The steel lid held her unfocused reflection within the logo of the Soviet Intourist Hotel. Three half brothers, now sixteen, eleven, and eight, had been conceived on that steel lid, none yet aware of the others' existence. A merchant with nicotine-stained fingernails, wire-rimmed glasses, and the long beard of a Wahhabi described the machine. "Gorbachev, Brezhnev, and the Bee Gees all had their drinks cooled with the ice produced by this magnificent machine. It is a celebrity among ice machines, envied and admired among its kind. All around Chechnya ice-cube trays have photographs of the Intourist Hotel ice machine pinned on their freezer walls, and they are all told that if they work hard, and believe wholeheartedly in the ideology of ice, they may someday rise to its ranks. And you might say, 'But Mullah Abdul, I don't *need* an industrial ice machine that can provide twenty cubic meters of ice an hour, when required.' To that I counter, what about clean water? You see, pure flawless $H_2O$ freezes

at precisely zero degrees, the temperature at which the carefully cali-
brated thermometer of this magnificent colossus is set. Water containing minerals and sediments and bacteria and parasites freezes at slightly
lower temperatures, and thus remains liquid and flows out the drainage.
The frozen water left behind is as pure as the virgins in Paradise, with
whom I hope to soon be acquainted, should God see me fit."

Sonja nodded, not unimpressed. On the card tables beside the
freezer lay guns of all sizes and caliber, brass belts of ammunition, septic
pipes fashioned into homemade Stinger RPG launchers, land mines, and
VHS recordings of *Baywatch*.

"What are you looking for?" the merchant continued. "Fragmentation grenades? Hollow bullets? If you give me a few days, I could find a
C-4 vest that would fit you nicely." She remembered him as the chemistry professor who had slapped her behind three times in as many months,
and expected her—a first-year university student then—to thank him
for saving her from the invisible bee that lived in his office. He'd been
a different man back then, arriving to class each morning with freshly
shaved cheeks and a stale-smelling corduroy jacket, but she recognized
his delicate bee-swatting hands, now curled around the butt of a rifle.
"Perhaps it would be better if I spoke to your husband," he said. "I'd like
to have a word with him about how he allows you to dress."

"Fuck off, you disgusting little man," Sonja said, in English.

"She speaks in tongues, too," the merchant muttered to himself.
"Another sign of the end times. Listen to me, woman. This is serious
business. If you dress with your hair and your face uncovered for the
devil himself to see, the Russians will come back, make no mistake, and
you women will be responsible."

Had he not had the contents of a small armory in arm's reach, she
might have kicked him squarely in his now-pious balls. Instead she shook
her head and turned toward the fabric stand.

She returned home with sheets of green and purple cloth, and unfolded them across the floor of her bedroom. As a teenager, she had

declined her mother's offer to teach her to tailor her own clothes; even at that age, such a domestic skill had insulted her ambitions. Now, eyes downcast, glaring as though a pair of trousers might materialize from the cloth by force of her concentration, she felt like Sonja the Idiot. Only one idea came to her. She took her measurements with a ruler and drew them on the cloth and cut outlines of her legs with nail scissors. For the next half hour, she stitched together the two cutouts with the same stitch she used to close wounds. When finished, she examined her creation. The stitching held tight when she pulled the seams, and her pinky just fit through the holes of the button fly. She envisioned pockets, perhaps even belt loops. If this worked, she might design a jacket and a blouse. Perhaps she could even begin a clothing line—*haute couture du guerre-zone*, all proceeds to support the hospital—and export handmade fashions to the boutique-lined avenues of London, where she had been privy to the conscience-balming Western consumption of Third World charity art and cheeseburgers.

It wasn't until she tried on the trousers that she realized her error. She had traced the exact measurements of her legs without allowing any extra wiggle room, and so she struggled with the trousers, falling onto the mattress and raising her feet toward the ceiling in the vain hope that gravity might pity her. An exhausting effort. It had been years since she had floundered this much without at least the prospect of an orgasm. When she finally pulled the trousers past her hips, she found Natasha's hundred-watt smirk in the doorway. "How long have you been watching?" she demanded.

"Not nearly long enough."

"You're always fucking asleep! You're always asleep when I'm making dinner or sweeping the floor or finding car batteries or crying or doing anything mature and useful, but then you always somehow wake up to witness me making a fool of myself. Do you have clairvoyance? If you do, you can see what I'm thinking; and if not, I'm thinking of a very rude gesture."

"Try to stand up," Natasha suggested, far too cheerfully. Sonja would rather have amputated her legs with the nail scissors than further humiliate herself, but what could she do? Refuse? Admit failure? No. She placed her palms on the edge of the bed. She pushed forward. Arms flailing, legs inflexible, she would have let the prurient chemistry professor slap invisible bees from her behind all afternoon for a pair of trousers that fit. At the apex of her ascent, when she saw Natasha, her eyes burst into coals, because was it really too much to be thanked? To be appreciated? To be assured that all the scones in England were worth less than all the potatoes and onions with one's own sister? *Yes, apparently that is too much to ask,* Sonja told herself, *or at least too much to ask from you, my potato-eating friend, you who believe you are the only person in the world to understand loss, and even that you're unwilling to share with me.*

But her glare broke with her balance. The wooden planks of her trouser legs pitched her forward and, arms flapping, she reached for Natasha. There was no one else to help her.

And Natasha caught her. The impact shimmied down Sonja's spine, loosening the tension coiled between each vertebra. How had they descended so far? How had they become so embittered that Natasha preventing her from falling on her face felt like an act of tremendous sisterly love? Tears squeezed through Sonja's closed eyes. A plug was pulled from the center of the floor through which the tension drained.

"Those are the ugliest trousers I've ever seen," Natasha said, still holding her. It was the first time they had hugged since she returned. Two and a quarter years would pass before it happened again. "They look painted on."

"I can't feel my toes," Sonja cried. "I don't think my blood is circulating past my knees."

"You should use them as tourniquets at the hospital."

"I don't want to be here, Natasha. I'm so fucking unhappy. I want to be back in London."

"It's okay. They're only trousers. Here's what we do." Clasping the waistline, Natasha halved them in one clean flourish. Sonja pulled the ends over her heels and stretched her sore thighs. She picked up the sheet of fabric stenciled with the silhouette of her legs, and tilted her head to see Natasha through the cutout.

"I think this is my knee."

"It is a lovely knee."

"What should I do with it?"

"I don't think you've ever asked my opinion before."

"I won't make a habit of it."

"You could."

"Tell me what to do."

Natasha looked to the fabric. "I could use a new pair of trousers, too."

Sonja smiled and gave Natasha the nail scissors.

Despite their moment of reconciliation, they soon returned to a policy of polite avoidance. When, after work, Sonja wanted less complex company, she visited Laina next door. Laina never looked particularly pleased to see Sonja, but she never looked particularly pleased about anything these days, and Sonja didn't take it personally. The old woman received daily visitations from ghosts, angels, prophets, and monsters, and some evenings, Sonja wondered if she herself was, to this old woman, a trivial hallucination.

"I saw an ice machine at the bazaar the other day," she said. Laina didn't look up from the scarf she was knitting, afraid to raise her eyes with so many visions crowding the air. "It once cooled the glasses of the Bee Gees, or so said the freezer merchant. Never turn your back to him, Laina. There is no bee."

"You can tell by the way I use my walk, I'm a woman's man," Laina said, without lifting her eyes from the needle tips.

"You know that song?"

"Of course. People used to recite it in the war. I didn't know it was a song. For the longest time I thought it was from the Qur'an."

Sonja smiled, glad she could still be surprised. "I never knew the Bee Gees were so profound."

"I saw six chariots in the sky today. I would have rather seen an ice machine."

For the next hour Laina described abounding supernatural phenomena. The angel Gabriel had fluttered into a rooster-less henhouse in Zebir-Yurt, and the next morning a farmer found eight immaculately conceived eggs. A boy in Grozny defeated his grandfather, a chess master third class, ranked one thousand six hundred and eighty-fourth in the world, after a game lasting thirty-nine sleepless days and nights that left the grandfather so bewildered, proud, and exhausted he promptly died. A band of corpse-devils rose from the earth at the Dagestan border to hijack three Red Cross cargo trucks, leaving the drivers hog-tied and blindfolded and magically suspended three meters in the air.

"Stalin has been resurrected," Laina said.

"I know," Sonja replied. "He's the prime minster of Russia."

On her way to work a week later, when the black Mercedes found her, she was sure she'd wandered into one of Laina's deliriums. The Mercedes braked sharply, drawing a curtain of dust along the street. The tires—before so dainty they could only drive in circles on a tennis court—were replaced with those of an armored jeep, raising the body of the car by a half meter. Swedish license plates, she noted, were still attached. The window descended and those gorgeous fingernails beckoned her.

"I thought we wouldn't see each other again," she said, pulling the door closed.

"And I keeping saying I'll never see Alu again and he keeps on being my brother. You intrigue me. You lived in London for several years, if my information is correct, which it always is. Had you stayed, you would be eligible for citizenship now. Even I can't get my name into one of those beautiful maroon passports. And yet you returned."

"I have family here," she said uneasily.

"I hide the toilet paper when my family visits so they won't stay too long."

"Could you get me back to London?"

"You could ask. But then who would I have to talk to? No one with your intelligence would return from London, which means you are either one of those idiot savants, light on the savant, or something entirely different. The only people who return are people like me, people who know how much money can be made."

Through the window, the city limits gave way to brown fields tilled by tank treads. They were on the road to Grozny. "I'm not here to make money."

"That's why you are so intriguing."

They reached the Grozny garage two hours later. Two dour-faced men met them at the door holding Kalashnikovs, one still three weeks from killing the other in an argument that would begin over driving directions, and Sonja feverishly hoped that the smuggler's love for Alu the Turtle still surpassed his loathing for Alu the Unluckiest Younger Brother in History. Three trucks sat at the end of the concrete tarmac. The brother led her to the first truck, whose shot-off lock clung by a half-broken, glimmering grip. He lifted the door and shined a flashlight into the trailer. A Red Cross first-aid kit sat in the circle of yellowed light. The circle spread to illuminate torn cardboard boxes and hundreds, no, thousands of first-aid kits. "These were stolen," she said.

"Of course they were, and not without some headache, I'll have you know. But as you said, nearly all of what you asked for can be found in a first-aid kit."

"What happened to the drivers?"

"Why do you care?"

She could feel him testing her, ready to blunt the slightest edge of moral outrage with a lecture on relativism in war, or maybe with another example of his contempt for Alu. She unsnapped the first-aid kit and surveyed the contents. Four absorbent compress dressings, eight adhesive bandages, a tube of antiseptic ointment, a breathing barrier, two latex gloves, a gauze roll, a thermometer, a packet of aspirin, and a scissors. She closed the lid, refastened the clips, had nothing but gratitude to give him. For all she cared, the drivers could be hog-tied and beaten, since she now had the ointment to disinfect their cuts, the gauze to bandage their wounds, even scissors to cut through whatever magical threads held them three meters off the ground.

"What about the morphine?"

"I nearly forgot." He pulled a black nylon duffel bag from the front seat, set it on the bumper, and unzipped it. A plastic-wrapped brick of white powder lay at the bottom. "Morphine is too expensive," he said, handing it to her.

"What is it?"

"Heroin."

The word alone weighed ten kilograms. This powder had been boiled and squirted between Natasha's toes twice a day for eight months. My god. And for the first time in how many days, she breathed the relief of knowing Natasha was safe at home, barricaded behind a water-glass moat, safe from the fangs of dragons. "Is it unadulterated?"

"Not enough sugar in there to sweeten a cup of tea."

"I asked for morphine."

"And even had you done me the favor of lobotomizing Alu while he was under your care, I wouldn't get you morphine. Heroin is much cheaper."

"I want something else, then."

"So do I. There are only a few departments open in your hospital, yes? If you rent me some unused space, we can continue this arrangement."

"For what?"

"My wares."

"No guns, drugs, or people."

"Of course not," he said. "I keep them at home. No, mainly national treasures looted from city museums that can be sold abroad."

"Fine. I want an ice machine. The hospital has been without one for several months. A bearded man at the bazaar is selling a nice one from the Intourist Hotel. Feel free to be rough with him. And where are the books I asked for?"

"You've chosen the wrong profession," he said, enjoying her stubbornness. "You're a natural swindler. You'd run me out of business. I've had difficulty finding them, but they should come in shortly. A third cousin in the West is asking for them from Amazon."

"What's that?"

"I haven't any idea. This kid can make your books appear from the ether. He'll run me out of business, too." He shook his head. "The whole world is conspiring to run me out of business."

"And another thing."

"Now you're really beginning to annoy me. If you keep it up, I'll have to bring my brother with me next time."

"I want new clothes."

And he laughed and laughed and laughed.

Two weeks later Sonja returned from the hospital wearing a maroon cashmere sweater, tan leather boots, and a pair of one-size-too-tight jeans displaying curves that the chemistry professor would have found a whole hive nesting on, had his eyes still worked. The weight of the psychology textbooks strained the rucksack straps against her shoulders. Her left hand, wrapped around a glass of ice, was numb.

In the hall she stopped at Laina's door, wanting to leave the ice for her neighbor. The murmur of voices inside stopped her. She crouched to the keyhole. Were Laina's hallucinations speaking back to her?

"There were twelve chariots in the sky today? That's two more than yesterday." Natasha's voice basked beneath a sun that never shone when she addressed Sonja. It was good to hear Natasha care, even if it wasn't for her.

"Twelve," Laina said. "I think they're up to something."

"Like what?"

"Who knows? Trying to steal the Moon to sell at the bazaar. Protecting the skies from Federal planes. Maybe trying to figure out how to get their horses down from the clouds."

Natasha's voice softened. "In the winter of the war, before I went to Italy, when the bombing was at its worst, I was afraid the apartment block would be hit. So I lived in City Park. I remember the City Park Prophet once said everything that isn't darkness or death is a vision. I remember he said we are all God's hallucinations."

"I remember once, on my birthday, when I was a child, I came into the kitchen and saw a huge wooden box on the table," Laina said. "I was so happy. I couldn't imagine what wonderful present lay inside such a big wooden box."

"What was it?"

"A casket. My aunt was inside."

Sonja bit her knuckle. When they were children they had pretended to have a third sister, a black-haired girl named Lidiya. Like Alu, the ghost sister was never around, and in her absence they had teased, chided, scorned, blamed, and hated Lidiya so they could love each other more simply.

"I'm afraid to leave the apartment," Natasha was saying. "I'm afraid of the city. There's just so much open air now. I'm afraid of nearly everyone. I don't know why. Everyone scares me but you. Even Sonja can be scary. Sometimes, if I let myself think about Italy, my body shuts down. It's like I'm not in charge anymore, my brain turns off, and I have to lock myself in my room and barricade myself with furniture. I feel so stupid. I'm such an idiot."

"Do you see the chariots?"

"No, not yet. I see a wallet, though."

"A wallet?"

"Yes, there was this man, and when he was dressing his wallet fell out of his trousers and he had a picture of his children in one of those plastic credit card flaps. That was the day when I gave up."

"It's good to talk about these things. It will keep the chariots and wallets of the world honest. They will know we see them, and are not afraid to sound like madwomen."

"Yes, I like talking with you."

"We're staying alive."

Sonja stood and walked to the flat, afraid of what she might hear next. At the kitchen table she examined the glass of ice. Each cube was rounded by room temperature, dissolving in its own remains, and belatedly she understood that this was how a loved one disappeared. Despite the shock of walking into an empty flat, the absence isn't immediate, more a fade from the present tense you shared, a melting into the past, not an erasure but a conversion in form, from presence to memory, from solid to liquid, and the person you once touched now runs over your skin, now in sheets down your back, and you may bathe, may sink, may drown in the memory, but your fingers cannot hold it. She raised the glass to her lips. The water was clean.

# CHAPTER

# 8

1994  1995  1996  1997  1998  1999  2000  2001  2002  2003  **2004**

FIVE HOURS AFTER his first successful amputation, Akhmed's hands
stopped shaking. The frost-caked road glared up at him, the more menacing since he'd seen, up close, what it could do. He had sawed straight
through that poor man's leg. He hadn't been able to grip the saw until
Sonja's fingers had wrapped around his. Until hers had pushed his hand
forward. The man he had imagined himself to be had died the moment
she set the blade against the bone and pushed his hand forward. He was
one more instrument for her manipulation. Her face had hardened with
a marble-like resolve unmoved by both his and the other man's suffering. As if she hadn't known that leg belonged to someone. As if she
hadn't known the hand she held did as well. Pushing the blade forward,
she had observed him as if he were the patient. And he had been. As the
saw teeth caught on the bone, she had performed a second surgery, one

less bloody but no less brutal, excising from his heart the impulse to run, to cower, to let the man bleed to death rather than face the horror of saving him. The amputation had left both patients lighter.

Watching for the slightest rise in the road, he still felt more like that young man than he did that doctor. He was nothing like Sonja. She was the strangest Russian he'd ever met, a riddle wrapped inside a mystery inside a set of unattractive but very white scrubs. What parts had she discarded for the sake of her sanity? What had she cut from herself? Had he stared into her pupils he would have emerged, bewildered and blinking, on the far side of the earth. Was he awed by her? Absolutely. Did he respect her? Unequivocally. Want to be anything like her? No, never, not at all. If he never again saw the beige corridors of Hospital No. 6 he would call himself lucky. But he had to go back in the morning; he had an agreement. A woman so casually capable of cutting off a leg was capable of throwing out an orphan girl.

Two hundred meters away, at a crook in the road, a diffuse fan of headlights turned into view. He ran. Birch trunks divided the beam into pale yellow blocks as he sheltered behind a half-rotted log, sucking on snow to mask his breath. Once the headlights passed he glimpsed the red of Ramzan's pickup heading toward the city. He bit his knuckle, unable to recall its Latin name. Ramzan couldn't know. He couldn't. When the taillights shrank to a distant scarlet flush he returned to the road, massaging the soreness between his thumb and index finger. In that busy afternoon his palm had had two more opportunities to callus.

A half kilometer from the village the flicker of a campfire jumped through the underbrush. With the pickup truck halfway over the horizon, curiosity rather than fear led Akhmed back into the forest. He crept with the faith that the flames spoke louder than the frost beneath his boots. There, in the clearing, a man made of shadow passed pamphlets to that shivering brightness. The dogs, lounging beside the fire, heard him before the man.

"It's Akhmed," he called over the dogs' growl. Never had he understood the obligation Khassan felt for those filthy, diseased animals. His son made him a pariah, but the dogs weren't helping. Another handful of pages fluttered into the fire. "What are you doing?" he asked.

Khassan was studying the sheet of paper in his hand, where in the fifth sentence of the second paragraph, in the gap of a missing comma, he found the sorrow of his life. The sentence described the upbringing of a minor eighteenth-century tribal leader, and it would be the last time human eyes would read the name of the tribal leader's mother. "A punctuation error," he said, with the tremble of more ominous inaccuracy. "I've read through that paragraph hundreds of times and never caught it."

"Don't do this," Akhmed said. He could have reached out, caught it, and kicked snow on the fire, but the page with the punctuation error was already smoke, and the name of a mother who died two hundred and twenty-three years earlier was already lost. He emptied his lungs but his sigh wasn't finished; it went on emptying him. One spring day, when Akhmed was a child, Khassan had led him to a logging field a half morning's walk from the village. Men with roaring orange saws had leaned into beech trunks and the trunks had spumed clouds of sawdust and groaned as the green treetops toppled. He was eight years old and the stumps were shorter than he was. "Hundred years to get that tall," Khassan had said, and turned for home.

"I was thinking of someone I lost many years ago," Khassan said. "She called me a coward once. It wasn't what she said, but the way she said it. As if her judgment just passed through me. As if I were a cloud."

The fire had thawed the overhanging branches. Droplets sliding down the slender fingers turned to steam before landing in it. Nothing Akhmed could say would put this man back together. "You were a good husband," he said. "Your wife loved you."

Khassan looked confused, as though he hadn't been thinking of his wife at all, and reached to the ground for another stack of pages. "My wife didn't, but thank you," he said, nodding to the fire. "Forty-four thousand three hundred and thirty-eight pages. It took five hours to count. Over twenty trips to carry them. No wonder these pups are so tired." He knelt and patted the bald dog's stomach with an awful affection. "Each page averages three hundred and fifty words. That's fifteen million words I've written."

"There are more words." The firelight twitched across their faces. It was all he could say.

"There are more writers."

"You can't do this." He spoke from a fear that closed his stomach into a fist, helpless like a child, his emotions a magnification of what he detected in the elder. If Khassan lost hope, where would Akhmed find it?

"You wouldn't understand, Akhmed, but you might, if you reach my age. I was thinking of the stories my mother used to tell me about princes and warriors who went to great measures to ensure their names would endure, and were punished by Allah for their pride. I want to be forgotten. There is something miraculous in the way the years wash away your evidence, first you, then your friends and family, then the descendants who remember your face, until you aren't even a memory, you're only carbon, no greater than your atoms, and time will divide them as well."

"What are you saying?" Akhmed asked, though he didn't want Khassan to say any more.

"I'm saying that I want to disappear."

Once, while hunting in these woods, Akhmed came upon a doe flopping on the ground and struggling to breathe. A distended pink wound spread her hind legs, and her snout held a long line of anguished groans, and to end her suffering he aimed for her neck. But before he pulled the trigger, the sac-wrapped end of a fawn split open the wound. His jaw slackened. He set the rifle among the leaves, hid his forefinger behind his back, ashamed of what it had nearly caused, and watched one life begin where another had nearly ended. And now, with the final sheets curling on the coals, fear rose to wonder as he witnessed a moment of equal profundity. Not once for as far back as he could recall had Khassan ever admitted to a shortcoming, a mistake, not even a lapse as trivial as a missing comma. Tonight he confessed total failure.

The returning headlights stretched their shadows across the clearing too soon to have gone all the way to the hospital. As the beam of light swung toward them, he saw, briefly, paw prints in the ashes of fifteen million words.


Held aloft by distant tacks of starlight, the night was a blackout curtain concealing Ramzan's truck until it was too late for Akhmed to turn back. Ramzan climbed from the cabin, lit a cigarette, and stared at what had been Dokka's house as Akhmed approached.

"Have you seen my father?" His face dipped into the orange orb with each inhalation. If he had the flat face of an ogre, or the many heads of a hydra, Akhmed might understand. If he had the cleft tongue of a devil, or the snake-hair of a Medusa, or the matted hair of a wolf-monster, Akhmed might understand. But Ramzan had two eyes, a nose, and a mouth, pairs of arms and legs and ears, hair greasy but not slimy and certainly not slithering, and Akhmed did not understand. They had been born in the same village, had gone to the same school, had their knuckles purpled by the same meter stick, kicked the same soccer ball down the same dirt patch where in summer the grass grew thick enough to block a penalty kick.

"What do you really want?" Akhmed asked, too tired to be intimidated.

Ramzan frowned, his cheeks the white of pounded metal. "Just to talk," he said. "It's been a long time since I've spoken to anyone. Two weeks. I keep a notebook and sometimes I write things down, and you can fake a conversation that way, for a little while, but—"

"I don't want to talk to you," Akhmed interrupted.

"The last person I talked to was Dokka. Two weeks ago. I came by to ask if he wanted more firewood. And now look what happened. Our poor friend. What did he get himself into?"

"Nothing. He couldn't kill a loaf of bread with a butter knife."

"And I'm told the girl, Havaa, even she was disappeared. But not by the security forces, praise Allah. No, she was taken by someone else. Someone else took her, but I don't know who. I think I have my finger near him. Or her. He could be a she. But I think he is a he. A him. A——"

"Where was she?" Akhmed asked, as calmly as he could manage.

"The security forces didn't find her. She wasn't there. She wasn't anywhere." Ramzan paused only to breathe. "Not in the living room or bedrooms or under the floorboards or in the closets, nowhere, nowhere, nowhere."

"Why do they even care?" he asked, hoping Ramzan, who sold information, might give a small piece for free. "What could they possibly want with a child?"

"No one is off limits because there are no limits. The *why* and *what* aren't for us to consider. Those are questions for philosophers and imams and not for people like us, whoever we are." His lips glowed in amber light. "The *who* and the *where* are all we must know and all we must answer."

"I don't see the why and what of a child."

"There you go, Akhmed. Asking the wrong question. She's wanted. That's it. It doesn't matter why. All that matters is where she is and with whom."

"If I see her I'll tell her you'd like a word."

"You're being smug, smug, smug." Ramzan's lanky arm wrapped around Akhmed's shoulder and the sweet, decadent scent of deodorant wafted from his underarm. The first time Akhmed became fully aware of his own odor had been on his wedding night, when, pressed against her in bed, awkward and struggling and generally doing it all wrong, he noticed Ula tilt her head to the open window.

"Dokka is gone," Ramzan said, close enough for his breath to warm Akhmed's neck. "He's gone. It makes me sad. He's gone. I wish he were here so I could ask him what to do. So I could say hello. I could talk to him. He always listened to me. He always spoke with me. He always answered when I asked a question."

All too aware of that, Akhmed said nothing. It hadn't always been like this. For years he, Ramzan, and Dokka had been friends. Every other Sunday they had gathered at Dokka's house to play chess, feast lavishly, and for just a few hours overthrow the fear and deprivation that had replaced the old order. In another life Ramzan's weaknesses would have manifested no tragedy greater than a cheated chess victory. Ramzan was the youngest of the three, so poor a chess player that Dokka had given him private lessons. He had learned well: made a board of the village, a pawn of the master.

"So tell me, where have you been all day?" Ramzan asked, his voice flat and solid, the voice of the anvil rather than of the metal flattened to it. "Tell me where you've been, who you've seen."

"Nowhere, no one."

"Come on, Akhmed. We both know that you will tell me. You are a clever man, you have a sick wife to consider, you know what will happen if you don't. Let's try it again. Akhmed, my dear friend, where were you today?"

Akhmed said nothing.

"Shy today, aren't we? Well, let's start small. Tell me something you've done today, hmm?"

"Praying."

"That's good. You should pray. I pray ten times a day. Five times for me and five for my father. I'm taking care of him, don't worry about that," Ramzan said. His lips were banks unable to seal the stream gushing between them. "Prayer is important. Prayer is very important. Especially now that we are living in the end time. You know that, don't you? The final Caliph will appear and the prophet Jesus will descend and he will slaughter the pigs and break the crosses. We don't have much time left, I don't think. That's why I pray ten times a day. I should probably pray fifteen or twenty times. My father needs it. You believe in the last days, don't you?"

"I believe in final judgments," Akhmed replied. "I believe we will each be called to account for our lives."

"When I was a child, my father brought me an eight-track tape player. Most of the tapes he brought me from the university library were violin concertos and operas and symphonies. Can you imagine anything more boring for a ten-year-old? But it was a wonderful present. I loved it. I enjoyed messing around with the speeds and knobs more than I enjoyed listening to it. If I slowed the speed of the tape, the whine of the violins sank to lower, more ominous pitches. It makes me think of Al-Haaqqa. Are you familiar with verse thirteen? *When the trumpet will sound one blast, the earth with the mountains will be uprooted and broken, that is the day when the inevitable event will come to pass, the heavens will fracture and fall, the angels will be on all sides, raising the Throne of the Lord that day, above them.* And I used to think that the trumpet blast would come sudden and all consuming. A true blast. An atom bomb. A pinprick in the balloon that is the world. But maybe not. Maybe not. Maybe the trumpet blast has been slowed like an eight-track tape, sounding on the lower frequencies, and maybe the trumpeter's breath lasts for many years, calling us not in unison, but each at a time."

"You forgot Al-Haaqqa's next line," Akhmed said. A swollen bead of sweat slid down Ramzan's forehead, following a thin ridge of scar tissue. When Akhmed was in his first year of medical school, he returned one November weekend for the Festival of the Sacrifice. Ramzan, still a teenager then, attempted a midnight liberation of the goat pledged for slaughter, partly because he believed the barbaric custom antithetical to Soviet rationality, but mainly because he wanted to see his pajama-clad father chase it through the night. In the ensuing struggle—Khassan, no fool, lay waiting—the goat, unable to distinguish its liberator from its executioner, grazed Ramzan's temple with a sharp kick. He became Akhmed's first patient. As Akhmed stitched a seam in his skin, the usually sullen teenager kept asking for Latin words. Ramzan spoke the words as if to spell them, holding the vowels like grapes between his rounded lips. And Akhmed couldn't have imagined that the teenager reverentially intoning *fellatio*, believing it the name of a Roman god, would grow into a man who spoke Chechen as a dead language, selling its words as he had sold firearms and explosives, without knowing their real worth, without regard for who they might kill.

"The next line in Al-Haaqqa?" Ramzan asked uncertainly.

*"On that day you will be revealed and nothing of you can be hidden."*

Ula smiled sleepily and rolled onto her side when Akhmed entered the room. He drew little eights on her forearm with his thumb until Ramzan's voice, addressing no one, faded with the splatter of gravel. In the kitchen he pulled a stool to the wood oven. He wanted to perch over the open oven door and bathe in the flicker until the ghost of this exhausting day disappeared into the chimney pipe. Havaa was safe. She was safe and he would have amputated his own legs for Dokka to know that. Thinking of Dokka and Havaa, he began sobbing. He'd forgotten the swell of pride, how it could overwhelm when least expected, how it could grow back—and how good it was to know there were parts of him a surgical saw couldn't remove. The flames dissolved in his eyes and through them an ache sounded: laughter. He couldn't explain it. His face couldn't express the thing in his chest. He was the most incompetent doctor in Chechnya, the single least distinguished physician to ever graduate Volchansk State University Medical School, and he had saved Havaa's life. He wiped his eyes on his sleeves, wanting to stay there, perched before the fire, but he had to feed his wife.

"How was your day?" he asked, after Ula swallowed her first bite.

"It was so busy," she murmured.

"Yours too?"

"I spoke to your father."

His father, a botanist and collector of pressed flowers, had passed ten years earlier. She had never met him. "He must have come a long way to see you."

"He did. He looked terrible."

"And what did you talk about?"

"Your mother," she said, as if it were nothing. He set the bowl on the floor and lay beside her with his arms folded so their noses and kneecaps nearly touched. Her forehead felt as though she'd spent the day in the sun. Maybe it was summer in the exile his father had returned from, and maybe he'd brought a bit for Ula. She didn't turn to the window when she inhaled; he kissed her nose for it.

"What did he have to say about my mother?"

She closed her eyes for so long he assumed she'd fallen asleep. "I saw a birthmark," she finally whispered. "An oval on her stomach."

Soon she slept. He finished the bowl of rice, disappointed by how little she had eaten, and rinsed it in the pail that had become the kitchen sink. After he stitched shut his pockets—to prevent checkpoint soldiers from planting contraband on him the next day—he brushed his teeth with baking soda and climbed into bed. He wiggled his toes. They felt wonderful there, at the ends of his feet. A question surfaced as he swam to meet Ula in sleep. By morning it would be forgotten, drawn back into dreams, but for a moment it sat there left by the tide. The oval-shaped birthmark on his mother's stomach. He had never told Ula, yet she knew.

CHAPTER

9

*This is about your father. I remember he wrote tracts of pure classification, every idea an -ism, every person an -ist, and when I once criticized him for this reductive habit, he said, "We know the meaning of nothing but the words we use to describe it." I remember he wanted to teach you to read and write but didn't know whether to teach you the Cyrillic alphabet (which would be used if the Russians won) or the Latin alphabet (which would be used if the rebels won), and so he taught you the Arabic alphabet instead, and said he would have taught you to read and speak in Japanese if he knew it. I can't write Arabic. I hope you can read this. I hope there are still people speaking Chechen when you read this. These are stray memories, plucked from the air. But if I closed my eyes and forced myself to find your father, to truly find him, I would find him at his chessboard. In his forty years he lost only three matches. One was to you on your sixth birthday.*

*I would find him peeling a plum. You haven't forgotten, have you, how he peeled the skin with a paring knife? A dozen revolutions and the skin came off in a thin, unbroken coil, a meter-long helix. He transformed the skin of that squat little fruit, smaller than your fist, into a measureable length. Then he held the blade to the naked flesh and rotated the plum vertically. One half fell from the other, the cut so clean not even a filament clung to the seed. Pale pink beads dripped to the plate. If Sharik was with me, the dog would contemplate his hands eagerly. But when your father finally let them fall within reach of Sharik's tongue, he tasted the disappointment of dry skin. Your father wasn't a graceful man, but he could cut a plum like a jeweler.*

*He pretended to prefer the skin, and always gave you the flesh. You devoured the slices because you had to wash your hands before touching the chess pieces. It was a beautiful set, hand-carved, purchased by your great-grandfather, before the Revolution, when a postal clerk could afford such intimate craftsmanship. He taught you to play chess, and on your sixth birthday, he let you win. Your father did many things in his forty years. Yet if pressed to recall his finest moment, I would choose to see him in the living room, with you, by the chess set, peeling a plum.*

# THE THIRD DAY

CHAPTER

10

THEY APPEARED FOUR years before her father was taken, one or two at first, eyes glazed as if they'd never before seen a house, then more. They came stooped and waxen, downcast and wary, from Grozny, Shali, Urus-Martan, one long exhalation toward the mountains. Some carried the most necessary provisions: boots, woolen socks, more woolen socks, bribe money. Those who had lost everything, even their reason, carried the most ridiculous things: a man who lost his parents and children in the same Uragan rocket blast carried the key to the flat they perished in; a thrice-widowed woman carried the framed portrait of a face no one had seen alive for over a hundred years, and no images of her husbands; a retired bureaucrat carried a twelve-hundred-page regulatory binder, convinced that these rules were forever inviolable. Others carried nothing at all. They kept coming and their clothes kept getting bigger on them. Havaa had just learned the Arabic alphabet, and she found the letter shapes in their figures. An eye raised to the mountains was ﻋﻞ, forehead sweat formed a stammer of ﻩ, each jawline was as sharp as ﺝ, the smoke dotting an old man's bark-loaded pipe was the point above ﺫ, and strung together they were an unpunctuated sentence the road wrote.

Her father seated the first one or two at the kitchen table and put enough food in front of them that they nearly refused to leave. Word spread through the refugee lines, and soon the number exceeded her parents' modest means. One day she came home from the forest to find her bedroom furniture scattered across the yard, her father and Akhmed modeling new beds on hers, the air pungent with sawdust, the sun glimmering off their bare backs. Two days later her bedroom was converted into a three-bunk hostel. The refugees—that's what they were, she could say the name in Chechen and write it in Arabic—paid for the night's sleep, two meals, and laundry line however they could. The shame that tightened Dokka's ventricles each time he asked for payment soon weakened to a slight, ignorable twitch. The first and thousandth refugees came from different peoples: the former deserving of his compassion and hospitality, the latter of nothing. Let them sleep outside for as long as their grandmother's jewelry will warm them. Let them eat their rubles. But since so few had jewelry or rubles, and since Dokka was incapable of turning away those truly in need, his parameters for payment expanded to include nearly anything. The tokens and trinkets went to Havaa, who collected them as souvenirs, and so rather than toys or homework she played with and learned from the plastic figurine of a ballerina in pirouette, the field guide to Caucasian flora, and whatever else her father and guest agreed was worth a rickety bunk bed on a winter's night. Now she slept on a mattress on the floor of her parents' room. Many nights she woke to find herself in their bed, her body heat held between theirs, distinguishing each in the darkness by the size of their fingers.

Others came on the weekends, strangers better dressed and rested, to see Akhmed. If they had heard rumors of the pedophile's ghost, they left their children outside when they entered the abandoned house, arms heavy with donations of linen bandages, fishing-line sutures, dry plaster, and slings of old magazines and bandannas. In the waiting room they sat straight-backed and motionless, afraid of breathing too hard, of squeaking the sensitive folding chairs and thus breaking the solemnity the proceedings demanded. Akhmed called them, one family at a time, as if they were his patients. And he wished they were, because they treated him with greater respect than his real patients, and he could do more for them. The family, as it entered Akhmed's office, likely knew he was the worst doctor in Chechnya. Sitting at the folding chairs before his desk, likely they knew he had followed the wrong calling. Likely they knew the worst doctor in Chechnya was its most talented portraitist.

The father might break the silence with a wet cough, and, praying that Akhmed not ask to examine his chest, describe the shape of his son's nose. Flat and wide, he might say, as if knocked in the face with a frying pan as a child. No, no, no, the mother might deny before Akhmed's pencil reached the paper. It is a normal nose, a shapely nose, a beautiful nose, and he was never hit with a frying pan, or a soup pot, or even a kettle; a ladle, yes, of course, that is to be expected because a mother's kitchen is her sanctum and she must maintain order. Then in might jump a cousin, a sister, an aggrieved daughter who too clearly remembered the slap of a ladle on her outstretched palm. The conversation might never recover if Akhmed didn't raise his finger to quiet them; he had heard these arguments before, had seen grief warp the fabric of memory such that a mother refused to recognize her son when described by the father, and the father, usually compliant to his wife's requests, truly believed his son's nose was so crushed he could only breathe through his mouth. He asked them to close their eyes, and hoped their mouths would follow suit. He asked them to concentrate.

Hunched over the steel-legged desk, a cup of lukewarm black tea within reach, Akhmed might think back to childhood, to the sketches of snake skeletons, knee tendons, and blood veins his father mistook for an interest in science. He might think back to medical school, when he skipped a year of pathology to audit art classes. By that point a career change was beyond consideration; he was a bottle, thrown to the sea, into which the villagers had folded their wishes, and though he was willing to give up on himself, he wasn't willing to let down those who believed he could carry them over the water. Yet he drew still-lifes when he should have drawn diagrams, studied models when he should have studied corpses. When he graduated from medical school in the bottom tenth he didn't know the disgrace weighing on him like a hundred rubles in five-kopek coins would one day be converted to less cumbersome denominations, when families, like this one, came, knowing he was too incompetent a doctor to save their son's life, but so skilled and well-trained an artist he might bring their son back.

Each half minute he would slide the paper across the desk and search their faces for the pause of recognition. Yes, those are his ears, just like that. No, my wife is right, his nose isn't so wide, and she never hit him with a frying pan. Mistakes would disappear beneath the corners of a pink eraser. That's him, they say. He is ours.

Some portraits found their way to kiosks where they stared out at the passing refugees, searching for their reflection in the line. Others rested in more intimate spaces: set in a glass frame over an empty bed, or folded in a wallet with nothing else in it, or locked in a bureau drawer beside the birth certificate documenting the exact hour, date, and place that life had entered the world. The missing remained missing and the portraits couldn't change that. But when Akhmed slid the finished portrait across the desk and the family saw the shape of that beloved nose, the air would flee the room, replaced by the miracle of recognition as mother, father, sister, brother, aunt, and cousin found in that nose the son, brother, nephew, and cousin that had been, would have been, could have been, and they might race after that possibility like cartoon characters dashing off a cliff, held by the certainty of the road until they looked down—and *plummeted* is the word used by the youngest brother who, at the age of sixteen, is tired of being the youngest and hopes his older brother will return for many reasons, not least so he will marry and have a child and the youngest brother will no longer be youngest; that youngest brother, the one who has nothing to say about the nose because he remembers his older brother's nose and doesn't need the nose to mean what his parents need it to mean, is the one who six months later would be disappeared in the back of a truck, as his older brother was, who would know the Landfill through his blindfold and gag by the rich scent of clay, as his older brother had known, whose fingers would be wound with the electrical wires that had welded to his older brother's bones, who would stand above a mass grave his brother had dug and would fall in it as his older brother had, though taking six more minutes and four more bullets to die, who would be buried an arm's length of dirt above his brother and whose bones would find over time those of his older brother, and so, at that indeterminate point in the future, answer his mother's prayer that her boys find each other, wherever they go; that younger brother would have a smile on his face and the silliest thought in his skull a minute before the first bullet would break it, thinking of how that day six months earlier, when they all went to have his older brother's portrait made, he should have had *his* made, too, because now his parents would have to make another trip, and he hoped they would, hoped they would because even if he knew his older brother's nose, he hadn't been prepared to see it, and seeing that nose, there, on the page, the density of loss it engendered, the unbelievable ache of loving and not having surrounded him, strong enough to toss him, as his brother had, into the summer lake, but there was nothing but air, and he'd believed that *plummet* was as close as they would ever come again, and with the first gunshot one brother fell within arm's reach of the other, and with the fifth shot the blindfold dissolved and the light it blocked became forever, and on the kitchen wall of his parents' house his portrait hangs within arm's reach of his older brother's, and his mother spends whole afternoons staring at them, praying that they find each other, wherever they go.

Every other Sunday Akhmed and Ramzan came to play chess with her father. Ramzan arrived first, knocking with his forehead, his arms hugging a stew pot; sometimes he brought self-awarded gratuities from the shipments he transported to and from the mountains, pickled trout or plum jelly, cured lamb, candied nuts. Then came Akhmed, entering without knocking, grabbing Havaa and hoisting her over his shoulder and threatening to marry her to a toad. In the living room Havaa would serve them tea, and rather than a chore it felt like her own modest contribution to the afternoon. In her eyes, the three men formed a family to whom she wasn't a daughter but a very young sister. This changed when Khassan joined them, once every few months, as the invisible structure built between them failed to support the weight of another man. In his presence the luster of Ramzan's laugh dulled and resentment built beneath his quiet face. Akhmed and Khassan monopolized the conversation and Ramzan observed, searching for an opening, but when one came he never knew what to say.

While the men ate she and her mother remained in the kitchen. The custom seemed so unfair, and she didn't understand why her mother, usually as stubborn as a sleepy ox, submitted to it. Her father allowed her to join them when they finished, provided she didn't bite her nails, and the ottoman provided the perfect perch from which to watch the chess game. It was a beautiful set of lacquered beech bordered with mother-of-pearl. The board had to have been carved from magical wood, since for all the time she spent in the forest she'd never come across so shiny a tree. The little figures, demarcated by color and bound by rules, made warfare a clean and orderly enterprise. The bulbous heads of pawns and imams, rubbed bald by the touch of too many fingers, were her favorite;

months later she would wonder why the rebels and Feds, most in their teens and twenties, still had so much hair. Her father was so skilled that Ramzan and Akhmed played in a team against him. The two consulted and conspired before making their next move, and her father would read a book while they decided, so confident in his mastery he didn't care if Ramzan cheated. Once he told her that a true chess player thinks with his fingers, and she would remember this, thirteen months later, when he lost his. When his turn came he probed the air indecisively; then, as if each digit independently reached the same conclusion, they came together on the wooden scalp of the imam who slayed Boris Yeltsin, like any good jihadist.

Her father only lost to them twice. The first was in 2001, the Sunday after a company of wounded rebels spent one night of an eighteen-month retreat in Eldár. They came from the hospital in Volchansk, a fact that Akhmed might have exploited when he later took in the girl, had he remembered. When they hobbled into the village square, arms in slings, eyes purpled by exhaustion, the assembled villagers thought the rebels had fled the hospital too soon. One was in a wheelchair. How had the Feds failed to catch them? Their green headbands proclaimed *Allahu Akhbar* in a golden Arabic script. The villagers, Havaa among them, approached the rebels with cautious curiosity. Many, Havaa among them, had never seen a rebel in the flesh. They were a land over the horizon; sons and brothers would go *to the rebels* and never be seen again. Several mothers spoke to them directly, asking after their sons, but most, Havaa among them, watched silently. A shudder passed through the entire assembly when the short field commander planted the green flag of national independence in the square. With this act the rebels—so weak a few children with gardening tools could have overpowered them—had officially seized the village, and thus damned it to a Russian liberation.

They demanded medical attention and were taken to Akhmed's clinic by a dozen villagers who introduced the rebels and disappeared, grateful for the clinic for the first time. Only after checking the linen closet for a potential Federal ambush were they willing to disarm. On the other side of the village, Havaa saw none of it. She sat with her mother, in the safety of the kitchen. Had she seen the short, squat field commander, she might have thought he looked like a half-emptied grain sack in fatigues. He addressed Akhmed courteously, reiterating the importance of communal sacrifice in the campaign to defeat the godless Russian scourge. Akhmed held his hands together but one couldn't stop the other's tremble. He warned the field commander that he wasn't a very good doctor, that a pedophile's ghost was said to haunt the clinic, and that he would much rather draw his portrait. In a deep, even voice as he unbuttoned his shirt, the field commander informed Akhmed that if he didn't become the best doctor in Chechnya within the next five minutes, he'd soon haunt the clinic as well. A surgical thread Akhmed had never encountered held the field commander's chest together.

"What is this?" Akhmed asked.

"Dental floss," the field commander said. Given the lichenous growth on the field commander's incisors, Akhmed assumed the floss hadn't seen much prior action.

"Dental floss stitches. I've never seen such fine work. Who put them in?"

"A doctor at the Volchansk hospital. She was both a woman and an ethnic Russian. Can you believe it?"

The self-doubt that had unfolded from the envelope with every hospital rejection letter again stole Akhmed's breath. "No," he said, dispirited. In three and a quarter years, when Sonja was to offer him a job, Akhmed would finally find that breath.

On the other side of the village Havaa was studying the pale blue flowers on her mother's skirt, annoyed she couldn't find them in the Caucasian flora guide. Why invent flowers when so many real ones would be honored to find their faces on a skirt? Her mother had spent the afternoon in the back garden and now chopped carrots, beets, and thyme lay on the counter. Havaa, standing on a stepstool and stirring the broth, found an unfamiliar gratitude for the smallness of her life. Everywhere beyond these four walls smelled of smoke and gasoline, but here, no calamity was greater than an egg falling to the floor. Later that afternoon the door would quietly close and her father would enter. He would speak with that deliberate, deceptive tone he used when reading her a story whose ending he already knew. She would ask if the army men would be staying with them and he would say, no, they're not refugees, and leave it at that. She wouldn't know that her father and Ramzan had spent nearly an hour conversing with the field commander. She wouldn't know that the field commander, impressed by Ramzan's experience as a trader in the mountains, had put him in touch with a sheikh who was looking for a capable man, a man like Ramzan, to deliver arms to the rebel encampments. All she would know was that the following Sunday, a day before the Feds arrived, her father lost Boris Yeltsin to a rook.

Three mornings after the rebels tottered from the village, Havaa woke to her parents' hushed panic. Her father hoisted her in his arms before she could change out of her nightclothes. The impact of each footstep jolted through her, and as he ran into the forest, she watched the village shrink over his shoulder.

"What is it?" she asked.

"We are being liberated," her mother panted from beside her.

A rotten log shielded them from all but the *zachistka*'s sound. When a ten-second spray of gunfire flooded the sky, Havaa couldn't have imagined it was directed at eight villagers deemed too dangerous to be transported to the Landfill. Lying on the mossy topsoil for hours, she thought of her father's defeat the previous afternoon. She knew that Russian soldiers could destroy a village, but she hadn't known her father could lose a chess match. He lay next to her, twitching at the slightest shift in the wind, his fingers white around the handle of the kitchen knife. The rising smoke was so thick dusk came at three o'clock. Her father peered over the log with a pair of binoculars. He passed her the binoculars, the two-night payment of an ornithologist, who was now homesick, studying birds in Ecuador. As she spied Feds through the gaps between tree trunks, her father explained the difference between *kontraktniki* and ordinary draft soldiers.

"The draft soldiers in blue uniforms are scared teenagers. They are what we might call the victims of absurdism," he said, not one to miss an opportunity to lecture a captive audience. "They would surrender if you waved a soup spoon at them. Most can't find Chechnya on a map and don't care if Putin, Maskhadov, or Father Christmas presides over the republic; most arrived by train in passenger carriages but most will return as Cargo 200, sealed within zinc-lined coffins in the freights. But the *kontraktniki*, the ones you see wearing sleeveless black T-shirts to show off their tattoos, they are nihilists, immoralists, or misanthropists, take your pick. They were released from prison provided they serve a certain number of years in Chechnya. They *want* to be here because this is the only place they can express their true nature, and, if I weren't hiding behind a log, I suppose I might even admire them because they are committed to the dialectics of their philosophy, no matter how horrid."

At that moment, a blond-haired conscript had pulled Khassan from the line of men that were to be taken to the Landfill. He hid Khassan in a tin-roofed shed and gave him his grandparents' name and address. "You must survive," the blond-haired conscript said. "You must survive and tell my grandparents. Tell them their grandson is not like the other solidiers. Tell them that they raised him well, that he's trying so hard to stay the boy they raised." Khassan would write a letter to the conscript's grandparents, but without access to a functional postal system, it would remain in his drawer for seventeen months, until the autumn morning when a Russian woman knocked on his door, asking if he had seen her son. It wasn't uncommon to see the mothers of missing Russian soldiers searching the Chechen highlands for their sons. Khassan wouldn't be able to help her, but he would ask her to post his letter from Russia. He wouldn't know that in Novosibirsk the grandparents of the blond-haired conscript would receive his letter eight days after they received word of their grandson's death and would read it as a eulogy at his funeral.

By evening the village still lay under an awning of smoke. Twenty-three had died. Fourteen from gunfire, three from collapsed houses, two from mortar fire, and one from suicide: a ninety-year-old man who had survived two world wars, three heart attacks, and, most debilitating of all, the shame of his firstborn son, a boy who could have been anything but chose to be a puppeteer. The Feds forced three into a cellar and lobbed in a live grenade before shutting the door. Another eighteen were taken to the Landfill, which meant forty-one villagers disappeared that day, to return only by the grace of Akhmed's pencil. Shortly after Havaa followed her parents home, Akhmed appeared in the doorframe and knelt to knock on the kicked-in door. He needed Havaa's fingers. In his clinic the wounded lay on every surface flat enough to hold a body. The butt of a Kalashnikov had forever shut a woman's left eye. The arm of a man who would go on to summit Elbrus bent as if it had three elbow joints. Akhmed's hand, flaccid on her shoulder, guided Havaa through the waiting room. His office was an operating theater. Mountainous tarpaulin topography spread across his desk, streams flowing into lakes of blood. A lamp sat on the floor, its light pinning the silhouette of Akhmed's head to the ceiling where it would blankly observe the scene. He spoke as if accountable to her, explaining that this wasn't a hospital and he wasn't a surgeon, that he could draw lovely sketches of the wounded but couldn't save their lives, that the doctors at Hospital No. 6 were unquestionably superior and had the *zachistka* cordon not blocked all traffic to the city, he would carry each to the hospital on his back to avoid the responsibility of their care.

Two neighbors helped him carry a limp body to the desk. He cleaned the wound with water, but he had run out of iodine solution and had to use a half bottle of *spirt* for sterilization. He made a homemade hemostat by wrapping clean bandages around the head of a pliers and clinching the handles with a rubber band.

Akim was thirteen, the first wisps of a mustache filled in with soot. Red dishrags were wrapped around his thigh, and between half-opened lids, his eyes found Havaa's.

"My fingers are too big," Akhmed repeated as he tightened a leather belt around Akim's thigh. The adults in her life all acted like children, and rather than compounding her fear, this forced her to be calm. Piece by piece she broke down the room, chopping the ceiling from the walls and the walls from the floor, amputating her shadow from her feet, until the one floorboard holding her was all that remained. Akhmed explained that Havaa had to help him ligate an artery with thread from a frayed skirt. A few months earlier her mother had taught her to sew and he knew that for her father's birthday she had mended the toes of all his socks.

"Okay," she said, though she didn't want to help Akhmed, though she wanted to hide in the forest, where birch branches were the only limbs that ever broke. But she did it for Akhmed, rather than for the boy, who once had found her talking to a pinecone and had teased her so badly she had wished him dead.

She couldn't sleep that night. In the quiet of her parents' bedroom she could still hear his screams. Everything was different now. She couldn't say how or when, whether it had happened when her father had carried her to the woods, or when her fingers had sunk into the hot ooze of Akim's open thigh, but everything was different. On either side her parents lay awake, and when she squeezed the flaps of their pajama tops, as she had always done for reassurance when she had a bad dream, her mother squeezed back.

No one wanted to risk moving the unexploded shells that lay scattered across the village, so the next morning Havaa's parents, among other villagers, pried toilet bowls from the rubble of collapsed houses and dragging them upside down and two by two gently set them over the unexploded shells. Havaa would never forget the sight. So many dozens of upside-down toilet bowls crowded the street that cars wouldn't pass for weeks, and in that time, she would occasionally hear the overdue explosions, the shrapnel ringing within the ceramic, but those bowls, the one decent legacy of the Soviet Union, never broke.

In the afternoon, she and her parents went to the clinic. Akhmed wouldn't meet their eyes when they entered his office. The blood-hardened tarpaulin lay on the floor, and in its red desert Havaa remembered streams. Akhmed slouched forward, his head propped against the desk by his pencil.

"I can't remember their faces," he muttered.

"Whose?" her father asked.

"I promised I would draw them, but I can't remember anymore."

"You should sleep," her father said, and beside him, her mother gazed at Akhmed with an expression of concern Havaa would only later recall.

When Akhmed woke, he kept his promise. He mounted blank pages on plywood boards, and over the next ten days drew forty-one meter-tall portraits. He used ink and charcoal, the cinders of burnt houses; there was a word for it, when artists used parts of the subject to recreate the subject, an -ism only Dokka would know. The portraits were larger and more detailed than anything he'd ever drawn. Eyelashes five pen strokes thick. Pupils the size of plum pits. When finished, he brushed the portraits with weatherproof finish and left them to dry overnight. By morning they shone like the lacquer of Dokka's chessboard. One at a time, he carried them to the street. Some he mounted within the doorless frames of abandoned public buildings; others he fixed into the walls of private homes, or hung over broken windows, or strung from empty planters, or raised to the top of flagpoles, or nailed to lampposts, tree trunks, or fences. One covered the hole punched into a wall by a mortar round. Another he staked upright in the cemetery, a tombstone for a man whose family couldn't afford one. They appeared with no commemoration louder than Akhmed's solitary hammer rap. Sometimes weeks or months would pass before the bereaved stumbled across the face of their disappeared, and when they did they might approach in awe, or pat their breast pocket for a cigarette, or laugh as if just understanding a joke, or ignore it entirely, having grown used to hallucinating their loved ones on walls, tombstones, and clouds.

Havaa experienced the sensation only once. After the *zachistka* she spent all her daylight hours in the woods. The village shrank to slender stripes as she receded into the trunks, meandering back and forth, building barricades of loose sticks, helping little bugs find fresh leaves, all while measuring distance by the diminishing volume of her mother's call. One afternoon she looked over her shoulder and froze.

A head, swollen and decapitated, hung from a tree behind her. A giant's head, she thought, and then, two steps closer, she recognized it. Akim had survived the night but died the next morning. Akhmed said that those hours were a gift she'd given Akim, that time became more important the closer to death one was, so an extra few hours to make peace with the world were worth more than years, though how he could have made peace while screaming, she didn't know. She stood close enough that her breath, chilled by the winter air, reached his lacquered lips. Akim once had found her talking to a pinecone and had watched, fingers barring his mouth, until snickers erupted from his nostrils. She had hated him then and still did. But standing before the portrait she felt something wrap around that hatred as a flame wraps around a candlewick, and soon there was nothing but a burnt taste in her mouth, his solemn face staring back at her, and the awful fact that it would never laugh again. Only then did she wonder how Akhmed had known to place the portrait where only she would find it. For a few more minutes, she stared at the portrait, and said good-bye.

When she woke the following Sunday, a single question pulsated in the cold morning air. What if there was no chess match today? The biweekly matches were the last heartbeats of the society in which she so badly wanted citizenship. She lay in bed until the sun had climbed into the first pane. When her mother, Esiila, asked her to help in the kitchen, she refused to answer, and poured a stream of indecipherable half words onto her pillow. The girl always surprised her mother. During the *zachistka* she had hid in the woods as quiet as the stones at her feet and twice as tough, calmer and more sensible than Dokka, who had gone on and on, lecturing them, knowing they were trapped. And now, the girl who hadn't cried once since the rebels arrived in town was bawling over morning chores. Believing the girl's endurance had at last reached its limits, Esiila quietly closed the door.

Havaa only left the bedroom when she heard the soft tapping of her father setting chessmen on the board. Later that afternoon, when her father lost Boris Yeltsin, again to Akhmed and Ramzan's rook, Havaa didn't care.

Quiet and cautious, the months moved like men slipping into mosque after *salat*. Villagers slid into the refugee lines without telling anyone and the taste of concrete dust hung in the air for a full season. Once a month, Ramzan's red pickup pulled up and her father sank into the cracked leather passenger seat, and she would watch through the window as the taillights shrank. When he returned a week later, his whole body would smell like an armpit and he would pause at the threshold, eyes narrowed, rebuilding his family in his mind before pushing the door open and telling them how much he had missed them. Though Havaa never discovered where her father and Ramzan went, or what they did, she knew from her mother's voice that they were probably doing something more dangerous than flipping blini on the skillet with their bare fingers.

The kitchen window was left open even in winter to ventilate the oven air and, in the mornings, her father's indigestion. She paused at it on the day before her father was to leave. Her parents' voices ran together like ribbons of smoke. Her father said it would ensure their survival, and her mother called him an idiot for thinking anything involving guns or Ramzan was safe, and Havaa dashed back to the woods, where songbirds spoke to one another in more pleasant tones. Ramzan's truck arrived before dawn. At the door, Havaa placed a pebble in her father's palm. "If you roll it in a hundred circles you get a wish," she said. He slipped it into his shirt pocket, and leaned forward, and his lips were two slats of sunlight on her forehead. The warmth glowed pleasantly, and after he turned to her mother, she pressed her fingers to her skin to hold it there.

Ula had taken ill in spring 2002, one year after the *zachistka*, and so when for the first three nights of her father's final trip Akhmed filled Dokka's seat at the table, it seemed only natural that he should come alone, as he had on other occasions when her father was in the mountains. It was January 2003. Havaa hadn't seen Ula in eight and a half months. On the first evening, as Havaa set plates on the table, Akhmed followed behind her and picked them back up, muttering, "These won't do." He left for his house and returned a few minutes later with a shorter, narrower stack of dishware. Between the knives and forks Akhmed's saucers looked like shrunken heads attached to enormous metal ears. Her mother frowned at the reconfigured table setting; men, she knew, would take everything from a woman, even her plates.

"To trick our stomachs," Akhmed told Havaa, loud enough for her mother to hear in the kitchen. "Tonight we dine like aristocrats on an elegant meal of modest portions. But I find nothing sadder than a small amount of food lost on a large amount of plate. But this," he said, holding a saucer in his palm, "is just the right size. If we trick our brains into thinking our dinner fills an entire plate, we might trick them into thinking our stomachs are full." On the kitchen window Havaa thought she caught a smile in her mother's reflection.

The tension that had seemed staked to the floorboards the previous night fluttered out the open kitchen window as her mother and Akhmed conversed. They reminisced about Dokka's arrival in the village. He had presumed the village had its own newspaper, a presumption some took as evidence of insanity. He had brought more boxes of books with him than there was floor space in his rented room, and rather than discard the precious tomes, he had turned them into furniture. He slept on a mattress raised on book boxes, and sat at a desk made of an old door laid across pillars of science manuals. It didn't help his standing among those already questioning his sanity.

Dokka had grown up and been educated in Grozny, and Akhmed, just graduated in the bottom tenth of his class with no job prospects and the noose of the village's expectations tightening around his neck, did his best to transform Dokka into a local celebrity, partly because he had never befriended a man from Grozny, but mainly so Dokka could replace him on the tongues of gossiping widows. An arborist by training, Dokka was assigned to a three-year position researching the potential environmental benefits of clear-cutting, the professional equivalent of Siberian exile. When the Soviet Union collapsed and the timber industry disappeared—along with Dokka's funding—he remained to take advantage of this rare opportunity to research new-growth forest. By then he had moved into a home large enough to accommodate both books and furniture, and the villagers, most anyway, didn't run to the other side of the road when passing him. Though Esiila's father belonged to the camp still questioning Dokka's mental health, Khassan fully endorsed the young arborist, and Dokka was willing to marry Esiila for such a small dowry, the father would have been judged insane himself for refusing.

Havaa watched the conversation as she would a chess match, each side testing the other, searching for weaknesses to exploit. Now and then her mother glanced at her and the reflection of candlelight revealed an unfamiliar intensity in her eyes.

"Has Ula shown any signs of improvement?" her mother asked.

"No. She hasn't left the bed for over eight months now."

"Are you any closer to a diagnosis?"

Again, Akhmed shook his head. "Her vitals are fine. Whatever she has exceeds my ability to detect, let alone treat. I make sure she rolls over every couple hours to prevent bedsores. What else can I do?"

"You don't think there is anything wrong with her, do you?" The question was a queen driven eight squares forward.

"I think the human mind isn't built to sustain trauma after trauma."

"Perhaps she needs to learn to care for herself. Perhaps your care is her paralysis."

Havaa focused on her fingernails. She wanted to speak but didn't, wanted to flee but couldn't.

"I've considered leaving her for a few days, seeing if her body might jump-start her mind. It seems too cruel."

"Both of our spouses have disappeared into themselves. Cruelty may be the line to draw them back."

The conversation then veered back down the unmined road to the past, but when they each reached for the water pitcher, her mother's fingers brushed his, and they all blushed.

Akhmed stayed with them the following day and night, and the one after that, spending most of the daylight hours planted in front of the living room window, staring across the street to his house. At night, when he thought Havaa was asleep, she heard him sneak into her parents' room. It wasn't until just after the *fajr* on the third morning that he finally left. He didn't return. Esiila stood at the window, where he had, and she could see him across the street watching from his living room window, and they stood there with a bridge running between their eyes. Something awful had happened, but Havaa couldn't put a name to it. She and her mother didn't speak for the rest of that day or the next, as if Akhmed had been the substance through which they communicated, and without him they were alone with what they knew. The longer they went without speaking it, the heavier that first word became. On the day her father was to return, her mother hummed while she swept, scouring the silence with the dust from the rooms. Daylight dissolved into marbled twilight and Havaa fell asleep waiting for her father to appear.

They steeped in that silence for eight more days and nights before the uneven crush of gravel broke it. The door edged open and her father's full weight collapsed against her mother's chest. She would remember the yellow-gray of her father's cheeks, how she'd seen that color frozen in deer urine but never on a human face. "Help me," he whispered. Only then, when he tottered forward, did she see the dark red rags rubber-banded to his wrists. Akhmed must have seen from his house because he ran in with his doctor's satchel before she could scream.

Akhmed would later explain that the bolt cutter had severed each finger so cleanly no skin remained to stitch over the bone. He would later explain that though ten strips of duct tape closed the wounds for the journey from the Landfill, infection was a greater threat than blood loss, and so he had no choice but to cauterize, no choice but to put out each finger like a cigar stub on the side of a heated butcher's blade. But when he ran in he couldn't explain what he was doing any more than could a man asked to put out a forest fire with only the water he could carry in his mouth. He asked her mother to start the stove and asked Havaa to go to her room. She hesitated. In the *zachistka*, she'd helped him when his fingers were too large and fumbling. Why wouldn't he let her do the same for her father? The thunderclap of her name, this time shouted by her mother, and she ran.

The clatter of kitchen utensils passed through her closed bedroom door. Akhmed shouted for the butcher's blade, and for more petrol, and with an intake of air the bar beneath the door brightened.

For three days her father slouched on the divan. Each night her mother unwound the gauze to polish the dark stumps with ointment. After a minute or two she cut a new strip of gauze, taped it around the shiny nub, and sighed, knowing she had nine more.

Late afternoon on the fourth day he stood. He paused at the coat stand, studying the buttons, and decided it was too warm for a coat. Havaa opened the door for him and he set his hand on the back of her neck and the heat of five missing fingers held her shoulder. They walked like that to Khassan's house. Ramzan opened the door. They both looked to Ramzan's fingers. Not even a nail was missing, and Ramzan blushed, and shoved his hands in his pockets.

"How . . ." Ramzan began to ask, but didn't finish. "You look better."

"I need a gun," her father said.

"What? No, Dokka."

"I need to know that my family can protect itself."

"Dokka, they let us go from the Landfill. Do you know what they'll do to you if they have even the idea that you are involved with guns again?"

"What, Ramzan?" her father asked, raising his hands. "What will they do to me?"

Ramzan looked down. "Fine," he said, after a moment. "Come in."

They walked past Khassan's desk to Ramzan's room. Ramzan popped the rigged floorboard and retrieved a Russian-made Makarov pistol from a cache beneath the floor. "Why did you bring the girl?" he asked.

"To pull the trigger," her father said, looking down at her. "She's six years old. It's about time she learned how to handle guns."

Ramzan took her outside, showed her how to load and unload the bullets, to set and release the safety. He told her to aim at the feral dogs clustered at the tree line, but she chose a tree trunk instead.

"It's a semiautomatic," Ramzan explained, "so you don't need to cock the hammer. Don't hold it out, that's for American movie stars.

You want to keep it just in front of you, your elbow against your chest, like you're carrying a water pitcher. This won't have the kickback of a high-caliber gun, but it isn't designed for children, so you'll feel it. Where do you think you should aim? The head? Never on the first shot. Too small a target. Aim for the chest, right in the center, that's the kill shot."

When she returned to the front of the house, her father sat back on the stoop, eyes closed, basking in the sun with a faint smile on his lips. She put the gun in his jacket pocket. He still hadn't said what had happened to his fingers. As they walked home, she was worried he might, but his feet ground into the glinting gravel, and hers did too, and they conversed only in footsteps.

Two women and a man waited for them at the front door. The man's hair looked painted and polished on his head; in another life he'd had a good job, a good flat, and a good wife, but now his lustrous head of hair was the only good thing he had left. "We heard you have beds," one of the women said.

Her father looked at his shoe as if just stepping in dog shit. With a sickle-moon smile he shook his head, but they all knew it wasn't in response to the question. Havaa would never know her father had spent the past three days paralyzed by the realization that his fingers would never again save Boris Yeltsin, or rake April soil, or flip the pages of a book, or wrap around his penis in the outhouse, where for the space of an inhalation he felt content.

"Yes," he said. The three refugees beamed with a gratitude that would fill him even longer than a final trip to the outhouse. "We have several beds."

SONJA DIDN'T SEE him when she crossed the parking lot, didn't know him when she unlocked the doors, didn't hear him when he greeted her good morning, when he climbed into the truck after her, when she released the brake, gunned the engine, and followed the gray road to Grozny. Twelve hours earlier he had nearly fainted at the sight of her palm calluses. But why think about this when the snow melted into muddy veins, when the blue of a peaceful sky radiated from all the metal of the jeep, when Havaa was safe and he was alive and Grozny waited like a great lake at the end of this river of asphalt.

To conserve petrol, Sonja accelerated for several seconds, then free-wheeled out of gear. Too much oil in the ground, never enough in the tank, he thought; it could be the national motto. They progressed halt-ingly, the truck leaping forward and then rolling to a near standstill.

He felt carsick, but knew better than to ask her to drive more evenly. Fifteen silent minutes passed before he flipped on the radio and gave the dial a quarter turn. A crush of warm static filled the cabin.

"There's no working radio tower in the country. It's all static," she said, without looking to him.

"I know. But 102.3 plays the best. Not too tinny. Full and robust. If a cello were to perform static, it would sound like this."

She shook her head and turned the dial. "I prefer 93.9," she said. She still hadn't looked at him.

"It's too thin and monotone. There's no variation. It just sounds like static."

"And that's why I like it," she said. "It sounds like static is supposed to sound."

He reeled the dial to the far end. "106.7," he said. "Just listen." Snatches of foreign transmissions laced the white noise. Syllables surfaced like glowing bubbles from the harsh swirl. Voices in a storm. She turned the dial back to 93.9 and they listened to static-sounding static. Fog fell over the fields. A bus was parked in a meadow. Paint chips pointed down a gravel road to the rusted remains of a tractor factory. Dormant smokestacks. Nowhere was a fire less likely to be found than inside a factory furnace.

"Do you worry about land mines?" he asked.

"Not really. There's a steel plate mounted beneath the driver's seat."

"Does it happen to cover the passenger's seat, too?"

She *had* to smile, but before she shook her head and said he could amputate his own legs now, her gaze hardened around a figure a hundred meters down the road. An elderly woman with the posture of a parenthesis. A twine-strapped bundle of blue tarpaulin hung from her shoulders. A lavender dress hem fluttered at her ankles.

"Don't you know this road isn't safe on foot?" Sonja asked through the open window. "Do you need a ride?"

The woman shrugged the blue tarpaulin, and watching her Akhmed wanted to reach out, to wipe the damp grooves of her forehead and tell her that he too had suffered Sonja's questions.

"Only a fool would sit in a truck," she said, pace unchanged.

"But we are doctors," Akhmed said, emphasizing *we*.

She glanced at him and back to the road. "And you're sitting in a truck."

Thirty minutes of empty fields passed without remark before Akhmed and Sonja reached the first checkpoint. An OMON lieutenant approached, followed by two scrawny privates who mimed his movements down to the way he chewed his bottom lip between his sentences; and contemplating these slight, unconscious facsimiles, Akhmed wondered if fear so consumed the young men that they would fuck, fart, and die on their superior's schedule. Sonja passed the lieutenant their documents: two ID cards, one expired medical license, and three letters penned by Federal colonels, which persuaded the lieutenant more compellingly than their legitimate documents. A hundred meters past the checkpoint she reached across his lap and slid the letters into the glove box. She still hadn't looked at him. He grabbed her wrist before she could shut it and pulled out more than two dozen envelopes. The letters varied in formality, from official endorsements typewritten on Defense Ministry stationery to a few approving words scrawled on the back of a rebel field map. The signatories formed an index of the top brass on both sides of the war: General of the Federal Army Valentin Vladimirovich Korabelnikov, Special Battalion Vostok Commander Sulim Yamadayev, Commander of the Northern Caucasus Military District Alexander Ivanovich Baranov, the deceased mujahideen leader Ibn Al-Khattab, separatist field commanders Ruslan Gelayev and Shamil Basayev, even a deputy from Putin's office, both rebels and Feds cohabiting peacefully by the thin partition of letter envelopes.

"Be careful with those," she said, pulling her hand away.

"Why do you have these?" he asked, as the first of long-overdue misgivings unsettled him.

"For unhindered travel. They take care of bureaucratic formalities."

"I wish you'd told me before I'd sewn shut my pockets."

She smiled.

"Have you actually met these people?"

"Of course not. Most are from the man we're going to see. He says he can steal the spots off a snow leopard."

"A criminal?"

She shook her head and glared at him with complete disdain.

"Is common decency too much to ask?"

"Excuse me?" she said, but he knew she couldn't claim affront. Common decency was the one thing he had that she didn't, and he held on to it as a rare, improbable triumph.

"You said every doctor and nurse to ever work for you has left but Deshi. Do you think that might have something to do with the way you treat people?"

"I think you'd better have brought your boots, because you're walking home."

He spoke in a measured tone as her knuckles whitened on the wheel. "You think I'm an idiot. An embarrassment to your profession. You are probably right. But that doesn't mean I'm wrong."

"I think you need to be quiet, Akhmed."

"Why?" He didn't dare turn to her.

"Because two days ago, I thought I was adding a competent doctor to my staff. Instead I'm babysitting a child who speaks in riddles and a man who couldn't identify his own foot if he tripped over it."

"That doesn't give you the right to treat me dismissively. I'm trying to help you."

"Actually that gives me every right to treat you dismissively. It gives me every right to dismiss you and the girl and fuck off back to London where even eighteen-year-old biology students know better than to give an unresponsive patient a questionnaire."

"The Feds are looking for Havaa," he said. "You're this prodigy surgeon, right? Leaving London to come back and save lives? You are saving hers, Sonja. Each day. And you don't even have to cut off her legs."

"How do you even know they want her? Why would they care about some child?"

"An informer was waiting at my house yesterday."

"I don't want to hear about it."

"I'm sorry," he said. "I'll be quiet."

"What could you possibly be sorry for?"

"I'm sorry for you. Something in you is broken."

"Another razor-sharp diagnosis, Dr. Akhmed."

"No, it isn't that."

"I've amputated one thousand six hundred and forty-three legs. You've done three, and you think you have the right to diagnose me?"

"I'm not diagnosing you."

"Then what the fuck are you doing?" She turned fully from the road and he saw her pupils, as wide as kopek coins, for the first time that morning. He shook his head at the windshield. Brown fields were everywhere.

And Grozny appeared, gray on the horizon as the road devolved to a basin of broken masonry and trampled apartment blocks. Cigarette kiosks slouched on the sidewalk. Akhmed wished he had taken paper and a pencil with him to capture his first trip to the city. Sonja brought the jeep to a crawl as they tipped into a crater. The street rose and disappeared somewhere above them, the whole world of dark wet earth, the tires spinning and reaching the lip. No scent drifted through the open window but the engine burn. No sewage or raw waste. Nothing. A flattened bureau basked in the sun, knobs pried out. The flicker of an oil-drum fire three blocks out came as a small, welcome signal of human habitation. Behind the flame a man turned a rotisserie fashioned from clothes hangers and a gardening stake on which was impaled a pink fist of flesh. Two pigeon claws revolved over the fire. Behind the fire, wooden gangplanks connected pyramids of rubble. Some lay over craters, others were suspended two or three stories high, bridging alleyways. This is Grozny? He should have visited sooner.

"It's like scaffolding," he said, the first words in many kilometers.

"Built by the street kids that live in the ruins," she said, and in a tone of apology added, "You were smart to bring her in."

No faces peered from the yawning walls. The thought of his dreary, soul-crushingly backward village sent an unfamiliar flare of pride up his chest.

"How do they survive?" he asked, glancing at a building with more plank bridges than floors. An ingenious strategy; these young engineers were clearly ethnic Chechen. Collapsed floors would take construction crews years to lift and rebuild, but plank bridges could be reassembled in minutes.

"They sell the rubble back to the Russians. Construction has begun on defense and petroleum ministry buildings. They buy back the bricks at two rubles each."

"More than I would have thought."

"Bricks purchased at dawn are cemented by noon, so the kids have to chisel off any remaining mortar. You see those white rubber casings in the rubble?"

"Like snake skins."

"It's electrical wire insulation. They strip and sell the copper wire. Just about any metal is worth its weight. Most of these kids can't read or write, but they've created metal-based currencies."

"Scrap metal and disappearances," Akhmed said, flat and without irony. "Our national industries."

The warehouse stretched wider than a soccer field with half its windows stained tar-black and the other half blown out, and when Sonja nodded to it he knew something was wrong. They passed a toppled chemical drum, its top peeled back like a bean-tin lid; a glowing blue sludge, too thick to evaporate, pooled at the bottom. A guard blocked the warehouse drive. His bloodstained bandoliers intersected at the sternum, the only red cross Akhmed would see that day. A dull glint, less recognition than knowing, appeared in the guard's face when he saw Sonja. "Only a fool would sit in a truck," the woman had said; if only Akhmed had met her a day earlier. The vise tightening in his chest had been there since the morning, since Sonja had refused to acknowledge him. She parked the truck, went to find the snow leopard–thief, and he was alone, brought by a woman who didn't trust him to a warehouse large enough to hold his village, a place where he shouldn't have been, in a city unworthy of even an imaginary plane ticket. Three Mercedes sedans sat at the center of the warehouse floor, Scandinavian license plates hanging from shiny screws. The walls were Western department stores: racks of leather and fur coats, refrigerators and dishwashers with warranties dangling from plastic ribbons, cardboard boxes stacked two stories high. A folding chair sat open on the floor, pliers and duct tape on the seat. A faucet turned on in Akhmed's mouth.

"It was the most remarkable thing I've seen in years. I couldn't think. I was stunned. Do I bow? I didn't know what to do." The thin, excited voice belonged to the thin, excited man entering the warehouse beside Sonja. "I never thought I would meet someone from China."

The two strolled with a familiarity—she touching his shoulder, he timing his footsteps to hers—that left Akhmed uncertain and unaccountably envious. The wide arc they walked around him drew a line of tension across the room. "What was he doing here? A journalist?" Sonja asked, avoiding his eye.

"An oil man. He wants to buy a refinery."

"You're selling refineries now?"

"Just the machinery," the man said simply. He wore a beige summer suit and a white dress shirt unbuttoned to exhibit a triangle of voluminous chest hair. His loafers reflected the pale light. A man dressed like this would be stripped, hog-tied, and beaten within one city block, but he didn't seem like the type of man that went anywhere alone. "Is this our friend?" the man asked, and nodded to the folding chair, pliers, and duct tape. "Have a seat, please."

Akhmed pivoted sharply, but the guard was behind him, the gun barrel leveled to his chest. A tourniquet gripped the corridor between his brain and body, and directions came to his limbs in halting dribbles that wouldn't save him. That morning Ula had been asleep when he left. He hadn't said good-bye to her.

"You haven't been honest, Akhmed," Sonja said. The way she studied him he knew his skull was just another bone she could amputate.

"I'm sorry," he gushed. "I lied about being in the top tenth of my graduating class. I was in the bottom tenth. In the fourth percentile."

No relief in her smile. "Do you think that's what this is about?" she asked.

What else could it be? The only lie he had told was that he was a good doctor.

"You knew my surname and patronymic, Akhmed." She had said his name twice now. The third time would be the last. "No one knows those. But you did."

"She wouldn't even tell me," the man offered. "Not that I had difficulty finding out, but still, she's rather cautious, don't you think?"

"You have to explain yourself," she said, and she paused for a breath. "Or I'll leave you here. I can't risk having an informer on my staff."

Had the gun barrel not pressed against his spine, he would have laughed. He would have treated the setup as another one of Sonja's tests. Treated the whole thing like the misunderstanding it was, because how could she mistake him for the man he had saved Havaa from? Havaa. The thought of her shucking the insulation from electrical wires reconnected his nerves. He couldn't swallow. In the mouthful of warm saliva a pearl formed; an irritant hardened into white gleaming fury at the possibility that the war would end his life as indifferently as it had a hundred thousand others, that he was no more privileged. He didn't want to die before an audience of stolen refrigerators. He had kissed Ula's forehead in the early morning and felt the flutter of her lashes on his chin but when he raised his face she had already gone back in the gentle wash of wherever it was she went when she wasn't with him. He hadn't said good-bye.

"I saw your work before I ever met you," he explained. "The rebels, they came to my village a few years back, and the field commander had a chest held together by the most magnificent dental-floss stitches. I was so impressed. The commander said it was the work of a Russian woman and I assumed they had kidnapped a Russian medic. But then, later on, I met a refugee from Volchansk who used to work at the hospital. She had stayed with Dokka when he was running a hostel for refugees."

"What was her name?" Sonja asked, eyes as fixed as constellations. She stood close enough for him to hear her teeth grind. There was so much of her, right here, in his face, and he would have stepped back, had a gun not pushed him forward.

"I mentioned the dental floss and the Russian woman doctor. It was only in passing. I wanted to know if the hospital was hiring. And she looked up and said, 'Sofia Andreyevna Rabina. Sonja.' I tried to ask her more, but she didn't want to talk about you. Your name was the only one I had when Dokka disappeared. I thought a doctor good enough to stitch a man with dental floss would be good enough to take in Havaa."

"What was her name!" she demanded. He was afraid to answer, afraid even to exhale; the hope wrapped within the question was so small and flickering a breath could extinguish it.

"Was it Natasha? Was her name Natasha?"

# CHAPTER

## 12

TALL, SWAN-LIKE, AND four years her sister's junior, Natasha stood in the spotlight of her family's affection. In his daybreak voice, cold from seven hours without the heat of a cigarette, her father would offer her good-morning first, even if she entered the kitchen two paces behind Sonja. Her mother treated her with the pride and envy of a woman who had fallen in love with sixteen boys in secondary school, none of whom reciprocated her affection. "My Natasha," she would say, running her fingers through the girl's long brown hair with a possessiveness suggesting the strands were an extension of her own. Natasha's eyes were brown spattered with glimmers of emerald and uncut diamond. Hazel, technically. Her mother stared in quiet awe of this more artful rearrangement of her genetic code, and slipped into a contentedness that usually appeared only after the red wine had fallen below the bottle label. Natasha's elevated station in the family left in her only the slightest scratches of arrogance. Better than anyone, she knew she had done nothing to deserve the beauty she was blessed with. Their parents' plain features, replicated predictably in Sonja, had reacted violently in Natasha to create something as surprising as a dove hatching from a pigeon egg.

Within the variations of beige composing the corridors of State Secondary School No. 28, the spotlight of attention expanded. As an ethnic Russian she belonged to the national minority that ran the republic. Her ethnic status propelled her into the elite echelons of adolescent popularity, where a personality cult had arisen around her, fueled by the adoration of obsequious underclassmen. In Moscow, Gorbachev's reforms barreled the Soviet Union toward the precipice, but in a far-flung city in a farther-flung republic, the old rules still applied. Ethnic Russians controlled all major positions of power, from headwaiters to heads of government, and the two-hundred-year history of imperial order reiterated itself within State Secondary School No. 28. With magnanimity, Natasha accepted her rank. She wasn't nearly as vicious as the girls who, in florid Cyrillic on the inner flap of their homework planners, graded boys on a twelve-point scale. Nor did she hold herself above the roiling sea of lunchroom gossip by pushing others under. Years earlier, when she was still young enough to need a good-night kiss, her father would plant his chapped lips on her cheek and, in a whisper of sweet tobacco, say, "Sweet dreams, my sweet tsarina." Even after she outgrew good-night kisses, she liked to imagine herself as the long-lost grandchild of Grand Duchess Anastasia Nikolaevna, and acted in a manner befitting a wise and humble monarch.

It was this—her ethnicity as a Russian, the stalwart minority defending the borders of Western civilization from the barbaric Muhammadans—that let her slip through her adolescent years with freedoms her Chechen classmates didn't enjoy. She could harbor lascivious thoughts of Ivan Yakov—a man her sister would revive three times in the second war—who was far more handsome than any literature teacher had a right to be. She could shave her legs without worrying if a prudish deity would smite those parallel beams of smooth skin. Overnight, it seemed, electrical lines were laid in her veins as she realized that the awkward, self-conscious boys around her were growing into men. The complications of puberty weren't further complicated by culture or religion. Only when comparing herself to her classmates, many of whom were subject to arranged marriages, did she come to understand that in Chechnya gravity pressed upon women with heavier hands. Her Russianness exempted her from its grip, and so yes, often she floated.

Though Russian, she'd never been north of the Chechen border. Her parents had been born in 1930s Moscow and had grown up in communal flats four blocks away from each other. They took the same buses, attended the same primary school, spoke an accent flavored by the same fog, ate eggs laid by the same chickens, watched the same setting sun impale itself on the bronze spire of the Central Pavilion of the All-Russia Exhibition Center. They each lost relatives to Stalin's purges. NKVD agents wearing uniforms the blue of a cloudless summer sky would stride into the apartment block past midnight, and the next morning residents would strain their tea without mentioning the scream-pierced night. Her parents blamed Stalin personally for the purges, and Natasha's state-approved history text confirmed that Stalin, and only Stalin, bore responsibility. But the terrible past of nighttime disappearances was locked within the pages of that history book; she never imagined she would one day disappear as easily as her forefathers.

In 1946 news spread of the deportation of Chechens and the need for ethnic Russians to resettle the empty republic. Her father was fourteen when he last drank a glass of rusty Moscow tap water. Her mother, eight. Trains carried them over the war-sickened land. They arrived in Grozny and stayed two weeks in a drafty university auditorium, sleeping on bleachers before receiving a residency assignment to Volchansk. They journeyed to the city by the same bus, two days apart. Natasha's mother and father each felt so lonesome in this silent country. They didn't believe they would ever find someone who had seen what they had seen, felt what they had felt. Twenty-one years after the end of the Great Patriotic War, they waited beside each other in a bread line. Their small talk surged to revelation. Neither could believe they had shared the same primary school, tap water, and sunset from adjacent apartment blocks. Neither imagined they would someday share two daughters: one beautiful, the other brilliant.

Though she was the elder, Sonja was always thought of as Natasha's sister, the object rather than subject of any sentence the two shared. She walked alone down the school corridors, head sternly bent toward the stack of books in her arms. To Natasha she was the Π-letter volume of the Large Soviet Encyclopedia: wide and filled with knowledge no normal person would ever need. On weekend nights, when Natasha returned from the cinema or discotheque, she would find a thin bar of light glowing beneath the door of her sister's room, and if she put her ear against the closed door, she would hear the whisper of a page turned every forty-five seconds. She believed Sonja to be a genius in the classical mold: a single great streak of lightning in an otherwise muddled sky. In all likelihood, Sonja had more academic journal subscriptions than friends. She could explain advanced calculus to her fifth-form algebra teacher but couldn't tell a joke to a boy at lunch. Even in the summer months, she had the complexion of someone who spent too much time in a cellar.

Everyone knew Sonja was destined for great things, but no one knew what to do with her until then. Even in academia, her natural habitat, she was an exotic species. Though her Russianness gave her certain dispensations, the idea that a young woman of any ethnicity could

so excel in the hard sciences was a far-fetched fantasy. Their parents encouraged her at a distance. Neither understood the molecular formulas,
electromagnetic fields, or anatomical minutiae that so captivated her,
and so their support came by way of well-intentioned, inadequate gen-
eralities. Even after Sonja graduated secondary school at the top of her
class and matriculated to the city university biology department, their
parents found more to love in Natasha. Sonja's gifts were too complex
to be understood, and therefore less desirable. Natasha was beautiful
and charming. They didn't need MDs to know how to be proud of her.

Sometimes, while struggling to earn average marks, Natasha
thought herself the only person in Volchansk who understood and envied Sonja for the wonder she was. Her existence was so narrow, her
energies so focused, she lived like a nail driving through the surface
of daily routines and disappointments. When, in May 1989, Natasha
needed to receive a three on her final chemistry exam to graduate from
secondary school, she forced herself to ask Sonja for help. They sat at the
kitchen table. Sonja opened the textbook and frowned at the landscape
of unhighlighted text. She didn't comment, didn't put her sister down in
any way, but simply said, "Let's start at page one." Natasha would always
remember that.

She passed the exam, but she wasn't admitted to a single university in Chechnya—probably because she didn't apply. She wasn't stupid, not even academically—she received top marks in history class,
and at that point knew more English than Sonja—but after nineteen
years living next to the searchlight of her sister's intellect, Natasha felt
ready to point her own little torch in a different direction. Instead of a
university acceptance letter, she received a secretarial position at the
Volchansk office of Grozneft, the Chechen branch of the Soviet Oil
and Gas Ministry, working for a leering, bloated man who assured her
that fifteen typed words per minute were more than sufficient. Natasha
kept the nails of her index fingers filed a half centimeter shorter than
the others, and from eight in the morning to five at night she punched

out reports on a black-ribboned typewriter. She worked in an office painted the color of cloud cover, but even in the ministry's somber shades, she felt all the exhilaration and uncertainty of the restructuring world. The Berlin Wall collapsed and soon the Soviet Union began to follow. Autonomous republics fell like pebbles from a crushed boulder. Anesthetically dull oil reports suddenly pulsed with significance. Chechen fields produced a relatively modest thirteen million barrels per year, but most of the region's oil ran through the republic's refineries. Ninety percent of Soviet aviation fuel was refined in Chechnya, along with much of the automotive-grade petroleum. With shortsightedness typical of a country whose first step in building an economy was to kill all the economists, the U.S.S.R. had built its energy production infrastructure on the far side of Russia's borders. When Azerbaijan declared independence, Moscow lost its oil-drilling-equipment assembly. When Kazakhstan and Turkmenistan left, they took extensive oil and natural-gas reserves. The sunken treasure of the Caspian could have lit Moscow for a thousand years, and that too was lost. In the urgent memos crossing her desk, Natasha read estimates of the Caucasus' total recoverable reserves that varied between twenty-five and a hundred billion barrels, the majority of which resided in the newly independent states, and the only available pipeline to convey Caspian oil from Baku to European markets ran straight through Chechnya. Then, a miracle. She began to enjoy her work. She read records of pipeline efficiency, the crude production rates, reducing the aggregate data into easily digested summaries, and, like an oracle that envisions but cannot intervene, she saw the prosperity of an independent Chechnya.

The ministry offices were housed in a six-story building bordering City Park, and each evening, on her way home, she passed a homeless man whose wispy beard reached his belt line. The man, a resident of the park, was known to most of Volchansk as the City Park Prophet. She gave him a few rubles each evening, and asked, half in jest, that he remember her poor tired feet in his prayers. The City Park Prophet's eyes would lower in gratitude, and he would promise to remember her when the end came.

She spent her Fridays at a nightclub called Nightclub, situated in what had been an aviation assembly plant. The floor spread across the eight-story hangar, wide enough to contain the gyrations of half of Chechnya. Nightclub never had reached, and never would reach, capacity. After downing drinks at the bar, Natasha and her friends shimmied their way to the center of the hangar. There, red velvet ropes created a ten-square-meter dance floor where the young, well-dressed, and secular could press against each other, shrieking and shaking in epileptic spasms of floodlight, freedom found in the ruins of empire. Natasha lost all elegance when dancing. Her heels hindered movement, but she couldn't take them off—no matter how often it was swept, loose bolts and rust-resistant rivets appeared on the floor, gently throbbing with the bass—so she listed. The majority of her dance moves consisted of attempts to stay upright. And one Friday night, in March 1991, with her hair, heels, and three-shot tilt no different from the previous dozen Fridays, she wobbled into Sulim's arms.

His 1990 black BMW convertible had been stolen in Belgium and driven across all of a European winter to reach him. He had three missing teeth—and one so black it was clearly on the way out—because for all his money, he still couldn't afford a decent dentist. He had the habit of raising his voice at the ends of his sentences, turning declarations into questions, as though when he whispered her name he wasn't really sure to whom he was talking. He had a bed the size of Natasha's bedroom, two Soviet pistols, his great-great-grandfather's *kinzhal* still brown with the blood of Imperial infantrymen, a short beard that never grew, eleven toes, and a long white curve of scar tissue on his pelvis that, in the seven months they saw each other, Natasha learned to desire and despise in equal measure. He had a cousin in the upper air of the *obshchina*, the Chechen mob. The cousin, educated at the London School of Economics, a man whose occupation reduced his life expectancy to that of a gulag laborer, had taught Sulim to open new markets with a crowbar. Their first month together was perhaps the happiest of Natasha's life. The following six, perhaps the most miserable.

The cancer in her mother's liver metastasized and she spent the last ten weeks of her life in the chlorinated air of Hospital No. 6. Through Sonja's connections, her father was allowed to spend the nights on the floor beside her bed, cocooned in his olive Red Army sleeping bag. Natasha gave Sulim a key to the flat. She fit her fingers in the furrows between his ribs, thought of them as rungs. The whole world was falling, but here was someone strong enough to hold on to. The two men with whom she'd been intimate previously had treated her like a slight, fragile thing, as if trying to fuck a Grecian urn. Sulim held her as if unafraid of crushing her kidneys. In her shoulders, he left perfect molds of his imperfect teeth that would turn red in the morning. He asked her to scratch him and her longer nails drew a tiger's coat on his back. Her body by itself seemed a beautiful but useless instrument. Sulim's grip on her wrists, his canines gnawing at her clavicle, this pressure in her chest, this flushed flesh.

But Sulim never stayed until morning. At two A.M., he began to yawn. He stood and ran his fingers across his stomach, pinching the skin. He had more money hidden in his mattress than the entire apartment block had in the bank, yet he had the waistline of a pauper. His navel had stretched to the shape of an almond. The waxen light of the corner lamp wrapped around his chest as he turned. His spine curved into a thin ridge when he reached for his socks, and she counted the rises of vertebrae. He wore wide-collared Hawaiian shirts. He fumbled with the spare button, slightly too big for his trousers' buttonhole. At times it felt like trying to build a meaningful relationship with a tooth fairy. He came at night, leaving behind presents, but always left by two. By the second month, he was leaving at one-thirty. Then one. He shrugged when she demanded to know why he hadn't introduced her to his family, why he didn't dance with her at Nightclub, why he dressed her as a mistress rather than a partner. "Because that's what you are," he said, and walked out the door.

The state police arrested him in November 1991 for fraud. An informer had linked him to the notorious *vosdushniki*—"air men," they were called, for their ability to draw billions of rubles from the air. Using falsified promissory notes, they authenticated bank transfers from an invented company in Chechnya to an invented company in Moscow. Enough paperwork went through for the *obshchina* men to withdraw the forged transfer in cash from Moscow banks. A bribe from Sulim's cousin released him from custody within two days, but the government still had enough thump in its baton to force him into hiding. He arrived at Natasha's flat at five in the afternoon. The living room curtains were drawn open and the smog-filtered sunset bathed his cheeks in ochre. She had never before seen him in natural light. In his left hand he held a blue nylon duffel bag. He explained the situation, drained of the swagger that had so entranced and infuriated her. He couldn't stay with family or friends, no one with whom he had a known relationship. He would stay here with her. She'd never seen him so in need. For the first time in their relationship, she realized that she had more power than he, and this was all she needed to let him go. He kept glancing to his feet. She would miss his eleventh toe. "I'm sorry," she said. "You need to leave."

Her mother passed a few weeks later. Natasha was at work, her sister at school, her father at the dessert counter in the hospital cafeteria. No one was there to see what the dying woman saw, in her final moments, when her uncle, the man who had disappeared when she was no more than twelve centimeters of fetal tissue in her mother's belly, emerged from the yellow wallpaper and led her the rest of the way. Ten days after the funeral, Natasha's father took a lorry job in Turkmenistan. On the morning he left, he wore a red sweater with golden diamonds woven across the chest. He had never filled it out, as her mother had predicted he would when she had given it to him five Christmases earlier. He would be wearing that sweater two and a half years later, just north of the border, when a stolen cement mixing truck would slam into his lorry cabin, cutting short his life, his final haul, and his five-week odyssey to return home to his girls.

Natasha went to work but couldn't pay attention to the reports she copied, collated, and conveyed. She lost her job soon after the declaration of national independence, when all essential oil ministry personnel were transferred to Moscow, her bloated boss included. She drifted, a kelp rope on the tide that washed away her country, family, and future. She made dinner one night, Sonja the next. Having graduated university at the top of her class, Sonja was now in her third year of medical school. She studied while they ate, paying more attention to diseases of the digestive system than to her dinner. Natasha tried to construct conversation with scraps of the day: *Did you see the car accident on Lenin Square? What classes did you have today?* But Sonja didn't believe in small talk and answered in monosyllables, a fact Natasha would remember when, sitting at the same table four and three-quarter years later, Sonja tried to convince her of its therapeutic qualities.

In the six months she lived without Sulim, without her mother or father, only one dinner was shot through with enough excitement to make her forget the awful cooking. Just before they were to eat, Sonja returned from the mailbox with a brown manila envelope riddled with international postage, and flung her arms around Natasha, panting and screaming joyous gibberish, with more life in her face than Natasha had thought possible. "London," Sonja finally said, and the word would remain with Natasha, its six letters stretching to accommodate every conceivable hope. "I've been given a full fellowship to finish medical school in London."

Natasha tried to smile, tried to pretend her tears were of joy rather than dread, but when Sonja threw her arms around her, when they embraced, Natasha held her sister tightly, so scared of letting her go.

.   .   .

Though Natasha had learned to sleep through the screech of tires, the curses, the celebratory gunfire, the explosions, the cries, the laughing, the whole hell of the street below, she stayed awake that night and watched speeding taillights stretch into crimson bars across the asphalt. The young men leaning on the hoods of European cars were gangsters and mercenaries and gamblers. They made dangerous bets with safe foreign currencies, laying on the dash the annual wages men of their education would earn in a lawful society. Some nights they tried to jump the decapitated Lenin statue in the square. That night was a simple drag race. Four cars looped through the city center along a course marked by trash-can fires. Reports of aerial bombing in Grozny had filtered in, leaving the city flushed and agitated. In the morning, she would take the bus to Grozny to meet with Lidiya Nikitova, a shuttle trader who flew through Tbilisi to Hamburg once a week and returned with suitcases packed with Western electronics and clothing. Natasha would fill two duffel bags with clothes, but also Walkmen, Game Boys, satellite phones, portable televisions, and the increasingly popular noise-canceling headphones to sell in the city bazaar. The Feds blocked the border, the airport looked like another shuttered factory along the Baku-Rostov motorway, yet the bazaar was flush with Japanese electronics, Burmese silk, Belgian chocolate, Brazilian liquor, Indian spices, and American currency. Only three cars came past on the next lap. She breathed against the glass of her bedroom window, summoning from the fog a smiling, finger-drawn face. It was November 1994. She hadn't seen her sister in more than two and a half years. She hadn't seen her father in more than three. She wondered if it would snow.

News came third-, fourth-, fifth-hand. Fact was indistinguishable from hearsay, so all was believed and all was disbelieved and all were right. *Grab as much sovereignty as you can swallow,* Yeltsin had urged, and Chechnya had opened its mouth. The president was still named Dzhokhar Dudayev, and he still had a fountain pen–drawn mustache. He was the first Chechen to make general rank in the Red Army and ten years earlier he had served in Afghanistan, where Russian bombs had fallen on Muslim civilians for neither the first nor final time. In bed Natasha listened to his radio address, his voice a lullaby compared to the screech of car tires. The fantastical marked his presidency. The government needed money, and so, after minting its own currency, Estonia sent its entire reserve of Soviet rubles to Grozny rather than to Moscow. The government needed an army, and, the previous year, when the Feds had abandoned their Chechen bases, they had left behind stockpiles of heavy artillery, ammunition, guns, armored jeeps, and more tanks than there were licensed Chechen tank drivers. She set the radio beside her pillow. The drag race had finished. She lowered the volume and rolled toward the black mesh speaker, imagining the voice of revolution to be the whispers of a friend talking her to sleep.

The rumors proved true; in Grozny, bombs fell. On the weekly trips to the capital, she paid attention to the crowds. The density of sidewalk debris ensured they only lifted their eyes at the murmur of planes. The traffic lights went out and policemen, still wearing the blue uniforms of Soviet road police, directed traffic with the tips of their cigarettes. She stood in a clogged avenue and scanned the skies. Only once did she see them fly over. Five planes in tight formation. She craned her neck while all down the avenue commuters left their car doors open as they fled. Five parallel lines of exhaust striped the empty sky. Kilometers above, men who didn't know her name wanted to kill her. A man in a bright purple suit grabbed her shoulder, shaking her, and asking if she was deaf or stupid or both. Following him down the line of abandoned vehicles, she pushed the driver doors closed, and in this simple act restored order to the world. He took her to the basement of a party supply store. They sat on sacks of inflatable plastic balloons. The man kicked over a box and whoopee cushions, Slinkies, and glasses with fake noses toppled out. "I can't believe I'm going to die somewhere so stupid," the man said, and began weeping. She asked how he knew this place. The man held on to his purple lapels. "This suit," he said, "I'm returning this stupid suit."

He was thirteen years into what would be a forty-eight-year career as a clown; he had an IQ of 167.

When the bombing stopped, she left the sobbing purple-suited man and went to Lidiya Nikitova's flat. She found Lidiya packing a suitcase on the unmade bed. Natasha expected to find it filled with Prada handbags, Gucci blouses, Ferragamo neckties, but instead found coarse woolen sweaters, baggy sweatpants, gray socks, a photo album. For ten minutes Lidiya shook her head in despair. Natasha worried the poor woman's head would fall off. "Chechens have family," Lidiya said, as she pulled out a pair of boots buried beneath a mound of toeless shoes. "They have their *teips* and their ancestral homes in the highlands to flee to. The barbarians. It's nearly the millennium and they still live in clans. Even now, in the middle of all this, they don't believe orphans or vagrants can ever exist because the *teip* will provide. The barbarians. What do we ethnic Russians have? No *teip*. Our countrymen are dropping bombs on us. No, back north for me. I've never been to Petersburg, but my cousin says it's much more civilized." After Lidiya Nikitova left, Natasha spent an hour browsing her apartment. She took a pair of high-heeled leather boots, cashmere sweaters, and silk evening gowns. She wouldn't have an opportunity to wear them, but beautiful things were so rare it seemed wrong to leave them behind.

Time no longer marched forward. The giant clocks hanging from office buildings began to confuse the minutes for the hours. They displayed June dates in November, August weather forecasts in December. Dudayev changed the national clock in an independence declaration from the imperium of Moscow time. His supporters set their watches an hour back, everyone else remained in the standard zone, and no one knew what time it was. At first, Natasha ate at preplanned points in her day to maintain the illusion of structured time, then only when she was hungry, then only when she had food. The phone lines trembled with static. The debilitated independence government promised at least five hours of daily electricity, but the five hours usually came in the middle of the night. The crumbling infrastructure turned time back farther than any presidential mandate. When had you last lived a day with the starting bell of your alarm clock? With breakfast *djepelgesh*? With news from Moscow and New York and Beijing beamed on the back of television waves? With the heat of that first cigarette in your throat and the Route 7 bus turning the corner, unfailingly three minutes behind schedule, just like you? With truant children pegging construction crews with snowballs, and the steam curling from the Main Department Store corner, filling your skirt, a convection tingling your thighs? With morning drunks, lining the sidewalks of City Park, switching from liquor to mouthwash? With a midmorning coffee break, sipping Nescafé that has probably a dozen actual beans per kilo, huddling within the yellow fluorescent wash of a bathroom stall, the only place you can be alone? With lunch? With a pause taken from work for the length of an afternoon cigarette? With the soft pinging of five-thirty streetlamps, coming to life as you pass, and the City Park Prophet waiting for you, his beard tucked into his trousers, his hand outstretched and humble, and you with ten rubles to press into his palm? With a home to come home to? With electricity in the wiring as you flick the lights, and heat humming from the radiators, and water in the tap, showerhead, and toilet tank, and voices saying *hello* and *how was your day* and *shut the fucking door it's freezing out there*, and you hearing them in your ears rather than your head, they who know your name? With a meal that is actually that, a meal, with family, both of which sustain in ways you will only understand in their absence? With soapsuds coating your forearms, the bubbles blinking out against your fingertips and rinsing away as you pass the plate for your sister to dry? With evening television, your parents on the divan, and you've never seen them hold hands, but they kick off their slippers, and on the floor their little toes touch? With your father's snores turning the hall into an echo chamber you walk through to reach the bathroom, warm enough you don't think of wrapping yourself in a blanket when you get out of bed? With toothpaste? With your sister's pencil scratches coming through the shadow-thin plaster walls, the mumble of rote memorization, her nightly prayers to a god you neither know nor comprehend? With your belief that no matter how badly you fuck up, you will always belong to these people, and that they will never let you disappear?

She went to Sonja's bookshelf. Extra brackets supported the heavy textbooks, and her index finger brushed past the spines of books too heavy to hold in one hand. How had civilization survived long enough to accumulate the knowledge contained in these books? The slimmer volumes stood on the upper shelf, a yellowed Red Army field manual the most useful of the bunch. Scanning the shelf, she recalled how Sonja always read the last page of a book first, how her sister had to know what would happen, where the story led, to see if it was worth the effort. She didn't open the torrid romance novels at the end of the shelf. The worn bindings had an intimacy absent from the rest. She imagined Sonja lying in bed, reading melodrama with an ache in her chest she couldn't quantify or explicate, and thus couldn't understand. Instead, she took a slender volume entitled *Origins of Chechen Civilization: Prehistory to the Fall of the Mongol Empire* by Khassan Geshilov.

She read by the slow burn of candlelight. Folklore said God had scattered ethnicities across the earth with a saltshaker; the shaker had slipped from his fingers when he reached the Caucasus, and a few grains of every nation had landed in its valleys. Other origin theories: the Chechens had descended from Scythian hordes, from the daughters of Genghis Khan, from a penal colony established by Alexander the Great, from a lost Roman legion. After finishing the first chapter, she flipped to the dust jacket. According to the three-sentence biography, Khassan Geshilov taught at Volchansk State University and lived in Eldár. This book was the first of a proposed multivolume history of the Chechen lands. In his photo he had clear brown eyes, a thick mustache silvered with gray hair, and a smile suggesting he was thinking of a flaky pastry or a woman's smooth calves rather than ancient hordes. Until the candle died, she read of ancient invasions: the Scythians in 850 B.C., the Greeks two centuries later, the Romans in the first century B.C., the Baltic Goths in A.D. 240, the Asian Huns in A.D. 370, the Avars, Khazars, Circassians, Mongols, and finally, ultimately, the Russians.

Without electricity or gas, the kitchen became a twilight mausoleum of dead appliances. One day, Natasha had an idea. Wearing latex gloves she found in Sonja's room, she scrubbed the innards of the oven and refrigerator with steel wool and bleach. She cut a broomstick to the width of the refrigerator compartment, jammed it in below the thermostat control, and pulled out the plastic shelves. In her bedroom, she gathered clothes from the floor in sweeping armfuls and deposited them before the refrigerator and the oven. Ever since she had begun working for the shuttle trader, her wardrobe exceeded her closet space. She hung silk evening dresses and cashmere sweaters on the broomstick bar, set folded jeans and blouses on the oven rack. When finished, she opened the doors to her new closet and bureau and felt pleased with her ingenuity. This is how you will survive, she told herself. You will turn the holes in your life into storage space.

Smoke turned the days into twelve-hour twilights. In the afternoons, when the chance of aerial bombing was the greatest, she wandered through the suburbs. She thought of her sister often. In their weekly conversations, Sonja described her boyfriend, Brendan, a Slavic Studies PhD candidate from Scotland, whose Russian was worse than Sonja's English. She described the international dormitory, which housed students from thirty-four different countries, none of whom tried to kill each other. She described pubs and monuments, black taxies that looked like bowler hats on wheels, a massive obelisk supporting the statue of a tiny man in Trafalgar Square, Buckingham Palace guards who wouldn't shoot her even if she openly mocked them, supermarkets with entire aisles devoted to breakfast cereal and salespeople who actually seemed pleased by the presence of customers. That first year, for the first time, the sisters had become friends. We are all the other has, Natasha had thought, but she knew Sonja had so much more. Sonja promised to find a way to bring her to London, promised to plead her case with the university, the Home Office, the goddamn queen, but nothing came of it, and Natasha wanted to flee but couldn't, didn't know how to, had heard horror stories of what happened to lone women refugees, and so their conversations grew shorter as civil society disintegrated. Teenagers with stolen firearms replaced policemen on the streets. Hand grenades cost less than jars of Nescafé at the bazaar. She didn't want to hear about the scones, and decided Sonja didn't want to feel guilty for eating them.

Days passed without speaking, then weeks. The telephone lines went weak from electrical shortages, but the central telecommunications exchange hadn't been hit. Natasha left the phone off the hook for days and the soft throb of the dial tone became the voice of stability in her solitude. When she wanted to speak with her sister, she went to the bookshelf instead. She read *Origins of Chechen Civilization* twice in one month, focusing on the last pages of each chapter, where the ancient invasions ended. After she wrung from Khassan Geshilov's words all the consolation she could, she returned the book to the top shelf, beside the romance novels, and kneeling on the floor, tugged at the largest reference book. A massive thing, a dining room table's worth of pulped wood. *The Medical Dictionary of the Union of Soviet Physicians.* She rested the book on her thighs and its weight soon put her legs to sleep. The four thousand eight hundred and eighty-four translucent pages held the most arcane and useless information. The names of buried blood vessels in Latin, Russian, and the official languages of the fourteen Soviet republics. The weight ranges of internal organs: 117 to 170 grams per kidney, 1.4 to 1.6 kilograms for a liver, 250 to 350 grams for a heart. She flipped through the book and found answers to questions no sane person would ever ask. The definition of a foot. The average length of a femur. Nothing for *insanity by grief*, or *insanity by loneliness*, or *insanity by reading reference books.* What inoculation could the eight-point font provide for the whisper of Sukhois in the sky? Based on the average life expectancy of a Soviet woman, she could expect to live for another forty-eight years, but the Soviet Union had died, and she hadn't, and the appendices couldn't explain this discrepancy in data, when the subject outlasted its experiment. Only one entry supplied an adequate definition, and she circled it with red ink, and referred to it nightly. *Life: a constellation of vital phenomena— organization, irritability, movement, growth, reproduction, adaptation.*

If she stood on the stool in the southwestern kitchen corner and pointed the radio antenna due south, she could occasionally pick up Russian-language news broadcasts from Nazran or Tbilisi. From there, she gleaned what information she could from the outside world. Porous enough to allow luxury cars, American cigarettes, and Russian firearms, the borders remained too dense for objective journalism. A Georgian accent raised the newscaster's Russian by half an octave and from that lilting, disembodied tenor she learned that Yeltsin had an eight percent approval rating and an election eighteen months away. The Communist Party of the Russian Federation, the primary opposition party, denounced him for losing the vast territories of the former Soviet Union. She understood precisely that this wounded pride would lead to punishment, would lead a crippled country to start a war to prove itself more powerful. On December 9, 1994, Yeltsin issued a statement ordering the Federal army to execute the disarmament of *all illegal armed units* in Chechnya, or, as they were known locally, *the government*. On December 10, 1994, he went to a hospital for a nose operation. On December 11, 1994, upon hearing reports that the first of the forty thousand troops amassed at the northern border had crossed the Terek River, she realized that the war had only just begun.

On the evening of December 11, 1994, when Natasha returned the receiver to its cradle, and the ringer burst into a tinny tremble, she let it ring for twenty seconds before lifting the receiver to her ear. "Hello," she said. "Finally, finally, finally," Sonja cried. "I've been calling you for days, weeks, all afternoon."

CHAPTER

13

1994  1995  1996  1997  1998  1999  2000  2001  2002  2003  **2004**

"I DON'T KNOW," Akhmed said softly. He watched her with such compassion it seemed he had forgotten the gun against his back. "I didn't ask," he said.

"You didn't ask? How could you not ask? How could you not ask her name?"

"Hundreds of refugees stayed at Dokka's house. I stopped asking their names."

"Where was she going? Didn't she say? She must have said something. Some hint or reference or mention. She must have said something. She must have. How could you not ask? How could you?"

"I didn't think I'd be asked to remember."

Her entire reflection fit in his widened eyes. Had Natasha's reflection once fit in his pupils? Drawn by light? Disappeared by a blink? "What did she look like?" she asked.

Akhmed could have filled a dozen lungs with that sigh. "Dark-haired and malnourished," he said.

The description would fit half the world. "Her eyes, what color?"

"Brown."

"But brown with shards of green and emerald? More hazel than brown?"

"Maybe. I can't remember."

"And her face?"

"She reminded me of Zakharov's portrait of the niece of Nicolas I."

"Nicolas I? What are you talking about? I need to know what happened. Where is she?" She felt nauseous. She had to know but he would not tell her. What had happened to her sister? When she died, this one need, so near to eternal it could be her soul, would survive her. "I need to know, I need to know," she repeated. "She was beautiful, wasn't she?"

"As beautiful as the Nicolas's niece, yes," Akhmed said. "She was probably headed to the refugee camps. They all were. Probably Ingushetia. Maybe the Sputnik or the Karabulak camp?"

He spoke, it seemed, as if he had been speaking to her for years, as if she was expected to follow the arcs of his cadence, landing on the period before he reached it. She was afraid to look down. "She was wearing traditional maternity clothes," he was saying. "And a green headdress."

"Where is she?"

Her hands tightened on his shoulders. She didn't remember putting them there. The loose handcuffs of his fingers raised them and held them and slowly placed them by her sides. She would remember this; with a gun to his back he was gentle. "I don't know," he said.

Far away Alu's brother nodded and the guard stepped back. "Our friend may be a terrible doctor," Alu's brother said, "but I don't think he's informing."

They walked to the supply crates shoulder-to-shoulder to avoid seeing each other. Akhmed helped her load the cardboard boxes into the truck and later she would remember him mopping his forehead with a gray handkerchief, asking if she needed help with a box of surgical saw blades, his poise as unsettling as any ruin she had seen that day.

As children Sonja and Natasha played hide-and-seek in the dust-thick catacombs of the apartment cellar. Light streamed through the high windows in long diagonals. On the floor each semicircle was a pool of lava, and light-caught dust motes were the remains of children who had stumbled into those incandescent rays. Natasha would drape a filthy curtain over Sonja and Sonja would count to fifty and the beat between each number would shrink as she neared that moment when she shouted "Fifty!" and sprang from the curtain and into that otherworldly place. Natasha was slender enough to hide behind a broomstick, but Sonja always found her. She always did.

"Who is she?" Akhmed asked as the warehouse shrank in the rearview. Ten minutes earlier she had told him they would stop at a phone bank and had said nothing else until she was behind the wheel and facing the mud-streaked windshield.

"My sister," she said.

"I'm sorry," he said.

Nothing could have made her feel worse.

"I'm the one who should be apologizing," she said to the gravel.

"Why does he help you?"

"Just after the first war I fixed up his brother Alu."

"And he still supplies the hospital?"

She nodded.

"He must cherish his brother."

She smiled. Poor, berated Alu, whose name was beaten more than a donkey's ass. Six months after they first met she had learned his brother's name was Ruslan, but she would always think of him as Alu's brother. She knew he had amassed a small fortune smuggling arms, heroin, and luxury goods for warlords, and had used that small fortune to rebuild his ancestral village after the first war. She knew his pet turtle was still alive, still named Alu, and housed now in the largest terrarium in the northern Caucasus. When his ancestral village was destroyed again in the second war, she knew he had paid passage to Georgia for his parents, brothers, aunts, uncles, cousins, in-laws, thirty-seven in total, even the oft-cursed Alu, plus the neighbors on either side of every uncle, cousin, and in-law, one hundred and seventy-four in total, where they lived in the Tbilisi apartment block he had purchased for the occasion, neighbor by neighbor, his ancestral village saved for a second and final time. She knew all this of him and more, but still didn't know why he didn't like Alu. "You may be right," she said, finally. "I think he just might cherish Alu above all."

The ruins opened onto what was once a central square filled with importunate street vendors, veiled mothers, and squirming toddlers. Pigeons missing eyes and wings hobbled on the granite stone like portents of a war still years away. There had been the statue of a Chechen, an Ingush, and a Russian poised in comradely unity, officially called "The Brotherhood of the People," but known locally as "The Three Idiots." Someone had dumped a few goldfish into the fountain and they had multiplied until the water thickened to a squirming orange mass. Rockets had demolished the five-story buildings that had floated on arcades of equilateral arches, the tree-lined pedestrian paths, the wooden benches dedicated to Party bosses, the fountain where in winter children ice skated over the suspended carcasses of two thousand goldfish. The ruins had been bulldozed to an uneven field of rock. She parked the car. Akhmed frowned. "I don't see any telephones," he said.

"We'll stop on our way back," she said. They climbed out. "You said you've always wanted to go to Grozny, so I wanted to show you the central square." She didn't look at him. It was the nearest to reconciliation she was able to go.

He smiled, nodded, held his hands behind his back. She exhaled. "Is that what this is?" he asked.

She shielded her eyes with a salute to the afternoon sun. "Right there, where the ground is blackened, just to the left of that cloud, that's where the Presidential Palace stood." Rotating in a slow circle, her index finger pressed the past into the empty panorama. The market selling Levi's two decades before any licensed clothing store. The music college, where some years earlier a prodigy had learned to play the viola by listening to the two-hundred-year history of chamber music lilting through those open windows. She reconstructed the square for Akhmed—her voice raised every edifice from the dust, replanted every linden tree—because that was easier than apology.

"Thank you. I've always wanted to see Grozny."

They passed through two more checkpoints before reaching a clean, freshly paved street. The anomaly of unmarked asphalt never failed to surprise her. A gray stone building filled most of the block. The sheet-glass windows, intact and absent of fractures, proclaimed the building's significance more eloquently than the Petroleum Ministry sign hanging over the entranceway. Armed soldiers stood at ten-meter intervals along the perimeters, as tall and broad as doorframes.

"I'm not going in there," Akhmed said, arms folded, refusing to leave the truck.

"Don't worry. All the letters in the glove box wouldn't get us in. We're going over there," she said, pointing down the block to what had been a shopping center. "The Petroleum Ministry has working international lines. Some clever entrepreneur tapped the outbound line and set up a phone bank in the basement."

The shopping center was a cave of broken storefronts, empty shelves, and stalagmitic glass. Even the plastic flowers had been looted from the planters. She led the way by her cigarette lighter.

"In London this would be an escalator," Sonja said as they descended a staircase.

"What's an escalator?"

"It's a moving staircase."

"Like a children's ride?"

"No, it's not a ride. It's just a staircase that moves. That's all."

"Then this is a broken escalator." In three years that staircase would become the first escalator in Chechnya. On weekends families from as far away as Lake Kezanoiam would bring their children to play on it.

She descended on the right side; even in a choice as arbitrary as which side to walk on she strove for order. At a brown door at the end of the basement corridor she knocked to the beat of an Umar Dimayev song. The deaf boy opened the door, and the blind man, his father, stood just behind him. Two spoonfuls were missing from his face.

"It's Sonja," she said. The blind man reached for his son, who tugged his left index finger in confirmation, then, looking at Akhmed, tugged the blind man's right middle finger.

"Yes, I've brought a friend. His name is Akhmed."

The blind man nodded to his son and reached for Akhmed's face. The first time the blind man had touched Sonja's cheeks she had known by his fingers that he would have made a great surgeon. "Don't make a face," she said, as the blind man parted Akhmed's beard. "You don't want to be remembered as a sourpuss."

Lightbulbs dangled from a brown electrical cord held by rusty staples to the ceiling. Somewhere a generator was humming. Card tables with rotary telephones sat evenly across the room. The whispers of five callers overlapped. She gave the deaf boy three hundred rubles and stepped over the braided wires to her telephone.

"City University Slavic Department," said the voice on the other end once she dialed.

"Good morning, Janice. It is Sonja. May I speak to Brendan?" Wrapped in the formality of proper English, her request sounded insincere to her.

"Hang on a mo', Sonja. He just left his office, but I'll see if I can't fetch him."

In the static hold she saw his chest, pale as a tadpole; she could have stood him before a bright light and seen his organs. Eights years on and he would have filled out, perhaps a paunch to accompany his promotions to Assistant Department Director, perhaps even a tanning salon gift token. When she backed out of the engagement he had spent three days on hold with the airlines and paid for part of the ticket when the cheapest, most circuitous route exceeded her savings. Going through her medicine cabinet, he had made a list of her favorite toiletries and purchased a half dozen of every tube, bottle, and canister for her to take home. She said she would come back. He said she would come back. The morning she left he wheeled the Samsonite, another parting gift, to the curb outside the international student dormitory, and sat beside her in the taxi, a cool perspiration on his palm, the city gliding past. When she said, half jokingly, as they reached the Heathrow turnoff, that he must be glad to be rid of her, because why else had he made it so easy for her to go, he buried his face in the crook of her shoulder and twelve hours later, in a lavatory twenty-five thousand feet over Ukrainian wheat fields, she found a streak of his hardened mucus and for a moment mistook it for her first gray hair.

"Sonja?" Janice said. "Brendan's left for a meeting. Can I take a message?"

They hadn't spoken since the previous month. He had contacts at Memorial and the Red Cross and if Natasha's name were to be typed into a computer he would know of it. Usually the moments before the call went through were honed with the hope that this month, this time, he would have an answer. But today was different. Today she just wanted him to know she was still alive. "Just tell him I called."

"And you spell your name with a *j*, yeah?"

She had asked him about it once, on their third or fourth coffee after classes. She wanted to know why Raskolnikov's love was transliterated as Sonia or Sonya but never Sonja. "Because that's how you spell it in English," Brendan had said. "Only Swedes spell it with a *j*." "Swedes are foreigners, too," she said, and held that *j* as the one letter in her name that was hers.

"Oh, and Sonja?" Janice said. "Is there a number where he can call you back?"

"How do the Swedes spell Natasha?" she had asked, but Brendan didn't know.

THE WINTER BRENDAN and Sonja fell in love, all of Volchansk became homeless; even those like Natasha, whose homes hadn't been hit,
found the cold easier to sleep through than the fear of falling rubble. She
spent the winter in City Park, a twelve-square-block refuge of brown
grass and barren trees, designed, it was said, by the dimwitted fourth
cousin of Boris Iofan, where the tallest man-made edifice was a corroded
jungle gym. The homeless, insane, and alcoholic reigned in this world.
Trained and experienced in the art of surviving a winter outdoors, the
city pariahs were inundated by professors and lawyers and accountants
whose degrees were worth the five seconds of warmth they could fuel.
Natasha and her cohort took direction from the City Park Prophet. The
great bib of gnarled hair, now reaching mid-thigh, shook indignantly
when he reminded them of his prophecy. No one had listened when he

predicted the fast-coming day when the sky would split open and God would fall upon the indecencies of man. Natasha remembered passing the madman each evening as she returned from the oil ministry, and he remembered the coins she had given him. "I told you I would remember you," he said when she first moved into the park; soon she realized that all of the City Park Prophet's flock had been daily alms-givers the Prophet now felt obligated to protect. He taught them to camouflage their tents and to scavenge for pinecones buried in the frost; to hunt feral dogs with cudgels and bait pigeon traps with the viscera; to pray five times a day and perform the proper ablutions, and Natasha, who had never stepped in a church, let alone a mosque, praised Allah because she knew better than to challenge a man who spent his life preparing for the apocalypse. In fourteen years those accountants and lawyers would collectively purchase for the City Park Prophet a studio apartment in a newly rebuilt apartment block. They would search for Natasha, hoping she would contribute to the considerable down payment, or at least be there when they led the Prophet into his new home, but the combined brainpower of six lawyers, three accountants, and eight PhDs couldn't solve the mystery of the former secretary's whereabouts.

By spring, when the Feds took the city, the bombing ceased and the siege settled into occupation. The City Park refugees dispersed to ancestral villages and *auls* scattered throughout the highlands, where they could count on the hospitality of distant family and clan. But Natasha had no family left. Her apartment block still stood, now the tallest building on the street. The windows had blown out but the bathroom mirror was still intact. She hadn't seen herself in months. Her options dwindled to subsistence and scavenging. Her reflection said she wouldn't last long in a city of drunken, vengeful, sex-starved soldiers. But avenues of escape still existed for women who could make themselves attractive without the benefit of running water.

Against the ringing of her last two kopeks of common sense, she found Sulim. He lived in the open now, in business with both Feds and rebels, and occasionally with the smuggler Sonja would later know as Alu's brother. They met in a bar that served nothing. No door, no liquor, no employees, no windows, but the regulars still returned each afternoon. Their lips were blue from drinking windshield wiper fluid.

In comparison to them, Sulim looked well. His eyes, unclouded by exhaustion, scanned her approvingly. The Parkinson's that would turn him into a quivering jelly mold in eleven years was already fermenting in his midbrain, but his hands didn't shake when he went to light his cigarette. War served him well. From mountain hideaways Dudayev's economic and police chiefs issued statements praising an economy and a police force that no longer existed, and in the vacuum of legitimate authority, organized crime provided the only meaningful order. He offered her a cigarette.

"You want to get out," he said. "Who doesn't?"

"I can do well in the West."

"Anyone can do well when they aren't dodging bullets." He scanned the ghost drinkers; those with the bluest lips had gone blind, and they reached out, touching the faces of their drinking partners. Sulim reached into his jacket pocket and pulled out a vodka bottle. "I don't know how they got it in their heads that we smuggle it in barrels of windshield wiper fluid."

"I'll work off the debt."

"Will you?" he asked.

"You know how hard I worked at Grozneft. I'm productive."

"Are you?" he asked.

"Please." He took a small sip from the bottle, savoring it as he watched her. He hadn't forgotten how she had denied him at her door, his skin sallow in the daylight. He crossed his legs, leaned back, waiting for her to beg. "I know there are trafficking routes," she said. "I know you can get me out. Please, Sulim."

"Under the Soviets, women who disappeared had to reappear on the other side of the world to make money. Now women can turn a profit simply by vanishing. Reappearance has too high an overhead. Chechen families will pay a higher ransom for the body of their daughter than they will for her alive. I've looked at the numbers."

She stood to leave.

"But you aren't Chechen," he continued. "You have no family to pay for your corpse. You have no afterlife for which your body must be prepared. You can have another cigarette."

He lit it for her with a bent match. She had kissed those knuckles. She had loved them.

"Will you help me or not?"

He was holding her index finger and he nodded it up and down. Crippled by tremors, unable to control his limbs, an embarrassment to his family, he would spend his final years in a windowless room with a television set for companionship. "You didn't really think I would deny you? Where do you want to go?"

"London."

"Then in London you will be an au pair. Do you know what that is? It's a French word. It means you will watch the children while the parents are at work."

"So I will be a grandmother?"

"Yes, something like that."

"I'm not my sister but I'm not a fool."

"There may be other things. Dancing, entertaining. Being, what's the word, enticing."

It meant prostitution. Waitressing, nannying, those were for pretty girls from poor countries, not pretty girls from war countries. Some repatriated women called it slavery, but even if it was true, so what? Paid sex with London civilians couldn't be worse than forced sex with Russian soldiers. And in London, Sonja would find her other work. Sulim watched her from across the table. His lips twisted into a slight smile, a challenge. Did he think she was afraid of him? Did he think he could possibly scare her?

"London," she said. "Make me an au pair. Make me reappear."


A young man with a soft, round face transported Natasha and five other women to the Dagestan border. They sat on crates in the near-darkness of a Federal supply van. The wind pulled against the olive canvas awning, and occasionally, a sliver of sunlight slipped through and was gone. She wanted to ask their names, where they were from, if they, too, were au pairs. Conversation seemed possible a moment after the round-faced man, looking like their younger brother, hoisted them into the truck bed. But the air clotted with doubt too thick for any words to pass.

Some hours later the van shuddered to a standstill and the round-faced man unlatched the back. Natasha shielded her eyes against the bright burn of noon and the light warmed her hands. A smock of dark evergreens wrapped around the nearest mountain. The round-faced man led them a hundred meters down a gravel path to a jeep flying the flag of national independence. Wooden benches replaced the backseats. They crowded in.

The jeep carried them up ravines of dried creek beds, along an unending jawline of pale stone. Conifer cones hung from drooped branches. The landscape appeared on the precipice of collapse. In the glens below, trickles of silvery light wound through empty pastures, glittering ribbons tied off at the horizon. It wasn't fair. She hated the outdoors. A sex worker was one thing, but a weekend hiker? The sun silhouetted wide circling wings. A pigeon, she first thought, grown to fit the monstrous proportions of this habitat.

The round-faced man parked the jeep when the incline became too steep. When she stood straight her hair hung off her shoulders, held back by the invisible hands of gravity. Sick, dizzied, she wanted a patch of asphalt she might sit on and feel whole. *Pretty Woman* wasn't anything like this. The round-faced man began climbing the rock-ridden slope and called for them. No, no, no, she wanted to say, the carabiner in my purse is only a keychain. But what could she do? The top was closer than the bottom. No threat or command, just his finger beckoning, and following it, she left Chechnya.

Dagestan was three unbearable hours of hiking, then another hour by jeep. The nod of the border guard's chin stubble was the only official record of their crossing into Georgia. Time was measured by bathroom breaks until they reached the water. The Black Sea was blue. They boarded a fishing trawler and the wind swept the scent of salt through her hair. Condominiums stood like dominoes on the coast, the white dots of lit windows numbering into the hundreds. When the sun fell below the water line the sea at last went black. She lay on the driest bit of deck she could find, used her duffel bag as a pillow, and fell asleep as the boat rocked on the water.

In Odessa they were divided. Three went with the round-faced man and as they disappeared into a Yugo something small and sharp panged through her; she didn't know their names. She and two others followed the man who had purchased their passports into the back of a delivery van. The door slammed shut. When it opened they were in Serbia. They stayed with eleven other women in a stone cellar. Manacles looted from the Sarajevo archaeology museum lay coiled on the floor, the implicit threat more constricting than the rusted cuffs. A tin pail tilted in the far corner; when one approached it, the rest turned away. Slurred voices seeped through the damp wooden ceiling. An argument over whether fire hydrants were a good idea. She touched the cheeks, forehead, and lips she had once gazed at in the mirror, proudly. Now she wanted scar tissue, missing limbs, cheeks buckshot with acne, teeth pointing every which way.

"What is this?" she asked.

No one spoke.

"Does anyone know where we are?" she asked again.

The girl sitting next to her, who couldn't have been more than four-teen, was the only one who answered. "The Breaking Grounds."

CHAPTER

15

"SHE NEVER TALKED about how it happened," Sonja said, thirty minutes outside Grozny's outer suburbs, ten since she had begun telling him. "How she got to Italy. If they took her on a plane or in a car or what. She never even told me who took her there, when she left, how she survived the first war. Nothing. She probably just didn't want to think about it, but I always thought it was her way of punishing me for leaving her." Akhmed had set the radio to 102.9. She barely knew him and that was the only reason she told him; he was, himself, static. She couldn't explain her confession any more than the calm that followed.

"War is unnatural," Akhmed said. "It causes people to act unnaturally."

"Even you?"

"Of course," he said. "I was never this charming." He stretched his hands in front of him; brown fields wedged between his fingers. "In the first war Dokka began classifying everything. He was an arborist by training, so he was used to dividing plants into species and genera and family, and one day he began doing that with everything else. With people. Everyone was a pacifist or an imperialist or a fascist or a classicist or any other number of -ists, and anyone who criticized his system was an anarchist."

"Havaa speaks in more -isms than a philosophy PhD."

"Yes, she really does take after him. She began making up her own and I remember hearing them discuss mustachism and shearistry and they were so excited. I had no idea what any of it meant. It was like a language they created to speak to each other more fully." He paused. He was breathing heavily. The flush of his cheeks had seeped to his neck. "I don't know why I'm telling you this."

"She plans to be a sea anemonist."

He laughed. "I bet. We were friends for years, Dokka and I and Ramzan. Every other Sunday we played chess, Havaa watching. Ramzan was the one who was waiting for me yesterday. The informer. We played chess every other Sunday for over a decade."

"What happened?"

"Ramzan began running guns for the rebels. He would invite Dokka on his expeditions, pay him well. I never understood why. He didn't need Dokka's help to drive a jeep into the mountains. The same way you thought Natasha was punishing you by her silence, I always thought Ramzan was punishing me with those trips. He never invited me along even though I needed the money as much as Dokka. We were friends, Ramzan and I, but I always felt Ramzan resented me for something I had done. Now I think it's more complicated than that. He was detained in the Landfill in ninety-five, and I think he resents me because I know what happened to him there.

"I was jealous of Dokka. Of his trips to the mountains with Ramzan.

Of the money he made. Of his wife. Mine has been bed-bound and senile for nearly three years while his had more vitality, more urgency in
her little finger than most men have between their legs. I was jealous of
his daughter. We tried for years but . . ." His voice trailed away. Beyond
him a single smokestack rose a hundred meters into the sky, no building
in sight. "Dokka was my closest friend and yet I wanted his family, his
opportunities, his life. He and Ramzan would go to the mountains for
a week or two and I would eat dinner with Esiila and Havaa. I would
spend the whole day and night there. On his final trip, in January 2003,
I slept in his bed for three nights. Of course I couldn't have known that
he and Ramzan had been detained and sent to the Landfill. I couldn't
have known that his fingers were snipped off with wire cutters while I
was at his house, sleeping with his wife, eating with his daughter, because I thought his life was perfect. Whatever we were to each other
was lost then. I'm not sure if Esiila told him or not, but he knew. Never
said anything but he knew. I would go over and talk to the refugees staying at his house when I wanted to talk to him. He didn't say a word to
me last year when I spoke to the woman who told me your name. If I
saw Dokka again, I wouldn't apologize or try to make it right. That isn't
what I would say."

"What would you say?"

Akhmed smiled, shook his head. "I don't know."


The shadow of a fresh crater darkened the road. At the bottom an arm
reached upward. The rest of the body lay there and there and there.
Lavender tatters, caught in an updraft, twisted in a wide ocean of sky.
"We offered her a ride," Sonja said, meaning *I told her so*, meaning *this
isn't my fault.*

Snow sprayed from the tires, cresting in the rearview. What would
she do if the war ended? Of all the possibilities and permutations she had

played out in her mind, peace was never among them. What would she do? The war that turned lieutenants into colonels, and unemployed men into jihadists, also turned residents into chief surgeons.

"Tolstoy was here two hundred years ago," Akhmed said. "There was a war then. He wrote a novel about it."

"I don't care for fiction."

"*Hadji Murád* it's called," he said. "I'll bring it for you tomorrow."

"Why aren't you angry at me?" she asked. The question had been burning in her all afternoon.

Akhmed folded his hands, but said nothing.

"I had you interrogated at gunpoint. If you were deceiving me I would have had you shot."

"If I were deceiving you, I would have been another man."

"You're a decent man," she said, and smiled. "A terrible physician, but a decent man."

"I know. I shouldn't spend so much time with you. You'll turn me into a first-rate surgeon and boor."

"I think it's the other way around," she said. A gauze of afternoon cloud cover had wrapped around the sky and she looked up and into it. "I'm overcome by the inexplicable desire to speak to you with common courtesy."

"I doubt that very much."

"I'm sorry I called you an idiot."

"You only implied it. Do you want to make it up to me?"

"Not really," she said.

"Then tell me who Ronald McDonald is."

"Very soon I'll have to apologize for calling you an idiot again."

"Imply," he reminded.

"No, this time I'll likely come out and say it."

"I already know he isn't the American president."

"I think you'll be disappointed."

"I almost always am."

"He's a clown."

"A clown?"

"A clown who sells hamburgers."

"Does he cook the hamburgers?"

"Does it matter?"

"I may be an idiot," he said gravely, "but I would never eat a hamburger cooked by a clown. Anyway, you were telling me about your sister. When she returned from Italy."

CHAPTER

16

IN THE WEEKS after she returned, Natasha traveled no farther than the three meters of gray carpet to Laina's flat. She drank weak tea, interpreted hallucinations, and returned, that fourth meter sealed behind an invisible wall of terror. Sonja watched distantly, wanting to take Natasha's hand and pull her down the hallway like a petulant child. Laina's flat—where, three weeks earlier, she had crouched at the door, a glass of ice melting in her grip, and heard Natasha's voice inside—seemed like the first step on recovery's staircase. But that step had stretched into a landing, then a floor, and Natasha couldn't have disappeared, not then.

Sonja, more talented as physician than as sister, withheld her diagnosis as long as she could. Then one Tuesday, Sonja returned from the hospital with feet swollen and shoulders heavy, too tired, really, to begin tending to her most difficult patient of the day. Natasha sat on the divan, a stack of books propped on the cushion beside her. *Origins of Chechen Civilization*, *The Third Soviet Guide to Ornithology*, *Life and Fate*. A yellowed tome covered her lap. *The Medical Dictionary of the Union of Soviet Physicians.*

"I can define any words you don't understand," Sonja offered, and immediately regretted it. Not the right tone to take. "Looking up anything particular?"

Natasha shrugged, of course.

"I hope you didn't read that all day." She turned to the bare wall. Her open mouth, pointed at Natasha, invariably projected condescension. "Surely there are more exciting books on the shelves."

"I don't want to be excited," Natasha said flatly. "I want boredom. I want to be lobotomized by boredom."

"Listen, Natashenka, something is wrong," she said, and hated her lack of specificity. Something? Wrong? How could a surgeon diagnose with such imprecision? "Have you heard of Post-Traumatic Stress Disorder?"

Natasha nodded without looking up from the page.

"What is it, then?"

Golden lamplight outlined the text as she flipped the pages. "It is a psychological reaction that occurs after experiencing a highly stressing event outside the range of normal human experience, which is usually characterized by depression, anxiety, flashbacks, recurrent nightmares, and avoidance of reminders of the event."

Natasha hadn't spoken a complex sentence in months, and even recited, the clause-heavy bluster made her sound alive again. "Sound familiar?" Sonja asked.

"The Italian head doctors went through this already. I don't want your help."

Help was the last thing Sonja knew how to give her sister. "Can you remember the last time you went outside?" she asked. Natasha could have lit a cigarette off the end of that glare. "I'll tell you when. When you were repatriated. You haven't set a toe outside this apartment block since you returned to it."

"You weren't there," Natasha said, shrugging. "So you don't get to tell me what to do."

For months she'd withheld, stopped herself, thought better, bitten her tongue to shreds. "I'm right here. Now. Here I am." She spread her arms, not to embrace her sister, but to show how wide she was, how much of her was here. "Do you know why? Do you have any idea?"

Natasha didn't move. She couldn't unlock the cellar door, not for Sonja, not for anyone. What had happened down there was still happening inside her, and she wouldn't let anyone, least of all her sister, into what she was still trying, still failing to escape from.

"Because of you. Because I was afraid you were here alone. Everything was so good in London. I was happy there. But I came back for you and that entitles me to your respect. You can hate me and think I'm a self-righteous bitch, but you will treat me with respect, because I came back here for you."

Again, that fucking shrug! Sonja couldn't imagine, then, with exasperation surging inside her, that one calm morning, eight and a half years away, after her sister had disappeared for a second time, she would wake on a hospital bed with her shoulders as stiff as her collarbones, and shrugging once, twice, failing to relax them, she would remember Natasha's shrugs, how fluid, how easy, and that would be the first definitive, the first known, that wherever Natasha was she would be shrugging.

"Do you want me to feel sorry that you left your nice life in London? Are you the victim here, is that what you're saying? Maybe you should talk with a psychiatrist about it, Sonechka. No, you made a mistake returning here for me," Natasha stated, as simply as if still reading from the dictionary. "Just as I made a mistake leaving here for you."

A window might have opened; a breeze might have slid across the walls, clearing the air, because Sonja smiled, and said, "We're sisters. In that way, at least, we're sisters." She took a clean breath, now that they had each said what they had to say. "I bought you a souvenir," she said, surprising even herself. "In London."

Exhibiting great restraint, Natasha didn't shrug. "What sort of souvenir?"

"I'm not telling you. I'm keeping it for myself."

"It's not a souvenir if you keep it."

"Of course it is. It's a gift to myself. I deserve it."

"Why didn't you give it to me?" Natasha had sat up and cocked her head to Sonja.

"Because," Sonja said, picking up the dictionary and fanning the pages with her thumb, "you're always on my nerves."

"All the time?"

"Stampeding on my nerves."

"I wouldn't want it even if you were giving it to me," Natasha said.

"Good, because I'm not."

"I bet it's a book about intestines."

"You know I'd keep that for myself," Sonja said. "I'll give it to you right now."

"Why?"

"How many intestines books does a woman need? I'll trade it to you for a promise," Sonja said. Natasha had taken up the clarinet when she was twelve, and Sonja, sixteen at the time, already sitting in on university classes, had heard every squeak, every warble, every pinched sharp through their shared, shadow-thin wall. She had paid Natasha, by the hour, not to practice. That same glint of easy opportunity returned to Natasha's eyes.

"What promise?" she asked.

"Promise that you'll come to the hospital with me tomorrow."

"And?"

"And nothing. Just that. If you think you're well enough."

"What, you think I'm not?"

"No, no. I'm not saying that."

"I know what you're trying to do," Natasha said. "Fine. I promise."

Sonja went to her room and returned a minute later. "Close your eyes," she said, and handed her a sturdy oblong object wrapped in a plastic shopping bag.

"What is this? A doll?" Natasha asked, pulling it from the bag. "I'm a grown woman."

"It's not a doll. It's a nutcracker of a Buckingham Palace guard."

"Who are they?"

"They stand outside the queen's palace. They're not allowed to laugh. They just stand there. They're not very good at guarding, when you think about it. They just stand there. You could dress up a lamppost and get as good a guard."

"Yes," Natasha agreed, cranking the nutcracker's mouth up and down. "A bad guard and worse souvenir. What should I call him?"

Sonja bit her lip. "What about Alu?"

"Alu the lousy, boring, worthless souvenir."

"Yes," Sonja said. "That is the perfect name for him."

"I'm a little disappointed. You spent five years in London and all I get is a doll?"

"The real gift was my absence."

Finally, a smile.

The next morning the hospital was quiet. The few patients Maali couldn't scare off with promises of an amputation cure-all waited for her: a sprained ankle, a case of the common cold, nothing urgent. She took Natasha through the ghost wards of deserted laboratories and examination rooms. Pigeons roosted in split IV bags. A manhole cover, leading nowhere, lay in radiology. The rooms would look unchanged eight and three-quarter years later when Sonja led Akhmed through. The powdered heroin, provided by Alu's brother, would still slouch against the canteen cupboard wall, but when she led him past she would do so without worry, without wondering if his veins, like her sister's, might tingle from proximity.

"This was once among the foremost oncology departments in the U.S.S.R.," she said, as they shuffled into a room relieved of its door-knobs and light fixtures. "Party officials came from as far as Vladivostok for treatment."

They paused at a hulking MRI machine which the former hospital director had sacrificed his pension, his marriage, and all the black in his hair to procure. "It's a shame we can't use this, but a single scan would kill the generator." A meter from her foot the bronze rim of a shell casing was silhouetted in dust. "Besides," she added, "there's so much embedded metal in here the magnetic field would turn the room into a shooting gallery."

The tour ended on the fourth-floor maternity ward, where a woman who had given birth the previous night smiled at everyone in placid exhaustion. Her child had emerged with a collapsed lung but the doctor on call had acted quickly and the child had lived. The mother held the infant to her breast. Its little lips bent the nipple. She beamed as they approached.

"God is great. She will live," the mother said in a slow cadence to make it clear that the two statements were logically dependent. She glanced up at Natasha, mistaking her white sweatshirt for scrubs. "I'm so glad you're here."

"I'm no one," Natasha said.

"Nonsense," the mother said. "You save lives."

Natasha crossed her arms, and Sonja couldn't see it, couldn't know it, but right then, when Natasha dipped her head, looked to her palm, to the floor, to Sonja and back, she believed that their body temperatures rose by some fractional degree, that this they shared. The baby finished suckling and tilted its square little face upward.

"Do you want to hold her?" the mother asked.

"No," Natasha said, ratcheting her frown.

"Nonsense," the mother said. "You want to hold her."

"I need to go, but you stay here. There is a case of the common cold in need of my attention," Sonja whispered as Natasha took the infant in her arms.

That morning, in the cavernous wards, Natasha's brain finally hushed. When the newborn sniffed strangely at her chest, she stared into its eyes and saw a world only two days old. Those two and a half kilograms righted her, turned her vantage to a future kinder than experience had taught her to expect. The next morning she woke when Sonja woke, left when Sonja left, and the next morning and the next.

Deshi and Maali, her superiors, were nurses and twins. Deshi, on the eleventh of her twelve loves, reminded her of Sonja, and she preferred Maali, the younger by eighteen minutes, who treated illness and injury as the practical jokes of a God wheezing with laughter, and suggested amputation for every cough, chest cold, ulcer, and eye infection that had the misfortune of seeking her counsel. In the maternity ward, Natasha cleaned towels, bedsheets, the linoleum floor, plastic tubes and hoses, bottles, baby bottoms, and bedpans. Her fingertips reddened in the bleach, and in this good hurt and those clean bottles, she found herself warmed by the small suggestions of her agency. In her day's rare pauses, she restored the view to the boarded windows. It began with a few right angles penciled on the plywood. She hadn't known what she was drawing until it took shape. Two squares, one atop the other. In the pencil's descent a stray line became a downspout, the pulsing overhead fluorescence became a blue afternoon sun, and a small curl of wood grain became a secretary's brown hair blown back by a desk fan. Drawing by division on the plywood, she parceled the building into floors, floors into windows, windows into panes. Familiar, but it still floated a centimeter off her memory; she placed a Soviet flag over the arched entrance, placed pigeons on the flagpole, placed a strong westerly breeze so the flag caught every squirt of pigeon shit. Pencil lead smudged on the thick of her palm as she dredged the building from its ruins. When finished she wrote its name in block Cyrillic above the awning. The Volchansk State Bureau of Vehicular Licensing and Registration. Of course it looked familiar; it had once stood on the other side of the window.

Over weeks and months, as spare minutes became hours and the hours days, she added linden and poplar trees, rusted streetlamps, drooping electrical lines, shingled roofs, a skyline of television antennae, clotheslines curved by wet laundry, smoke ribbons unwinding from tailpipes, the sidewalks and cigarette kiosks and everything she could remember. She added no fire hydrants.

Behind her back, and later to her face, Deshi and Maali opined.

"A dreadful thing," Deshi said when she thought Natasha had gone to the parking lot for a cigarette.

"Completely inaccurate," Maali concurred. The nurse understood what it was like to be the younger sister, if only by eighteen minutes, and her criticism hurt Natasha the most. "The perspective is skewed. It isn't possible to see so much of City Park from this window."

"Perhaps we shouldn't be so hard," Deshi said. "She's never actually seen the view from this room."

"That's the problem, isn't it? She's drawing something she's never seen."

"She isn't even Chechen."

"Her greatest shortcoming."

"She deserves pity rather than scorn."

"We retired three years ago," Deshi lamented. "What are we even doing here?"

The unlit cigarette somersaulted from her fingers as she pushed open the door, dashed between her critics, and closed the curtain over the boarded windows. She had felt more humiliated before, but never by people whom she trusted. She grabbed her lighter from the counter and pushed past the nurses, but Maali's grasp, surprisingly firm on her wrist, held her.

"Let me guess," Natasha said. "The only way to fix the mural is to amputate the hand that drew it."

Maali smiled. "It's not quite so serious."

"Really?" She felt strangely honored that Maali didn't want to chop off her hand.

"It's just that there was never a bus stop at the intersection of Lenin Prospect and City Bureaucrat Street. I know because I stared at that corner for thirty years."

"We'll help you," Deshi added, and under the combined guidance of eyes that had spent some sixty years in front of the maternity ward windows, she erased and redrew, swept up the eraser lint, erased and redrew again. Deshi and Maali argued over every signpost and streetlamp, every tree in City Park, every storefront, kiosk, and traffic light; they had stared from different windows onto different cities, and in trying to bring back both, she created her own. She shaded the buildings with ash and coal, sliced advertisements from unread magazines still stacked in the waiting room and pasted slivers of color across the plywood. The blue waves of a Black Sea resort became sky. Mint gum became linden leaves. Some afternoons the nurses would become lost in the mural, pointing to the distant corners and alleyways like faded pictures in a photo album. The finely detailed ventilation grate that had once suspended a thousand-ruble note in its draft, where Deshi plucked three months' rent from the air. The aboveground gas pipes from which their mother had hung laundry and their father a hammock. Or the school-yard blacktop, where Maali's son had played soldiers years before the war took him. In sixteen years, when glass replaced the plywood boards, Natasha's murals would find their way to Sonja's bedroom closet, where they would remain a private treasure for some sixty-three years, until Maali's great-great-grandson, an art historian, put them on display in the city art museum.

She was studying her city when the nurses arrived on the morning she was to perform her third solo delivery. "It's going to get busy," Maali said, with no small amount of glee. With her rain jacket, windbreaker, and overcoat hung on different pegs, the coat stand suggested a fully staffed ward. "We heard land mines on the way in."

Deshi wagged her head. "You enjoy this job too much, sister. I worry your head has broken."

"It's too bad you can't amputate a head."

"You can. It's called a decapitation."

Maali noted it excitedly on her clipboard.

"We're all working trauma today," Deshi said.

"What if there are deliveries?" Natasha asked.

"Then you'll do them, Natashenka. It doesn't take much to deliver a child. The mother does most of the work."

The first casualties arrived a half hour later; red heat radiated from their skin. Natasha disinfected the ropy ends of a calf when Deshi came calling. "We have a delivery. Go."

The patient lay gowned and supine on the maternity ward bed. Her face throbbed against the white sheets, as flushed and anguished as those four floors below. Two men stood beside her, each holding one hand. She recognized the cleft in the older man's chin, but now wasn't the time for pause, for reflection; now was the time to act. She stood between the woman's pale open legs, trying not to look down.

"The contractions are three minutes apart," the younger man volunteered. He spoke with the halting formality of an outsider.

It was all she needed in order to remember what to do. "Lasting how long?"

He didn't know. Sweat grew heavy on the woman's forehead and trickled toward her temples. After washing her hands to her wrists, rubbing sanitizer to her elbows, she snapped on a fresh pair of gloves. Another contraction came; they all heard it.

"Do you feel like you have to shit?" she whispered into the woman's ear, afraid of embarrassing her in front of her husband.

The woman nodded.

"What did you ask?" the younger man asked. "Is she okay?"

"The child is in the birth canal, putting pressure on the rectum, that's all." These people knew nothing of her, and she drew enough confidence from what they did not know to keep her voice level. They didn't know that her name was Natasha; that she had performed only two solo deliveries, one and three weeks earlier; that six months earlier, as she detoxed in a Rome psych ward, God had pulled her through a needle's eye so narrow that this thread in front of them was all that remained.

She told the woman to lift her pale little legs, place her feet in the stirrups, and the woman did. She pulled the woman's dress into a crumpled hoop around her stomach. They thought she knew what she was doing and she made their faith hers.

"My chest hurts," the woman said.

"You need to breathe."

"My eyes hurt," the woman said.

"You need to blink."

She set two pillows on the floor, beneath the woman's open legs, just in case. The vise of the woman's grip crushed the older man's fingers to squirming scarlet tendrils. "I've seen you before," Natasha said, but was swallowed within the woman's wail. "Push," Natasha said. "Push."

A mat of damp hair ringed by pubic curls began to crown.

"Gently," she said, extending her hands as the mat of hair became a head. "Take deep breaths. Slow breaths. Imagine you are inflating a balloon. Your breaths are slow and deep. Blow through your mouth at the most painful point of each contraction. Try to whistle."

She steadied her hands beneath the crowning skull. Instinct told her to palm the back of the child's head so its first sensation was of warmth and comfort, but she kept a finger's width between the child's skin and her own. Maali had warned her never to touch a child's head before seeing its face; doing so could cause the child to inhale amniotic fluid. But it wasn't the child who gasped, it was Natasha as she watched the damp forehead emerge. The birth canal sheathed every slip of skin as the mother slid her child into life. Its little eyes didn't move. Far away, the mother emptied her lungs in an unshaped melody. They all inhaled her whistle.

"The head has come out," Natasha announced, trying her hardest, for the sake of professional decorum, to stifle the smile widening across her face. The mother pushed and the room hushed, dampened, narrowed by her exertion. The shoulders stuck. With the most tender turn of her gloved hands, Natasha rotated the child's head so its lids looked into the fleshy pale of the mother's thigh. The right shoulder slid through. She lifted the child's head and when the mother's next whistle pushed out the left shoulder, the rest glided into her hands like an afterthought.

She lifted the umbilical cord over the child's face, and the warm wet weight of the head pressed to her palm. She angled the child toward the floor. "A girl," she said. The child opened its eyes and a sharp chill ran through her to know that hers were the first hands to hold the girl.

"She doesn't look right," the father said.

Natasha rubbed the girl's back through a towel, then tilted her head to open the airway. She stroked the girl's nose, dried the girl's mouth, suctioned residue through a plastic syringe, tickled her feet, but still the girl hadn't cried. Should she run downstairs for help? Could she perform CPR on a newborn? She pushed her fingers into the child's soft, soggy soles, and begged them to kick back. At the ends of her feet the protruding toes seemed in error, so curled and delicate they might sink back into the doughy flesh. These are the feet of a human being you brought into the world. She will not die.

She didn't. Lips drawn to the pink edges of her toothless gums. A sharp gulp.

"She's breathing."

"I can hear," the father said. The girl wailed. "She breathes like her mother."

She placed the girl on the mother's bare skin. The mother stared through a frame of damp hair and recognized her daughter; they were both breathing. Pink liquid trickled from the girl's mouth, striping the incline of her mother's still swollen stomach. With a fresh towel Natasha wrapped the two together.

"You should start nursing as soon as you feel able," Natasha said. She didn't need to borrow their confidence. It was hers. "It will help the placenta come out and stop the bleeding."

The mother nodded weakly, happily. Her voice was unfamiliar when she spoke. Natasha had only heard it in screams. "This is my daughter?"

"Yes," Natasha said, finally allowing herself a smile. "She's yours."

The older man approached as she washed her hands under the sputtering tap. There was much yet to clean, but first, her hands. He thanked her.

"The mother did most of the work," she said. In his wrinkles she recognized his face as she might a photograph crumpled and flattened. "I've seen you before."

"Have you been to Eldár?"

In a truck, with five other women. "In passing."

"What about the city university? I taught there. Or the Café Standard? I enjoyed their bebop nights. Do you like bebop?"

"I don't like trumpets."

"But what if a trumpet is playing the music you like?"

She thought of loose screws trembling on the Nightclub dance floor. "The music I like can't be played on a trumpet," she said.

"If it can't be played on a trumpet, it's not music."

"My name is Natasha, " she said, smiling.

"Khassan Geshilov."

Repeating the name aloud, she saw the black-and-white dust jacket photo. "I've read your book."

He gave a bashful laugh. "You're the one?"

"It ended before the Russians arrived. A stupid decision, if you ask me."

"If only you had been my editor! *Origins of Chechen Civilization*," he said fondly, as if he had also forgotten the title. He turned to the boarded windows. "This is the whole city, isn't it?"

"As much as can be seen from the window."

He strolled the ash-shaded streets and verdant leaves, reading the city so he might later remember. He lingered at an intersection between City Park and the university library, hesitated, then pressed his finger into the street. "The love of my life was nearly killed by a bus here. She had been following me, and I only found out then, with the screech of bus tires."

"You have stalkers? No wonder you didn't have time to write about the Russians."

"That's a story for another day." He glanced back to the newborn. "Let's introduce ourselves."

The father and the historian embraced, all gratitude and congratulations silently locked between their arms. The father lifted the girl from the mother. His long fingers held her.

"What will you call her?" Natasha asked.

"Havaa," the father said. "Havaa."

# CHAPTER

# 17

HAVAA'S FATHER NEVER again played chess after returning from the final trip to the mountains with Ramzan in January 2003. He spent his days caught like a coin between the divan cushions. Sweat seeped into his shirt collar, leaving a rim the color of crushed mustard seed. His fingers had, well, *healed* wasn't the right word. The stumps had hardened into pink lumps rising from the webs of his palms. He struggled to button his shirt, open the door, eat, tie his shoes, and Havaa, insistent and unrelenting, became his hands.

The heat of the following summer weighed so much it would take an extra autumn to fully lift. Her mother kept her waistline hidden beneath wide skirts and aprons, refusing to wear maternity clothes. She still slept in her parents' bedroom on a mattress so thin she felt the pattern of nail heads in the floor. Refugees still arrived, still overdressed and bewildered, and her father still took them in.

That summer the leaves drooped in the heat. Decay baked at her feet and in it crawled little insects that made homes in her boot prints. She hiked as if the forest were a fragile thing, careful to sidestep saplings so slender they bowed with the breeze. Her father told her that Soviet timber interests had controlled the forest before the wars, but she couldn't find a tree stump on her side of the forest, and rust-chewed saw belts, buried like relics of a prior civilization, were the only evidence of past industry.

Flocks of migrating birds clutched shaded branches. Lizards hid in dewy deer tracks. Once, she saw a wolf slaloming between the birch trunks; its pink tongue lolled from its open mouth and the sunlight glimmered on its fangs. When the wolf spotted her, half hidden behind a hornbeam, its ears snapped skyward. It found her eyes amid the leaves and studied them, questioningly, and she stared back, unnerved but not quite afraid, until they came to an understanding, and the wolf continued its saunter through the long, lovely shadows. Despite her sprinting pulse, she had only pity for the wolf, sweltering, as it was, under that heavy silver coat.

She visited Akim often that summer. His portrait survived the February frosts and March thaws, but even the varnish, smeared like sunblock across his cheeks, couldn't save him from the summer heat. His face slumped and faded. How the summer aged him. In life he had preferred the cold and dreamed of visiting the North Pole. In eighteen years his oldest brother, a geologist, would bury what remained of Akim's portrait in Arctic snow, not quite at the North Pole, but close enough to make a compass needle spin in circles.

The sight of Akim's half-erased face left Havaa crestfallen, but an hour's trek from the village, she found the solution guarding a fallow field. The scarecrow wore a burlap sack and sun-bleached blue trousers, its straw-stuffed waist wider than that of any villager. A faceless cloth crammed with dead leaves sat where the head should be. Crows perched on its brim and mice nested in the sags of its shirtsleeves. Her parents warned her against venturing into the fields, but the chance to extend Akim's life, once again, outweighed her fear. Each step planted with cautious deliberation, she reached the scarecrow. A wooden post, rooted in the soil, impaled the limp straw body. She kicked the post, then excavated its base. The dirt scratched her knees and she scratched the dirt back. The scarecrow tilted with the post, arms and legs hanging back like a refugee collapsing into bed. Mice scurried from the sleeves when they at last brushed the ground. The whole glaring sky focused on her as she tied a rag around the splintered post end, gripped, and pulled. The scarecrow's head nodded as it fell along the furrows. His arms stretched across the dry soil as if searching for mines.

It took three afternoons before she joined the straw body to Akim's head. When the sun set on the first evening, she left the scarecrow to sleep in the driest part of a roadside ditch. The next evening she hid him in the shadow of a fallen tree. Finally, she had the wilted torso leaning against the tree, and taking gardening shears by their blue rubber handles, she decapitated the faceless cloth head with a few rusty snaps. She dug a small hole, slid the post in, and the scarecrow stood. Browned straw jutted from the scarecrow's neck, bearding Akim, but another few clips shaved him. Though the scarecrow looked better, it was still no more than a lax, lifeless body propped up beneath a fading portrait, requiring resuscitation. She snipped her hair with the gardening shears and pasted the clippings on Akim's crown. She pricked her finger with a sewing needle and rubbed her warm blood onto Akim's cheeks. Reenacting Akhmed's movements, she thumped on the scarecrow's chest, as he had thumped on the boy's chest, and when the breath of life erupted—her own—she stood back and wiped the sweat-sting from her eyes. The air was clean. Her hands brown with dirt. Pride surged through her, raw and immense; she had believed happiness to be an absence—of fear, of pain, of grief—but here it roared in her as powerful as any sadness. She looked at her fingers and loved them. They had carried the scarecrow for three kilometers of field, road, and forest without setting off a single mine. They had saved Akim for a second time.

As the summer burned on she would lie on her back and describe to Akim the shapes of clouds spotted through breaks in the trees. She would lie on her stomach and report the gross and fascinating news from the insect world. She would complain about her mother and father, how the Landfill had changed them both and how the dry evening air combusted without refugees to douse the tension. Silence, she had learned, was safer than questions. Even as her mother's belly grew, Havaa kept her questions and comments for Akim, who, in death, treated her more graciously than he ever had in life.

Havaa was sitting beside Akim when she heard her mother's screams, first mistaking them for the breeze through thicket, but the air lay thick and still, and wind couldn't call for help. She ran home. Her mother lay on the floor beneath a blood-soaked apron. Her father and Akhmed knelt beside her. "She's hemorrhaging," Akhmed was saying. "I don't know what to do. We need to get her to the hospital." She waited with her father while Akhmed hurtled toward Ramzan's for his truck. In a shuddering voice her father kept asking the pale-faced woman—who looked like her mother and wore her mother's apron but couldn't be her mother—for forgiveness. If she had been dying every minute of every day, they might have been a happy family. The blood consumed every centimeter of apron cloth and Havaa was afraid the wound would become hers if she came too close. Her mother stirred, looked to her father, and wrapped her five fingers over his none. She opened her mouth, but he shook his head, told her to save her breath, and Havaa would always remember how he had shushed what might have been her goodbye so that she could breathe.

The splatter of gravel outside and Akhmed ran in, now in the living room, now kneeling on the floor, now lifting the head of the woman who would not be, could not be, but was her mother. Her father tried to help but he couldn't even lift the hair from her eyes. They left Havaa at the house with instructions shouted from the open passenger window and swallowed by the road before she could ask for clarification. The road distended, becoming a cloud the truck fell into. She asked Allah to save her mother, and, as her prayer vanished in dust, wondered if she should ask again in Arabic.

Back in the house she went to her parents' bedroom and opened the top dresser drawer. She plodded over the cool circles of coins, rummaged through silk handkerchiefs and leather wristbands. She found it in the back of the drawer. It was wrapped in a cotton bandanna, next to the jewelry her mother tried on when she thought she was alone. Even through the bandanna her fingers remembered the grip. The knot was simple, loose, gone with a tug. The silvery finish shone as if in those months of darkness it had reserved its reflection for this. She held it as Ramzan had taught her. Close to her chest. As if carrying a water pitcher. What lay at the other end of the barrel didn't matter. She couldn't see past the trigger. The whole world was howling and if it kept on, if it didn't stop, she would let the barrel reply.

She would remember the cool metal warming in her hands, how she gripped it like a banister. Later she would learn that Akhmed had shouted instructions as he drove; her father performed them as well as his hands allowed. She would never understand why Akhmed hadn't thought to bring her when he needed a second set of fingers. In the panicked departure no one remembered her mother's ID card. The sergeant at the checkpoint nodded often, sympathetically, and then explained there was simply no way he could allow her through without proper identification. There are few rules in war, he went on, but those that do exist must be upheld, because if so simple a rule as this is broken, then couldn't the more complex, convoluted, one might even say absurd rules of the Geneva Convention break with even greater ease? Her father raised his hands in response, but the sergeant, a man who had grown up in a mining town above the Arctic circle, and found the Chechen climate so fine he had renewed his contract three times, had seen worse. Her mother died and the argument went on for several more minutes before anyone noticed.

The gun was buried in the back of the drawer before her father returned. The look on his face told her what had happened and that hurt burrowed deeper than anything she'd ever felt, deep enough to change from the thing she felt to the thing she was. Love, she learned, could reduce its recipient to an essential thing, as important as food or shelter, whose presence is not only longed for but needed. But even on those days when she ran to Akim in the woods, her pain wasn't complicated by guilt. She hadn't caused or contributed to her mother's death. She couldn't have saved her.

That was the difference in how she mourned each parent. One and a half years since her mother had died and she grieved for her cleanly because she wasn't at fault. But when the security forces had come for her father three nights earlier, she could have taken that pistol and aimed it at the first face appearing in the kicked-in door. She could have fired all twelve rounds, let the magazine drop, ducked and reloaded, just as Ramzan had taught her.

But she didn't. Instead she'd followed her father's hoarse command and run through the backdoor and into the safety of the woods with her prepacked just-in-case suitcase. The shadows of the Feds moved across the windowpanes. The bookcase tipped and the book covers opened like wings over an underbelly of white feathers, dirty with ink. In the living room the men gathered with their faces to the floor. From behind the moldering log, she couldn't make out what the men were laughing at, and because she couldn't see she could still believe it wasn't her father. She sucked snow, breathed through her mouth, her breath invisible in the cold. Their shoulders strained with an unseen weight. They vanished, reappearing in the next window, and she crept to the edge of the clearing until she could see the parked truck. The duct tape stretching over her father's mouth wrinkled. When she saw that they had even taped his hands together, she would have fired three shots right then, if she had had the pistol. But there was no gun. The silver Makarov was not in the dresser drawer. It hadn't been there for some time.

1994 1995 1996 1997 1998 1999 2000 2001 2002 **2003 2004**

THE SILVER MAKAROV pistol was all Ramzan thought about for the two weeks preceding Dokka's disappearance, in which he failed to produce a single bowel movement. Each morning, venturing into the cold in nothing but a robe and lambskin boots, he turned the corner of the house, passed icicles filling the gutter's missing segments, passed the frostbitten fingers of fallen birch limbs, and waded down the sharp incline to the scattered pinecones that had amassed into an ankle-deep mound at the outhouse door. Inside, he sat with his elbows burrowed into his knees, a full-bodied clench that left him red-faced and winded. Snow flurries fell through the roof's missing half, landing on the back of his neck, and melted into sweat. His scrotum was an empty coin purse flattened between his legs. He was unable to father even a soft dollop of excrement. As the stagnant days stacked one atop the next, he altered his diet, already limited to what his father hadn't thrown to the dogs. He stopped eating his favorite meal of cured beef spiced with paprika, chilies, and coriander, the one sumptuous dinner his father allowed him each week. He left the butter off his bread and by daylight ate only the apples his father once favored. He yearned for vegetables. Vegetables! Raw and leafy, flavorless and coarse, yes, cucumbers and turnips and beets. Haunted by what he knew to be feminine cravings, he was unmanned for a second time, but not even the intimacy of his shame could repel his yearning for cabbage and sprouts, for roughage sweeping through his system like the bristles of an enraged broom. Even if he broke down, debasing himself by requesting greens in his biweekly provisions from the state security forces, he would receive only a few yellow heads of frozen lettuce, which his father would, no doubt, feed to the yapping beasts in the yard. But he felt increasingly certain that it was neither the surplus of cured meats, nor the dearth of vegetables in his diet, but rather the conversation with the Cossack colonel that had fossilized his lower intestines. He considered prayer, but asking for spiritual laxative was surely sacrilege. Inspired by the long, leaky shits he'd taken as an eighteen-year-old Red Army private, he performed post-*fajr* calisthenics. He vomited twice from the exercise, but still failed to coax even a pale, watery squirt. The weather, at least, provided solace. If ever there was a season for constipation it was winter. Beneath the wooden toilet box, the cesspool had frozen into scentless stone. Surely that was preferable to the fecal fever baking beneath the wooden seat in summer. He sat. He pushed. Struggling against his body, he came to the dismaying conclusion that his viscera had betrayed him. Even when his rear end felt tied closed with drawstrings, he checked himself. But each time he examined the rough square of military-issue toilet paper, it was white. Even after he spoke with the colonel for a second time, two weeks after their initial conversation, and gave up Dokka, no relief arrived. And three days after Dokka disappeared, when Ramzan closed the satellite phone and ended the last of the three conversations he would have with the Cossack colonel, he considered what his father had suggested that morning about Akhmed. Could it really be true? No, it couldn't be, not really, and he couldn't believe it, couldn't allow it, because it was no more than a ploy to trick his conscience into mercy. But would his father break his two-year vow of silence to tell a lie? Not that it mattered now. Ramzan had given the Cossack colonel Akhmed's name. The plea spoken from his father's prideful lips earlier that day had quickly betrayed itself, degenerating from appeal to denunciation, and yes, he would take away the one person in the village his father loved if only to teach his father what it was to be alone. Wherever Akhmed was, wherever he had hidden the girl, he was no more than a ghost still ignorant of his death.

It was the Cossack colonel, Ramzan came to believe, who had tied the knot in his intestines. His deep timbre could constipate the Volga. The smoke of three daily packs blew through his sentences. He spoke with a velvety menace as he asked Ramzan if the sun was shining over the village, and the collision of the colonel's tone and the childlike question gave Ramzan the impression that to the man on the other end of the line death was an unremarkable hazard of his trade. The sun was shining, beaming even, yet Ramzan felt compelled to lie, to say the cloud cover sat as thick as spoiled milk, as though enough small lies would absolve him of the larger truths divulged. But he didn't lie. He said yes. The sun shone. The colonel grunted in approval, then read from the military meteorological report for the village. Static breathed through the transmission. Ramzan lifted the antenna toward the sky like a lightning rod pulling the full force of the colonel's voice from the heavens. When reception returned, the colonel asked about the silver Makarov pistol.

But when Ramzan left his house in early December 2004, two weeks before Dokka was disappeared, he still had forty-five minutes before hearing the Cossack colonel's voice for the first time. A blue nylon duffel bag the size and slump of a dead cat dangled from his wrist; inside swung the satellite phone. He opened the back door and, stepping into the wind, crossed the field. The sun filled the frozen slant of the out-house half roof, but the privy hadn't yet consumed his hope and dread, as it soon would, and he passed without looking back, walking as snow hardened into the deep treads of his leather boots, following the narrow corridor of bedsheets left stiff on the clothesline, over the brittle yellow grass, over his grandparents' plot, to the uneven edge of the field and into the forest.

Snow had thickened the ground. The quiet of his house followed him into the woods. Two hundred meters in, raising his head in a long scream, he tore a hole in the silence through which he could walk more freely. His father, he hoped, would mistake it for the wounded bawl of his pack. Before the wars, the winter had been warmer. A meteorologist might beg to differ, but weather prediction was an act of infidel witch-craft that could not be trusted.

For the duration of the three-kilometer hike, he scanned the snow but found no tracks wider than a rabbit's foot. The conditions that al-lowed the forest to flourish had devastated its wildlife. The village economy depended upon logging, and when the enterprise and its ad-ministration vanished with the Soviet flag, the villagers were left with-out the means or infrastructure to extract any real money from the forest. So they hunted. Aided by the wartime influx of munitions, they hunted deer, wild boar, brown bears, and wolves like men who believed they would always be hungry and the forest would always be full.

The cell of subsistence hunting eventually metastasized into the gun-running operation that would take Dokka's fingers and trans-form Ramzan into a man who hiked three kilometers in December to make a phone call. His first taste of trading came when he worked for a small crafts concern that bloomed under the relaxed regulations of perestroika. He scavenged the mountains for the stone sculptures of shaman artisans. The hamlets he found were no more than high-altitude islands in a sea of mining waste, and he exchanged petrol, medical supplies, and tinned food for the carved stone. The artisans always chose to bargain through a *shura* of elders, upon whom time had acted like a substance that repeatedly dissolved and refroze their faces, and Ramzan, in his early twenties, felt like a foreigner among these aged creatures, and nearly always gave much more than the carvings were worth. To his mind, the stone sculptures of goat hooves, a child's hands, and a mutilated deer weren't worth the last spittlely sip of a shared vodka bottle. He took the sculptures to an industrial park outside of Grozny, where they were examined, priced, crated, and shipped to distant countries where wealthy cosmopolitans would pay vast sums to display the hoof of a Chechen goat.

In 1999, years since Ramzan had ventured into the mountains for sculptures, he traded cured meat for shotgun shells in a neighboring village. A welder there made homemade ammunition. New buckshot was prohibitively priced on the black market, so the ingenious man packed the casings with ball bearings cannibalized from trolley wheels. They exchanged words before ammunition and meat, and soon realized that each had worked in the industrial park. The welder explained that immediately following the birth of his first son he had begun working as a night watchman at the industrial park so he could, at the very least, get a good night's sleep. They talked about how, in 1991, the crafts concern had stopped purchasing authentic mountain sculptures and begun mass-producing them in Grozny with the help of a professor at the Fine Arts College and the serf-labor of his undergraduate sculpture class. The recollection was a tunnel through which trust traveled. They shared nothing in common but the memory of the industrial park, and it was enough. Ramzan took the welder fresher cuts of meat, and in exchange the welder gave Ramzan a Kalashnikov. Ramzan returned to the welder several days later with the hind legs of a brown bear bleeding in his truck bed.

And one day the welder vanished to join the independence fighters. For the next year, Ramzan struggled to survive. The task, already a great challenge, was compounded by his diabetic father. In a country where clean water was scarce, insulin should have proved impossible. But Ramzan found a way.

In a small, unassuming collective farm, known locally as the Miracle Fields, Ramzan worked as a petrol farmer for the insurgents, or the Feds, or more likely both. The pipeline running through the untended pear orchard conveyed oil from local wells to a regional refinery, but the pipe was riddled with so many bullet holes that the refinery had long since ceased operations. The reek of rotting, unpicked pears filled the air as Ramzan dug pits, called barns, alongside the pipe. Dark fountains of oil filled the barns, which fed into a system of irrigation channels that, in earlier times, had been used to water the pear trees. Perhaps as much as half of the oil seeped into the soil, into the groundwater below, but the oil spouted from the pipe in such abundance that no one ever thought to seal the barns with concrete or plastic. Twice a day, a tanker truck arrived to siphon the oil through a long rubber hose and distribute it to covert factories, where the crude oil was refined into a highly sulfuric diesel with eighty-year-obsolete machinery looted from the National Museum of Oil Production. The women who bottled the diesel in glass jars and sold it on street corners were the nearest entity to a working gas station for several hundred kilometers. Sometimes the moonshine diesel worked, and sometimes it caused the cars to explode, but it always filled the coffers of the insurgents, or the Feds, or more likely both. Ramzan, for his part, was well paid, and he used his earnings to buy insulin and syringes on the black market. Due to regular territorial disputes along the pipeline, the work was more dangerous than the war itself, and Ramzan was sustained not by love for his father but by the fear of failing him.

In 2001, when a band of wounded rebels briefly occupied the village, Ramzan recognized the welder among their ranks. They embraced as brothers, as though bonded in a crucible more dramatic than an industrial park. The welder introduced him to the field commander, a man with very bad teeth and dental-floss stitches in his chest. Impressed by Ramzan's familiarity with the mountains and eager to set up supply routes for the coming winter, the field commander referred Ramzan to a Saudi sheikh who had come to Chechnya to support the holy warriors in their *ghazawat* against the infidel oppressor.

The sheikh wasn't the first foreign Wahhabi Ramzan had seen break sharia law, but he was the first to break it in the name of Internet poker. "The Qur'an specifically says, '*He who plays with dice is like the one who handles the flesh and blood of swine,*' but makes no mention of playing cards," the sheikh explained at their initial meeting, conducted between bets in the midst of the quarter-final round of one of his tournaments. The sheikh had perhaps the only working computer in Volchansk, and connected to the Internet—a technology that surely allowed far too much freedom to be pious—via a portable satellite dish. The sheikh, a short, brimming, gourd-like man, smiled at the computer screen. "I play in the morning," he said, "when it is still late night in Western Europe and America, and the judgment of the other players is clouded by whiskey. All my winnings, of course, go entirely to jihad."

No fundamentalist undercurrent ran through the national culture before the first war. Sufism had always been the predominant Muslim sect, and Wahhabism was a foreign, wartime import. A few times a year, Arab Wahhabis came through the village in search of recruits. They promised rations, shelter, an eternity in Paradise, and, until that day of glorious martyrdom, a monthly salary of two hundred and fifty U.S. dollars. Few young men followed the monochromatic Wahhabi faith, but many were quite willing to be radicalized for a monthly salary that eclipsed what they would otherwise earn in a year. The war of independence so quickly conflated with jihad because no one cared about the self-determination of a small landlocked republic. Arab states would gladly fund a war of religion, but not one of nationalism. And in this way it didn't matter who won the war between the Feds and fundamentalists: the notion of a democratic and fully sovereign Chechnya would be crushed regardless. Martyrdom was the easiest way to make a living, but death didn't appeal to Ramzan, and he was pleased when the sheikh, gleeful after winning the ten-thousand-dollar tournament, crossed his spindly legs and offered a different proposal.

The real war was one of supply, explained the sheikh, who had been trained as a tax attorney before giving his life to Allah, and would return to tax law in five and a half years, when Allah failed to warn him, for the final time, of his opponent's full house. The *dzhigits* had to be restocked and rearmed, the sheikh said, and failing to do so was more destructive to morale than a barrage of mortar rounds. At times, the sheikh continued, when the fighters were encamped in mountain caves, without the firepower to defeat a pack of wolves much less the Federal army, the jihad subsisted purely as a prayer in the hearts of its devout adherents. By this point, it was difficult to pretend that a few thousand men hiding in the mountains could overcome one of the world's largest armies. Yet they had to pretend. The illusion of victory in the minds of the newly converted was, in itself, victory. And morale was essential in maintaining this ancillary conquest for Chechen souls. If the foot soldiers died in bomb blasts, they would blame the Russians. If they died of hunger, they would blame the Wahhabis. Trustworthy transportation was needed more than all the prayers of the Arab world, yet was so difficult to obtain, for the sheikh was a foreigner and didn't know the land. Ramzan did. In the end, he was easily coaxed. The sheikh gave him an envelope with ten pale green twenty-dollar bills and Ramzan pinched the money with his fingertips. For some reason, he'd always imagined American bills would be thicker.

While his neighbors slogged farther into the forest in search of game, Ramzan drove to Volchansk, Shali, even Grozny. The weapons he would deliver to rebel encampments all came from Russian munitions factories. Some he purchased in bulk from a crooked Federal captain who would order his company to attention when Ramzan arrived, and would then walk down the line with an open parachute bag as Ramzan read aloud from the sheikh's handwritten list of needed munitions; in reports to his superiors, the captain would refer to such incidents as rebel ambushes in which his soldiers had no choice but to surrender. Others came through the smuggling routes that ran through the border regions like veins through marble. One day, when discussing supply routes, the sheikh showed him a map of the entire republic, pasted together from a dozen low-resolution pages printed from the Internet. "What's wrong?" the sheikh asked when Ramzan goggled at the misaligned segments held by peeling tape. It was the first time he had seen a map of his own country. The Soviets had banned maps of the entire republic for fear that such a symbol would serve to foment national solidarity, or, at the very least, make long-haul truckers a little too complacent. In the frenzied smuggling following the Soviet collapse, no one, to Ramzan's knowledge, had ever thought to sneak a map across the border. And here was one, right in front of him. His country looked like a rectangle drawn by a man suffering from delirium tremens. He hadn't known that. It did make him feel patriotic. "This is a beautiful map," Ramzan answered, at last. The sheikh let him keep it.

Over the sixteen months he worked for the sheikh, Ramzan transported semiautomatics, machine gun belts, Makarov pistols, aluminum pails of loose bullets divided by caliber, telescopic sniper rifles, hand grenades, clothes-hanger trip lines, brown paper–wrapped blocks of Semtex, stopwatches, coils of multicolored rubber-coated wires, black-and-white photographs of Russian military bases, maps redrawn to include road blocks and checkpoints and ruins, jars of thick dark grease, red plastic jugs of petrol, batteries, butane lighter fluid, compasses, bandannas, powdered soap, iodine tablets, cigarettes, sacks of rice, spotted potatoes, plum jelly, dried apricots, condensed milk, lentils, ground pepper, communiqués, translucently thin rice paper, pens, envelopes, letters from family members, pay, prayer rugs, paperback Qur'ans, and steel septic pipes used to launch homemade rockets, which he also transported. Compensation was subject to the exigencies of combat. Sometimes it came in envelopes: U.S., Russian, British, or E.U. currency. Other times as a cut of the delivered goods: a pair of dull leather military boots, a basket of fresh corn, a boar's hide, a sheepskin overcoat, a silver Makarov pistol. When he felt like a criminal, he reminded himself that a land without law is a land without crime.

Combat enlarged the resupply journeys beyond the simple calculations of time and distance. Covering a hundred kilometers could take weeks to prepare for and days to execute. He packed his truck to capacity and used only a frayed blue blanket to conceal its contents. It didn't matter if the Feds caught him with a butter knife or an atomic bomb. A gunshot would announce the same sentence. He drove toward ridges that sawed farther into the sky as he approached. Danger resided beneath, on, and above the main roads—land mines, patrols, and helicopters—and so he instead followed the trails of shepherds, flattening the tall grasses. Plains grew to foothills and foothills to mountains. He ascended switchbacks so sharp they required three-point turns. Both side-view mirrors snapped off. The rock scraped the paint from the door. Now and then he'd glance down to the gullies of indefinable green funneling toward slivers of water that marked the depth and decline of the land. Cloud cover dwarfed distant cities and villages. Invader and invaded held on to their fistfuls of earth, but in the end, the earth outlived the hands that held it.

He drove until the mountains no longer let him. Then came the shortest and most arduous distances. He loaded the supplies on a plywood frame and strapped the frame to his shoulders with strips of canvas and bungee cord. If properly balanced he could carry forty kilograms up the mountain. The rebels would not assist him, believing such labor beneath men of their pious patriotism, and he carried the forty kilograms up boulders and bluffs while the drop of the valley glared up at him.

Every ten minutes he checked the compass and mountain line. He tied a bell to his wrist so the lookouts would hear his approach before their scopes saw him. They materialized in camo fatigues faded to the same moss-spotted tan of the stone. Beards hung from their sun-darkened faces and the martyrs greeted him with imperious gratitude. Depending on where the rebels were camped and where the road ended, he would invite Dokka, never Akhmed, to join him.

There.

The hoofprints of an elk.

He squatted to the ground, stopped by a set of prints that marked the snow like a long ellipsis leading nowhere. The tracks hadn't yet frozen and the elk was likely within a few hundred meters. To come upon an elk again. To admire rather than shoot. He stood and checked his watch. The sunlight turned the silver hands golden. Twenty minutes before he was due to check in. Staring down the trail of prints, he tried to follow its line through the birches and pines. Somewhere in that distance of frost and shadow, movement disrupted the stillness and the disturbance had carved a distance within him. He continued. The call couldn't come late. Not even the sighting of an elk would excuse it.

The trees opened to the most recently clear-cut swath of forest. Already the saplings had grown taller than him. They loomed over the short, frost-buried stumps of their antecedents. His footprints wove among them, larger and more apparent than the elk's, halting at the deep-treaded tires of a dilapidated logging truck. The loggers had abandoned the truck when they fled, and in the intervening decade its yellow paint had faded, chipped, and been recolored in a maroon coating of rust. The tire treads were so deeply cut he used them as rungs to climb to the cabin. Spiderweb fractures spread across the windshield, but the glass still held the snow. Seated in the driver's seat, he unzipped the duffel bag and assembled the phone. The satellite consisted of three metal rectangles coated in hard resin, which, when set up and positioned at a fifteen-degree angle on the cabin roof, looked like a cooking sheet basking in the sun. He connected two black rubber wires to the satellite. One led to a battery pack, which he left sitting beside the satellite on the roof, and the other ran through the cracked window and attached to the receiver. The pea-green keypad lit up. Three minutes remained before his call was due. Though wrapped in shame and remorse, these phone calls constituted the best moments of his month; for nearly two years, the military men on the other end had been the only people interested in speaking to him. He measured the cold by the length of his breath, which grew and vanished, like a tusk that kept dissolving from his face. The entire forest's quiet was concentrated in the cabin.

Later he would store the memory of this moment with that of his mother's rolling pin, how just the sight of it emerging from the kitchen cabinet would make him salivate. He would treasure it as he treasured the ball of yellow yarn, still attached to the amputated sleeve of a sweater she had been knitting for him when she died. He would weave those three minutes into the fabric of his mother's memory, because she had loved him, and believed him a kind and generous child, and died before she could see the half man he had become. For nearly two years he had worked as an informer for the state security forces. He had given up neighbors who had wished him a happy birthday every year of his life. And still he believed himself the victim as much as the perpetrator of his crimes.

At eleven o'clock he punched the nine-digit number into the keypad. An adjutant answered, and in the cramped cold of the cabin his voice trilled like a clarinet. The adjutant passed the phone to the colonel, whose voice—if he were being honest—had no effect on his bowels until it spoke of the silver Makarov pistol.

·   ·   ·

Nearly two years earlier, in January 2003, he drove into the mountains for what would be the final time. The morning of his departure, he woke early and performed his ablutions and prayers on the trapezoid of dawn light that lay like a prayer rug on the floor. The winter sun kept the same hours the Soviet post office once did, and he prepared to leave without even the light of a kerosene lamp. Nine years had passed since the house he shared with his father had received reliable electricity, and darkness no longer felt like an absence, but rather a thickening in the air, a viscosity that slowed his movement and called upon his spatial memory. His long underwear had stretched in the knees and as he pulled the elastic band to his hip, he mourned the fact that he could obtain a crate of Special Forces sniper rifles more easily than a decent pair of thermal underwear. Before leaving his room, he reached into a wicker basket of unwashed clothes. The wool socks and gray undershirts parted and compressed as he pushed through them, but at the bottom, the Makarov pistol kept its shape.

In the kitchen, steam surged from the kettle spout. Ramzan opened the stove door and cupped his hands in the orange heat. Pages rustled in the living room. His father knew he would leave for the mountains today. A fan of mustard light fell from the living room doorway, and after preparing a cup of tea, Ramzan walked toward it. The light rose from the floor to his feet and up his legs, outlining the droops in his long underwear and then jaundicing his hands, wrists, forearms, elbows. "You are leaving soon," his father said with a foreknowledge that made a statement of the question. His father sat at his desk in the pool of lamplight. Ramzan took a seat on the brown ottoman; the backside had paled from years facing the morning sun.

"What are you reading?" Ramzan asked.

His father gave an abashed smile, as if caught eating *manti* from the pot with his fingers, and tilted the cardboard cover toward the light. It was a conspiracy story about an inept American spy who infiltrated the

Kremlin and was discovered by a commissar whose proletariat spirit
and exceptional good fortune compensated for his lack of deductive reasoning. His father only read these potboilers when Ramzan was in the
mountains. For a man whose life revolved around academic texts, the
shift to pulp fiction announced his paternal worry with the volume of a
bullhorn.

"You've read it before?"

"Twice."

"Who wins? The Americans or the Russians?"

"Both," his father said, glancing to the frost-filled windowpane.

"Then who loses?"

"Everyone else."

"I should be back in a week."

His father nodded, and looked down to his book. Two years would
pass before he had another conversation with his father.

"I'll see you soon," Ramzan said. His father marked his place with
a pencil, stood, and wrapped his arms around Ramzan's shoulders. His
father's breath warmed his cheek like a small, surviving cloud of summer humidity. On the desk, beneath the novel, the typewritten carcass
of his manuscript bled red ink. "If you were writing your book instead
of reading others, you might be finished by now."

"Perhaps," replied his father. Their embrace didn't break off so much
as dissipate, an exhalation releasing whatever tenderness was briefly
held between them. His father's hug was an act of precaution rather than
love, so that if Ramzan did not return from the mountains, his father
would have the consolation of knowing his final gesture toward his son
had been one of kindness rather than disappointment.

In his bedroom he popped two rigged floorboards and felt through
the shadows for the frayed tail of rope. Coiling the rope around his
wrist, he drew the wooden pallet across the concrete foundation. A
duffel bag with his most treasured possessions sat on the pallet. In it
were three fragmentation grenades, a Kalashnikov and eight full maga-

zines, a hunting knife, an old membership card to the village *banya*, two hundred thousand rubles divided in eight shrink-wrapped stacks, and a small sandalwood box containing a single yellow sweater sleeve still attached to the yarn ball.

He slid a stack of bills into the upper right pocket of his old Red Army jacket—a jacket that appeared to be composed entirely of pockets—and slid his arms into sleeves that felt like the largest of the pockets. He looked like a fisherman. He pulled the silver Makarov from the wicker basket, wrapped it in an undershirt and set it in the duffel bag, to keep for himself. The sidearm was one of the twenty he was supposed to transport to the mountains that day, a small gratuity he had awarded himself. In three weeks, he would teach Havaa to shoot it.

Outside, the rising sun flashed on the frost as he stomped toward his truck, carrying his backpack and the teakettle. He popped the hood and, after letting the kettle cool in the snow, filled the radiator. Antifreeze was an unaffordable luxury, so each evening he drained the radiator and each morning refilled it, and he did this until spring. The weapons and supplies—the nineteen other Makarov pistols among them—were already packed in back. It was a risk leaving the weapons outside overnight, but less of a risk than bringing them in. The temperature difference could easily fracture the rifle operating rods. His father stood in the doorframe, his frown the largest wrinkle on his face.

In two minutes his home was indistinguishable from the other snow-capped dwellings scattered in the rear view. He honked twice when he reached Dokka's. Through the living room window, an argument between Dokka and his wife halted with the second horn blast. Havaa stood in the doorway, watching Dokka forlornly as he slung a knapsack over his shoulder and clomped through the snow to the passenger's side.

"Difficult morning?" Ramzan asked.

Dokka smiled. "I'm married. What morning isn't?"

No vehicles had passed since the last snowfall and without tire tracks to follow he couldn't be sure where the road was. As long as he didn't run into a tree, he figured, he was going the right way. Slouched in the passenger seat, Dokka pushed a pebble in small circles around his palm.

On the road, the snow rose from ten to twenty centimeters as they drove south. Ramzan kept at forty kilometers an hour for so long the two digits seemed skewered on the speedometer needle. They stopped to eat lunch and relieve themselves beside a thicket of pines, whose snowy boughs provided camouflage for the red truck.

"The snow is like my wife's mother," Dokka said, kicking it over the tire tracks. "She will name every place we've been."

"Have a cigarette."

"You haven't hunted this year. You've forgotten that a buck is easiest to track in fresh snow."

Ramzan hoisted himself on the warm engine hood. What accounted for Dokka's sudden anxiety? Yes, they would likely be shot if discovered by the Feds or state security forces, but that could happen as easily in Eldár or Volchansk, in their homes or in the street, while they slept, or while they played chess, a fate so likely to befall a Chechen man it seemed silly to worry about it too much.

Before them stretched a white field that had, for eight years now, grown nothing but weeds and dust. The snow erased all measure of distance and the field expanded past the horizon, wide enough to extinguish the sun.

"You won't be able to do this much longer either," Dokka said. "The war is over. Grozny has fallen. These skirmishes are final breaths."

"You're an optimist, Dokka."

Night fell and they drove through terraced valleys until they reached a hamlet built of the same pale stone that crowned the slopes. Centuries earlier, the hamlet had been home to several thousand; but in 1956, when the Chechens returned from Kazakh exile, Soviet authorities prohibited them from returning to their ancestral homes, and this hamlet of pristine ruins was one among hundreds scattered throughout the highlands. It seemed so unnatural to Ramzan to see a village decimated not by bombs and bullets but by time and neglect. The thirty-nine residents who gathered around the truck shared the blood of common great-great-grandparents. The men wore lambskin hats and tall leather boots, the older women wore gray and black headscarves and long plain dresses, and the younger women wore blue and pink hijabs folded to the width of a hunting blade. The children stood just outside the splay of headlight, afraid it might burn them.

They were met by the tall, arboreal elder, known for eating snow to numb his stomach ulcer. After washing in a tin basin, they dined at his home. Slabs of white stone sealed with clay-lime mortar formed the walls. Weathered petroglyphs adorned each stone: spokes of light jutting from plum-sized suns. In the main room they ate on the mats they would later sleep on. They chewed differently here. Their bowls full, their bites unrationed. No need of words when the tongue could converse with mutton.

Unaccustomed to such portions, Ramzan and Dokka finished last. As soon as they set down their bowls, the women filed in through the backdoor. The women waited for the men to leave before taking their places on the lambskin blankets. Ramzan, the last out, heard whispers and suppressed laughter as the door closed behind him and very much wished he could have remained behind. The men followed a deer trail past the ice-glazed remnants of a stone tower. In earlier centuries, it had been a fortress, watchtower, signal light, and anchor to the long-since-scattered *teip*. Past the tower they reached a clearing. A series of elevated planks formed a flat, dry, tire-shaped platform in the center of the clearing. Its axle was a ring of stone containing the ashes of a bonfire. The men carried logs from a lean-to deeply entrenched in the hillside. Within minutes the fire reached above Ramzan's head, so bright he could count the rings of the logs yet unconsumed. It had been years since he had last participated in a *zikr*.

Ramzan and Dokka removed their boots and joined the others in a circle around the fire. The elder began the *zikr* with prayer. A steady call, the voice of a man, he thought, in a country bereft of men. *La ilaha illallah, la ilaha illallah.* The elder repeated the cry, and its slow rhythm sliced the words into syllables that stood alone as if locutions of a higher language. Voices on either side joined in harmonies that buoyed the elder's call. Then clapping, not to keep the rhythm, but to propel it. The silver of the moon and the orange of the flames entwined on the elder's tilted face. *There is no god but Allah.* The men swayed from side to side as the pace increased. Swaying grew to stomping, and sawdust rose from the shaking platform, and the men shed their outer garments. Against the burn of bonfire, the men combusted. The flailing arms of overcoats, the falling hands of woolen gloves, but the cries were not the cries of a land mine or shelling, and the pain of the elder's call was the merciful ache of longing. *There is no god. But Allah. No god. But Allah.*

Ramzan clapped and he stomped and he shouted as sweat slicked his face. Without warning, a man three down from Ramzan let out a long wail, and though Ramzan couldn't tie one word from the string of utterances twisting from the man's throat, he understood precisely what the man meant. The man's eyes were closed, and the uncommon serenity of his features suggested he had seen all that could be seen. The elder's voice dropped an octave and in unison the men's stamping became a dance. They marched joyously, counterclockwise, sliding the left foot across the platform and dropping hard on the heel of the right. In unison they spun. Three hundred and sixty degrees flattened to an indivisible plane. The pressure had built in his chest and he tried to contain it with reminders that he was no longer Sufi, that these weren't his people, that human sorrow was the prophecy of an empty heaven, but it built, and built, like the memory of a long extinguished orgasm, and the pressure closed the space between his cells, and he was released. No melody ran through his wail. His voice was hoarse and broken and he raised it. The other men took no note above the tremble of palms and planks, but Ramzan's next breath brought peace.

The following morning Ramzan woke with a sore throat. After

breakfasting on nuts, dried fruit, and goat's milk, the elder led Ramzan and Dokka to their truck. In exchange for the hospitality, he gave the elder ten kilos of rice and a liter of butane. The elder refused any offer of munitions besides buckshot, and despite his protestations, Ramzan pressed the issue. He couldn't recall when he had last felt so moved to ensure the safety of a stranger. But the stiffness of the elder's frown made it known that he would never be persuaded of a hand grenade's safety. Driving away, Ramzan struggled to focus on the road. The lives lived behind him were so small and anonymous they had escaped the notice of state socialism, of the first and second war. The previous night, for the first time in a long time, he had felt whole, and his eyes returned to the rearview, where his dignity was held within a few square centimeters of glass.

They drove another five hours, through mountain passes so narrow the side mirrors would have snapped off, had they not already, and back down to valleys; five hours of listening to Dokka praise his wife's resourcefulness and her gardening and her talent for creating sumptuous dishes with only a third of the requisite ingredients, five hours of compliments so lavish and exaggerated that Dokka could only mean them as insults, for why else sing the praises of marriage to a man who could never marry, why else recite the wonders of companionship if not to wound Ramzan, who, for those five long hours, felt so deficient he would have given his right hand in dowry for a wife who could neither cook, nor sew, nor raise children, a wife who committed adultery and passed gas in public, a wife who treated him like an animal—yes, he would take it and be fine with it because a disgraced man is still a man, and Ramzan wasn't a man, not really, yet the whole world expected him to be one; and the neighbors, dear god, *why haven't you married, a handsome man like you still living with your father*—and when his quiet demurrals spawned rumor—*he doesn't like women, that's why he's thirty-one years old and unmarried*, he couldn't decide if truth or rumor dishonored him more, but ultimately, he decided it better to allow the hearsay of homosexuality to flourish so long as his silence could cast doubt upon the whole matter, and yes, his silence engendered doubt, though mainly in himself, converting shame into rage and propelling it through his veins, his kidneys, his forearms, his little toes, and then returning to that second heart on which the names of those who slandered him were etched, and much later, he would recite those names over a satellite phone and those who had created those stories would fall victim to his own stories, *homosexuality* replaced with *rebel sympathies*, *Wahhabism*, *jihad*; but those stories were still unspoken, still unimaginable, and the purgatory of Dokka's wife, within which he was the unfortunate audience, remained interminable even after five hours of driving when he crested a hill and slammed on the brakes because right there, not two hundred meters away, was a platoon of Russian troops, and he viewed them as both conquerors and liberators, who might kill him but would free him at least from the perdition of Dokka's voice, and trembling with terror and gratitude he spoke the words that had been on his tongue for five hours. "Stop talking, Dokka."

A welcome quiet suffused the cabin, and Ramzan basked in it before fear retook him. There were two armored personnel carriers, two UAZ jeeps, and a tank crowned with a machine-gun turret.

"Turn around!" Dokka shouted and shook Ramzan's arm by the sleeve of his jacket. "What are you doing? Let's go!"

But he kept the ball of his foot pressed to the brake pedal. "They have already seen us."

It was true. The machine-gun turret had swiveled to face them and snow shot up behind the jeeps as they accelerated toward the crest.

"If we run, we're fucked. If we wait and are reasonable, we might survive. We're just sitting here. It's not yet a crime to be alive. You might even get a chance to finish telling me about your wife."

The jeeps stopped twenty meters ahead and idled, while behind them, the tank gradually ground up the incline. The soldiers who emerged were not the tattooed *kontraktniki*, like those Ramzan remembered from the *zachistka*; no, compared to those hulking Russian bears these were half-starved jackals. *We may live to see the sunset,* he thought.

Four soldiers bearing machine guns approached. He raised his open palms to the Feds. Dokka followed suit.

"You went to a filtration camp before. You survived. They didn't hurt you," Dokka stammered, unable to convince even himself. Ramzan wanted to grab Dokka by his ears and shake that stupid self-deluded skull until its one grain of logic rang out. Leaning forward, he felt the empty space between his legs.

"Stop speaking, Dokka. Just be quiet."

One of the soldiers approached the driver's door. He had gone at least a week without shaving, but the growth couldn't conceal the concavity of his cheeks. All around the snow stretched indifferently.

"Water," the soldier croaked. Misunderstanding the request, Ramzan held out his identification card.

"Water," the soldier again said. "We've been eating muddy snow for days. We need clean water. Can't you speak Russian?"

"I think we should give him water," Dokka whispered, his opened hands still facing the windshield. It was the first sensible thing Dokka had said that day.

"I have water at my feet," he told the soldier. "Don't shoot me."

The soldier accepted the grease-smeared canteen, sighing as he brought the brim to his lips, and his relief became Ramzan's. The soldier didn't suspect that the water had spent the previous day circulating through the engine radiator.

Dokka's hands remained skyward when they were ordered out of the truck. Ramzan protested briefly and halfheartedly; he had, after all, given that first soldier a canteen of water, and was this how his hospitality was to be repaid? But he dropped the remonstration when that first soldier, his thirst now quenched, pressed the gun barrel to Ramzan's forehead. They lay facedown in the snow with their wrists bound behind their backs in plastic zip-strips. To keep his head above the snow, Ramzan had to arch his back and puff out his chest and flail like a beached whale. From that uncomfortable vantage, he watched the soldiers unpack the sacks of rice and grain from the truck bed. A few more seconds and they would find the Makarov handguns, fragmentation grenades, Semtex bricks, and lead wires, and he would die here, flopping like a goddamn sea mammal, many kilometers from home. How he wished he had stitched his address into his trouser inseam. He hadn't taken the precaution for fear that the security forces would implicate his father, but now, with snow melting through his jacket, he could think of no inhumanity grimmer than an unmarked grave. Perhaps he would be forced to lie upon Dokka to save ammunition. Such a death would insult the gunrunner. He would demand his own bullet. For the water canteen, they could at least do him that small honor. Beside him, Dokka had given up. The heat from his face had thawed a soup bowl in the snow. He wept into it.

"Don't worry," Ramzan said. His tone surprised him. He could see the end and he was calm. "Today, we'll find out whether the imams or commissars were right."

"You're brave," Dokka said. "Here I am, crying. I dishonor you."

How often is immense unhappiness mistaken for courage? He opened his mouth and filled it with snow. It melted as he listened to Dokka's sobs. The soldiers at least would remember which of the two had faced his bullet with clear eyes.

But the soldiers, in an act of unexpected compassion and restraint, decided not to summarily execute them. After finding the weapons, they pulled Ramzan to his feet, then Dokka. Shaking their heads at the mucus frozen to Dokka's lip, they turned to Ramzan, and spoke only to him. They were lost. Three nights earlier, the cold had killed their radio, and they had driven through blanketed fields in vain search for human habitation. They hadn't been tracking the red truck. It was an accident. As the gun barrels pointed them toward the UAZ jeep, the commanding officer asked, "Are you familiar with the Landfill?"

Ramzan nodded.

"Can you give us directions?"

"Directions?"

"I told you. We're lost."

He could not believe it.

"If you take us there, you'll live. At least until we get there. That much, I guarantee. And likely after. I know a lieutenant there."

"Okay." He didn't know what else to say. The commanding officer beamed gratefully. Afraid the man would kiss him, Ramzan made the first move to the jeep. His captors followed.

The soldiers led them down the hillside, tenderly, so they didn't lose their balance. The commanding officer opened the jeep door for Ramzan and cut the zip-strip with the serrated edge of a hunting knife.

"Watch your head," cautioned the commanding officer, who would never tell another soul of his military service. The woman he was to wed in three and a half years would know him as a hundred people—a husband, a father, a churchgoer, an elementary school teacher, a charity worker—and would never find a commanding officer in that population she so dearly loved.

Ramzan slid to the far side of the seat. Dokka sat beside him. A few uncomfortable minutes passed before the commanding officer reappeared in the passenger seat with a Marlboro Red, the rebel field commander's favorite brand, dangling from his lips. The officer and other soldiers watched him expectantly.

"What?" Ramzan asked.

"You haven't fastened your seat belt," the commanding officer observed.

"My seat belt?" He glanced around. All the soldiers were wearing seat belts.

"We're not going anywhere until you buckle up," the commanding officer said.

Ramzan nodded, yes, of course he was required to wear a seat belt, just as he was required to give directions to a torture camp, because stupidity was the single abiding law of the universe. He buckled up, and took a compass from his jacket pocket. "Turn around," he said. "The Landfill is behind us."

Within an hour Ramzan directed the jeep to the road that would take them to the Landfill. Ovals of melted snow appeared in the fields. Strangely curvaceous patches of damp dirt. The sun shone. At one point he yawned and felt the nudge of Dokka's elbow. The hollow-cheeked, grease-lipped soldier dozed beside him.

"I think Akhmed is sleeping with my wife," Dokka said. Ramzan turned back to the window. Silvery branches darted past. The following summer would be beautiful. He had heard all he cared to hear about Dokka's wife.

Early December 2004. Two weeks before Dokka disappeared. In the cabin of the abandoned logging truck. The first conversation with the Cossack colonel.

"Ramzan Geshilov?"

"Reporting, sir."

"Do you recognize my voice?"

"I don't, sir. Are you filling in for Captain Ivan Fyodorovich?"

"Is he the officer you report to?"

"Yes."

"Yes, who?"

"Yes, sir."

"I have fucked the wife of your superior officer eighty-seven times, and only the first three were before they married. Do you understand me?"

"Yes, sir."

"I am told you are among our less incompetent assets in the Volchansk region. Is that true?"

"I don't know, sir."

"At last, someone who tells the truth."

"Yes, sir."

"What's the weather like in Eldár Forest?"

"It is . . . it's sunny. And cold."

"That's what the meteorological report states. I'm glad that the meteorologists are honest, at least for today."

"Yes, sir."

"Where are you this very moment?"

"The cabin of an abandoned logging truck. Three kilometers from the village proper. Sir."

"Good. You are speaking with me rather than the cuckolded captain because a situation has arisen of the utmost importance. Since the captain can't solve the case of his missing wife, who disappears into my bed each Thursday, I wouldn't trust him with this. You see, the ballistics report has come back on a gun used in the assassination of an FSB colonel last year."

"Last year?"

"Yes. A year to get a simple ballistics report. It's December 2004, and it's just come in. When I was last in Moscow I read that Chinese assembly plants can produce a new car in a few hours. And it takes a year for us to produce a ballistics report that connects the bullet in the head of an FSB colonel to the gun lying meters away."

"Yes, sir."

"The report has come back, and I want you to find where the gun came from."

"Pardon me, sir?"

"Did you break wind?"

"No, sir."

"Then don't waste a request for my pardon."

"Yes, sir. It's just that I'm not sure how I'll find the origin of a gun fired a year ago."

"It's one of those needle-in-a-haystack situations, is it?"

"With all respect, sir, it's a needle in a needle-stack."

"On that account, you're in luck. It's one of your needles."

"You must be mistaken. I haven't run so much as a toothpick in the past two years. Ask the captain, sir."

"How about I ask his wife instead. No, I'm not concerned about what you claim not to be selling, but rather about what you've already sold. You see, the serial number on the Makarov pistol used to kill the colonel in December 2003 corresponds sequentially with the serial numbers of the Makarov pistols found in the back of your truck when our brave lads ambushed you and took you to the Landfill in January 2002."

Silence.

"Are you still there?"

"Yes."

"Who?"

"Sir."

"This puts us in a rather difficult situation. In seeking information on the supplier of a gun used to assassinate an FSB colonel, we are immediately led to a person whom we pay to provide us with just that information."

"I swear I had nothing to do with it, sir. Who was the assassin, sir?"

"A Black Widow. A *shahidka*. A separatist trained and sent by those animals in the mountains."

"Was she taken alive . . . sir?"

"The *shahidka* was detained at a filtration point. Cleverly, she seduced the colonel, a man, I am told, so very well endowed that only the cavernous cunt of a Chechen has the latitude to accommodate him. No doubt hearing of the colonel's great girth, the *shahidka* used her powers of seduction. When they were alone, she shot him."

"But, sir, why wasn't she checked for weapons?"

"If you still had a pair of stones between your legs, you would know that the average cunt of your womenfolk is capacious enough to conceal a rocket launcher. The colonel was a fool, no doubt, but nonetheless, he was still a colonel."

"Yes, sir, but wouldn't it be more prudent to trace the *shahidka*, rather than the gun?"

"A gun can be identified more easily than a person. There is a lesson in that."

"But the *shahidka* . . ."

"Irrelevant."

"I'll do what I can, sir."

"No, you will not do what you can do. You will do what you are told."

"Yes, sir."

"Numbers are the amoral language of absolute truth. These serial numbers do not lie. At some point you were in possession of that Makarov, and I will know the name and location of the next hands who held it. I was promoted to replace the departed colonel. I now hold his rank and command, and so, understandably, it is my chief priority to kill the architects of his assassination. Should I fall victim to a similar fate, and should the cuckolded captain be given my rank, I truly fear the fate of the Russian nation."

"Yes, sir."

"I see from your file that you have a father."

"Yes, sir."

"And he lives with you?"

"Yes, sir."

"He turned seventy-nine this year?"

"Yes, sir."

"He survived the Great Patriotic War?"

"Yes, sir."

"And the deportations to Kazakhstan?"

"Yes, sir."

"And eleven years there on the steppe?"

"Twelve, sir."

"And you would like him to see his eightieth birthday?"

"Yes, sir."

"Then give me names, Ramzan."

"Yes, sir."

"Or I'll sew your stones back on just to chop them off twice."


The Landfill filtration camp was so named for having been built, or rather sunken, into the site of a partially constructed garbage dump. Once, when Ramzan passed the site as a younger man, he watched a brontosaurial backhoe bite into the soil and scoop out a bathtub's worth of loose earth. But after the collapse, and the subsequent wars, plans to finish the landfill were postponed then abandoned completely. Only two of the eight proposed pits, each twenty meters deep, with the surface area of a soccer field, had been excavated. The concrete and plastic foundation, which would have trapped runoff effluvia, was never installed, and so rain and snow dissolved into a knee-deep sludge at the bottom of the two earthen pits. When Ramzan was taken there in the first war, he spent three days in Pit A before two guards lowered a sixty-rung ladder, doused his feet and legs in frigid water, and led him to the two-story white building whose entranceway still bore the sign REFUSE DISPOSAL ADMINISTRATION. Petitions calling to fill in the pits circulated after the first war. An unfortunate group of sixteen women widowed by the Landfill shoveled for a month, but failed to visibly alter the swampscape. Ultimately, the symbolic benefit of filling the two pits didn't hold up to the actual benefit of rebuilding roads, houses, schools, power plants, refineries, and hospitals. No one imagined the pits might again be used. No one imagined there would be a second war.

But there was a second war, and now, in January 2003, having encountered the lost Federal patrol, Ramzan was imprisoned for the second time. He spent eleven days belowground, this time in Pit B, while

Dokka was taken to Pit A. At the very least his ears would receive a welcome rest. He descended the now-rusty sixty-rung ladder and the guard shook him from it before he reached the final rungs. The sludge had frozen to a snowy dampness that only reached his ankles. The pit held two dozen others. Over the coming days, he would pray to the sky with them all, but only his conversations with the blue-eyed imam would remain etched in his memory. The guards lowered food and fresh water in tin pails attached to yellow cords that came irregularly, sometimes five in a day, sometimes one, sometimes in the middle of the night when the men would wake, gather, and divide the provisions. The one thing the pit had no shortage of was space. Ramzan spent the daylight hours walking alongside its walls, wondering if somewhere the Feds had a modern prison, with electricity, bunks, cells, and roofs, in which they housed not prisoners but banana peels, and potato skins, and broken shoelaces, and apple cores, and last year's calendars, and deflated tires, and balled-up paper, and used tissues, and cigarette butts, and the last worthless slivers of bar soap. Some compassionate guard, whose soul the imam would teach Ramzan to honor, had tossed in thin wooden planks, and a sidewalk the width of a balance beam stretched around the pit's perimeter. The names and villages of captives were carved into the clay walls. Men packed snow on the walls as far up as they could reach to moisten the clay, and after a few minutes scraped it off and identified themselves in block letters drawn by stick or finger. Information the Feds would torture them for was written here on the walls for all to see. It was well understood among the men that the Feds had as much sense as two bricks smashed together. It was also understood that pain, rather than information, was the true purpose of interrogation.

In the afternoon of the fourth day, Ramzan balanced on the slender sidewalk when the blue-eyed imam stopped him.

"Give me a boost," the imam asked, nodding his bearded chin toward the wall where he had written half his name. At first, Ramzan refused. Since arriving he had done his best to keep his distance from the filthy, brutalized men, as though his refusal to acknowledge them were the tightrope he walked upon, saving him from falling into their ranks.

"Are you a general, hmm?" the imam asked. "Or a Persian prince? Are your hands too delicate to help an imam old enough to be your uncle?"

"I'm not a Persian prince."

"Then climb down from your throne and help me."

The imam placed his muddy boot in the stirrup of Ramzan's woven fingers. He hoisted the imam, whose weight, held in Ramzan's straining hands, was greater than his size suggested. After an endless moment, the imam tapped him on the forehead with a muddy finger and Ramzan let the old man drop to the ground.

"Take a good look at it," the imam said, pointing to his name and village. "If it turns out you are a Persian prince, and they let you leave, you must remember me."

"If they let me leave, I will forget everything here."

"No," the imam protested, wagging his muddy little finger at Ramzan. "You must remember."

"Why?"

"So that my nephews will know where to buy my corpse."

Ramzan nodded.

"I can afford it, you know," the imam said, proudly. "I still have my retirement account."

When Ramzan turned, the imam asked, "What did they get you for?"

"Smuggling weapons. You?"

"Height."

"Height?"

"Well, the lack of height. The Feds came to my village for a counterterrorist operation. They were looking for some Wahhabi mastermind that was supposedly hiding there, but their only physical description of the man was that he had a beard and was less than two meters tall. They rounded up every short, bearded man, and many adolescents who didn't have beards but met the height description. On the reason-for-arrest line of my report, they wrote *too short*." The imam shook his head and stared up at his name written in the clay wall, now beyond his reach. Ramzan was glad he'd stopped to lift the imam.

"It's funny," the imam continued. "My generation grew up in the Kazakh resettlement camps, and because protein was so scarce, it's not at all uncommon for men of my age to be short, but I've always been ashamed of it. My younger brother used to tell me that my shortness wouldn't kill me. He was only two centimeters taller than me, but I swear, he lived his entire life in those two centimeters, lording them over me, always asking if I needed help reaching the upper shelves. I wish he were still alive, just so the Feds could arrest him for being too short, too."

"What can one do?" Ramzan said, shrugging.

"Pray," the imam said.

The imam held court in the southwest corner of Pit B, perched on the seat of honor, an upturned water pail that had come loose from its cord. Each morning he led prayers and performed ablutions with snow that turned his hands a numb white. He insisted that God, in His mercy, would forgive their unclean state. He had memorized the entire Qur'an and lectured on the nature of evil, which, like a shadow, cannot exist independently of the good it silhouettes. Unlike the sheikh and mujahideen, he never tied politics to Qur'anic verse, and instead explained the righteousness of the faithful and the wisdom of the Prophet and the joyousness of a Paradise that is the summer to the winter of the world. Above all, he spoke of the end times and God's judgment.

But the interrogator would judge Ramzan before God would, and it was the interrogator's judgment that he feared. Each day he watched the ritual of men called forth. First the sixty-rung ladder was slid down the wall of the pit, and then the name of the summoned was magnified through a bullhorn speaker, so loud and static-laced it sounded like it truly came from the heavens. If the summoned hesitated, a warning shot was fired. The summoned climbed all sixty rungs to the sixty-first, street level, a place so distant the sky seemed closer. None of the summoned returned. An optimistic man might believe they had been found innocent, released, sent home to their families; but not even Dokka, in whatever comparable perdition he lived, would be capable of such optimism. As soon as the summoned reached the top of the ladder and stepped onto the snowy soil of the sixty-first rung, the imam began the funeral. The service was unlike any Ramzan had attended. No body. No shroud. No friend or neighbor who had known the summoned in any but this desperate condition. They were all dead, just a step or two behind the summoned, and they honored him not as one who departs, but as one who has fully entered. The imam congregated the others around the damp plaque where the summoned had written his name and village. They read the name aloud, softly at first, then growing to a chant that rivaled the *zikr,* and made prayer from the name and sent it skyward. For twenty-four hours, or as close as they could calculate, the name and village of the summoned was left on the clay wall. At the twenty-fifth, the men gathered around the inscription. Each took a palmful of earth from the thawing ground and pressed it to the wall. Without the body, they could only bury the name, and when they could no longer read it, they knew the man was gone.

"According to *hadith,* he who nightly recites the sixty-seventh surah will be spared a torturous death," the blue-eyed imam lectured one evening from the upturned bucket. "You must all know that. You must all count on that. The surah describes the Merciful's creation of all seven heavens, each one above the other. The Throne of God sits atop the highest heaven, and lanterns adorn the lowest. The lanterns are our stars and comets, this firmament above our very heads."

He glanced to the sky and lowered his face. He pulled a matchbook from his pocket and struck it. Soft yellow light gloved his hand. "Take heart, my friends; we are already among the righteous. We are already with God." He raised the match to his face, and his shadow was cast across the Landfill clay. "Here is the lantern of our lowest heaven."

From somewhere far above them, a name was called through the bullhorn speaker. The imam stepped down from the bucket and walked toward the ladder. "With God," he said, as he stepped onto that first and lowest rung.

Night fell. The moonlight covered Ramzan like a flimsy bedsheet. He lay on a strip of once-burgundy carpeting, which would capsize in the mud if he sat up, turned over, yawned, or thought too hard. The stars shone much brighter here. The gauzy light of the Milky Way canopied Pit B, the nearest thing to a roof. Nothing in this or the next world was worse than physical pain. In the afterlife, as no more than a soul, he would be without a body to beat, skin to peel, blood to flow, eyes to gouge, fingernails to pry, lungs to drown, ventricles to stop, and so the retribution of God would always be gentler than the retribution of man. He held on to this one truth the next morning when his name was called through the bullhorn. He held on to it as he climbed the ladder and saw, framed by the rungs, the names of those to follow. When ordered to disrobe, he complied. When one of the interrogating officers wanted a better view of the cratered skin that had been his scrotum, he complied. Those scars were seven years old. During his first detention in the Landfill, in 1995, in the first war, he had refused to inform. They had wrestled down his pants, shown him the bolt cutters, and still he had said no. Screaming, thrashing, with his manhood half severed, he had said no. He had done that, and now he was ready to start saying yes.

He would have confessed everything, but they didn't ask, weren't interested, threatened to cut out his tongue and put pliers to his teeth if he spoke one more fucking word. Electric wires were wound around his fingers. A car battery was drained into his bones. God might have been watching, but it wasn't God's finger on the battery switch. The interrogating officers didn't speak. Instead he was an instrument they played, performing a duet, and in their own way they conversed through his sobs. They both wore very shiny shoes. That was all he would remember.

He passed out and was resuscitated by buckets of cold water so frequently that even the electricity in his veins couldn't warm him. The interrogating officers stepped out of the room to have a rest, and new officers entered. He had been in interrogation for three hours and they still hadn't asked him a single question. In a moment of calm, when the interrogators were asking each other about their weekends, he tried to find the beat of his heart among the burps and squelches, real and unreal, emanating from his blistered body. Before the second car battery was attached, the new interrogator guided Ramzan to the next room. He had trouble walking. He had forgotten torture could be so exhausting. The new interrogator, the one with less shiny shoes, held him upright, using his whole body as a crutch, and helped him walk. He carefully wiped Ramzan's forehead with a handkerchief before opening the door to the next room. A white wooden table scored with fingernail scratches stood in the center of the room. In this realm of ceased expectation, the aquarium at the far end didn't surprise him. The blue-eyed imam was brought through another door. He didn't recognize Ramzan, or if he did, he refused to acknowledge the fact of his shame before a disciple. The imam was held down against the table. One of the guards pulled down his trousers and underwear. The interrogator with less shiny shoes, who had, moments earlier, so tenderly guided Ramzan down the corridor, went to the aquarium. He put on a pair of thick rubber gloves. He reached into the aquarium. The blue-eyed imam didn't know what was happening. From his vantage, he saw only the wall and the arms holding him. The imam couldn't see what Ramzan saw. He couldn't see the interrogator with less shiny shoes approach with the bucking, writhing black belt in his gloved hands, and the interrogator couldn't see the imam's face. The imam didn't understand what was happening, and neither did Ramzan. But when the interrogator with less shiny shoes pressed the eel, teeth first, between the imam's pale buttocks, it could be nothing else. The room went blurry, then black, and the imam's shriek followed Ramzan into unconsciousness. When he woke, he was back in the first interrogation room. The interrogator with less shiny shoes crouched behind him. His hands were wet. Ramzan promised everything, and the interrogator, like the parent of a child too old to believe in ghosts, watched him with disappointment, his clear eyes saddened by Ramzan's sincerity. The interrogator took off his jacket, rolled up his sleeves, laid the live wires on Ramzan's chest and mapped the border of their shared humanity. Ramzan offered his soul. He begged to be enslaved. The known universe contracted to the limits of the cement floor, and on it, the interrogator was both man and deity, prophet and god. By ten o'clock the interrogator with less shiny shoes asked his first question. By eleven the electrical wires were unwound from Ramzan's fingers. By noon he was allowed to dress. By one he was on the FSB payroll. He kept thanking the interrogator with less shiny shoes. Again and again and again, he thanked the man, and never before had he expressed such earnest gratitude. He would have followed the interrogator with less shiny shoes anywhere. It was God he found at the other end of the electrical wires. He was given a satellite phone and a three-hundred-page manual written in German, French, English, and Japanese. He asked after Dokka, asked if he could buy back his friend's life. Yes, the interrogator with less shiny shoes told him, provided the village could raise a fifty-thousand-ruble ransom within a week; otherwise, the ransom would jump to seventy-five thousand for his corpse. Ramzan reached into one of the many pockets of the overcoat they returned to him, and timidly pulled out the plastic-wrapped bills. No one had thought to check his pockets. "This is only half," the interrogator with less shiny shoes told him. "But I am, above all, a reasonable man."

Ramzan waited for Dokka on the concrete stairs of the Refuse Disposal Administration. A hundred meters away, at the bottom of Pit B, his funeral was taking place. Perhaps one of the others sat on the imam's upturned pail, intoning the name of Ramzan Geshilov, the good and righteous man who had refused to inform and had died for it in the Landfill seven years earlier and only now was having his funeral.

The pebbles at his feet were round and pockmarked. His bare toes curled around them. There was no guilt, no shame, those would come later, but for now, just the blanketing white noise of relief, of this breath, of non-pain. He wore the rings of ten burn marks on his fingers. For the first time in his life he believed without reservation in the existence of a kind and generous God, as desert thirst teaches one to believe in rain. After an hour his red truck turned the corner, followed by a dust billow that swept past when the truck stopped. Dokka's gasps filled in the open passenger window. Leaving the engine idling, the interrogator with less shiny shoes climbed from the driver's side. He held up a red plastic bag, like a fish he had proudly caught. Ten fingers floated in the blood. "Your friend gets these back when I get the other twenty-five thousand," said the interrogator with less shiny shoes.

After Ramzan climbed into the driver's seat, after he bandaged Dokka's hands with bandannas and duct tape, he looked to the dash and saw that the interrogator—whose shoes, wet with blood, now shone in the afternoon sun—had left them with a full tank of gas.

And, now, two years later, December 2004, two weeks before Dokka disappeared, when the dial tone severed the Cossack colonel's threat, and Ramzan packed away the satellite phone, and descended from the cabin of the abandoned logging truck, he did so with the same numbness that had allowed him to drive away from the Landfill two years earlier. Both times he heard Dokka's beseeching voice, and both times he did his best to ignore it. For the two weeks after the Cossack colonel's call, the two weeks in which his bowels clenched in a constipated fist, Dokka, not yet a ghost, haunted Ramzan. He ran through the twelve names he had already given the Feds, the twelve who had disappeared because he had become an informer two years earlier at the Landfill. What did a thirteenth matter? What did any one person matter when pounded against the anvil of history? He sat quietly and remembered Dokka as if he had already gone. Dokka always ended his questions with *or*, as if anticipating he would be denied: *Would you like to play chess, or . . . ? Will the G-3 rations be handed out tomorrow, or . . . ?* His generosity in opening his home to refugees, and his intransigence in demanding rent, even if payment was no more than a dull button, or a paper clip, or a piece of stationery for his daughter's souvenir collection. His brown eyes had twice grown dull: first after he lost his fingers, then after he lost his wife. His paddle hands. His slender toes taught the dexterity of a left hand. He could clasp a pencil between his first and second toe, and write in awkward letters so large only a sentence would fit on the page. His genius for chess.

The more Ramzan thought about it, the more awful it became. The Dokka unearthed in no more than a trowelful of memory was enough to break his heart. Dokka insisted on wearing button shirts, and how he dressed each morning, if the girl helped him, if he was too proud to ask his daughter for help, if he woke before dawn to begin the long arduous task of buttoning his shirt with his toes, Ramzan didn't know. On that frantic truck ride back from the Landfill, Dokka had thanked Ramzan for saving his life. Somehow they had survived and not even the agony of ten amputated fingers had been enough to make him forget his manners.

Two weeks after his first conversation with the Cossack colonel, he trekked back into the woods, back under the ice-encased branches, to the cabin of the corroded logging truck. He called the colonel and gave up Dokka, explaining that Dokka harbored refugees, and also likely rebel sympathizers, though he didn't add that most Chechens sympathized. He described, truthfully, how Dokka had asked for a weapon when they returned from the Landfill because he had feared he couldn't protect his family. He described, truthfully, how he had taught Havaa to shoot the Makarov pistol because Dokka no longer had the fingers to pull the trigger. It was the first unembellished account he had provided. The silver Makarov pistol was the sole piece of evidence, and though he gave extenuating circumstances, mitigating factors, and reasonable doubt, the colonel wasn't interested in building a prosecution against Dokka. The colonel asked about Havaa, and Ramzan, with a tightening in his gut that promised no parole of his captive bowels, understood that when a man is implicated in the assassination of a colonel, his entire family must disappear, even if his entire family is an eight-year-old girl.

When it was done, and Ramzan emerged from the woods after speaking with the Cossack colonel for the second time, he forced himself to walk to Dokka's house. An ache radiated from his temples. He closed his eyes. What did you do with that gun, Dokka? You stupid man. I can't buy your life this time. With each step he discarded a piece of himself. Even as he gave up his neighbors, he cocooned himself in the rationale of exigency. Whether eating scavenged food or selling an old friend, they had all shamed themselves to survive. Greed didn't motivate his informing, at least not primarily; primarily, he informed by necessity, to survive, for his love and hate and above all awe of the power wielded by the interrogating officer with less shiny shoes. But by giving away Dokka and the girl, he had stepped into full accountability, and lost the shadows that had saved him.

A few seconds after the knock, the door opened by the ingenious foot-operated pulley system Dokka had designed from a timber saw band, a shopping-cart wheel, and a stirrup.

Dokka welcomed him, invited him in. Not a trace of suspicion. Dokka, he realized with painful clarity, was the only person, besides the Feds, who would speak with him. The only person who tolerated his voice, who would listen and respond, and it was at that moment, he would later realize, that the universe went silent. He could have pinned the gun on Akhmed, on anyone. Why, this one time, had he told the truth? Again Dokka invited him in. Only then, with Dokka's hospitality, friendship, and conversation before him, did Ramzan understand why he had inflicted this visit upon himself.

"Oh, no," Ramzan said, when Dokka beckoned to the kitchen table. "I just stopped by to see if you needed any firewood."

"You left a heap in the backyard just the other day."

"Yes, I know, I just wanted to see if . . ." He bit his lip and glanced to the threshold, scuffed and worn by the feet of hundreds of passing refugees. It would record the footfall of those who would disappear Dokka and his daughter that night. He looked up into Dokka's brown eyes.

"Are you all right?" Dokka asked. "You look ill."

I'm sorry, Dokka. Look at you. I'm sorry.

"Ramzan?"

I came to say good-bye, he thought. "I came to say hello," he said.

1994 1995 1996 1997 1998 1999 2000 2001 2002 2003 **2004**

"SO THIS IS why they keep you around?" Akhmed said to the one-armed guard, who just then, in the hospital parking lot, floundered under the weight of a heavy box. A blue throbbing vein surfaced on the guard's valiant left forearm. "Do you moonlight as a professional mover?" Akhmed asked. He leaned against the jeep, casually smoking a cigarette. "Half-off moving?"

"May I shoot him, Dr. Sonja?" the one-armed guard asked, hopefully.

She smiled at these two buffoons—the one-armed guard threatened to kick Akhmed's ass with his *two* working legs—and they had to be buffoons, because every hospital employee with a kopek of common sense had left. "I need his arms," she called after the guard, who was chasing Akhmed across the parking lot. "Don't shoot him until we get all the supplies inside."

When they finished unloading, she went to the canteen cupboard. Behind the shoebox of loose cash, the clattering ID cards, the plastic bag of heroin, stood the good stuff: cans of sweetened condensed milk. The sweet syrup gurgled from the cut triangle, a thick coating on her gums, and for a few succulent seconds her mind narrowed to the width of that sugary stream. "Sweetened condensed milk will rot your mouth but preserve your soul," advised her father's aunt Lena, who died in a Grozny nursing home at the age of one hundred and three, having outlived two husbands, six children, three grandchildren, and thirty-two teeth. The maternity ward was empty, the trauma quiet, and Sonja closed her eyes, slipped into this unexpected peace as she would warm, cleansing water.

She climbed to the fourth floor. The swinging doors of the old maternity ward crooned as she entered. The droplet flame of her cigarette lighter guided her to an oil lamp and expanded to fill the glass chamber. When she lifted the lamp the light peeled back the shadows. In the years since their completion, Natasha's murals had faded and smudged as if a fog had fallen across the city. Even so, the degree of detail still amazed her. There, in the window that held half of City Park, a dog had been, for eight years now, relieving itself on a commissar's leg.

"You didn't show me this on the tour."

He had changed into those ridiculous woman-sized scrubs and leaned against the doorframe, trying and failing to act casual. Buffoons, imbeciles, orphans, lunatics, and visionaries; family. "I'm sorry," she said. "For earlier today."

He shrugged; was there no end to the number of shrugging shoulders she was asked to decipher? "What is this?" he asked, glancing to the walls.

"The old maternity ward."

"On the fourth floor?"

"The genius of Soviet engineering," she said, shaking her head. "The hospital was designed in the early Brezhnev years entirely without the input of practicing physicians. After the Feds shot a rocket at the storage closet, we finally decided to move everything to the first floor."

The shadows slipped from his face as he stepped into the pool of lantern light.

"Did you draw these?" he asked, nodding to the nearest window mural.

"Natasha did."

"What was she like?" he asked, tilting his face to her.

She had described Natasha to border guards, camp officials, and aid workers. Hazel eyes, brown hair, one hundred seventy centimeters in height, sixty kilograms in weight, no tattoos or piercings, no visible scars but cigarette burns clustered on her left shoulder; she incanted the litany, scribbled it on paperwork as an unconscious doodle, but how could an instrument as blunted as language express one as strange and fleeting as Natasha? Metaphors failed her; Natasha could not be summarized. What she possessed were losses: the loss of Natasha's laugh, the loss of Natasha's scorn, the loss of Natasha's begrudging love; and as a phantom limb can ache and tickle, her lost Natasha was still laughing, still scornful, still loving begrudgingly, burgeoning with enough life to make Sonja wonder if she, herself, was the one disappeared.

"Natasha was complex," she said finally, which was as near to the truth as she could articulate.

"Is," he corrected. "She will come back. Like a George Bush."

Smiling stupidly, she shrugged, at long last discovering the gesture's utility. Akhmed's cheeks bunched at the corners of his grin. His confidence was so big and brash she might believe it if she wasn't careful. It was that hope, lingering in the slimmest margins of possibility, that hurt her more than the loss; unlike Natasha, it never disappeared entirely. "Talking about it doesn't do any good," she said, glad, at least, that Natasha wasn't there to hear her admit it.

"Dokka was disappeared once, and he returned. Without his fingers, but still. I hope he does again."

This is the hardest part, she could have told him, before time dulls the loss to a manageable ache. But he and the girl still joked with a levity Sonja couldn't have summoned a year after Natasha left, and that capacity for joy unsettled her.

"Would you love her," she asked, unable to mask her unease, "if you had children of your own?"

"It's hard to know," he said. "I've always loved her. But she is mine, now, more than anyone's. If I had a family, I might know better what to say. But she's mine. That I know."

Once, after she had renounced her family in a childhood tantrum, her father had said, "Your family isn't your choice." Nearly thirty years later, while walking through City Park, she had seen two homeless men wedged into a single sleeping bag, their soot-stained arms wrapped around one another, and finally understood what her father had meant.

"It's funny," he said, walking to the window. "A friend of mine told me about this mural years ago."

"Did he have a child delivered here?"

"I doubt it." He stood in reverent concentration a hand's width from the ply boards. "He's nearly eighty."

"She worked on them for such a long time. I'd never seen her devote so much of herself to anything. I was so proud of her. Deshi and Maali helped her." Natasha had once described it as transcribing their memories, a turn of phrase so lovely Sonja was unwilling to share it with him.

"I'd forgotten completely, otherwise I would have asked to see them sooner. When Khassan told me about them, I was so moved that someone would go to the trouble. It seemed like such a big beautiful waste of time. You can imagine how much that would appeal to me. So I did something similar."

Her heart rose a centimeter. Even disappeared, Natasha was still surprising her. "Because of my sister's murals?"

"Yes, I suppose so. I told you about the wounded rebels that occupied the village? The Feds came next. Forty-one of my neighbors were disappeared. I remembered what Khassan had told me about the room with its view recreated on boarded windows, and I drew portraits of all forty-one on plywood boards and hung them throughout the village."

"Everyone here is a fucking artist," she said, shaking her head. "If you people spent more time fighting and less time drawing, you might win a war now and then."

"It was medical school that did it to me." He leaned to her and dropped his voice to an exaggerated, conspiratorial whisper. "I used to skip lectures and labs to sit in on art classes. That's why I'm a better drawer than physician."

"I can't believe you told me that."

"I'm trusting you with my darkest secret," he said, so pleased with himself she couldn't avoid laughing with him.

"I could lose my job for knowing that and keeping you on. Criminal neglect."

"Obviously you are a criminal, look at the company you keep. International smugglers and amateur artists." His left arm had steadily edged toward hers. "You could fire me."

"It's too late for that," she said, and focused on the women's scrubs cinched around his biceps, how ridiculous he looked. There had been fourteen since the elevators last ran: four Russians, six Chechens, two Ingush, one French physician, and a Finnish journalist, who she fucked before granting an interview. None knew her surname or patronymic; anonymity was the most comprehensive prophylactic. And the sex itself, infrequent and illicit and often awkwardly impersonal, fulfilled her more wholly than anything a husband could provide. As someone whose days were defined by the ten thousand ways a human can hurt, she needed, now and then, to remember that the nervous system didn't exist exclusively to feel pain.

"Even before those portraits, people from neighboring farms and villages would come to my clinic, people who didn't have photographs of their lost ones. I'd draw them." He said it as if it had happened centuries ago.

"Like a police sketch artist?"

"If I must be an -ist I'd prefer portraitist."

And then it was so obvious.

"Draw her for me," she asked. "Now. Draw the face of the woman who told you my name."

When he returned with a notebook and pencil, they sat at the counter. He opened the notebook.

"I only barely remember her," he said, in apology or indemnity, she couldn't tell.

She nodded at him to begin. If she opened her mouth, if she tapped that reservoir, nothing would stopper it. He folded the notebook at the spine and drew a line so soft it looked halfway erased. An oval. It could be anyone's head, even Natasha's. Next he drew two smaller ovals, right in the middle of her head, too long, until she imagined bangs. The two eyes watched her from the page. When he began drawing the wrong nose, she squeezed his wrist.

"That's not . . ." She struggled to push words into the sentence. She would regret this. She knew she would. But she hadn't seen her sister's face in twelve months, two weeks and three days, and even more than Natasha's face, even more than her return, she wanted Natasha to end. "Her nose was smaller," she said.

For the next half hour she gently corrected him whenever he strayed. He hadn't forgotten her face, she told herself; she was only helping him remember. And if she was deluding herself, so what? Weren't delusions better than desperation, false hopes better than none at all? As Natasha's calm, untroubled face emerged, Sonja's heart climbed her ribs. It drummed against each one, then rose to her neck, pressing against her throat. In a refugee camp or foreign country, somewhere far away, Natasha was safe. He drew a chin she would recognize in a crowd of thousands, then down to her perfect, unblemished neck. Not one cigarette burn; she hadn't told him to put them there. Something spectacular was happening in her chest. She hadn't expected this. On one sheet of paper in a notebook of two hundred and twenty, and with no more than a few millimeters of pencil lead, he returned Natasha to her and to the maternity ward.

"Please stop," she said.

"I thought you wanted this?"

He reached for her shoulder and she turned away. "I'll see you tomorrow," he said after a moment.

"Take this with you."

He lifted Natasha from the counter and carried her from the maternity ward.

CHAPTER

2 0

1994 **1995 1996** 1997 1998 1999 2000 2001 2002 2003 2004

SHE WAS SOLD to a brothel within bullet range of Kosovo, and from there south through the cinderblock city of Tirana and across the Adriatic, where, rocking on the dull green water, she saw the face of the moon for the first time in five weeks. It, too, was cratered with cigarette burns. Her passport was her deed, her title, and bill of sale, carried by whoever owned her today, traveling within reach of her hand but never in it. Through it all, she could count on a ritual as fixed in the day as sunrise and set. Every morning a shot of heroin inflated her head so it floated a meter above her neck until noon. By afternoon she's itching. By evening she'll do whatever they ask to get a shot that night. She's not the high-priced, high-class call girl she had imagined, borne by limousine to fancy hotels, where she knows the doormen by name and tips them generously when she saunters into the night a free woman. She couldn't buy a full bag of groceries with what the johns pay for thirty minutes. It feels like autumn, but maybe it's spring. She can't tell, fifteen stories above the nearest leaf. She can't remember the year or the city, the taste of fresh air or the feel of her passport, her sister's voice or the love and desperation that compelled her to flee, but she stands by the window and remembers the view; in eight months, when it's all over and she's taking three-hour showers in a women's shelter, she will walk to the bathroom mirror and, angle by angle, she will draw it on the steamed glass. The men call her Natasha, but she doesn't know how they know her name. Finally Katya tells her that's what every girl from Eastern Europe is called, we're all Natashas to them. An average day consists of ten men, three cheeseburgers, eight glasses of tap water, and two shots. A toothbrush, no toothpaste. A roll of Certs, one after each man. The repatriated women are right: modern-day slavery, but there's nothing modern about it. Eight of you sleep on four bunk beds crammed into a bedroom. In the early morning, midafternoon, whenever the clouds part, when the heroin slithers into your blood and you forget your name, you stand at the window and thread the eternity of sky through needle-head retinas. Block after block the city goes on and every last building, right up to the horizon, stands. Sergey, the pimp, whose brother was sent back from Grozny in a zinc can, quit smoking last week or last month and the spent pieces of his nicotine gum, spat out and dried on the floor, look like little gray brains. One Natasha died, seven Natashas left; a new Natasha walked in the room and asked if this was where the au pairs slept. You are all replaceable, all disposable. Sergey reads business books and listens to lectures on free-market capitalism and, sometimes, in the middle of it, you can hear the lectures through the wall, through the grunting flab atop you, and listening to *free trade* and *commodity economy* leaves you with a rich nostalgia for the relative generosity of totalitarianism. There is the night, the last night, the next night. The belt around your ankle, the two taps of the syringe, the blood into the barrel, the plunger pushing in. There is the woman named Anzhela but called Natasha. The woman named Nadya but called Natasha. The woman named Natasha, called Natasha.

# CHAPTER

## 21

AT DAYBREAK KHASSAN left for the service road half hoping to intercept Akhmed, but all he found was a fresh set of footprints. Not knowing what else to do, he walked back and forth, urging the dogs to do likewise, and together they turned five kilometers of snow into a riddle no one could solve. Khassan had taken off his gloves, periodically oiling his fingers with butter, and for five kilometers lapping tongues warmed his knuckles. The bald one, Kashtanka, shivered like a prenatal rat, and several times Khassan paused to reattach the blanket tied by twine around the dog's pale torso. In summer he bathed the dogs. If one fell sick he cared for it. At the village edge, he knelt and they gathered to him, leaping, licking his cheeks, leaning their paws on his back and panting in his ears, diseased, unwashed, his, his, his. When he stood, all six followed with Sharik at the rear. It wasn't yet nine o'clock. The day stretched out and his path in it lay as meandering and meaningless as the one he had left. Before the bend in the road he saw Akhmed's house and across from it the gap that had been Dokka's. If he had seen Akhmed that morning, he would have had to ask permission to visit Ula; if he had asked permission, he might have been denied. It was a better excuse than the frigid air to stay curled under the covers those extra minutes.

The dogs lounged in the snowy lawn to wait for him. He crept through the shadows of the living room, careful not to disturb the curtains, and into the bedroom where Ula slept fitfully. He hesitated to wake her, as if he were no more than her troubled dream and would dissolve if he touched her. Her hair clumped in greasy cords and she smelled of talcum powder. In the kitchen he filled a stew pot with clean water and set it beside the bed. He drew the covers to Ula's chin, so when she woke she wouldn't worry about her decency. Then, reluctantly, he rubbed her arm.

"Why are you here?" she asked without even the suggestion of surprise in her face.

"Do you remember me?" he asked, more urgently than he had intended.

She narrowed her eyes.

"I must have lived a thousand lives before this. I was a bird. I was a bug. I lived in the leaves. I don't know which life is the hallucination."

"You're Ula," he said. "You're married to Akhmed."

"Why are you here?" Again she asked the question; again he didn't answer.

Because his son was the reason she spent the day alone. Because keeping her comfortable, keeping her company, caring for her was the least he could do. Because he was lonely. Because he had forgotten a woman's companionship. Because the thought of talking himself senile to a pack of feral dogs didn't appeal to him this early in the day. He looked to the stew pot of water beside the bed. Because she forgot. Because she forgot everything he said. "I'm here to wash your hair."

She nodded and he peeled back the blanket, her skin whiter than a Russian's. Sometimes Akhmed carried her outside to the rocking chair and she would sit without rocking, swathed in blankets even in the sticky summer months. Khassan turned her so her hair hung off the side of the bed and into the water. The soap gave a fine lather, and he ran his fingers through the water, and broke the bubbles against her scalp, and washed away the grease and dead skin. After it was washed and rinsed, he wrapped her hair in a towel and propped her upright against the headboard.

"You look like a sheikh with that turban around your head," he said.

"Why are you here?" she asked.

"I'm here to finish telling you a story."

She smiled, pleased with his answer. "You might have to repeat things. You may not know but my memory isn't what it once was."

He began where he had stopped, on the steppe, where the next morning he and Mirza boarded the train from Kazakhstan to Chechnya. Eldár was a ghost town when the survivors among its former residents returned. Soviet soldiers tasked with building a new thoroughfare had uprooted all the tombstones from the village cemetery. Khassan entered the village on a street scrawled with epitaphs. Dust added an extra half centimeter of height to the tabletop, the shelves, and floor. The air was too thick to breathe, and so on his first night home, he slept outside. The next morning, under an awning of bulbous gray clouds, he buried the brown suitcase in the back garden.

He was thirty-one years old and enrolled in the history doctoral program at Volchansk State University. On the day of Mirza's wedding, he barricaded himself in the university library. He had considered kidnapping her, as Chechen grooms had done since time immemorial when failing to receive the approval of a bride's parents. But he didn't want to earn a reputation as a bride kidnapper, particularly not among his professors, and besides, it was too late. That afternoon she would marry the botanist she'd been betrothed to since her ninth birthday, and if botany wasn't bad enough, the man also had a clubfoot and a collection of pressed flowers. All through the day Khassan read thick philosophical tomes, but not one explained the injustice of a world in which he would lose Mirza to a clubfooted botanist with a passion for pressed flowers. The botanist was a decent man, but Khassan was in love, and thus capable of infinite hate.

About the time he began writing the book that would occupy his life, Khassan embarked on a smaller, secondary project of historical reclamation. On notecards he recorded the recollections friends, neighbors, and distant relations had of his family, and pinned them to the walls of what had been his sister's room. All were small and ordinary—his sister's hiccupping laugh, his father's wish for the smallest denominations of change so his pockets would jingle like a rich man's—but when he read them, alone in the house they once had shared, these unremarkable memories returned with an unforeseen force. When one wall was covered from floor to ceiling, he began populating the room with artifacts of Mirza, as though she too had receded into the past that had claimed his family. He followed her. When, at the bazaar, she purchased a ball of ruby-red yarn, he purchased the tangerine ball adjacent; when she wore a gray cardigan with silver buttons, he found that same gray cardigan, with brass buttons. While the clubfooted botanist collected flowers, Khassan collected his wife. The notecard-papered room soon filled with the headscarves she'd never worn, the cigarettes she'd never smoked, and in the evenings he would flop into the teal-striped armchair, so similar to the navy-striped armchair in her living room, and would read while sipping from a teacup a centimeter narrower than hers, and for a few moments, if lucky, he would forget and she would be standing just out of sight, refilling the samovar, or perhaps knitting a pair of tangerine mittens, and his happiness became the one real artifact in the room.

So it went. Seven years passed before he spoke again to the real Mirza, on an autumn afternoon as uninspiring as every afternoon that autumn, when the blast of a Volchansk bus horn broke the silence. He had just left the library in a frantic search for matches when he heard the punched blare. He turned, and had the Prophet himself stood there, he would have been no more surprised. She wore the gray sweater; the silver buttons really did look better than brass. The flailing ends of a ruby-red scarf tossed at her shoulders. The bus had braked less than a meter from where she stood; he could have bowed down and blackened his lips on that hallowed pavement. Their eyes met. She blushed; not with surprise or astonishment, but with the downcast embarrassment of one who has been caught.

He invited her to the university cafeteria. They picked awkwardly at a pastry plate, and she tried to convince him that she had come to the city for a dental appointment, and he gave assurances that he believed her. But her sheepishness dissolved as quickly as the spoonful of sugar in her second cup of tea. Her short, filed fingernails darted across the partition of silverware. They spoke for two hours, and when the cafeteria lady's disapproving glances lingered too long, Mirza asked for a tour of the library. She hurried from one stack to the next, wide-eyed and awed, and only later, when he'd checked out a dozen books for her, did he learn that this was her first time in a library. He carried them to his office, which did not, he could safely say, have the same impact. It was, quite literally, the broom closet. The brooms were gone—he'd thrown them out when he'd been assigned the office—but the closet was barely wide enough to accommodate the smallest university desk, which was wedged in so tightly tissue paper couldn't have slipped between it and the wall. Her days were empty, she confessed; would it be possible to come to the university a few days a week and read in his office? This Mirza was entirely different than the younger one who had smashed Stalin's plaster nose with the heel of her boot. Perhaps he had changed, too; but he loved her no less.

Twice a week they met at the corner, mindful of oncoming buses. He saw her in the gray sweater with the silver buttons, the blue sweater with the fake ivory buttons, the green sweater with no buttons. They passed a cigarette back and forth, and when he felt the damp of her lips on the filter, the world became big and beautiful. His office could only accommodate one chair, so she would read her books there while he worked in the library. One afternoon he returned a half hour earlier than usual and found her hunched over a huge stack of typewritten paper. From the flipped-over pages, he could see that she was at least two-thirds through *his* manuscript. A breeze would have broken him. "This is wonderful," she said, standing, as if baffled that he was capable of anything wonderful. His tilted gaze found her ankles. They were lovely ankles. She praised his book and he embraced her from gratitude rather than lust, but she didn't let go. Neither did he. She kissed his cheek, his earlobe. For months they'd run their fingers around the hem of their affection without once acknowledging the fabric. The circumference of the world tightened to what their arms encompassed. She sat on the desk, between the columns of read and unread manuscript, and pulled him toward her by his index fingers.

It was over in ninety seconds. He walked her to the *marshrutka* stop. When she boarded the shared taxi-bus, he followed. He sat beside her and angled his leg against hers, and they rode silently, two strangers with a secret held like a sheet of paper between their knees. She met him at the back of his house and at the door she stood red-cheeked and shivering, and he took her hands. She was his home. The only land that bound him. He led her to the notecard-papered room and didn't have to explain a thing. She saw the yarn and knew. She unwound the ruby scarf from her neck and added it to his collection. This time they undressed before making love. The birthmark he remembered so vividly was still there, a purple ink-spill across her kidney, the only part of her that hadn't aged. The affair lasted another eleven months, until she became pregnant. For several years she had tried with her husband, who had resorted to root-based aphrodisiacs brewed by an elderly widow— after the story spread, the widowed herbalist received enough business to become the wealthiest woman in the village, and soon received a number of marriage proposals herself—and whether the father was he or the root-remedied botanist, Khassan never knew. Akhmed was born on July 1, 1965; that was all that mattered. Mirza died when she was thirty-nine. Akhmed was seven. The cancer in her stomach was just eight months old. After she passed, Khassan and the botanist became friends. Both shared the same object of love and loss, and though they never discussed it, Khassan suspected the botanist knew. The botanist allowed him to be an uncle to Akhmed, a figure whom Akhmed could love without having to rely on, and in this way, regardless of true paternity, he was a better father to Akhmed than he ever was to Ramzan.

"Even you know that, Ula. You just have to look at how each turned out."

When Khassan returned home, Ramzan was sitting at the table, though sitting generously described his posture, which slumped so low the chair back loomed over his head. The sharp reek of liquor coated the air. Perhaps it had dissolved his son's spine.

Teetering against the table, Ramzan kept his voice steady; he still hadn't seen his father at the door. "There's nothing to eat and I can't shit. I don't understand it, do you? How can I be constipated when you've given all the meat to those filthy dogs? The sleeping pills. Maybe it's that. Maybe it's the weather. Maybe December has frozen my bowels." He spoke in the vacant monotone of a man who knew no one was listening, and it was awful for Khassan to hear his son's voice, whittled by loneliness, addressing an empty chair. A few years earlier, Khassan hadn't been able to get him to answer a yes-or-no question; now no question Ramzan posed and answered was so simple.

If not for Ula, Khassan would have shut the door and returned to his dogs. He would have followed them through the alleyways, through the refuse-strewn gutters, to the thin strips of twig shadow that made mazes on the forest floor, until their upturned snouts pointed to him, eager, hungry. If not for Ula, he would have ignored his son's voice in the morning and at midday and in the evening, when he said good-bye to his pack and returned home to prepare his insulin shot. The day would have silently joined the hundreds of others, if not for Ula. But he had spoken to Ula, and the relief of unburdening still lifted him, and today, he decided, would be the day he spoke to the one person who was waiting to hear from him.

"You can't shit?" he asked softly. He had forgotten the tone of chastisement. "It could be the sleeping pills you take to fall asleep among ghosts. It could be Alman, or Musa, or Omar, or Aslan, or Apti, or Mansur, or Aslan the Hirsute, or Ruslan, or Amir, or Amir Number Two, or Isa, or Khalid, or even Dokka. Probably Dokka." He layered his voice with all the animosity it could sustain. He had never spoken this way. For one year, eleven months, and four days the pleas, admonitions and prayers he had wanted to utter never left his lungs. The weight of all he hadn't said hung like a dead organ in his chest. He could barely breathe. He, too, knew what it was to have waste you cannot dislodge.

Ramzan's face lit with surprise. "I've been waiting to hear you say that," he said. A beaming grin stripped the shadows from his features. Khassan's silence had been so long and lonesome that to Ramzan this voice of denouncement was both victory and absolution. The sound of his father's voice was all that mattered; its message was irrelevant. "But you can't speak to me like that," he added, clasping tightly to the thread and hoping argument would unspool more of his father's voice.

"You're telling me how to speak?" Khassan's temples throbbed. "A son tells his father? A boy? A . . ." He stopped before belittling Ramzan's manhood.

"You think you live ten centimeters off the ground, but who gets you the food you throw away to mutts?" Ramzan spoke with slow, savage joy, pinning each word to his father. "In fifty kilometers I couldn't find enough aspirin to dull a hangover, but every other week I bring you insulin. You should be grateful. I allow you both to survive and to resent me for it."

Khassan's breaths couldn't come fast enough. A dull, vise-like clarity crushed whatever fatherly affection survived the silence. For all the lies Ramzan lived by, he was still capable of speaking the truth, and it was for the truth, rather than the lies, that Khassan hated him. He had once held his hand over Ramzan's bassinet and the boy's fingers had wound around his like little vines. He had once lifted the boy and seen miracles in his deep, unblinking eyes. "You are nothing to me," he finally said.

But Ramzan, still grinning, still unaccountably joyous, said, "Just like your book? Are you going to carry me to the woods and burn me?"

"I treasured that book more than anyone."

"I know, more than my mother."

"She knew exactly who I was when she accepted my proposal."

"She thought you were Albert Einstein, that the honor of your genius would compensate for your neglect. You treat your dogs better."

"That's not true," Khassan said, uncertain how the conversation had turned against him.

"A genius, she thought. As if Albert Einstein would forget his wife's birthday."

What had possessed him to speak? Two more silent years would hurt less than one more minute of this. He had expected Ramzan's vehemence, his blather, but hadn't expected his concision. Hadn't expected that the son who had destroyed his reputation, his name, his faith in human goodness, would find new ways to ruin him. More than his paternal failures, it was the grinning joy his son took in describing them that Khassan would remember. Eyes skewed with jubilation. Khassan recognized them as his own. It was the conversation he'd feared since Ramzan's birth. Since the woman who wasn't Mirza had said, in an exhausted ache, a word that should have wrapped them together: "Ours."

Since he had held him, no more than a bald head and blankets, and wished the child in his arms were Akhmed. You poor thing. You never had a chance.

"I haven't been a good father, I know, I know, I know, I know, I know, I know, I know, I know, I know, I know," and he kept repeating it, the needle stuck on this one proclamation he stated and restated so Ramzan wouldn't. "But I never hurt you," he said finally. "I never laid a finger on either of you."

"You were a mouth that only opened to eat. Just like now. And what's worse is you squandered what you had. You were physically capable of having a wife and son, but you didn't want us."

"I'm sorry for what happened to you," he said. Even in apology he couldn't name it. March 2, 1995, eight days after Ramzan's twenty-third birthday, he'd never forget the day. The transport truck didn't slow down when Ramzan was pushed from the back. The adult diapers they'd dressed him in were maroon. Finding his boy, right there, in the road, my god, his horror had left him speechless. Akhmed had treated Ramzan's wound and was the only other villager to know of it. For weeks Khassan had tended to his son, taking him meals in bed, reading him pulp fiction, coaxing the spark of life from his dull, brutalized eyes. Ramzan had never recovered, not fully, not physically, not existentially. The Landfill had snapped him as cleanly as a branch and all the tea and small talk in Chechnya wouldn't put his halves back together. He never spoke of what had happened there. His pride for what he had done and his disgrace for the consequence were so entwined that he couldn't even tell his father that he had been castrated for refusing to inform on his neighbors. "I mourn the life you weren't able to experience," Khassan said. "For the father you might have become, for all our sakes."

"And I mourn the father you might have been," Ramzan said. The taunt peeled from his voice and behind it lay unvarnished, unfathomable need. Khassan's face felt so heavy. He had expected false accusations, dissemblance; he hadn't expected honesty. The floorboards ached as he turned to the door. In his head he heard the jingle from the television show that had followed the nightly news in the seventies, a stupidly cheerful song, sung by collective laborers, whose melody had once worked on his ears like a reverse alarm clock, a ringing that had let him know it was time to sleep, to rest, to dream; and though he hadn't thought of the song in years, it came to him now, every note, and he hummed it beneath his breath as he held the doorframe, and wanted to die.

"You think I'm selfish, but I'm not," Ramzan said, behind him, with unbearable sincerity. "I meant what I said about the insulin. This will all be over, eventually. We just need to survive it. You can't survive without insulin. We both need food, right?"

"I'm seventy-nine years old. Seventy-nine. The rest of my life is not worth the rest of Havaa's or Dokka's or Akhmed's."

"I'm not holding a gun to anyone's head."

"Ramzan." Khassan sighed. A wave of exhaustion seeped through him. "You're putting the bullets in the chamber."

"I'm just like you! You said you never laid a finger on my mother or me. I've never laid a finger on anyone either!"

"That's all?"

"That's all."

"Just a name over the phone?"

"That's all!"

"Then another name, no? And another, and another, and another, and another, and another, and another, and another, and another, and another, and another, and then Dokka?" He found his own bewilderment reflected in Ramzan's eyes. His stupid, stupid child didn't understand what he was doing or why any more than Khassan did.

"It was for us. So that we'll survive together. You're the only person I have. You're my family." It was the saddest, sweetest thing he'd ever heard. In another world he would have embraced Ramzan, kissed his forehead, held him so that his son's heart beat indistinguishably against his own.

He walked to the table, cupped Ramzan's shoulder. His grip was strong and consoling. He imagined Ibrahim on the mountaintop and the verses returned unbidden: *My son, I dreamt that I was sacrificing you.*

"You speak of family; then let Akhmed and Havaa be."

"I know you want him for your son. I've known that my whole life."

"And so what if he is, Ramzan?" Khassan asked, clutching Ramzan's shoulder. "What then?"

Ramzan's face went flat, cold, depthless. "None of us is bound to anyone by so trivial a distinction. Do you think paternity even matters? No, Father, no. We are the children of wolves. That's all, Father. He could be your son, your brother, your nephew, your neighbor, your friend, and I wouldn't save him."

"And yet you save me. What a waste."

Khassan walked to the door, opened it to the wind. He looked back. Ramzan watched him, as frozen and impenetrable as a winter pond. *You are mine. I recognize you. We twist our souls around each other's miseries. It is that which makes us family.*

Outside, his dogs were waiting for him.

CHAPTER

2 2

THE VILLAGE CHIMNEYS were sending up smoke among the birch trunks when Akhmed heard a low whistle from the trees. Khassan, surrounded by his guard of feral dogs, stepped into the road with an orange hand cupping the flashlight. The dogs, watchful, ears erect, studied him warily.

"I didn't want Ramzan to see me waiting for you," Khassan said. His fingers glowed.

"He was waiting for me last night, asking about Havaa."

"I spoke with him today. For the first time in two years. My own son. I begged him."

The statement knocked Akhmed a step back. Surprised, honored, grateful that the man would break the silence for Havaa's sake, his sake, he set his palm on those radiant fingers and the road was dark again. "It's all right."

"I'm sorry, Akhmed, I'm—" A sob halved the old man's voice and Akhmed gripped his fingers. When his mother died, Khassan wept at the burial. When Akhmed's father died, Khassan provided the shroud. Akhmed had always remembered this, how Khassan had shared his mourning as if he were family. Dog paws pattered in the undergrowth.

"So they will come for me." For years he'd lived with the fear of murder, torture, or disappearance, as all men of his age did, and it was the senselessness that truly frightened him; that the monumental finality of death could come arbitrarily was more terrifying than the eternity to follow. But if his death severed the connection between city and village, it would be neither futile nor insignificant, and he would be more fortunate than many thousands of his countrymen.

"I don't know," Khassan said. His hands shook under Akhmed's.

"And Ramzan doesn't know where I've been these past three days?"

"I don't think he wants to know. So long as the burden of disclosure is on you, some small corner of his conscience can stay clean."

He imagined her right then, annoying Sonja, asking her to explain why feces are brown, why ears bend, so young and silly and smart. She was a child without parents, and he was a man without children. Ten years earlier he couldn't have imagined claiming her, but the rules of that society had broken. There was no one left to say whom you could love.

"I won't say a word," Akhmed whispered.

"I'm sorry."

"Havaa is my only allegiance." The moon outlined Khassan's face. Tears rimmed his eyelids, and his lips pressed into a tight frown, but he didn't appear contrite. If Akhmed hadn't known better, he would have thought it was an expression of overwhelming pride.

"Do you remember in the first war, Dokka carried a book with him everywhere?" Akhmed asked. "Whenever the Feds passed, Dokka would open his book and start reading."

Khassan gave a relieved grin. "The Feds thought the rebels were il-
literate, so by reading a book he proved he wasn't a rebel."

"But it wasn't even a book, was it?"

"No, a journal. All the pages were blank. But they couldn't tell that."

They laughed and the flashlight beam tore hoops in the shadows.

"And he wasn't shot," Khassan mused.

"No, not then."

Khassan pulled a manila envelope from his overcoat and passed it to
Akhmed. The exchange, Akhmed thought, was the nearest thing to a
postal service in many years. "I was hoping you could give this to Havaa.
It's a letter, some memories of Dokka before he became a father. So
she'll have something to look to when she's older."

"I'm glad you're optimistic," Akhmed said.

"What do I do? I know what honor requires, but *that*? To my own
son? With my own hands? Am I expected to do *that*? Tell me what to
do, Akhmed. You know that your name is the next he'll give the Feds.
You tell me, what should a father do?" Khassan had leaned forward, his
stale, quick breaths warming Akhmed's cheek, his hands reaching for
Akhmed's shoulders. It was a peculiar sensation. They had never hugged
before.

"I don't know," Akhmed said. There was no right answer and he was
too tired, too cold, and too close to home to sift through all the wrong
ones. "I've never been a father. I don't know what you should do."

"I'm not asking for your approval. I'm asking for your advice."

Akhmed nodded. "I'll think about it."

Khassan stepped back and his face, paled in moonlight, shifted violently. He opened his mouth, but for a moment only his eyes spoke.
Akhmed would have filled the fragile space between them with gratitude. He would have thanked Khassan for the advice, the stories, the
meals, the cigarettes, the silences, everything, even the interminable
history lessons, they had shared over the years. He would have said that
Khassan had been like a father to him, in the ten years since his own

father had passed. He would have said it, but Khassan spoke first. "I feel fortunate to know who you are, Akhmed. I've wanted to say that for a long time."

Their eyes met and broke away. Such naked acknowledgment of their relationship embarrassed them both, and nodding, turning toward the village, Akhmed said nothing.

He entered the musty blindness of the living room and crept toward the bedroom's lantern light. "It's me," he said, in the doorway. "How are you?"

Beneath the blankets, Ula turned and smiled lazily. "Oh, just fine. Fine and fine. Your father came again. He told me a bedtime story."

He prepared a dinner of lentils and canned apricots, pulled a chair beside the bed, and ate with her. His poor Ula. She really was losing her mind. Her health had improved in recent months, but this insistence that she spent her days with his ten-years-deceased father dispelled hope for recovery. Just as well. Her mind was one less thing she had left to lose. In a cigar box beneath the bed he hid a hypodermic needle and a vial of heroin he had swiped from the hospital.

After cleaning the dishes, he found his copy of *Hadji Murád*, steadying the wobbling dresser leg, and set it by the door. He secured the living room blackout curtains before opening Khassan's envelope. Brass fasteners bound forty or fifty sheets. He parted the pages at random. *Your father loved your mother's nose. It was a big, ungainly thing, and he said it was still growing, and was slowly taking over her cheeks and forehead, so her entire face would soon submerge beneath her nose.* He couldn't start, not now, and slid the sheets back into the manila envelope.

In bed he cupped Ula's bony hip. It wasn't the hip he'd held on their wedding night as he fumbled and grunted, so self-conscious about his performance he wasn't prepared for the embarrassment that accompanied the turn of her nose to the open window. But he loved it more, would miss it more. They used to argue about everything, quarrels that left them both hoarse the next morning, and they forgave each other in silence, with a cup of tea, a hand on the shoulder, unencumbered by the voices that divided them. He missed her scorn more than anything. How she looked at him as if he weren't there. How she knew what the whole village suspected: that he was an incompetent physician, a worse bookkeeper, a romantic, a man who was never happier than when sketching birds in the woods. How she knew that and still loved him. He ran his fingers through her hair. Days since he had last washed it, and still so clean. Praise Allah she is speaking with my father. If she is looking so far over the horizon, she won't see what's in front of her.

"Do you remember who I am?" he asked, but she had already fallen asleep.

"You know how those things were invented?" Sonja asked with a nod to the stethoscope the girl was using to listen to her own heartbeat. "It was invented by a French physician who had a very fat patient. The patient was so fat that the French physician couldn't hear the heartbeat through his chest. So he invented a stethoscope."

"That's weird," the girl said, shifting the bell like an indecisive chess piece. "I've never seen a fat person before."

"Never?"

"Never. But in my souvenirs I have the autograph of a man who used to be fat."

The girl noted her heart rate on the chart Sonja had given her. Overcome by an inexplicable interest in medicine, the girl, draped in a lab coat that swished against the linoleum, had been following Sonja since dinner. It took the better part of an hour before Sonja realized the girl was imitating her. Her raw exasperation softened to a more delicate displeasure when the girl began scolding the air for carrying contagions. Poor child, she thought, let's hope she finds a better role model.

The girl held the stethoscope bell like a microphone and, while kicking a drooping tail of bedsheet, began interviewing Sonja. "What's it like being a surgeon?" she asked.

"Wonderful. Next question."

"Why don't you have kids?"

"They ask too many questions."

"Who did you bribe to get into medical school?"

"Surprisingly, no one at all."

"And are you the only woman surgeon in the world?"

"It feels like it."

"What's your favorite disease?"

"Chlamydia."

"If they let you become a surgeon instead of a wife, would they let me become an arborist instead of a wife?"

"Who's 'they'?"

"You know."

"Tell me."

The girl's face hollowed with resignation; it had been a long time, but Sonja remembered what it was to have that face, what it was to feel you were no brighter than the dumbest man, no stronger than the weakest boy, and with those ideas crowding your head no wonder subordination was the only inevitable outcome. She sat on the hospital bed beside the girl, remembering what it was like to have that face, and pitying it. "Listen, Havaa," she said, summoning as much generosity as she could muster at this hour of night, "you can be exactly the person you want to be, okay? It may not seem that way, but things change when you get a little older. If you work hard, and give up certain things, and yes, resort to bribery now and then, you'll be an arborist, or a sea anemonist, or anything else you want."

And they kept talking, passing the stethoscope bell back and forth.

"Do you have any questions for me?" the girl asked at the end of the interview.

Since Akhmed had left that evening, Sonja had held the question as she would a long-awaited letter, terrified of what the envelope contained. "Did a Russian woman ever stay at your house?"

"Which one? Lots of people stayed with us."

"Her name was Natasha."

"Probably thirty Natashas at least."

"She looked like me."

Havaa gave her an appraising look. "Then no."

"Like me only beautiful."

The girl tilted her head. "I can't imagine that."

And it struck her. Why hadn't she thought of it sooner? Akhmed's sketch. She was upright and out of the room before Havaa could ask where she was going. Why had she asked him to take the portrait? Where would he have put it? She climbed to the fourth floor and worked her way back to her room, checking the new and old maternity wards, the land-mine man's room, the empty administrative offices, the waiting room. While searching, her mind flashed to the day she had purchased the Buckingham Palace Guard nutcracker. True to form it had endured flights across Europe, every bump of the Samsonite, and even the shame of Alu's name, without once breaking composure.

She had found the nutcracker in a convenience store sticky with the residue of spilled soda, where she stopped for cough drops before attending a lecture. It was four weeks to Christmas. The first war wouldn't officially begin for twelve more days. She had bought it without once thinking of Natasha, on a whim, because Buckingham Palace was what foreigners thought of when they thought of London and she, Sonja with a *j*, was nothing if not foreign. Gray clouds lined the horizon as she climbed the escalator at Holborn and crossed Lincoln's Inn Fields to the Royal College of Surgeons. There, at a neurosurgery lecture, she transcribed the snaking syntax of British academia in a bright pink notebook she had found in a fifty-pence bin. Attached to the Royal College was a museum dedicated to the history of anatomy and pathology. After thanking the lecturer, and pausing in the atrium for a cigarette and cough drop, she strolled through the museum's curious exhibitions. There was a display detailing the history of non-Egyptian mummification. An alcove devoted to the tibia. One room exhibited the 1,474 skulls collected by nineteenth-century physician Joseph Barnard Davis. A fractured skull of a Roman woman found at Pompeii. The skulls of nine Chinese pirates hanged in Ningpo. Congolese from Leopold's rubber plantations. But the skull that haunted her was that of a Bengali cannibal. Fully intact, the mandible still locked against the temporal, the twenty-two bones that constitute a human skull all accounted for. The eight bones forming the neurocranial brain case bathed in halogenated light. From the size of the plates, the prominence of the supraorbital ridge and temporal lines, as well as the overall size and solidity of the skull, she knew it belonged to a man. The skull appeared no different from those of the Chinese pirates, the Congolese plantation workers. She read the placard written a century and a half earlier by a Victorian phrenologist. *There are no characteristics to distinguish the cranium of a cannibal from that of an ordinary man.*

That morbid association between the cannibal and the nutcracker, one which she never mentioned to Natasha, was all she thought of while searching for the portrait. She finally found the notebook on the canteen counter, beneath a stack of folded linens. From the last page Natasha observed her calmly, through eyes unclouded by judgment or resentment, her hair held back with a headband she had never owned, her ears heavy with earrings that didn't exist. Clearly Akhmed hadn't met her.

Her footsteps, slowing to a processional as she neared her room, tapped like the last drops falling from a stopped faucet. She wanted to know and didn't want to know; the two were always there, always tearing at her, a tug-of-war in which she was the rope. But that was okay, she told herself. The truth was one more rumor passed along the refugee lines, another hallucination she could freely disbelieve. When she entered the room the girl was already asleep. She slid the portrait into one of the drawers, thankful to postpone the answer for one more night.

THE SECOND WAR, when it came to Volchansk, came without bomb blasts or mortar rounds, tracer bullets or tank treads. It came through the bazaar at first, a few more kopeks per gram of cardamom, a few more rubles per carrot, the deprivation subtle enough to blame on currency inflation, or global markets, or natural disasters. Then the electricity went. But the municipal power lines, restrung after the first war, never had carried a current for more than two hours at a stretch anyway, as likely to come at daybreak as midnight, fifteen or twenty minutes for Natasha to charge her batteries, pull news from the airwaves, hop in the shower and blow-dry her hair before the lights flickered and the city collapsed back into darkness. The tap water went next. With the remaining civilians she drew buckets from unboarded wells and strained the water through pillowcases before boiling it. Then food shortages.

No milk, then no plums, then no cabbages, then no corn meal. Even the feral animals quieted, the dogs stopped howling, the songbirds stopped singing. And though Federal forces invaded Chechnya in August 1999, the second war didn't begin for Natasha until the afternoon in 2001 when it marched through the doors of Hospital No. 6.

The skies of the maternity ward mural were as placid as on the day she had drawn them when she mistook the first crack for thunder. Gunshots followed as quickly as her footsteps as she ran downstairs. In trauma, Sonja and the nurses huddled by the aluminum filing cabinets.

"We could evacuate them to a village," Sonja suggested. "We have a truck."

"No," Deshi said. "We keep them here. This is a hospital. They belong here."

Maali assented. "Let's use them as human shields."

Natasha tried to wedge herself into the conversation, but as usual the triangle wouldn't widen into a square. She took a deep breath and turned. This isn't about you, she told herself. Your reaction is the only thing you can control. Who would have thought those books Sonja had brought with her the day she found ice were worth reading? In the five years she had worked here her emotional spectrum expanded beyond the monochromatic depression that had tinted her early days of recovery. *Recovery*. What a strange, wondrous word. None better defined her gradual reintegration into humanity. Nearly nine months of confinement, forced prostitution, beatings and heroin addiction, but she had come back. No one was more surprised than she herself, and no one was happier than Sonja. When Natasha was a teenager she once fell asleep on the roof and woke the color of borscht. The following week all the popular girls at school came in sunburned, and a week later the girls that wanted to be popular, until the principal, in an impromptu assembly, explained that girls had been known to roast alive while sunbathing. The memory was still there, tucked away in folds of time, and she found it again, with a smile, on the afternoons she climbed to the hospital roof to lie in the sun. Entire hours passed without her once thinking of Italy.

The nurses didn't want to hear from her, but the patients did. An elderly woman, Xenia, patient number 29395, repeatedly asked *what is happening*, more confused and hesitant with each reiteration, as her neighbor, her first cousin, begged her to shut up because her insufferable voice would kill him faster than any bullet or bomb. When the Whites had swept through Volchansk eighty-one years earlier, Xenia had asked her cousin the same question and her cousin had answered. Xenia had been six, her cousin seven. Her voice had been lovely then.

"We're figuring it out," Natasha said. "Don't worry. Can I get you some ice?"

Xenia gave her cousin a smug smile and nodded.

"Bring me the tongue depressor!" the cousin shouted after Natasha.

Two days earlier, when Xenia had arrived with pneumonia, Sonja had treated her lungs with the respect a plumber shows to blocked septic pipes. Her sister's work was undeniably good, but its execution bothered Natasha. To work in these circumstances a surgeon must reduce each patient to her body, but this was an attitude shared by the traffickers, pimps, and johns populating Natasha's private perdition. So while Sonja examined a cracked pelvis without once meeting the patient's eye, or addressed the patient by placard number rather than by name, Natasha sequestered herself in the fourth-floor maternity ward, where whole days passed without their paths crossing, where the wails of newborns reminded her that life is louder than its pulse. While Sonja debated the merits of evacuation, Natasha fed Xenia crushed ice with a plastic spoon and told her exactly what was happening.

Boot fall, echoing down the corridor, ended the debate. The security guard ran through the double doors, his arms pumping, his shirttail flapping behind him. "They're here," he called. He ran right past Sonja and out the back door, announcing his immediate resignation in a breathless shout.

"Who?" Sonja called after him. "Feds or rebels?" No answer. Xenia held an ice cube in her mouth, afraid to break it. No one spoke. The shuffle of military boots paused at the closed double doors. The air was stretched so taut Natasha could have walked across it. A sharp kick, initially mistaken for a gunshot, jolted them all and flung open the double doors. Four bearded men entered with machine guns raised.

"I retired seven years ago," Deshi said to no one in particular.

"We hereby liberate this hospital for patriotic use for the glorious campaign for national independence," the shortest rebel declared. Dirt powdered his cheeks. Blood stained his shirt and trousers. He glared at the room, daring them to blink. "Who's in charge?"

Across the room, with an exasperated roll of her eyes, Sonja raised her hand.

"I am the field commander of the fourth brigade of the National Military of the Chechen Republic of Ichkeria," the shortest rebel said. He lowered his gun and took small, plodding steps to Sonja. "There are forty of us. Most need medical attention. Everyone needs food and water."

"We could amputate all their legs," Maali suggested, but the limping entrance of thirty-six more rebels made permission a formality. Sonja agreed to treat the wounded provided they removed their boots. They corralled the rebels in one of the ghost wards, sharing an unspoken consensus that the quicker the work was done, the better for all involved. The rebels asked for treatment by ascending order of rank, rather than by triage. The lower ranks were first into battle, the commander explained in a clipped northern accent, and thus had suffered the longest. Natasha's throat tightened as she cut through the trouser leg of a curly-haired private. Nothing but pale down on his cheeks and pink clouds in his eyes. She hadn't touched a man's trousers in five and a quarter years.

"What are you doing?" he asked, supine on the hospital bed.

"Giving you shorts. You have lovely legs."

"Where are my legs?"

"Still here. Don't worry."

She tried to be gentle, but shrapnel had cratered his left calf. "Hold on," she said. "Just hold on." Her sweat-slickened bangs stuck to her forehead. She wanted to ask his name, but what if he died and she was left here with his name? The name Natasha wouldn't learn was Said. He came from a Grozny suburb, where his mother, a veterinary's assistant, brought home the litters abandoned on the clinic doorstep. The war had already taken his mother, but he would live to return home to her cats, which had multiplied to the population of a village during the war years, feasting, as they did, on the burgeoning estate of rats and mice. Working odd jobs and sacrificing the comforts of wife and family, he would spend his life caring for the descendants of his mother's cats. Eight hundred and eighty-two, all named for his mother, though he would never know that exact figure. In sixty-six years, on his deathbed, he would remember that distant afternoon, when the fingers of a beautiful nurse had mined metal from his legs. He would remember it as the moment of greatest intimacy he ever had had with a woman. Then he would remember his cats.

Natasha called to Sonja, asking for pain relief. The young man was incoherent, addressing his mother in a jar of cotton swabs. Across the room, the surgical saw paused, but Sonja didn't look up from the half-severed arm. "You'll have to get it yourself," she said calmly. Given her history with the drug, Natasha never prepared or administered the heroin. Dreams of bent spoon handles persisted, and five years clean she was still afraid a cigarette lighter could reheat her cravings. But she peeled off the latex gloves and jogged to the canteen. Now wasn't the time for caution, not with that boy on her hospital bed. In the cupboard, behind an armory of evaporated milk, she found it. It compacted in her grip, filling the corners of the plastic bag. Alu's brother had claimed there wasn't enough talc in the bag to powder a baby's bottom. The Italian junk Sergey had shot into her had contained enough to service a nursery, and even that had laid electric lines where her veins had been.

But this? Ninety-eight percent pure? She spat in the sink; she was sali-
vating. You *can* control your reactions. You *can* control your reactions,
she repeated. It took two minutes to cook. She only had to take one
syringe to the trauma ward, but for the twenty-meter walk, when she
was alone with it, she felt vastly outnumbered.

When it came time to treat the commanding officers, the last pack-
ets of surgical thread had already disappeared into the limbs of their
subordinates. The field commander, the last to receive medical attention, lay on Sonja's cot. The blood of his command soaked the sheets,
and when his bare shoulders touched it, he sighed. Between his beard
and his eyes, a slim band of soil-colored skin suggested many months
of sunshine and malnutrition. Natasha watched while her sister treated
him. A long, semicircular gash split his left pectoral. "My chest is grinning at me," he observed.

Sonja flooded the wound with saline and iodine. With forceps she
pinched through the gash for shrapnel fragments. It had begun to clot,
but wouldn't heal without stitches. The rebels looked on with reverent
interest.

"We have a problem," Sonja said. The commander nodded to the
ceiling. "We need to get you stitched up, but we're out of surgical
thread. We simply don't have the supplies on hand to treat so many field
injuries."

"He can have mine," murmured a thin man, whose beard was half
shaven to accommodate thirteen stitches on his left cheek. A chorus of
offers followed. Even those without a single stitch vociferously pledged
their surgical thread.

"It isn't sanitary," Sonja said with a finality that ended debate. None
appeared too disappointed that his offer was declined. "Don't you have
field medical kits? Anything we can sterilize and sew into you?"

A junior officer appeared with a small green bag. Natasha sifted
through it while Sonja held a compress to the wound. She pulled out a
pink toothbrush with a fan of gray bristles, a small bottle of nonalcoholic

mouthwash, a tube of fluoride whitening paste, five tubes of toothpaste, on which the five daily prayers were written in black marker, and three rolls of unwaxed dental floss.

"The floss," Sonja said. "It might work."

The field commander grimaced as the alcohol-wetted floss followed the needle through his skin. He refused the offer of pain relief. Natasha admired his abstinence.

"Have dentists begun enlisting?" she asked as Sonja slipped the needle in a fifth time. If he refused anesthetic, she could at least offer the distraction of conversation.

"No, it was a captain's private supply."

"Did he have fine teeth?"

"Yes," the field commander said. His open mouth revealed a more relaxed philosophy toward dental hygiene. "They were beautiful, beautiful things. He brushed five times a day, always before prayer, as if performing an ablution on his mouth."

"Was he conscious of his health in general?"

"Not really. He smoked no fewer than two packs a day."

"He sounds like a strange man."

"You get that way. In the first war I fought with a man who went through a roll of antacids every day."

"That can cause an electrolyte disturbance: hypercalcemia. Stones, bones, moans, groans, thrones, and psychiatric overtones. That's the mnemonic," Natasha said, and repeated *psychiatric overtones* to herself. She wondered if Maali had a taste for antacids.

"I doubt it matters. He's very dead now. Besides, we ate nothing but buckwheat kasha. No, he took antacids as a calcium supplement. He was terrified of osteoporosis."

She nearly laughed. "How old was he?"

"Twenty-two."

"You are all insane."

The field commander winced as Sonja pulled the stitches tight. "It just becomes easy to convince yourself that caring for a small part of your body will act to protect the rest. As though Allah wouldn't be cruel enough to steal the life from a man with perfect teeth."

"Did it work?"

"We left his mouth open when we buried him so that in Paradise he can flaunt his teeth to the angels."

The rebels spent the night in the ghost ward. None snored; even in sleep they were wary. In the morning they pointed the hospital beds of their wounded comrades toward Mecca. Natasha ladled a dense pulp of oats and powdered milk into their bowls. With Sonja and the nurses, she checked the bandaged burns, stitched lacerations, the broken bones splinted between sterilized wooden strips. Only the rebel with the amputated arm would be left behind. The field commander prayed for him, then rooted through the man's rucksack for anything that might connect him with the insurgency.

"You're a civilian now," the field commander said. "Enjoy the peace you have fought for. We'll take your arm for burial, but must leave you here. If you want to stay, the lady doctor said the position of security guard has recently opened."

Complying with his insistence to be treated last, Natasha served him the final bowl of oats from the canteen. The surface had cooled to a carapace the field commander tapped twice with his spoon before breaking.

"Where are you going next?"

"South," the field commander said. "To the mountains."

"Try to find a doctor or veterinarian before then. If this gets infected, the Feds will be your smallest problem."

"In our condition we probably won't make it farther than Eldár today."

Only two of the field commander's shirt buttons matched the brown fabric, whose original color would be anyone's guess. Natasha pulled the shirt past his shoulder and covered the stitches with a fresh bandage.

The dental floss had worked. "I was in the mountains once," she said. "I climbed right across the border."

"In winter?"

"Spring."

"The winter will be difficult. We need supply lines. Good middlemen. Maybe we'll find someone in Eldár. You're not looking for a new profession, are you?"

As his contribution to the hospital, the field commander left the bag of toothpaste. He stood stiffly by the door as his command shuffled out. Alone, he turned to the sisters.

"Thank you," he said, bowing slightly. "You are kind, decent, and if I can risk impertinence, quite attractive. There must be some Chechen in you."

"I have a favor to ask," Sonja said. "Would you write us a letter of safe passage, so we can, should we need to, travel through rebel land?"

The field commander had two sisters of his own, older by one and three years, who teased and chided and always took care of him. He kept their names written on the sheet of paper stitched in his trouser seam. He trusted them with the name of his first crush and would trust them with his eternity. He smiled and searched for a pen.

When the field commander departed, and the double doors swung closed, Natasha returned to the maternity ward almost believing the war had left with him. Six days later the Feds would enter the city. They would launch a single mortar round at the hospital in retaliation for sheltering rebels. That round would hit the fourth-floor storage room. Maali would be searching for clean sheets. She would land atop the rubble, four floors below, her pulse slowing in her wrist. A syringe would be prepared and half injected, but death would relieve Maali's pain before the drug took effect, and the senseless, screaming world would go quiet when Natasha slipped that same syringe between her toes, and with a push of the plunger, sent Maali's blood into her own.

# THE FOURTH AND FIFTH DAYS

CHAPTER

2 4

1994 1995 1996 1997 1998 1999 2000 2001 2002 2003 **2004**

HAD HE SLEPT on the divan, he would have seen the letter to Havaa. Had the side lamp still held even a spark of electricity, he would have seen the letter to Havaa. Had he risen an hour later, when dawn threw its bright beams across the floor, he would have seen the letter to Havaa. But he hadn't seen it, and now Havaa was galloping across the waiting room, her face a flower head, a moon, a cannonball, and then it was there, punching into his gut, knocking the breath from his lungs, and only then, with her arms belted around his waist, did he remember the letter from Khassan which he had forgotten to bring.

"You're here," she proclaimed to his hip bone.

"Where else would I be?" He didn't fully appreciate what the girl knew, that *here* was a special, unlikely place. She thought he could have disappeared by now, too. That he could be with her father, wherever that was, and whatever that meant. But he was here. The sharp sting of bleach preceded Sonja's footsteps and they both looked to the door before she appeared. Her bright white scrubs could belong to a doctor in Moscow or London or Berlin. Should he ever disturb a sleeping land mine, or cross the path of a bullet, he would want to be treated by a doctor wearing those scrubs.

The previous night, as he had sketched the portrait of her sister, he had fought the urge to lean in so his left knee would touch her right. Two years had passed since he last touched a knee like that. And before that? When had he touched Ula's knees with anything like desire? Caretaking had refined his passion, once as raw and combustible as crude oil, into a dimmer, longer-burning love.

"So this is the Tolstoy book?" She nodded to the chair where *Hadji Murád* lay. That, he hadn't forgotten.

"Yes, the one he wrote about Chechnya."

Pulling back a stray lock of hair, she drew a question mark around her ear. He handed her the book. She flipped to the last page.

"What are you doing? Don't read the last page."

"I always read the last page first," she said, without looking up.

"That ruins everything. The whole book is working toward the last page."

Her lips pursed to a pebble. The paper cover bent in her grip, as if she were steadying her hands. The amphetamines? But she spoke in a flat, uninspired tone. "If it's not an ending I think I'll like, then I won't read the book. " She handed it back to him.

"Are you serious?"

"He gets decapitated on the last page. That's not an ending I want to read."

She was harder to pin down than the last pickle in the jar. Here he had thought he would impress her, thought they would have conversations about the book's images and themes, a literary salon in a city without electricity.

"But it's the great book. It's a century and a half old and still the best book about the first and second wars."

"Why would I want to read what I'm living?"

"You prefer escape?"

"You've been here four days," she said. "Keep coming back, and we'll see if you still think books are worth arguing over."

Akhmed, Deshi, and Havaa went to the weekly aid distribution point, so shortly after eight, when a man was carried in with a tailpipe lodged in his chest, Sonja received him alone. The man, an army contractor, had been plagued by asthma for all of his twenty-one years. After living his life as a drowning man, his final breath, nineteen seconds after the car bomb detonated, entered him effortlessly, the easiest inhalation of his life, through the metal trachea jutting from his chest, and into his collapsed lung.

But Sonja only knew him as a corpse. The handful of amphetamines that had propelled her through a sleepless night lingered in her veins. She wheeled him into the trauma ward on a hospital bed, and sat beside him as moths fluttered overhead. His head lolled to the side and his eyelids snapped open. She began speaking with the corpse—who was, in all respects, a wonderful listener—and became so engrossed in the hallucination she lost track of the real world behind her where Akhmed's footsteps sounded in the corridor.

"Honor the dead?" Sonja was saying, her face level with that of the corpse. Akhmed watched from the doorway. "Yes, but only if the dead are honorable. No, of course I'm not casting aspersions. It's okay if you feel rotten. You just died. Don't be too hard on yourself. Now, I must ask if you can see my sister down there. Yes, I know it's crowded, but please have a look. I can wait. And while you're at it, would you save me a chair? Oh, I should have known it would be standing room only." Akhmed couldn't see her face, but her exhausted voice was enough to make him ache. "You say you've had trouble breathing?" she said, speaking into the tailpipe as if into a microphone. "It appears you have a bronchial growth." When she took the man's face in her hands, Akhmed stepped into the room to save her from whatever was happening inside her head. "There are no characteristics to distinguish the cranium of a cannibal from that of an ordinary man," she told the corpse. "But I can tell we would have had a grand time, you and I."

Two hands, on her shoulders, pulled her gently from the corpse before it could answer, before it could tell her if Natasha was down there with him.

"Not you, too," Akhmed said, wearily. His skin was a degree or two warmer than the corpse's. His navy *pes,* a size too small, still roosted on the back of his head. "Someone here has to stay sane."

The big oaf led her to the office that was her bedroom. He was like a pool of water she'd fallen into; she hit, hit, hit and he was still there, around her. She'd been awake forever. The flap of moths was overwhelming. In the office, he pushed her into the overstuffed executive chair. "You need to rest," Akhmed said, in a tone of authority obviously an imitation of her own.

"And who do you think you are to order me around?" she asked. Already she missed the corpse. He was a much better conversationalist.

"I think I'm someone who slept last night." He scanned the bookcase, selected the thickest book from the bottom shelf, and dropped it on the desk. "A medical dictionary. If you won't read Tolstoy, read this. It will put you to sleep in no time."

When the door closed behind him, she scrutinized the dictionary, wary of subterfuge. She hadn't opened the book in years. A surgeon of her skill had no need. Slowly, fearing further hallucinations hid between the covers, she opened the book. It was just as dull as she remembered.

But she was already in, and the crowded little script calmed her. The definitions had the stately reassurance of orthodoxy, reminding her of the prewar years, when she had relied on the reference book to complete her weekly assignments, when she had sat at her desk, her ears plugged with cotton balls, as that awful thudding Natasha called music had pounded from the next room, when she still believed the meaning of a thing was limited to a few tersely worded clauses, but nothing, she now knew, could be defined in exclusion, and every bug, pencil, and grass blade was a dictionary in itself, requiring the definitions of all other things to fulfill its own.

Her fingers shadowed the thin pages and the words appeared written on her skin: the average weight of a hand, interpretations of a knuckle. A shawl of post-high drowsiness wrapped itself around her. She hated to admit it, but Akhmed had been right. Then, halfway through the book, at the bottom of the 1,322nd page, circled in red ink:

*Life: a constellation of vital phenomena—organization, irritability, movement, growth, reproduction, adaptation.*

The breaking sky could release no more striking a pronouncement. She repeated it to the unmade bed, to Havaa's still-packed suitcase, to the desk of the former geriatrics director. Not once had she ever marked a dictionary, but here this was, encircled by the same red pen she'd kept on her nightstand. She stumbled into the corridor, reached out but couldn't find a wall. Her legs felt as stiff as they had been on the day she had tried to make her own trousers, but when she lost her balance, when she fell forward, Natasha wasn't there to catch her.

When she woke on the floor, the insides of her cheeks felt like the insides of lemon rinds. She rubbed her temples and checked the unlit overhead lights, but, thankfully, the ceiling was still. In the storage room she pulled a pack of Marlboros from the fresh carton. The crinkle of plastic wrap followed her down the corridor. At the door the one-armed guard declined her offer of a cigarette. Shards gleamed in his ashtray. His name was Mohmad. He didn't particularly enjoy this job, but he knew enough to know that any man was fortunate to have work these days, particularly amputees. In Ingushetia he had an eleven-year-old daughter he didn't know about, who was waiting for him to call. In two and a half years he would hear her voice for the first time.

She smoked three cigarettes before Akhmed appeared behind her, warming his hands around a mug of steaming water. "Marlboro?" she offered. He lit the cigarette from her ember.

"You look much better," he said. The corners of his lips inched toward a grin.

"Shut up."

"Nothing like a little beauty rest."

"I'll light your scrubs on fire if you say another word."

The incipient smile sagged into an expression of surrender. "They came back for him," he said. "Whoever dropped him off."

"Bringing a dead man to a hospital. Do they think we're magicians?"

"Medical miracles are the only miracles most of us will ever see."

He had her on that one. "You're a believer," she said. That explained his incompetence as well as anything.

"I believe in some things."

"In God."

He shook his head.

"But I've seen you pray at noon."

"That's like asking if I believe in gravity," he said. "It doesn't require belief."

"I've always thought Marx's view on religion was the one thing he got right. Faith is a crutch."

"If you step on a land mine," Akhmed said, "the crutch becomes the leg."

Westminster Abbey was the only steeple she'd ever stood beneath, a tourist guidebook, rather than a prayer book, in hand. God, like everything kind and good, lived in London. She dropped her gaze to her hands and picked at the white calluses that scalloped her palm.

"My goodness. These belong to a lumberjack," he said, lifting her hands, examining them with a mixture of awe and pity. "Woodsman hands."

"I hate my hands." Aloud it sounded as small and petty as it had in her head, but they were horrid things, these hands, a crime for which she felt the immediate relief of confession. "How could such things grow from a woman's wrist?"

"You've chosen the wrong profession. If not a lumberjack, you would have made a marvelous strangler." With the unexpected sensitivity of a surgeon, his fingers drifted up her forearm.

"I keep thinking in Latin," she said. He paused on her ulna. "The names of bones."

"Latin is a problem with which I have no experience." He squeezed her bicep. "You should think about anatomy like I do. This is your arm. It's only your arm. This is your shoulder, nothing less than your shoulder. Your neck is only your neck." His finger rose to a chin that was simply her chin, cheeks that were her cheeks, a nose that belonged to no one else. "And lips," he said, leaning to her. "Our lips."

A moment and she pulled away, frowning back at the hospital and smoothing out her scrubs. Of the varying shapes of love, grief, anger, and terror that had inhabited these scrubs, optimistic anticipation was a new one. She looked to his big, stupid face, blushed, and turned away. What would Deshi say if she saw her like this? The shock might very well make her act on her ten-year-long threat to retire.

"I'm going to the fourth floor," she said, finally. "You could meet me there in a half hour."

"Even though I'm not a very good doctor."

"Even though you are criminally incompetent."

He opened his hands. Not one callus.

"Don't make fun of my lumberjack hands."

"I'm not," he said.

"You are," she said.

He squinted across the parking lot to the armored truck, thinking of the previous day, perhaps, how she had ambushed him in Grozny, how repellant a woman she was for putting a gun to his head one day and her lips to his the next. When he asked for the keys to the truck, claiming he had forgotten his scarf in the passenger seat, she felt too relieved to dwell on the fact that he hadn't worn a scarf the day before.


Their footsteps from the previous evening were still evident in the dust of the fourth-floor maternity ward. Natasha's murals seemed to study her, as if she were their creation. Unsettled at the thought of standing alone among these ghosts, she went to the corridor and opened the storage room door for fresh air. The smashed city stretched to the frozen river. International law prohibited the targeting of medical facilities, which explained why, in a city where eighty percent of freestanding structures had been flattened, the hospital still stood. The shell that had crashed into this very room had been an act of reprisal rather than war. Natasha had collapsed with the walls, fallen with Maali, kept aloft by momentary updrafts, then plunged ever downward, until the earth had yawned open and she had entered it. Sonja knew the two had been coconspirators and confederates, sisters to ambitious, demanding women. She knew Natasha hadn't been right after Maali's tumble. She didn't know that Maali, eighteen minutes Deshi's junior, had lived her sixty-seven years in those eighteen minutes, finding room there for every dream, fear, and exasperation, setting her watch eighteen minutes ahead so she could pretend she had Deshi's experience, always wondering what her life would have been like if she were just eighteen minutes older. Natasha had loved Maali for this as much as for her demented enthusiasm for amputation, but Sonja didn't know it. In four months, when cleaning out a file cabinet, she would find municipal buildings drawn on the back of payroll forms. Long, uneven lines of Maali's penmanship disfigured Natasha's sketches, her critiques sometimes playful, sometimes damning, but always invested, and in those sketches, framed and hanging in the waiting room, as they would be within an afternoon, Sonja would see what the two younger sisters meant to each other.

The stairwell door slammed shut. They walked to each other until their silhouettes converged. In the darkness she found his eyebrows with her thumbs. They went to the third maternity bed, and she sat on the edge, and he stood between her legs. Her thighs clasped his hip bones. From the far side of the room the lantern dimly bathed them.

"I think there is a bee on my behind," she said.

"You're still hallucinating," he said.

"You should slap it away, just in case," she said.

She reached under his shirt, spread her hand across his abdomen, and tried not to think of which organ lay beneath which finger. "This is your stomach," she said, mimicking his tenor. "Not your brother's stomach, not Stalin's stomach, but your stomach."

"You make me sound like a serious man."

"You certainly aren't that."

They undressed by degree, a button here, shirtsleeve there, making a show of their shortcomings, their bodies androgynous with deprivation. It was remarkable to trust someone enough to be silly like this. She lay back. It was dark. Her lips found his.

"Good night to you and your ugly nose," Deshi told Akhmed as he was leaving. A buoyant confidence swelled in him and as he stepped into the navy twilight and trekked toward the village he finally felt part of the top tenth percentile. Never had he been so honored by being addressed in the second person.

But the radio antenna listing from the hood of Ramzan's truck, parked before his house, punctured the sweet feeling inside him. Akhmed smiled sadly and trudged forward, balling his fists in his coat sleeves. The coat was fifty-eight years old, canvas military grade, about the only thing the Red Army had ever done right. It kept him as warm as it had kept his father and his father's father and the idea of three generations sheltered by the same stiff, unyielding fabric gave him greater comfort than the coat itself ever could.

Again Ramzan questioned him, and again he claimed ignorance.

"You disappoint me, my friend," Ramzan said. Ramzan's coat was six months old. It would never warm another set of shoulders. "You're a doctor. Think logically. Think about your wife. Think about yourself. Think about your silence. It's reckless."

"I owe Dokka my silence more than I owe you anything," Akhmed said.

"Owe? We're beyond obligation," Ramzan said. "We wear clothes, and speak, and create civilizations, and believe we are more than wolves. But inside us there is a word we cannot pronounce and that is who we are. I know you think you are being noble, that this is some terrific act of sacrifice. You probably believe that because you fucked Dokka's wife two years ago, you owe it to him to save his child. But let me be clear, Akhmed. You don't. She is not yours." Ramzan's voice cracked, and he steadied himself with two deep breaths. It wasn't an act. "I know you think I'm a traitor and a coward, Akhmed. And you're right. But that doesn't make me wrong. I'm telling you this because we were friends. You don't owe this to Dokka."

Akhmed hadn't lusted for Esiila before the wars, hadn't thought of her as more than the wife of his closest friend. She could have been anyone. He had just wanted to hear his name breathed in his ear, a body warm and damp beneath him, whole and alive and a world away from pain. Was it such a sin? No, of course not. But Dokka. There was Dokka. Now he stood up for them, as if he were a hero rather than a hypocrite, as if he hadn't betrayed, dishonored, and broken the family whose last living member he now offered his life to save. Ramzan stood across from him, but he knew that in their hearts, they stood on the same side.

Pale moonlight fell across his snowy boot tracks, and Akhmed suddenly saw the fragility of the plan he'd designed over the past day. The girl would be safe, he had assumed, if he severed the link between the village and the city, and the link was him. But this meant trusting that Sonja would care for the girl. It meant trusting an erratic, overextended surgeon, who had put a gun to his back a day earlier, with the girl's life. It meant pushing through his endless doubts and trusting, however misguidedly, the decency he believed was buried inside Sonja.

"Why do they want the girl, Ramzan? You still haven't tried to explain."

"Revenge," Ramzan said flatly. "Dokka fucked up."

"But what did he do?"

"Akhmed. So many questions. If you had learned to keep your mouth shut, your eyes on your feet, you would have had a happier life."

"They already have Dokka, Ramzan. Why do they need the girl?"

Ramzan shook his head. "Because the life of a Russian colonel doesn't equal the life of a Chechen arborist."

"You can't mean that—"

"A few days after we returned from the Landfill, Dokka asked me for a pistol. He wanted to be able to protect his family, so I gave him one of the Makarovs I'd kept from our final fucked-up gun run. That same Makarov was later used to assassinate a colonel."

"But Dokka couldn't have been an insurgent. He couldn't hold a gun in his hand, much less fire it!"

"That doesn't matter when the serial number on the pistol used to kill a colonel sequentially matches the serial numbers of the guns those lost soldiers took off us before they left us at the Landfill. The Feds made the connection. I couldn't give Dokka up, because they already had him."

"But why do they want the girl?"

Ramzan gave him a sad smile. "You know the saying, *As the son inherits from the father, so the father inherits from the son*? The Feds have made it official policy. There is a campaign to disappear not only suspected insurgents but their relatives as well. The idea being that you are less likely to go into the woods with the rebels if you know that your house will burn and your family will disappear. Rebel recruitment has plummeted in recent months. It's part of the new hearts-and-minds strategy. It's how they will win the war on terror. They will kill Havaa and call it peace."

Akhmed's head hummed with the shock of how not shocked he was. What Ramzan said made sense to him. He understood why the Feds would want to kill a child. Accompanying that understanding was a second, equally shameful recognition: this incomprehensible war would take from him even the humanity to find it incomprehensible.

"Why are you telling me this?"

"Because I'm trying to save you."

When Ramzan returned from the Landfill the first time, with that wound between his legs, Akhmed had saved him. They never said it, Ramzan never thanked him for it, but they both knew that the week he spent treating the infection was just that. If a stranger were to put his ear in the space between them, he would hear the dull roar of that knowledge.

"Isn't it too late for that?" Akhmed asked.

"No, not yet."

"Yes, it is."

"If you give up like this you really will be the stupidest doctor in Chechnya."

Akhmed allowed himself a smile. This was the Ramzan he remembered. "That honor has been mine for some time."

"You probably think you are a hero or a martyr, don't you?" Ramzan asked. "You probably think you are a saint for refusing the Feds. I know, Akhmed, I know what you're thinking. You're thinking that by refusing me you're refusing them. But let me tell you, my friend, I am nothing. I am no one. I am so much easier to refuse than those to come. You're thinking that you will be as silent to them as you are to me. But you won't, Akhmed. You just won't. You might believe that you will be brave, that you will hew to your convictions, but you have never been to the Landfill. They won't ask you where the girl is. They will make you bring her to them, and you will watch yourself do it. Look at me, Akhmed. Once I was like you, and soon you will be like me. They are in the business of changing lives, Akhmed, and they are the very best."

This was his greatest fear. Could he stay silent? Could he withstand what awaited him? He told himself that his love for the girl would fortify him against any torture, but this, like so much of what he told himself, was a lie. After all, he was squeamish at the sight of blood; what would he say when lying in a puddle of his own? But he saw no other way. He would pray for the strength to stay silent, for a quick heart attack, and leave the rest to God.

"You remember in ninety-five, my first trip to the Landfill?" asked Ramzan. "It was my twenty-third birthday and I had the bad luck of bi-cycling to the city on the day of a rebel ambush. That's the only reason they took me. I was a young Chechen man on the day rebels decide to attack the Feds outside of Gudermes, so they took me to the Landfill and you know what they did. You stitched me back together. For so long I worried you or my father would ask why it happened, and I was always afraid of it, afraid of the asking and how I would answer. But neither of you ever did. You're both too polite. But don't you want to know what happened? You're always asking *why*, Akhmed, so let me tell you. It hap-pened because they asked me to inform on my friends and neighbors, Akhmed. When they threatened to beat me, I said nothing. When they threatened to electrocute me, I said nothing. When they threatened to castrate me, I said nothing. I said nothing, Akhmed. Whatever you think of me, you remember that once I said nothing when a wiser man would have sung. And the interrogators, they couldn't believe it. They called in others to examine me. I was there on the floor, and above their faces were dark ovals silhouetted by the ceiling lights. They had beaten me hard and I couldn't hear right, but I kept saying no, with every breath I had. The only reason they let me go, the only reason they didn't shoot me right there was out of perverse respect, some sort of professional courtesy. But I wish they had shot me, Akhmed, because the good part of me died there, and all this, everything since, has been an afterlife I'm trying to escape."

Akhmed had never been in a fight before, but right then he had to concentrate on controlling his hands. On their own they would have strangled Ramzan to keep him from saying one more word. Whether this was confession or ruse, Akhmed couldn't say, but the anguish was there for him to see in Ramzan's face. "Why did you start saying yes?"

Ramzan trembled beneath his folded arms. "A second war. A second trip to that place. I knew what was coming. I knew it never stops. They put a shame inside you that goes on like a bridge with no end, the humiliation, the fucking humiliation of knowing that you are not a human being but a bundle of screaming nerve endings, that the torture goes on even when the physical hurt quiets. People treated me differently when I came back the first time. They gossiped, told rumors about me because I still lived with my father, couldn't marry, and then I was a fucking joke to those for whom I'd sacrificed a wife, children, family, a life. When the Feds took Dokka and me to the Landfill, when I said yes, when I told them what they wanted, when I agreed to inform on anyone, I wished I had done it in ninety-five, in the first war, *that* is my biggest regret. If I had said yes from the beginning, I would still be a man. I'm not asking for your friendship or forgiveness, Akhmed, just tell me you understand. Please give that much to me."

Ramzan stepped forward to embrace Akhmed, and in the moment before he came to his senses, before he planted his hands on Ramzan's chest and gave him a sharp shove to the ground, Akhmed wanted to take

Ramzan in his arms, as a patient, as an old friend, and fix all that had gone wrong in him.

"I don't," he said as he pushed Ramzan. Ramzan tumbled and the next moment Akhmed knelt over him, fist raised, ready to beat Ramzan as the interrogators had beaten him, for what he had done to Dokka, to Havaa, to the entire village, to himself. Ramzan covered his face with his hands and tried to crawl away on his elbows. "Don't hurt me, don't do it, don't hurt me, mercy, have mercy," he pleaded, eyes closed, collapsing into a fetal position, weeping into the brown snow. Akhmed stood, disgusted with himself, with the man at his feet, with the war that had reduced them to this. "I don't understand," he said, but Ramzan could hear nothing above his own calls for mercy.

After checking on Ula, he drew closed the blackout curtains and lit the living room oil lamp. Khassan's letter lay on the divan, where he had left it the previous evening. How could he have forgotten it? He really was an idiot. Through the closed door he could still hear Ramzan's faint crying. The previous night Khassan had asked his advice, and he thought he had understood what was the right and honorable answer, but no longer. Crammed in his jacket pocket were the two letters of safe passage he had taken from the glove box of Sonja's truck that afternoon on the pretext of searching for a nonexistent scarf. The glove box held dozens of letters of safe passage and he hoped she wouldn't miss or need these two. He slipped them into the larger manila envelope that had held Khassan's letter, added a one-word note to Khassan, then sealed and addressed it: *For K, 56 Eldár Forest Service Road.*

Back in the bedroom, he undressed Ula. He carried her to the bathroom and the water rose, so slightly, when he set her in the tub. She had never learned to swim. As a girl she would scoop carrots from her mother's stew and feed them to the rabbit that lived in the back garden; her mother trapped the rabbit one autumn afternoon and made stew from it, and for all their time together, Ula refused to explain to Akhmed her aversion to carrots. He washed her neck and shoulders. He lifted her elbow and scrubbed the divot of soft underarm hair. Her mother had spoken of lust as if it were a loaded firearm, and when, one summer, the big-eared boy who lived across the village transformed into something right-sized and beautiful, she concealed her affection, holstered it to her chest, because she knew the shame of it could kill her mother. He washed her elbows and wrists. With a toothbrush he scoured the rims of her fingernails. He washed her nape and her back and slalomed his fingers down her spine. Her older brother was born touched, kept in a room with the curtains always drawn shut, this wailing, incomprehensible heart beating against the walls of the family house. For nearly as long as she had feared him, she had been ashamed of her fear, and wanted to reach through his madness to the part of him that could, at times, be so gentle, and embrace it. He washed her chest, the skin that had been breasts. He washed her hips, her stomach, swirling soap into her navel. She had been so afraid of Akhmed when she met him for the first time, on a June morning, on her porch, the branches clutched by blackbirds. In the eight years since their betrothal he had become a local celebrity. He could have any girl. He could have anyone. Her mother invited him in without fear of embarrassment because a cousin had taken her older brother for the day. He washed her pubis, vagina, and anus. He washed her thighs. He washed her knees. He washed her calves. For as far back as anyone could remember, she had wanted to be a mother. He washed the tops of her feet, her soles, all ten toes and the gaps between. She would have had eight girls, treated them like the very reason her lungs drew breath, whether they were normal or touched, whether they ate carrots or not, she would have loved them, and given herself to them; she would have given each a pet rabbit; a mother, she would have been a mother if her body and Akhmed's had only worked the way they were supposed to work. When he finished, they were both clean.

He wrapped a towel around her shoulders and with long, vigorous caresses, rubbed her dry. He couldn't stop worrying that she might catch a cold. Four hours earlier, he had come inside Sonja, and now he was brushing his wife's hair. Nagging doubt was the nearest he came to guilt. He looked into the eyes of the wife that had become his ward. A smile was buried in his beard. He had never loved her more.

He helped her into a nightgown, pulled the covers to her chin, and lay beside her. "Any visitors today?" he asked.

"No," she said. "I was waiting for your father, but he never came."

So much of his marriage was a disappointment—childlessness, ailing health—but they were blessings, now, in the end, when he had to let go. Yet he'd grown to depend on the act of longing. He performed his nightly ablutions and prayed, but the ritual was empty, mechanized, and he recited the words as he would a recipe. The pearl of faith had dissolved, and at its core was a sand grain of doubt, and he held on to it, knowing that doubt, like longing, could sustain him.

Later that night the wind carried the low rumble of approaching trucks. He was fully dressed, wearing thick wool socks and his fifty-eight-year-old coat, because wherever they took him would be cold. By the time the trucks pulled up to his house, he'd already loaded the syringe with enough heroin to stop the heart of a healthy man. Her long, slow breaths filled the room. He took the time to disinfect her skin. Outside, truck doors slammed shut. Praise Allah for her hallucinations. Without them he wouldn't have the strength to push the plunger and forever numb that precious vein. But she was convinced that his ten-years-dead father had visited her this week, so even when her eyelids flashed open, and a bleary, misapprehending plea poured forth, he looked away, because a woman who spoke with ghosts was nearly one herself and would forgive him for taking her the rest of the way.

Her breaths slowed. Her eyes drifted to the left, to whatever came next. He held her hand. It stayed warm. Once, three months after their wedding, he had held that hand through two kilometers of sunshowers that had left them drenched and shining and purified to each other.

He closed her eyes. He put a small bandage on the pulseless vein. This was it. God could ask no more of him. The fists of the security forces pounded at the front door. The manila envelope containing the two letters of safe passage lay on the floor, beside the bound pages of Khassan's letter to Havaa. Would she ever read it? Would she ever know her father made furniture from his book boxes? The pounding grew to splintering. The underside of a corpse was the only place the security forces wouldn't look, and he slid the manila envelope and Khassan's letter beneath Ula's body. He kissed her forehead. She was gone and he still couldn't say good-bye. "We will never be dry," Ula had said. The sky was pouring. She was there.

When the men broke through the door, he was on his knees. He prayed for his wife, that in Paradise Allah would give her a body that worked. He prayed for Sonja, that she would find companionship. He prayed for Havaa, that she would live to die a natural death. He prayed for Khassan, and for Dokka. But when the men started beating him, when they taped his mouth and threw him in the back of the truck, he prayed only for himself.

# CHAPTER

## 2 5

THE TUESDAY NATASHA departed had been the third warmest December day in living memory. Sonja's coat still hung on the coat stand, where she had left it earlier that morning, after raising the window sash to test the air. The illness Natasha had claimed, when Sonja tapped on her door with fingers still warm from their reach into sunshine, was, in fact, withdrawal. Ever since Maali had fallen with the fourth-floor storage room, Natasha had numbed herself with pinches of heroin. Not counting the first dose, stolen from the syringe intended for Maali's forearm, she only snorted the powder. No more than once or twice a month for the first year, infrequent enough for her to believe, with some justification, that she was in charge of the heroin rather than the other way around. But then there was the time she delivered three stillborns in one week, the time the winter freeze slid right into the third week of May, the time an ache crept its way into her left ankle and stayed for months, the time she woke feeling as rotten as sunken squash and twice as ugly. The world must have grown crueler, because soon she was finding reasons to snort on a daily basis. Maali's fall, Sonja believed, was the cause of her malaise, as if Natasha had been tethered to the nurse, as if her regression could be so neatly explained. Even as Natasha broke her standards faster than she could lower them, one was immutable: she would never use a needle again. So late the previous night, when she had found herself planting a syringe in that familiar place between her toes, she had promised herself she would leave the next day. To her great surprise, she woke in the morning. To her greater surprise, she kept her promise.

She made her bed, cleaned her room as best she could, and packed what she needed in Sonja's black Samsonite. Before leaving she sat at the kitchen table her father had built for them himself from ash wood. It was a rickety thing, with nails that kept falling out and matchbooks under two of the table legs, a table the poorhouse would refuse, but one she had eaten from her entire life because spilled tea and tetanus wouldn't kill anyone as fast as a pride-wounded father. She tried to draft a note to Sonja but all alphabets failed her. What could she say? Wouldn't any excuse read like an insult to the sister that had, she could now acknowledge, given up a decent life in London for her? No, better to say nothing for now. She would get word to Sonja from the camps, when she had gone too far to turn back. Had she known the heartache her wordless departure was to cause, she would have written down the sentence pounding in her head: *Thank you, Sonja.*

She marched down the service road away from the city, toward the border, on the trodden path of some fifty thousand previous refugees. Where would she go from the camps? Turkey, Armenia, or Azerbaijan most likely, but she would rather go to China or Hawaii, a country where no one could speak Chechen or Russian. She wanted to hold foreign syllables like mints on her tongue until they dissolved into fluency.

The wet leaves paving the service road caught in the suitcase's wheels. Such a warm day, but she was cold. By sunset she had walked only the eleven kilometers to Eldár.

The last time she passed through Eldár had been in the bed of a canvas-canopied truck with five women. She hadn't known its name then. The service road widened into the trunk of the village road, from which unnamed side streets branched into the shadows. Even if the overhanging electrical lines carried a current, no streetlamps stood to light those crevices. She came to a porch where two women knitted and gossiped in the warm air and she asked for a room. They nodded down the road.

A third of the houses were ruined by fire or explosions, or even by the former occupants themselves, who, like farmers sowing their fields with salt, believed destruction to be the final act of ownership. Portraits hung eerily from electrical poles and doors, their faces staring blankly at her. She asked an elderly man for a room and he directed her farther down the road to a house with a green door where a man named Dokka kept beds for refugees traveling toward the border.

The man named Dokka opened the front door with his foot. He regarded her suspiciously, and she worried her skin, paler since September, revealed her ethnicity. But then his hesitation burst into a firework of recognition. "Natasha!" he exclaimed, opening his arms in welcome. Attached to them were two hideous, fingerless hands. She stepped back. He knew her name, but they had never met. Those things at the ends of his wrists wouldn't have slipped her mind.

He asked if she remembered him.

"I'm sorry. How would I?'

He laughed, loud and brightly, while she stared at his hands. Those, at the very least, were no laughing matter. "I met you seven years ago in the maternity ward of Hospital No. 6. I'll never forget you, not for the rest of my life. I am Dokka. You delivered my daughter, Havaa."

She repeated the name, but couldn't match it to the several hundred newborns in her memory. Behind him stood a little girl with almond-brown hair, green eyes, and ten fingers, all there. Natasha began to ask about the refugee beds, but Dokka cut her off. "Come inside. You can stay as long as you'd like."

The rooms themselves appeared amputated at waist height; nothing stood out of a child's reach. Dokka, politely declining her offers of assistance, used his hands like forceps as he bustled around the kitchen. He pinched a matchstick between his teeth, struck it against the wall, and spat it into the open stove. Over four years he had brewed tea for perhaps two thousand refugees, but there had been no pot he wanted to taste finer than this one. Again she offered help, but he had brewed tea for two thousand without faltering, and only needed her help drinking it.

"You're going to the refugee camps?" he asked. She nodded. She'd heard stories of overcrowded camps, where a single spigot left running would supply water for three thousand souls, but the blessing of rumor was its boundlessness, and she could disbelieve what she wanted. Despite all that had happened, Sonja's description of London lured her. She wanted to live there.

"You shouldn't be traveling alone. There are soldiers and bandits, often the same people. You should travel in a group with at least one man."

She couldn't help smiling. "I've done that before. It didn't work out."

"And you're ethnic Russian? No, no, no." After a moment Dokka gave a knowing nod to the empty seat beside Natasha. "Before you leave, we will think of something."

When the girl returned a half hour later with a treasure trove of pinecones, bird feathers, and dried leaves divided by color, her father, in a tone of familiar exasperation, asked her to remove her muddy boots. She carefully placed her findings on the kitchen table and followed them into the bedroom. She still hadn't said a word to Natasha. Standing before the open closet, Dokka explained that his wife had died that spring. He missed her greatly, not least because her passing had left the household with only one pair of functioning hands, still too small and weak to chop firewood, but he had a closet full of her clothes, which the moths would feast upon before Havaa could grow into them, so she should, he said while walking out, in short, have at it. As she undressed she turned to hide her burn scars, but the girl had seen worse and studied her without judgment or disgust. Without a mirror, she had to ask the girl's opinion of each dress. The girl shook her head no, no, no. She had seen her mother in this dress and that dress, each one of which pained her to see worn by a stranger, and she nodded yes only when Natasha put on a maternity dress, the only one in the closet she hadn't seen her mother wear.

After dinner, Dokka gave her a clean bedsheet and showed her to the room that had been his daughter's. In the world beyond were two thousand and eighteen souls who had slept in that room, and remembered that room, and would harbor it in their thoughts for no fewer than ninety-nine years, when a little girl that Havaa had once watched sleep, the last living of the two thousand, closed her eyes for the last time.

Havaa lay on the bottom bunk of the bed beside Natasha's, and, propped on her elbows, peering into Natasha's upside-down eyes, asked to see Natasha's hands. "You still have yours," she said, bending Natasha's fingers.

"I intend to keep them."

"My mother kept hers and she still died."

"They usually don't play much of a role in that."

The girl wasn't so certain. "My father said your hands were the first to hold me." She had stopped flexing Natasha's fingers and was now holding them, squeezing them, firm.

"I helped your mother give birth. I made sure she was clean and comfortable. When you popped out, I made sure you were, too."

"I saw baby rabbits once," the girl said proudly. "Did I look like that?"

"No, not at all. You were beautiful."

A grimace crowded the girl's face. "I wanted to look weird."

"You did look weird," Natasha said, a beat too quickly.

"I don't believe you."

"Your legs were growing out of your shoulders, arms came out of your knees, and you were breathing out of your bottom. I had to fix everything. I missed lunch that day because of you."

The girl beamed above her. "Are you going to help children in the camps?"

"It's been a long day. Let's talk about that tomorrow."

The girl snuffed out the lamp and thin, tapering smoke unwound from the wick, drifting into Natasha's yawn. She could count the bed slats through the limp mattress. The heavy blankets, gray, coarse enough to clean a skillet, smelled of every body they had ever warmed. Where was her sister right now? And was she asking the same question? There would be time for guilt, for second guesses, for turning back, but this was the time for rest, and as she slipped into sleep, a sleep so deeply peaceful not even the long fingers of dreams would reach her, she heard the girl say, "I'm glad you have yours. Otherwise I would have fallen."

At breakfast Dokka urged her to stay for another night or two. Another group of refugees might pass through, one she might join. It was wisdom a child might summon, but coming from him, from his kindness and hospitality, she decided to stay, even though she was only a dozen kilometers from home. The girl hid her smile behind a spoonful of kasha. Havaa wanted to show her the forest, and after washing their dishes they returned to the bedroom to dress.

"Do you want to see my souvenir collection before we go?" Havaa asked. "I have a collection of all the people who've stayed here."

She opened the drawer before Natasha could suggest they see it when not dressed in enough layers to roast themselves alive. There was a pressed flower head, plucked from Ukrainian soil twenty-two years earlier, the only entry in an otherwise empty journal. Three brass buttons that had fastened the blazer of a thrice bankrupted businessman, who, in Hoboken, New Jersey, had already put in the paperwork to open the collection agency that would make him a millionaire in eight years' time. A key ring with two keys that opened the front door to a house that no longer existed.

"You have to give me something before you go," the girl said.

"I'll give you the teeth from my mouth if we can just go outside now. There is a wetland forming in my underwear. I can feel tadpoles."

Taking her by the hand, the girl led Natasha through the undergrowth until the forest forgot the service road and the birch trunks blocked out the village chimneys. The loose soil felt odd under her boots. When was the last time she'd lost the texture of asphalt, concrete, or linoleum beneath her toes? When she hiked over the border with five women whose names she still didn't know. This was nicer.

In piles of wet, rotting leaves they found maggots and larvae and crustaceous creatures, which they both agreed were better suited to oceanic depths. They found a mountain range of deer dung scaled and mined by a brigade of red ants. The sun was burning a hole in the middle of the sky, and Natasha was wondering if Dokka's hands were capable of making *siskal* for lunch, when the girl stopped suddenly. "What's wrong?" Natasha asked.

The girl nodded to a parting, twenty meters away, where two lengths of aquamarine lay like misplaced strips of sky. As they edged forward, Natasha saw the aquamarine didn't belong to the sky, but rather to the legs of straw-stuffed blue trousers.

"A scarecrow?" Natasha asked. A faded Red Army–issue shirt languished above the trousers. Nine soldiers had lived and died in that shirt. The scarecrow, drunk, judging from its borrowed birch-trunk backbone, had been decapitated. Nailed to the tree, where the head should have been, was a moss-devoured board.

"No," the girl said. "It's Akim."

"Who's Akim?"

Too young to explain in words, the girl's face was old enough to show the loss that was that name. Natasha, not understanding what this meant, was briefly annoyed, believing it profligate to expend pity on a scarecrow when there were more deserving life forms, but of all people, who was she to judge how a girl disburses her empathy. She wrapped her arm around Havaa. The whole of the girl's bony shoulder fit in the cup of her palm, and the girl reached up and held on to her fingers. If Akim could have seen the two of them, he would have taunted them for weeks.

After dinner that evening they were joined by a man, tall, slender, and bearded, in whose presence Dokka grew aloof. His name was Akhmed. He asked about the hospital, showing particular interest in the hiring process. The hospital hadn't adhered to those formalities since before she arrived—she had never even taken a first-aid course, she confided—and if he still wanted to work there Sofia Andreyevna Rabina would surely hire him. The brilliance building behind his eyes faded when she added that no hospital employee had received a salary in many years. And then he asked a peculiar question: had she ever used dental floss for stitches? Natasha was questioning his sanity when he described a rebel field commander who, two years earlier, had arrived in the village with his chest held together by dental floss. That would be Sonja, Natasha said, she could stitch a lion to the back of a wildebeest. He had never seen finer stitching of any other material, much less dental floss, and could vividly recall the twenty-three stitches curving along the crescent wound, which the commander had called the grin on his chest, and the memory had haunted him, reminding him of the unexpected wonders a capable mind might conceive. Natasha wholeheartedly agreed, and encouraged his misconception that Sonja worked miracles, not from malice, but from a budding pride that stretched all eleven kilometers home.

Dokka didn't say a word to Akhmed, not even in greeting or farewell, and when the man left, Natasha asked if he had come invited.

"He comes once a week," Dokka explained. "Usually when travelers are staying. He likes talking to people, getting news from the outside. And he helps with the tasks Havaa's hands are too small to perform. Chopping firewood and the like."

"But you don't care for him?"

Dokka gave a sad smile. "He was my closest friend once. It pains me that I can't decline his assistance."

In the bedroom, Natasha undressed under the girl's inquisitive stare. "Did they take you to the Landfill, too?"

"No," Natasha said.

"Then why are there marks on your shoulders?"

Instinctively she reached back and covered the knotted scars. Some three dozen stippled her left shoulder and neck, and had Sergey not switched to nicotine gum, there would have been some three dozen more. "It's nothing," she said, quick to throw on a nightdress. "I fell asleep in the sun once. I couldn't sleep on my back for months after. Just a reminder of my foolish younger self." After she brushed her teeth, she asked, "Did the scarecrow walk into the woods by itself?"

"I helped him," the girl boasted.

"He must have been heavy."

"It took me three days. I dragged him along the road and hid him each night so no one would take him."

"Why?" Natasha asked.

"For Akim."

"You mentioned him earlier. Who is he?"

"No one really."

"Is he like an imaginary friend? My sister and I, when we were children, we pretended we had an imaginary sister."

"No!" the girl said, horrified by the suggestion. "Akim's not imaginary."

"I'm sorry, I was just asking."

"You're mean." Natasha felt like she had stepped into a foreign country whose customs and manners she didn't comprehend, where her gestures of concern were taken as affronts. The Samsonite was still unzipped from when she had retrieved her wool sleeping socks, and through the opening she saw the black fake fur hat of the Buckingham Palace Guard nutcracker. Without pausing to consider the thousands of kilometers the souvenir had already traveled, or that she might need this totem to draw strength in the uncertain days, she pulled the toy from the suitcase and presented it to the girl in appeasement.

"Here," she said. "A souvenir."

The nutcracker was as wide as the girl's hand and twice as long. As she studied it, her curiosity consumed her anger. "Who is this?" she asked.

What was the name they had given this little wooden man that never laughed? She lay back, more afraid of losing the name than the nutcracker itself, but there it was, years since she last spoke it and it was right there.

"Alu," she said.


Five nights and the refugees Dokka promised still hadn't come; on the morning of the sixth day, she announced she was leaving. After breakfast Dokka asked her to join him in the bedroom. Six ribbons looped around the six dresser drawer knobs, and Dokka fit his wrist into the first, opening a drawer that contained jewelry, foreign coins, wristwatches, and billfolds, a more extravagant version of his daughter's collection. "Right there," he said. "You see the red bandanna? Take it."

The bandanna wrapped around an L-shaped object. Its weight substantiated her fear the moment she lifted it.

"It's a Makarov semiautomatic pistol," he said. "You simply unlatch the safety, point at the target, and shoot."

But for the beige handgrip, the gun was silver; a passing cloud dulled its luster. She had seen guns on television and at the bazaar, in the hands of rebels, soldiers, and gangsters, pointed at her in City Park and the

Breaking Grounds, but she had never stood on this side of the barrel before.

"I'm just as likely to shoot off my own head as anyone I aim at," Natasha said. She didn't want the gun and told him as much, but he insisted, saying Comrade Makarov would keep her safe on those dangerous roads. "Do you arm all your guests?" she asked with a smile.

"You're our first."

"Why?"

"After I lost my fingers, I thought Havaa should learn to shoot. But when I think about her shooting at the Feds, and what would come after that . . . She knows to run. It's better if we don't have the gun."

"But why give it to me?"

"Because I want to protect the person who gave me Havaa." She could think of no refutation. He insisted she keep it on her person, and it pressed against her left breast as she hugged Havaa good-bye. The girl clung to Natasha's fingers, and Natasha shook them both away, with gratitude, and hurried into the cool daylight before their affirmations of goodwill crippled her. Her boot heels bit into her ankles but she wouldn't stop to slip on extra socks before she had traveled far enough from Dokka's house to preclude the possibility of returning. The wood, brick, and cinderblock dwellings grew smaller as she reached the village's southern end. A stubble of dead grass filled the ungrazed fields. The forest closed around the road. Hanging from a tree was a final portrait, a woman with long, dark hair and an aquiline nose, whom Natasha recognized but couldn't identify. Of all the village portraits, this was the most detailed and closely observed. In the center of the otherwise serene portrait, the woman's lips opened, just a centimeter, revealing no more than a sliver of her tongue, the forty-second portrait, if Natasha were to count, the only one whose subject opened her mouth in speech or sigh, a word spoken and heard for eternity, or an expression of longing, though whether it belonged to the woman or the artist, Natasha couldn't say. She stared at the portrait for several minutes before understanding, belatedly, why the woman looked so familiar. Perhaps those chestnut-sized eyes recognized her. Natasha was, after all, wearing the woman's maternity dress.

She made it twenty kilometers by the time the sun set. She had hoped to come to a village where she might enjoy a morsel of Dokka's hospitality, but the scavenged remains of logging encampments were the only signs of prior habitation. All else was woodland. She went deep enough into the trees that not even the glimmer of a campfire could be seen from the road. Recalling the lessons of the City Park Prophet, she built a fire from dried branches and dead leaves. Dokka had given her a G-4 humanitarian aid ration: three cans of evaporated milk and one tin of processed meat. The Feds who doled out the G-series aid claimed it was enough food to support a man of average height and build for three days, thus corroborating her long-held suspicion that everyone in Russia was either a midget or a fucking idiot. She cut the evaporated milk with canteen water, shaking the concoction until it came out in glossy, fire-soaked dribbles that beaded the canteen lip like golden roe. When it came time to sleep, she extinguished the flames and, as the City Park Prophet had taught her, spread her sleeping bag across the charred ground so it would pleasantly toast her backside as she drifted away.

The next day she hiked ten or twenty or forty kilometers. The following day, maybe more, maybe less. A thousand times she considered turning back but the huff of every cloud in Chechnya was no bleaker than another afternoon in the hospital corridor, fighting the ten steps to the canteen cupboard. And my god, the Samsonite suitcase, why had she thought this was a good idea? Gravel and dirt caught in the wheels as it slowed from a rolling suitcase to a dragging suitcase to an anvil with a retractable handle. What sort of lunatic shows up to a refugee camp with a Samsonite? She packed so much emotional energy into that suitcase she had none left to consider what she had done to Sonja.

Each day the mountains grew taller. Filtration points and checkpoints abounded, most manned by young soldiers too timid to investigate movement in the woods. But on the evening of the fourth day, carrying on her shoulders all twenty-eight weary kilometers, Natasha came to a filtration point larger and better lit than the others. The chain-link fence, crowned with razor wire and stretching along the pasture and into the woods, prevented the usual circumnavigation. Had she arrived at the checkpoint when the sun warmed her bones, she might have turned back and taken the connecting road she had passed two hours earlier. Had it been summer, and the ground hadn't needed to be warmed and dried by fire, she might have bedded in the woods and waited for the morning to illuminate her options. But it was neither earlier that day nor earlier that year. It was night; it was cold; her bones hated her; she just wanted to get to the other side, warm the ground, and sleep and sleep and sleep. Besides, she was a refugee destined for a refugee camp, and in her exhaustion she believed the soldiers would honor the international law guaranteeing her safe passage.

A halo of floodlight surrounded her; whether it guided or followed her, she couldn't say. A bullhorn demanded she keep her hands in plain sight. Fatigue and haste had clouded her judgment, and only now, as she walked in that brilliant circle with one arm raised, the other pulling the suitcase, did she begin to worry. She'd imagined that homesick boys a year out of school would man the filtration point as they had the others. But when she saw the prison tattoos on their hands, when the bespectacled official frowned at the fifty-ruble note she presented in lieu of a passport, she saw her mistake beyond all doubt. These were *kontraktniki*, and this was the front line rather than a checkpoint. The Makarov weighed more every second it went undiscovered. The men found her sanitary napkins suspicious enough to inspect, yet hadn't searched her. They gathered around her portable alarm clock like uncomprehending tribesmen. All the while the gun grew heavier on her breast.

She drew her mind to the Rome women's clinic, which, despite every aspersion she had cast at it, was in memory another term for rescue. Her blood had been drawn and filtered through a vending machine that flickered with red and yellow numbers. She had tested positive for a half dozen sexually transmitted diseases, all of which sounded like geometry terms. In group, listening to the confessions of women who missed their pimps, who were terrified of what their families would say, who didn't sleep for fear of waking up in the brothel, she had nodded in recognition. Strangers from Poland and Turkey and Siberia had spoken with her breath. Her hope of rescue had taken so long to die. It had survived the Breaking Grounds, Kosovo, the beatings, rapes, and heroin. It had survived longer than denial and indignation, longer than three of her teeth. It had survived until the day a john's wallet had fallen from his trousers, opening on the floor. The transparent plastic sleeve had held a portrait of a boy and girl dressed in matching sweaters and smiling uncomfortably. She had begged him, a father, a family man, to rescue her. But he had just looked at her as if she'd asked him to staple feathers to her arms. When her turn had come, she told the other women and they had looked at her and nodded.

But rescue was another country, and she didn't know if she would make it there. The soldiers kept unpacking and unfolding, unraveling and unwrapping, while on her chest the Makarov grew to a Kalashnikov, then a Katyusha rocket launcher. The soldiers were ripping the wheels from her suitcase and still hadn't touched her. As she tightened her headscarf, she finally understood. The soldiers thought she was a traditional Chechen woman.

An older officer, fragranced with enough aftershave to inebriate lesser men, emerged from the camouflaged outhouse that constituted the checkpoint office. Golden stars glimmered from his epaulets. A double-headed-eagle perched on his tie clip. His hair parted above his left ear and was plastered across his balding crown. Nothing escaped his wide blue eyes. The soldiers addressed him as colonel.

"I apologize for the inconvenience," he said, in round-bodied Russian. "You will be on your way shortly."

He spoke a hushed order to the soldiers. She had no reason to doubt him when the soldiers obligingly began to fold her clothes and tie her suitcase back together with twine.

"This way," the colonel said. Guiding her by the arm as a gentleman might, he walked her toward the forest. "You need to sign a few pieces of paperwork before we can let you through. Unfortunately, it's located at an outpost a half kilometer west of us."

She didn't know at which step the truth crystallized in her mind, whether it was the fifth step or the sixth, the eighth or eighteenth, but long before they reached the woods she knew what this man would do to her. The colonel, a man who blamed the wars on the fact that his first wife once lived here, still hadn't decided.

The whole way the colonel spoke in the honeyed, empathetic tone of one every bit as frustrated by bureaucracy as she was, who would, of course, let so sweet a refugee pass through unhindered were such a decision his to make. He didn't slur his words. His arm held her so gently she wanted to believe they really were walking toward an outpost in the middle of a forest filled with paperwork. Every so often, he smacked his bubblegum.

When they reached the edge of the woods, he told her to stop. The light of the filtration point shone in his eyes, but they were beyond even that questionable society. He untied her headscarf and slithered his fingers through her hair. His first wife had been the first of five. Each one met the others after her divorce and with each other they pieced their lives together. His five wives would be bridesmaids at each other's second weddings. Their children by second husbands would be christened together, and much later, two of their thirty-nine grandchildren would join in a marriage that would not end in divorce. The friendship of his ex-wives was the one decent thing the colonel had created in his forty-seven years.

"Take off your clothes," the colonel instructed wearily, as if this were one more duty the bureaucrats asked of him.

"No," she said. She had never denied a man like that. Her mouth had gone dry and her whole body hummed as she said it again. "No."

"Take them off," the colonel repeated.

"No."

The back of his hand crossed her cheek with a violent crack. He massaged his knuckles. Had he been angry or lustful, she might have surrendered, but his face revealed no emotion, nothing to suggest either of them was human. In four brothels she had met every shape of desperation God had given testicles, and the only men she couldn't forget were those who needed to impart pain rather than receive pleasure. The colonel's backhand burned against her cheek. Beneath that cemented hair, the colonel was every man in the Mediterranean she still remembered.

"Okay," she said. "I will." Even her surrender didn't stoke a flicker in his eyes. She reached for her coat buttons. A marching band had taken residence in her chest. Her veins vibrated. She unbuttoned her overcoat but would not then, or ever, shrug it off. It took all her strength to lift the Makarov from her inner coat pocket. Her palm held the burden of battalions, the mass of a hundred thousand lost limbs, and her hand didn't tremble. She unlatched the safety and aimed the pistol at the bridge of his nose. Judging from the colonel's expression, she might have been aiming a pastry. He smiled. Had she not walked through all of Hell's flames, she might have believed she could forfeit her dignity. But she knew better, and then he knew she knew better, and her glare crushed the air between them and in it was, for him, finally, the understanding that he would never return from here.

"I—" he began, and she squeezed the trigger without hesitating. More than anger or fear or hate, she felt a deep disappointment in the colonel for speaking. He should have known words wouldn't lead them from the woods. She was a poor shot. Though she aimed at the man's forehead, the bullet raked the left side of his skull. His ear yanked off as if held by wet clay. Mucus ran from his nose and melted into sweat, blood, tears, and whatever else pasted the moonlight to his skin. He shrieked, and she smiled at the great bellows he had hidden in his chest. His pain broke the register of adult expression, exiting his lips in the high-pitched and familiar wail of an infant. She knelt beside him. She leaned to his face. His screams rose in bursts of hot steam from his lips. So this is what it's like. This is just how much you can make a person feel. She didn't know she was the deepest wish come true of five women a half continent away. She pressed the pistol to his temple and stared into the wide wound of his eyes with the righteousness of one rendering a service to a stranger. She was patient. He stared at her and she waited until the terror of what was to come dissolved the stones of his eyes. Blood gurgled from the opening that had been his ear, but his hair, parted just above it, was unmoved.

"You'll have to walk into the forest alone," she said. He thrashed his arms before three squeezes of the trigger forever stilled them. A silence followed. She closed her eyes. Her hands finally began to tremble.

Then sprinting footsteps, shouts of *colonel*, parabolas of torchlight scanning the ground. The bare branches gestured welcomingly. She could flee, but how long would she last? A few hours? A day or two at most until tracking dogs pulled her scent by the lungful from the Samsonite and found her? No, she was done hiding, done bargaining. She had known that from the moment she reached for the pistol. To live with dignity meant a premature death. One of the roving circles of torchlight caught the fingers of the colonel's outstretched arm. A few minutes later another flashlight fell upon them, and this time Natasha and the colonel were not overlooked. The shouts of *shahidka, shahidka*, made her smile. She stood firm, steadying herself against an oak tree, and managed to fire twice more before a machine-gun round opened her stomach and dropped her to her knees. It was supposed to hurt, but this much? The first-time mothers said it hurt more than they had ever imagined. And was it worth it, she would ask. Oh yes, they would say. Oh yes. The torchlight fell upon her again. The second bullet put a hole in her chest, and she felt her breath leave, but neither the third, nor fourth, nor fifth, nor sixth, nor seventh, nor eighth, nor ninth, nor tenth, nor eleventh, nor twelfth, nor thirteenth, nor fourteenth, nor fifteenth, nor sixteenth, nor seventeenth was seen, or felt, or heard.

# CHAPTER

## 2 6

THE HOUR HAND reached eight, eight and a half, nine, nine and a half hours in the morning, and still no sign of Akhmed. The girl asked for him as soon as she woke, but Sonja had sidestepped his name as if it were a puddle on the road, and they hadn't spoken of him since. "Talking accomplishes nothing," Natasha had said, and for once, in her heart, Sonja knew her sister had been right. It was the fifth day after Dokka had disappeared.

When the hour hand reached eleven, Sonja went to the canteen for a glass of ice to calm her nerves, and found a slip of white paper on the counter. *If you find my body*, it said, *return it for burial.* She crushed the note into her pocket but then took another look. The full address was *38 Eldár Forest Service Road.* Akhmed's village. Was this what he had kept stitched in his trousers? Sixteen hours earlier they had lain on the narrow maternity ward bed and held each other so neither would roll off. When he stood and hitched up his trousers, she had noted a small tear near the knee, which he had blamed on a stray line of razor wire, even though she didn't ask. She ironed out the wrinkled slip of paper with her thumb. It was the penultimate message she would receive from him. In a shoebox in the canteen cupboard, atop six dozen others, his ID card was to be the final message, though she wouldn't find that for another five days.

With the note now folded in her jacket pocket, she drove to Eldár. Bereft of leaves, the trees looked skeletal. This was the road Akhmed marched down to and from the hospital. The one he *marches* down, she corrected, careful to keep him alive while she still could. Clouds veined the sky. Grain stalks swayed with what little breeze there was. The forest had overtaken much of the farmland, but as the road curved through a field, she came upon the frozen carcass of what had been a wolf.

Eldár was no more than a saucer beside Volchansk, the type of village one would only stumble upon when lost. Save for the street portraits, its name was all that distinguished it from a thousand other ruined villages. She tracked the addresses, no small feat when so few doorways stood, and parked in front of number 38. Across from Akhmed's house, frozen ash stretched beyond the charred foundations of a house, across the field, and into the woods. It had been Havaa's home, and the realization pulled a wire of grief straight through her stomach. Havaa and Akhmed had only become real when they were plucked from nowhere and deposited in her life. She knew what had happened to Havaa's father and her home, but here the girl materialized in her mind as she hadn't before. She turned her back on the ruin.

The door to number 38 hung from its top hinge. As she entered her stomach clenched, as it did each time she stepped into the operating theater knowing she couldn't save the life before her.

For her first nine years, she had traveled to her maternal grandmother's flat in Grozny for Christmas and New Year's. Her grandmother had moved from Moscow to Grozny in the late forties, among the ethnic Russians sent to repopulate the republic after the deportation, and had taken with her the goose-down mattress she had inherited from her parents. The grandmother's parents, Sonja's great-grandparents, had hidden the goose-down mattress in a haystack for three years following the Revolution, when the price of owning such an extravagance had been nine grams of lead. The grandmother's parents had lost to the state nearly everything of lesser value than their lives: the farmland, the farmhouse, nearly all their clothing and furniture, even the donkey they had named Vladimir Ilyich. Through it all the goose-down mattress lay beneath the haystack that neither the commissars nor the Cheka agents had thought to disturb. When they moved to Moscow, they prized their rescued mattress as a happy memory of what life had been like before a band of angry men overly fond of facial hair had deigned to liberate them. Even in the Great Purge, when they hid the goose-down mattress beneath their bed and slept instead on a thin mat of straw, they pulled it out on birthdays and anniversaries to remember the way life once had been. Sonja's grandmother was conceived on that mattress, birthed on that mattress, and sixty-four years later she died on that mattress. For its long life, a life that outlasted the Soviet Union, the mattress retained the damp reek of haystack. It marked Sonja's first nine Decembers, and now, in her thirty-fifth, she pushed open the rickety door of Akhmed's house and found the scent of her grandmother's mattress inside.

The living room had been violently shaken. A fallen bookcase leaned against the divan. On the floor were twelve kopek-sized circles connected by slender shafts of light to twelve bullet holes in the ceiling. She called his name, but the house wouldn't respond with even an echo. A trail of glass led to the kitchen where the kettle and two cans of evaporated milk were the only intact containers. In the bedroom, a body rested beneath the sheets. A hypodermic needle lay on the floor beside the bed. Akhmed's wife, Sonja realized. She slowly peeled back the sheet. Out of habit, she felt for a pulse. The woman's hair smelled of pears. Her hands were smooth, uncalloused, beautiful. Pressing her fingertips to the woman's forehead, she found herself for the first time in many years standing before a corpse without guilt, a mourner rather than a failed surgeon.

She didn't know the woman's favorite color, or her favorite food, or whether she had, as a child, preferred her father's company to that of her mother; she didn't know the sound of the woman's voice, whether it was as small as her body suggested, or much larger, growing as her flesh shrank. She didn't even know the woman's name. But she knew this woman had a husband, and he had been a decent man, yes, *had been*. Akhmed died the moment she saw his wife in bed. He wouldn't return. Whoever came upon this house next would find fallout, chaos, and would not see the way Akhmed had lived; a stranger, a refugee, would discover this place and never the man and woman it had belonged to.

She found a broom and dustpan in the kitchen closet and swept up the broken dishes and jars and teacups. She righted the living room bookcases and, unsure of how Akhmed had ordered the books, she arranged them alphabetically. She wiped up the plaster shaken loose by gunfire and nailed a wooden board over the bullet holes. She scrubbed the black grime from the basin with steel wool. For more than two hours she tidied the house. The rooms contained so little they were quickly restored, and by early afternoon she had no choice but to face the bedroom. Dust blanketed the bureau, carpeted the floor, filled the frame of their wedding photograph. She pulled a fistful of white athletic socks from the drawer. "Do you mind if I borrow these?" she asked, and took the silence as permission. She cleaned the bureau, floor, windowsill and panes. The edge of the bed, rim of the lamp, and the books stacked beside the nightstand. *Hadji Murád* was among them and she set it aside knowing this once she'd break her long-standing policy against sad endings. In one of the bureau drawers she found several dozen charcoal-drawn portraits of the woman now lying dead in the bed. In the drawings her cheeks were fuller, her eyes open and clear. In every one she smiled.

When she finished dusting, she turned her attention to the bed. "Several hours after death the sphincter and bladder muscles relax," she said softly. "It isn't right to spend an eternity in soiled underwear. I'll clean you, okay?" She pulled back the covers and stripped off the night-dress. Wearing the socks like gloves she washed the woman's thighs and buttocks, and then dressed her in a tan skirt, a garden-hose-green sweater, and a burgundy headscarf. She looked like a bouquet of roses. Akhmed had told her that his wife hadn't walked in more than two years, so after pulling on the last pair of clean socks, she wedged the woman's feet into a pair of sneakers. "Now you can walk wherever you want."

After cleaning and dressing the woman, she returned to the manila envelope and collection of pages she'd found hidden beneath her body. The manila envelope was addressed: *For K, 56 Eldár Forest Service Road.* This K, whoever he was, lived only a handful of houses away. She set it aside and picked up the fastened pages. They appeared to form a letter or journal entry. The first sentence read: *This is about your father.* She flipped to the last page to read the last sentence, as was her custom, then moved up to the last paragraph, and then the last page:

> *There is little ink left in the pen, even less energy in my hand, and the time has come. This story ends where you begin. You were born in a hospi-tal. I drove your mother and father in the truck I purchased my son for his sixteenth birthday. Your mother's face was as red as the paint. Your father kept telling me to drive faster. The maternity ward was on the fourth floor of the hospital. Your father and I helped your mother climb the stairs. When her feet failed, we carried her. She was worried her hips would crush you. Even before you were born, she worried for you. It was amazing to see*

*her love you before you even met. Perhaps our deepest love is already in-scribed within us, so its object doesn't create a new word but instead allows us to read the one written. For their entire lives, even before they met, your mother and father held their love for you inside their hearts like an acorn holds an oak tree. You were their rain and sun, their morning and night.*

*In the maternity ward the nurse put your mother in a bed and I held her left hand and your father held her right. Custom says that a man shouldn't be present at a birth, but we didn't listen, we were there. On the boarded windows were drawings of a city that no longer existed. You were born within the memory of a kinder past. Your mother's screams opened her jaw so wide you could have come from her mouth. Never have I seen your father so afraid. Then, you arrived. We were all there, waiting for you. The nurse held you in her hands. You didn't breathe. We held our breaths waiting for you to find yours. And when your mouth opened, and your lungs burst, we knew they would never be empty. And your father, I have never seen a man more joyful.*

*The nurse who delivered you was named Natasha. All these years later I remember her name because she had remembered mine. She had read my book,* Origins of Chechen Civilization, *one of the four score who ever had. Hers were the first hands to hold you. When you were suf-focating, she taught you to breathe.*

*Your mother's were the second hands. She looked at you as if she had been born to you. She passed you to your father. The corners of his eyes crinkled. His heart had been the acorn. Now it was the oak tree.*

*Those are the first three pairs of hands that held you. How I hope you will live long enough that I will never know the final three.*

*"What is her name?" the nurse asked, as your father held you to his chest.*

*"Havaa." He spoke your name like the rhythm of a pulse.*

*When they took him, he held your name right there in his chest, and you were with him, even if you didn't know it. When he reached the end, he did not die. He called your name and began to live in you.*

She set down the letter. If her pounding heart spoke a name, it was one she didn't recognize. Her sister had delivered hundreds of newborns in the seven years she had worked in the maternity ward, hundreds of Havaas, and they were her patients, not her children, neither more nor less loved than the other lives begun and ended, saved and lost, revived and mourned within the gray granite walls of Hospital No. 6. But Sonja couldn't name those countless others, had not shared with them a mattress or a room or an energy bar, would not recognize their faces on the street or in the bazaar or at the cemetery, did not wish for them what she wished for Havaa, a need, newly made, to save this one life her sister had brought into the world.

Before leaving she surveyed the rooms a final time. Akhmed's wife lay peacefully, her hands at her sides, her bright white tennis shoes ready to take her anywhere. Sonja propped the front door as best she could and wondered who would enter next. The vacant house would become a haven for refugees who had heard of a hostel in the 30-block of Eldár Forest Service Road. It would never again be as clean as it was the afternoon Sonja left, as one might expect, as some three thousand souls were yet to shelter there.

She drove to the address marked on the manila envelope. A red pickup truck parked in front of the house was better kept than any others on the block. Green antifreeze beads lazed in the sludge of the half-shoveled walk. She knocked on the door. A minute passed before an elderly man opened the door and gaped at her, his unhinged eyes filled with such bewilderment she wondered if he saw her as a ghost.

"I'm sorry to bother you. I'm Akhmed's . . ." What? Employer? Supervisor? Colleague? Lover? Five-day acquaintance? She held out the manila envelope. "I'm his friend. Are you K?"

"Khassan," the old man mumbled. He reached for the envelope as if it weren't there, as if his hand would pass through the paper, through her, into eternity. "Where did you . . ."

"In his house. I found it there. He was taken last night."

"I know. And Ula?"

"Ula?"

"His wife," the old man said.

"She's there, but she's gone too."

The old man nodded, barely there. He squeezed the manila envelope and traced the address with his index finger.

"Are you okay?" she asked. He looked like he might fall over.

"Thank you for bringing me this," he mumbled.

She was halfway to her truck when she heard the manila envelope tear behind her. Her truck was right there, next to the red pickup, and she just wanted to leave. That manila envelope contained a final message, but it wasn't hers, and she didn't want to know what it said. She slid the letter to Havaa in the glove box, between the letters of safe passage, without noticing that two were missing. Driving away, she fit her lips around the round, sonorous name. *Ula. U-la.* The name made her lips pucker, waiting to be kissed by the reply. Had she known the name earlier, she would have dressed the wife in a gown and shawl, rather than a skirt and a sweater, so she would, for all time, look as elegant as she sounded.

1994 1995 1996 1997 1998 1999 2000 2001 2002 2003 **2004**

BENEATH THE STARS, without the interference of cloud or wind or leaf cover, the low rumble of diesel engines murmured through the open window where Khassan waited and listened. When the nightstand clock read 12:15 A.M., the splayed headlights of three trucks parted the darkness. A minute later, in front of Akhmed's house, the trucks were parked, engines idling, passengers disembarking, men from the security forces, whom Khassan, with his head craned out the open window, saw only as black silhouettes lit up by the headlights before returning to shadow. It was 12:16. Entire years had passed when he was rich enough in time to disregard the loose change of a minute, but now he obsessed over each one, this minute, the next minute, the one following, all of which were different terms for the same illusion. At 12:17, the knocking began. Khassan couldn't see the masked security forces first pound then kick at Akhmed's door, and at this distance the thuds might be mistaken for a less violent act, an insomniac carpenter, a couple keeping themselves warm in bed, but a minute later came the unmistakable splintering of wood, twisting of door hinges. Khassan gripped the sill. He could see nothing but the pale flood of headlights. *You are a coward,* Mirza had said a half century earlier, and he heard her as if she stood just behind him. *You are a coward.* But what could he do? Run out? Reason with the masked men now entering Akhmed's house? At best, they would arrest and take him wherever they were taking Akhmed. At worst, both would be shot for his intervention. And Havaa, what would happen to her? His face broke out in a cold sweat and his hands tightened their grip against the sill. He tried moving his feet toward the doorway, but they weren't listening. Not once in his seventy-nine years had he felt more useless, more powerless, more afraid. *You are a coward,* Mirza said in his ear, but she didn't know what they do to people in the Landfill. At 12:21 came a burst of twelve gunshots, enough to kill twelve Akhmeds, but no shadows crossed that wide wound of headlight. Unable to see, unable to move, he tuned his ear to the frequency of Akhmed's broken bones, his bruised flesh, his gouged eyes, his ruptured organs, his snapped fingers, his busted cheeks, his smashed temple, his collapsed skull, his sobs, his surrender, his defeat, his gasps, his pleas, his promises, his prayers, his final breaths, his last memories, of his mother's embrace or Ula's thigh or a dog's bark or a bullet rushing through a pink brainy cloud, whatever Akhmed might hold to as the whispers cease and the silent ascension begins. Akhmed's pain would be the only sound loud enough to break through Mirza's flat incantation, *you are a coward a coward a coward,* but Akhmed made no shout, no plea, no call for mercy that Khassan could hear. The only sound to escape the house was the clatter of dishes, the white plates with chipped edges, the small saucers Akhmed used to use to fool his stomach, the teal blue teacup, the one with the crimson rim from which Khassan had sipped the fancy Indian tea someone's in-law had given one of them, and how could a teacup shatter when padded in so many layers of memory, how could this be happening again, how could Khassan stand at this same open window where four nights earlier he had listened to the same smashing dishware, had stared into the same unblinking headlights, had felt the same disgrace rip through him when Dokka was disappeared? At 12:27, shadows lumbered into the stream of headlights and among those shadows was a flailing form, so faint a contortion no one save Khassan would recognize it as Akhmed. A moment and the shadow vanished back into blessed darkness, and the truck doors snapped closed, and Mirza's accusation clamped him to the windowsill, and the headlights pulled the trucks back to the underworld they had emerged from. As the last truck passed Khassan's open window, Akhmed's muffled cry finally reached him.

The sun had risen by the time his mind slowed enough to slip away. He dozed, but didn't rest. In his dreams he wandered through grass frozen into fields of stiff white ribbon. He had hated Kazakhstan so much. He'd never imagined he might look back on exile as his happiest years.

At ten he woke and for three hours stared at the ceiling as he marshaled the courage to stand. The house was silent. He slid through Ramzan's half-opened door, as he had dozens of times before when he had something to tell his son. Ramzan lay on the bed, mouth agape. Khassan crept to the bureau, where he withdrew the *kinzhal* from the top drawer. He had received it from his father, and his father had received it from his father's father, and so it went, a century and a half of fathers and sons. It was the oldest thing he had ever owned not counting the trees in back. Near the handle the blade went brown with the blood of an Imperial conscript, or perhaps it was just rust. His father had taught him to thrust it forward, turning the blade before ripping it out, in case Tsar Alexander II might rise from the dead to pillage Eldár.

The edge followed the grooves in his palm, his life line, his love line. He carried it to the bed and wrapped the blade in the blanket so it wouldn't wake Ramzan prematurely. He took a breath and the air filled him completely. The previous night was a place he wouldn't return from. After the headlights had faded, he had crossed and uncrossed his fingers, picked up and set down the water glass, and amid these trivial gestures, he had died. "You are nothing without love and pride and family," he had once told Akhmed. The first two had disappeared the previous night in the back of a truck; he was on his way, fingering the blade that would soon cut through the third.

"Did I ever tell you the story of the cobbler's drunken son?" he softly asked. Ramzan heard nothing. "When I was a child, our village was plagued by a cobbler's son, an eighteen-year-old who inflicted more property damage than could be expected from a man who couldn't make his two feet move in the same direction. The cobbler was respected throughout the village until his son discovered the effects of fermented beet *samogon*. The liquor made pariahs of them both, proving right the aphorist who first stated that as the son inherits from the father, so the father inherits from the son. For years the cobbler appealed to the imam, apologized to the fathers of the women his son dishonored, and paid for, replaced, or returned the stolen goods. He offered to mend the shoes of any soul his son had wronged. So it was. But there came a point when the son's capacity for ruin outpaced the cobbler's capacity for restitution. He was in debt. Half the village walked on shoes paid for by his son's drinking. One day the son vanished. No mention of him, no funeral, no gossip of work on a distant collective farm; he just disappeared. A month later my grandfather visited the cobbler with the village elders. They took him honey and raisins and welcomed him back. I, still a boy, was told to honor and respect the cobbler, as all the villagers were, because he had put the good of our small society, our *teip,* above his own. His son's name became a blasphemous word, erased from the collective memory, stricken from even the whispers of women. The story, when told, always ended at this pinnacle of honor and sacrifice. It never went on to tell how the cobbler, who didn't mend another boot in his life, lived to the age of ninety-nine as a hermit, drinking himself senseless every day and night, alone but for the ghost of his son, whom he pleaded with in unbearable calls that I could hear from the far side of the village.

"They never tell you about that part, about how long you might live with it," Khassan continued. He held Ramzan's limp fingers. Thirty-two and three-quarter years had passed since he had first felt those fingers and they had astonished him, delicate as sparrow feet and holding on to his thumb as if he were the sturdiest branch in the forest. "They never tell you about that part."

For two long years he had hated himself for imagining this moment. Disappearance by disappearance he had tallied the lives his son had extinguished—and if Ramzan hadn't snuffed them, he'd held them to the wind—Alman, Musa, Omar, Aslan, Apti, Mansur, Aslan the Hirsute, Ruslan, Amir, Amir Number Two, Isa, Khalid, and Dokka, postponing this inevitability until the next day, the next disappearance, until he watched Akhmed's beaten shadow eclipse the flood of headlights, and knew the next day would be the last. Twenty-one years and five months earlier, Ramzan had bounded from this bed and out that door to the kitchen, shirtless and wide-eyed with awe; he had pointed to a single hair sprouting from his underarm, as thrilled as if he'd found a diamond there. "You were right about the trumpet blast," Khassan said. The regret was already there, a blank wall he'd spend the rest of his life staring at. "These are the end times. There can be nothing after this." Now that it had arrived, all his talk of mountaintop sacrifices seemed the absurd, grandiose fantasies of a confused old man. There was no voice in the sky.

Ramzan's chest rose and fell, oblivious to the decision already made by the hand holding his. Khassan had held that chest when it was no wider than a chicken's, had held it to his own and felt something so tender and precious pass between them that he would have done anything for this boy. But this? Had the bottle of sleeping pills not sat open on the nightstand, he would have acted sooner. But from the many times he had perched on the mattress, he knew the pills would keep Ramzan comatose until evening. He could wait. Now that he had, in his heart, stepped over the edge, it didn't matter how long he fell before hitting the ground. "I want to tell you something," he said. "But I don't know what. I don't know." Pride wouldn't allow apology, not even now. "You are my son. You are mine," he whispered, as a spell, as a gift, a last lullaby, a branding. Ramzan's head turned, so slightly, into the pillow, and it nearly broke Khassan to see this shimmer of life. Sleep, just a while longer, that's it, where else can you go where you neither suffer nor cause suffering? Khassan lay on the bed and breathed with his son. He followed Ramzan's lead. Together they drew from and gave to the communal air, his open hand on Ramzan's chest, rising and falling in this silence they made.

Three knocks broke it. Khassan sat up and carried the cavern in his chest to the front door. No one in the village, not even Akhmed, had visited the house since Ramzan's collusion became known. Were his former friends standing on the other side with honey and raisins to welcome him back into society? You are too soon, he wanted to cry. I haven't done it yet. I'm still climbing to the summit. He blotted his forehead with a purple handkerchief before opening the door.

On the other side stood a woman foregrounded against the teal sky. She wore a padded gray coat over scrubs. "I'm sorry to bother you. I'm Akhmed's . . . I'm his friend. Are you K?" She passed him the manila envelope he had given Akhmed two days earlier. His pulse quivered as he accepted it; if it still contained his letter to Havaa he would give up. But his address was written on the manila envelope by Akhmed's hand. The contained correspondence was thinner than his. "In his house," she said in explanation. "I found it there. He was taken last night."

That shadow floundering through light to the dark bank on the other side. The dementia that was to consume his memory in nine years would leave him that. When all else had faded, those headlights would still shine; they would be the light at the end. He could hardly speak, think, act, breathe. What was happening? What was this? He discovered Ula's name between his lips. The woman dropped her eyes and shook her head, respectful but firm, perhaps accustomed to delivering bad news.

As soon as she turned to the road, he tore open the manila envelope. It held two letters. One was written by an FSB colonel, the other by a rebel field commander. Each letter gave orders for the unhindered passage of its unnamed bearer. A third message lay at the bottom of the manila envelope, written on a scrap of paper so slight he nearly missed it. *Mercy,* the note read. *Mercy.*

The dogs, dozing beside the house, stretched their legs on the ground and lumbered after him, Sharik last, as he hurried to Akhmed's house. He held the manila envelope against his chest, blocking it from the wind.

The front door was propped against the doorframe. He passed over a clean living room floor, an inexplicably alphabetized bookcase, and the dogs followed, Sharik last, because the front door wouldn't close, and what did it matter, they were cleaner than the last beasts to enter.

Ula lay fully clothed on the unmade bed. After the past hour watching the rise and fall of his son's chest, he knew immediately that she was gone. White tennis shoes jutted from the end of her baggy brown skirt, as if in death she would be reborn in good health, given a newly wired nervous system, allowed in her private paradise an afterlife of marathons. He closed the bedroom door, afraid the dogs might nibble at the body. Claw patter trembled through the thin walls. If he had to come back, he would be a dog.

For a moment he stood by the door, surprised by the scent of soap. Then one foot forward. Then the other. He folded her hands together and placed them on her stomach. The room was clean, as was the body, and though he could explain neither, he wasn't surprised. A burgundy headscarf framed her face. Cupping her skull like a fragile bowl into which he had poured his most valuable possessions, placing his thumbs on her lids, he opened her to the dead afternoon light. She stared straight through him, to the unfolding infinities that bookended her thirty-five years, through him to the place where they would soon meet, when the trumpeter's breath failed, when he would descend the notes of the final melody to the silence where Mirza waited.

He could have wrapped her in a white elasticated bedsheet, the nearest to a burial *kafan* in the depleted closet. The body was usually washed in scented water, but a martyr was buried unwashed, in the clothes she died in. He could have enshrouded her. She weighed so little. Even a man of his age could have carried her outside. In the backyard he might have set her on a cushion of snow. The ground was frozen. He could have plunged the spade head but the ground would hold. He knew no burial prayers, but he could have stood quietly and let canine panting mark the minute. He had spent his entire life burying, and unearthing, and reburying the dead, and he could have done it once more. The spade would have scraped through the frost. A shovelful of snow scattering on her torso. Three thousand years before a Russian empire existed, native tribes buried their dead in kurgans that grew so large they became part of the land, surviving the construction and collapse of subsequent civilizations. He would have thought of this as he entombed her. He would have shoveled until he couldn't lift the spade, until the tomb reached his chest, until it compacted into a monument that would last until the spring thaw. But he didn't have the energy to do more than close her eyelids, fluff the pillow beneath her head, and point her toward Mecca.

At home he picked three sets of clothes. Extra layers, heavy on wool; no longer could he rely on the comforts his son provided. He searched his closet for something to pack his clothes in but only found a laundry bag. He'd never thought to replace the brown suitcase after he buried it, never thought he would leave Chechnya again. At the center of his small bundle of clothes was the ruby-red scarf Mirza had unwound from her neck and placed in his hands, one afternoon, long ago. In the kitchen he packed alcohol swabs and syringes and insulin vials and all the food he could find in withered plastic shopping bags. On the kitchen table Ramzan's keys radiated from their ring and he placed them in his pocket. He didn't know where he would go. He had journeyed through Poland, Czechoslovakia, and Germany. He had, once, taken a victorious shit on a Reichstag commode. And from there to the Kazakh steppe, where, to the horizon, nothing sounded louder than the wind. He had traveled a quarter of the way around the globe without taking one step voluntarily. This was his home. For every barrack floor, muddy trench, outpost tarpaulin, bunker cot, and fallow field he had ever slept on, the memory of home was his only rest. Returning in 1956 he had vowed to never leave. Better to die here, he imagined, than endure another exile.

He crossed the hall to Ramzan's room. Neither his *kinzhal* nor his boy had moved. If he could reach back he would hold his son, love his son, and untangle the knot his soul had become. He would find the ends. "Why are you my father?" the boy had asked one August afternoon, twenty seconds after asking, "Why is the sky blue?" and forty seconds before he asked, "Why do people get old?" They were sitting outside. Khassan had been teaching his son to eat shelled sunflower seeds and he held his breath long enough for the question to pass. "Why are you my father?" the boy asked again. It was two years before he stopped asking for a bike, five and a quarter before he stopped asking his father for anything. Khassan had never found an answer. If he could go back he would make one.

He closed Ramzan's door behind him. The time for answering had ended and the peace of the afternoon articulated all he wanted for his son. The shopping bags, laundry bag, and two letters of safe passage waited at the front door, and as he reached for them, a question hit him like the face of a wall. Who was that woman and why had she come to deliver Akhmed's answer? Had she known she would deliver him from his son? It didn't matter. He would forever remember her as an angel dressed in an overcoat and scrubs, sent to stay his hand.

He locked the door behind him and crossed the packed snow to the red pickup. The dogs followed him, sniffing at the plastic bag of insulin, syringes, and chicken thighs. He set the bags in the passenger seat and turned to the dogs, six in all, lean-boned and matted and blind and bald.

"I'm leaving," he said. His voice cracked with sorrow as the dogs tilted their snouts to him. Killing his son had seemed less reprehensible than abandoning these dogs. "I don't know where I'm going. I don't know what will happen."

Tears fell down his cheeks. Two of the dogs ran after a hallucinated mouse, while the rest stared up at their broken benefactor with the same incomprehension that had made a home between his ears. "I can't promise anything, but I will try to take care of you. If you want to come, I will take you."

He climbed into the truck, set the two letters of safe passage in the glove box, and started the engine. He eased the brake and let the truck roll at a walking pace, waiting to see what would happen. In the rear-view the dogs licked each other, tumbled on the ground, and went on in a world without him. Gravel shot back when he pushed the accelerator and the ears of the bald dog perked, and when she turned the other dogs noticed, and their snouts swiveled toward the truck as they galloped as one animal, a twenty-four-legged, twelve-eared beast, racing to reclaim their seventh head. He unlatched the back and one by one they jumped into the bed of the pickup truck, Sharik last.

Passing beneath the portraits of the disappeared he saw them as if for the first time. No one else would remember the artist's face, but he would. When he reached the end of the block, he kept driving. When he reached the end of the village, he kept driving. Wind tossed the dogs' tongues and they shook their heads wonderfully. The serrated ridge of mountains cut into the horizon and he drove toward it. The passing refugees had speculated wildly, believing any rumor large enough to hope on. He didn't know what lay on the other side. He didn't know that the disease that would in nine years erase every memory but the headlights was already brewing among his neurons. He didn't know that his son would live alone in the village for three grief-stricken years, wondering and waiting for his return before moving to a mountain hamlet, where he would keep wondering what had happened to his father, without ever finding out, for another fifty-seven years. Khassan didn't know and he drove. He was seventy-nine years old. He was beginning a new life.

CHAPTER

2 8

1994  1995  1996  1997  1998  1999  2000  2001  2002  2003  **2004**

"IF YOU COULD go back, would you leave London?" Natasha had asked the question on a cool Tuesday morning in March 1998. They were on good terms that month, sharing the last drags of a cigarette in the hospital parking lot as loose debris rustled under what seemed too pleasant a shade of sky. "If you could go back, would you leave London?" Of the thousands of times she had considered and still would consider the question, that had been the only time it had been posed as if an answer lived on the other side of it. "If you could go back . . ." There was a time when she had indulged in the hypothetical for hours a day, plotting the map that had led her here. But no life is a line, and hers was an uneven orbit around a dark star, a moth circling a dead bulb, searching for the light it once held.

The visit to Akhmed's had taken longer than she anticipated, and as she parked the truck and crossed the lot, the premonition of impending disaster pressed on her. But Deshi's heavy, dozing breaths were the only sound in the waiting room. Sonja jiggled her chair. The knitting needles began working in her hands before Deshi opened her eyes.

"Anything?" Sonja asked.

"No, slow week. The land mine's brother took him away, our only visitor."

"That's it? Nothing else?" She held the edge of the check-in counter, where a pen, long dry, remained tethered by a thin metal chain. How could it be that today, of all days, the emergencies of God and of man rested?

"Nothing else," Deshi said, without lifting her gaze from the needle tips. "Not a single patient in the hospital."

"We could shut it down."

Deshi smiled; not a day passed that she didn't regret asking Maali to fetch clean linens; not a day passed that she didn't hold Maali amid the rubble of the falling fourth floor, holding her as she had when Maali fell from a swing set, four years before the deportations, when Maali was crying and Deshi was the only one who knew how to comfort her. "Where would she go?" Deshi asked.

"Holiday."

"All that education and she finally says something smart."

"I can't remember the last time the hospital was empty."

"No, I can't either."

"It won't last."

Deshi shook her head. "Why spoil such a lovely afternoon with talk like that."

"I'm just being realistic."

"I bet she'd be realistic on a summer day, too," Deshi said.

"I thought you were done gambling?"

"I would have liked to play cards with Akhmed. I'd have won the trousers from his legs."

Harboring the small joy of that achievement, Sonja smiled. "I'd have liked to see that."

"I don't suppose we'll be seeing him again, will we?"

"No, I don't think so."

"A shame," Deshi said. That simple epitaph was the last they would ever say of Akhmed. A finger materialized from the tips of Deshi's needles. "Who are you knitting that for?" Sonja asked.

"Our young friend. She's had her hands balled in her sleeves all week."

The girl. Sonja hadn't considered what Akhmed's disappearance meant for the girl, who had, in less than a week, lost everything she had known. The day had spared legs from land mines and hearts from cardiac arrest, but it hadn't spared her. "Where is she?"

"I retired ten years ago," Deshi said. Another ten would pass before she acted on it. Three after that she would die of throat cancer, but not before falling in love with her oncologist. "Go find her yourself."

Eventually Sonja found the girl on the fourth floor, cross-legged within the doorway that framed the charred canvas of the city. Sonja sat beside her. "I'm sorry."

"Will he come back?"

"I don't know," Sonja said, and immediately regretted it, knowing how much false hope one can cultivate in the soil of those three words. "Probably not."

The girl nodded to the city.

"It's hard, Havaa, I know. The same thing happened to my sister." But that was a lie, wasn't it? She spoke of Natasha as if her sister was one of the disappeared. She wanted a share of the national suffering, to blame the Feds for the fact that her sister didn't love her enough to say good-bye. There was, at the center, an unnamable darkness around which she circled but couldn't touch. "I don't know where she is. I don't know if she's alive or dead. I know nothing."

"How do you find them?" the girl asked. She lifted her gaze to Sonja as if teetering on the precipice.

"I don't know, Havaa. I'm sorry. I don't. Maybe we try to find them in other people. In kindness and generosity; those things don't disappear."

The girl gave a deep, mucus-rattled snort. The answer wasn't the one she wanted, but Sonja had learned to be realistic when discussing death. Even if the answer put no distance between the girl and the hole the war opened within her, it was, Sonja hoped, enough to keep her holding on.

Havaa reached for her hand, and without thinking, Sonja felt for her pulse. Her radial artery rose and fell against Sonja's finger as a gentle reminder. She pressed her palm to Havaa's forehead.

"Am I sick?" the girl asked.

"No, you are in perfect health." And as she said the words, they seemed like a small miracle. She held Havaa's wrist, bending the joint back and forth. Through faded blue sweatpants, she felt the shape of Havaa's calves and knees. These legs would stand and walk and run. These arms would lift and embrace and let go. This person would grow and adapt and live; Sonja would make sure of it. "Your family isn't your choice," her father had said, to quell a tantrum, many years earlier, and without wanting to, she kept discovering what he had meant.

"What are you doing?" Havaa asked.

Spools of raw gratitude unraveled in Sonja. She was an idiot to be so impressed by legs that walked, wrists that bent, hands that held. Instead of explaining, she focused on the sensation of good fortune, of undeniable blessing, so she could later return to this memory to marvel at the girl's body, how remarkable it is, this human matter.

"I have no idea what I'm doing," she said, and helped the girl to her feet. "You kept your suitcase packed just in case you had to leave again, right?"

Havaa nodded.

A half hour later they left the hospital. Block after block passed unchanged but for the location of craters, the dispersion of brick. A one-way sign pointed to the sky. Three emaciated black dogs watched them from across the canyon of a grocery store basement, but thankfully didn't follow. All through it Sonja's head hummed. She held the girl's suitcase in one hand, and her hand in the other. She tried to remember the name of the street she had lived on.

This is what there is. Scorch marks fanning like massive seashells across the ground. Clouds gathering at the horizon. The unevenness of earth. The small heat she holds in her hand. A hand that is her hand holding a hand that is the girl's hand. This is it.

Somehow her feet recalled what she had forgotten. They led her. Her apartment block hadn't fallen. Blast tremors had opened the windows, but the building stood. They climbed the stairs.

"A nice woman lives here," she said as they passed Laina's flat. "Maybe you could spend time with her while I'm at the hospital."

The girl nodded. They stood at the front door. "I haven't been here in many months," she said. She unlocked the door. Dust covered everything but the ceiling. She would deal with it tomorrow, or the day after that; she had cleaned enough for one day. The entranceway bore no sign of break-in. The looters had long since emigrated. She lit a candle.

For dinner Havaa skinned and cut the sprouts from two potatoes, while Sonja found a car battery with enough juice to put a pot of water and rice to boil on the hot plate. When they ate, Sonja described the chopsticks people in Asia use to eat rice. The girl attempted it with two pencils, and after five minutes of failure, declared Asia an invention of Sonja's imagination. When they finished, Sonja led her to Natasha's room. Out of habit she knocked before opening the door. The bed was still made. The desk chair sat at an angle, as though its owner would return any moment to write a note, a letter, an explanation, or an apology.

"This is where you'll sleep," Sonja said. She set the suitcase on the edge of the bed and cleared the lower drawer of Natasha's jeans and sweaters. Natasha had taken the burgundy cardigan Sonja had given her for her eighteenth birthday, the one she hated and never wore, and wherever she was, Sonja hoped the temperature dipped enough for her to try it on. "You can put your things here."

"Am I going to live here?"

Sonja hadn't thought that far ahead. "Do you want to?"

The girl surveyed the room, inspected the closet, checked under the bed. "I get the whole room?"

"The whole room."

"And I don't have to share it?

"It's all yours."

The girl slowly nodded and leaned into Sonja, listening to the gurgle of her organs, these marvelous things we ignore, forget, and take for granted. "Come on," Sonja said. "You should unpack before either of us changes our minds."

Havaa unlatched her suitcase and pulled out balled gray socks, a sweater, a skirt, two headscarves, white underwear patterned with little pink bows. Then came the strange and wonderful artifacts. A marriage license from 1942, given by a couple who had been married for sixty-one years and no longer needed the document. A photograph of a slender man wearing a pea jacket that now hung in a closet in Saudi Arabia. The eighty-first draft of a love letter. The uncanceled stamp that would have sent the unwritten eighty-second draft. A prayer book opened by two hundred and six yearning hands.

"What is all this?" Sonja asked. In three weeks, when she would help Havaa build a case to display these treasures, Sonja would use her surgical saw, for the first time, to create something.

"My souvenirs," Havaa replied. She spaced them across the drawer with greater reverence than she'd shown her clothes. "From the refugees that stayed at our house."

There was a silver ring that had made a thirty-eight-year-old mother of two feel like the most glamorous woman in Grozny. An address book that an unfaithful husband had given Havaa so his wife's ghost wouldn't find it among his possessions. A dried seahorse that a father gave his six-year-old daughter in lieu of a pony. A Taj Mahal keychain that a refugee in southern Russia regretted giving away. A tie clip that a cosmonaut carried to space and back. And a Buckingham Palace Guard nutcracker.

"What's that?" Sonja barely got it out.

"That's Alu," the girl said. In three weeks and one day, with her palm aching wonderfully from sawing through wood, Sonja would tell her about Buckingham Palace. "He's an idiot."

"Who gave you Alu?"

"One of the women who stayed at our house."

"One of the refugees?" Sonja asked. In eight months, she would begin telling the girl about Natasha, and it would take her the rest of their time to finish the story.

"I introduced her to Akim," the girl said. "She was nice."

"What was her name?"

"I can't remember. Lots of people stayed at our house."

"But you remember Alu's name." In eight and a half years, she would have already taught the girl every lesson she had scribbled in her secondary school notebooks. In ten and three-quarter years, the girl, then a first-year biology student at the newly constructed Volchansk State University, would begin teaching her.

"Alu didn't leave."

"But what did she look like?"

"She had all her fingers."

"What else? What else?" In twelve and a third years, the girl, now a woman, would accompany Sonja on a five-day holiday to London. When the night porter asked, "Would your daughter care for an herbal tea?" it wouldn't cross Sonja's mind to correct him; it wouldn't have crossed her mind for some time. At the end of five days, they would leave London. Sonja would never see the city again. Havaa would.

"She was very pretty. I was nervous she wouldn't think I was pretty."

"Was she happy?"

"I don't know."

"Where was she going?" When the girl, she would forever be the girl to Sonja, went to Lake Baikal for two years to write her dissertation on the effects of climate change on freshwater microorganisms, Sonja would briefly consider sleeping in the hospital. But the world had long since stopped shaking, and no one would tolerate such eccentricity, not even from the distinguished head of surgery.

"Probably to a refugee camp."

"But where, which camp?"

"I don't know."

"Think hard. Where?" In twenty years Sonja would find Natasha's name beside her own, in the final sentence of the acknowledgments of Havaa's dissertation. The dissertation would be published to some acclaim, and on dusty university bookshelves in a half dozen countries, the two sisters would share an afterlife in that final sentence, one comma away from Akhmed and Dokka.

"I don't know."

"Was she alone?"

"Yes, she was alone." In twenty-eight years and seven months, at a limnology conference in Cologne, the girl would meet the man she was to marry nine years later. At the age of forty-six she would have her one and only child in the same maternity ward she was born in, a boy to carry her father's name; hers would be the second hands to hold him. At the age of sixty-eight she would hold her first grandson, also to carry her father's name; hers would be the third hands.

"And she left your house?"

"I said good-bye and she left."

"What direction, then? What direction did she go?"

"Down the road. There's only one direction you can go." The girl would outlive her husband, her son, one grandson, and every soul she had met before the age of eleven. She would outlive twenty-three of her teeth, three of her toes, one of her kidneys, and all the brown of her hair.

"Then where is she?"

"I don't know."

"But you saw her."

She would die at the age of one hundred and three, in the geriatrics ward of Hospital No. 6, in a room that had been the director's office, then Sonja's bedroom, and finally a regular hospital room, a room Havaa would remember as many thousands of refugees remembered her own childhood bedroom, a room that had been there when it was needed.

"Where is she? Please, Havaa. Please."

The girl wrapped her fingers around Sonja's. She looked up. Her eyes were green. "We don't know where she went," she said.

They never would.

THE MEN IN Pit B would remember him as a quiet man, if they remembered him at all. They would remember how he fastened his shirt buttons with his toes, how he had learned to live without his fingers. He was anxious, hungry, and scared, but they all were. At night they slept in the brown snow on sheets of carpet, slabs of plywood, whatever they could find. Though they all had nightmares, some would remember how the fingerless man kept repeating *is she . . . is she . . . is she . . . is she . . . is she . . .* before another man shook him awake.

Four nights after the fingerless man arrived, another man climbed down from the sixty-first rung. He curled near the side of the wall and slept. In the morning, the new arrival scanned the prisoners. His eyes found those of the fingerless man through the small crowd. It was clear that they had known each other from their past lives on the sixty-first rung, but whether they were brothers, or friends, or rivals, or enemies, none could say. The men, those who had been there for months, had seen how the Landfill could twist one's sense of honor and obligation, how in this underworld even a hated face was a welcomed one.

The new arrival examined their wounds, and though he didn't do a very good job, they called him the doctor. He was quiet. By night he neither screamed nor snored, and by day he rarely answered questions with more than a nod or shake of his head. When they commented on his reticence, he said he was practicing for his interrogation. The men, those who would leave without their fingers, their mental health, and parts of their souls, but would leave, might remember the carving of epitaphs on the clay wall. Though surprisingly self-sufficient, the finger-less man was unable to write his name. The doctor helped. The two epitaphs were carved so close together they looked like one.

A few days later, the fingerless man and the doctor were summoned to the sixty-first rung. The fingerless man had difficulty climbing. The doctor helped. For the following day and night, the men at the bottom of Pit B, those who would survive and those who would not, prayed at the epitaph of the fingerless man and the doctor. Twenty-four hours after the two ascended to the sixty-first rung, the men of Pit B, those who would break and those who would not, each packed a fistful of clay into the wall. Their palms were wet and cold, and they were solemn. When the names of the two men were buried, everyone knew they were finally gone.

But if they were to remember anything of the fingerless man and the doctor, they would remember the initial conversation, when no one was sure what the two meant to each other. The doctor had approached the fingerless man. For a moment they stood apart, each uncertain of the other. Then the fingerless man opened his arms, and the doctor stepped into them, and the two men swayed as they held each other, revolving in a private *zikr* that they alone understood. No one knew what to make of these two men who had found each other in the mud of the Landfill and begun dancing. No one had ever seen anything like it. The doctor whispered, wary of the other men, and no one could say what passed between the two as they turned together, whether a confession, or a story, or an apology. Someone claimed to have heard the doctor repeat *she is safe*, three times, but the man who heard this received regular visits from his deceased in-laws, and no longer trusted his senses. What all heard, what all remembered, was the fingerless man leaning back in the doctor's arms, lifting his face, and laughing, a sound none had heard in many days, his cheeks wet as he roared a name—*Havaa, Havaa, Havaa*—and those who witnessed would remember how here, in Pit B, a man who had lost his freedom and his fingers, and would soon lose his life, had found in that name an immense, spinning joy.

IN WRITING THIS novel I drew from the following sources, all of which I would urge anyone interested in Chechnya or modern Russia to read.

To get a glimpse into the day-to-day life of a wartime Chechen surgeon, I relied on Khassan Baiev's magnificent memoir, *The Oath: A Surgeon Under Fire*. Anna Politkovskaya's haunting, harrowing *A Small Corner of Hell: Dispatches from Chechnya* was always in arm's reach, and I have included several of her anecdotes in altered forms. Baiev and Politkovskaya are two of the few heroes of the Chechen conflict, and their writing is essential and courageous testimony.

For descriptions of and insights into wartime Grozny, the deportations, and the Caucasian petroleum industry, I turned to *The Angel of Grozny: Orphans of a Forgotten War* by Åsne Seierstad and *Allah's Mountains: The Battle for Chechnya* by Sebastian Smith. In chapter 12, a number of the descriptions of Chechnya between the collapse of the Soviet Union and the First Chechen War are drawn from Smith's journalism; additionally, Sonja's attempt to re-create for Akhmed the ruined Grozny square is based on Smith's account of a Chechen woman doing the same for him. Both Smith and Seierstad have spent extensive time reporting from Chechnya, and together their books form a panorama of the past two decades in the Northern Caucasus.

In writing the *zachistka* I drew from Andrew Meier's description of the Aldy *zachistka* in his vast and powerful *Black Earth: A Journey Through Russia After the Fall*. While researching his book, Meier traveled from Chechnya to the Arctic, from the Pacific Ocean to the Gulf of Finland,

and has created the most encompassing single-volume account of post-Soviet Russia that I've yet read.

For Natasha's journey through the Breaking Grounds and into Western Europe, I turned to *The Natashas: Inside the New Global Sex Trade* by Victor Malarek and *Sex Trafficking: The Global Market in Women and Children* by Kathryn Farr. *One Soldier's War* by Arkady Babchenko, *Towers of Stone: The Battle of Wills in Chechnya* by Wojciech Jagielski, *The Chechens: A Handbook* by Amjad Jaimoukha, and *I Am a Chechen!* by German Sadulaev provided valuable historical and cultural context. Joseph Barnard Davis and his 1,474 skulls come from *Human Remains: Dissection and Its Histories* by Helen MacDonald. I owe debts of influence and inspiration to the body of fiction dealing with political disappearances, particularly Daniel Alarcón's *Lost City Radio* and Michael Ondaatje's *Anil's Ghost*—both novels include scenes of artists summoning images of the missing, which inspired Akhmed's portraits. Sonja's scene with Ula owes a debt to "Old Boys, Old Girls" by Edward P. Jones. The axis on which this novel rests is formed from two narratives shared by Islamic and Christian traditions—that of a parent asked to sacrifice a child, and that of an orphan delivered into the family responsible for her orphanhood—and in thinking of these, I'm grateful for N. J. Dawood's elegant translation of the Koran and *The New Oxford Annotated Bible*. Finally, *Hadji Murád*, the last and among the most powerful of Tolstoy's novels, appears in a beautiful translation by Richard Pevear and Larissa Volokhonsky in *The Death of Ivan Ilyich and Other Stories*.

ACKNOWLEDGMENTS

MY GRATITUDE TO the Stanford Creative Writing Program, the Iowa Writers' Workshop, the Truman Capote Literary Trust, and the Patricia Rowe Willrich Fellowship for supporting this novel, and to the Bread Loaf Writers' Conference and the Sun Valley Writers' Conference for their votes of confidence.

This book couldn't have found a more phenomenal editor and advocate than Lindsay Sagnette. My thanks to her, Becky Hardie in the UK, Anne Collins in Canada, Molly Stern, Christine Kopprasch, Rachel Rokicki, and everyone else at Crown. I'm grateful to Tom Jenks, Carol Edgarian, and Josh Clark at Narrative magazine, where Sonja, Akhmed, and Havaa first appeared, and to Olga Zilberbourg, for fielding my many Russian-related questions. And a big thanks to Austin Ratner and Christina Minami, brilliant novelists and physicians both, for pointing out my many medical inaccuracies.

Chechnya has been utterly transformed in the past decade, in large part due to the efforts of a younger generation determined to rebuild the republic. My thanks to those whose help and hospitality made my travels in Chechnya possible. All these pages aren't enough to convey my appreciation and respect.

At Stanford, I'm grateful for the support and feedback of Eavan Boland, Adam Johnson, Elizabeth Tallent, Tobias Wolff, and the Stegner Workshop that graciously read long pieces of this novel: Josh Foster, Helen Hooper, David Kim, Dana Kletter, Justin Perry, Shannon Pufahl, Nina Schloesser, Justin Torres, Juliana Xuan Wang. And at Iowa: Erika Jo Brown, Scott Butterfield, Ethan Canin, Andres Carlstein, Lan

Samantha Chang, Patrick Haas, Michelle Huneven, Allan Gurganus, Alexander Maksik, and Elizabeth McCracken. Jay Muranaka for his friendship. Christina Ablaza, Connie Brothers, Krystal Griffiths, Deb West, and Jan Zenisek for having the answer to just about everything.

To my family, my friends from D.C., and people who still know me as Hal: thank you.

Peter Orner, my thesis advisor, was the third person to read this novel.

Janet Silver, whose insight and generosity is felt on every page, was the second person.

M. was first.

# A Constellation
of Vital Phenomena

# A Reader's Guide

Garnering rave reviews coast-to-coast, *A Constellation of Vital Phenomena* is an unforgettable debut novel that deftly explores the human cost of war—and the healing power of hope. In this haunting masterwork, award-winning author Anthony Marra transports us to a snow-covered village in Chechnya. It is 2004, and an eight-year-old girl has just watched Russian soldiers abduct her father and set fire to her house in the middle of the night. Accused of aiding Chechen rebels, her father has suffered the brutality of the Feds before. Fearing the worst, their lifelong neighbor Akhmed rescues the girl and seeks refuge at the bombed-out hospital run by Sonja, a brilliant but tough-as-nails female surgeon. Resistant at first, the doctor soon discovers that her new visitors may hold the key to finding her missing sister. Over the course of five extraordinary days, their worlds will unravel in unimaginable ways, culminating in a breathtaking, ultimately affirming turn of fate.

This guide is designed to enrich your discussion of *A Constellation of Vital Phenomena*. We hope that the following questions will enhance your reading group's discussion of this stirring meditation on loss and redemption.

## Questions and Topics for Discussion

1. Before reading *A Constellation of Vital Phenomena,* how much did you know about Chechnya? Which of the novel's cultural details surprised you the most? What can fiction reveal about history that a memoir or history book cannot?

2. How did your image of Akhmed shift throughout the chapters? Despite his many weaknesses, how does he become a source of strength for the loved ones in his life? How does his art restore the humanity around him?

3. Why is Sonja able to remain clear-eyed and resilient? What does she teach Havaa about being a woman, and about the limits of being a healer?

4. Discuss the betrayals that drive the storyline. Would you become an informant if your life depended on it? Can suspicion and corruption ever rise to a level that makes loyalty impossible?

5. What is Dokka's greatest vulnerability? What do his daughter's memories of him say about his hopes and fears?

6. Discuss the title (in chapter 24, Sonja stumbles across it in a Russian medical dictionary's definition of life). What is phenomenal about the life force and the body's intricate capabilities?

7. What is Khassan's key to survival? Is his image of homeland and heritage accurate?

8. What is the effect of the timeline, encompassing five days in 2004 and flashbacks from a decade earlier? How does this approach echo the reality of memory and longing?

9. What does it mean for Sonja and Natasha to be ethnically Russian? When is this an advantage, and when is it a disadvantage? How are cultural identities shaped in the

midst of political, military, economic, and religious power struggles?

10. What accounts for the very different fates of Natasha and Sonja? Is Natasha's beauty an asset or a liability?

11. How is the concept of family—from the sisters' relationship to Akhmed's marriage to Ula—transformed in a land of warlords?

12. In his review for the *Washington Post*, Ron Charles describes the novel as "a flash in the heavens that makes you look up and believe in miracles." Discuss the book's closing lines in that context. What does *A Constellation of Vital Phenomena* ultimately say about anguish and joy?

*Guide written by Amy Clements*

# A Conversation with Anthony Marra

**Q. Why write about Chechnya?**
A. I first became interested in the region as a college student in St. Petersburg. I arrived to Petersburg shortly after the journalist Anna Politkovskaya was assassinated, presumably for the reporting she did from Chechnya. I realized that Chechnya was a place I didn't know how to spell and couldn't find on a map, but the ramifications of the wars there had reached as far north as Petersburg, where on a daily basis I saw Russian veterans soliciting for alms in the Metro stations. I began reading nonfiction accounts of Chechnya and quickly became fascinated. Its history and culture has inspired writers like Tolstoy, Lermontov, and Pushkin. The accounts I read of ordinary people in remarkable situations were the kinds of stories that I felt needed to be brought to life through fiction.

But to answer the question of why set a novel in Chechnya, my answer would be that it is a setting that magnifies and dramatizes the moral conflicts of characters in extraordinary ways. This cast of characters wants what we all want—to live peacefully and provide for our loved ones—but their circumstances require them to make decisions the reader will hopefully never have to make, but nonetheless will understand.

**Q. Readers and reviewers have commented on the beauty of the language in this novel. Can you talk a little about how you wrote it?**

A. I ended up writing four first-to-last-word drafts. Each time I finished a new draft, I'd print it out, set it in front of my keyboard, and retype the entire novel. Because retyping mimics the original act of creation, it taps into whatever creative well the sentences first rose from. The novel changed from draft to draft, then, from within, organically, rather than from changes that were superimposed on it. There's a scene early on when Khassan despairs as he realizes that he must again retype his 3,000-plus page history. Thankfully, *Constellation* isn't nearly that long, but I still knew exactly how he felt.

I also kept a daily word-count record. My goal was to hit a thousand words every day. The days when I recorded zero words felt like wasted days. I grew up going to church and Sunday school each week, and at long last, I was able to put that Catholic guilt to good use.

**Q. The novel has some dark moments, but at the same time, it's filled with moments of humor and hope. How, and why, did you blend instances of death and loss with levity?**

A. I once heard Allan Gurganus say that writers should strive to make readers laugh and cry on every page. It's a tall order, but I absolutely agree with the reasoning. Novels need the high as well as the low notes in order to be true to the emotional reality of life. When I traveled to Chechnya, I was repeatedly surprised by the jokes I heard people cracking. It was a brand of dark, fatalistic humor imprinted with the absurdity that has become normalized there over the past two decades.

A book I thought of while writing *Constellation* was *City of Thieves* by David Benioff. Benioff's novel pays tribute to the immense suffering caused by the Siege of Leningrad, but it's filled to the brim with life, love, humor, even joy, all of which only enhance and make more real the underlying historical tragedy. Hopefully, *Constellation* works in a similar fashion.

**Q. Your writing style is unique in that you move back and forth between the present and the past. Was that a conscious choice?**
A. War breaks cities, buildings, and families, but also time and the way stories are constructed. To tell this story in a straightforward, linear fashion would fall short of capturing the absurd, recursive manner in which its characters assemble their chaotic narrative. All the characters in *Constellation* are trying to piece back together their fragmented lives, and I wanted to embody that in the novel's structure. As each character attempts to rescue what has been lost, the novel mends their individual stories into a communal whole.

**Q. What has been the greatest influence on your writing?**
A. My mom has six siblings and my dad has four sisters, and between them all there are more cousins than I can count, which means that family events have always been filled with voices, stories, and laughter. From an early age I learned from them that stories are how we understand one another, how we preserve the past, and how we make meaning from the chaos of our lives.

# Recommended Reading:
## *Far-Flung Fiction*

*State of Wonder* by Ann Patchett (Brazil). A perfectly constructed and beautifully told story of ambition and loss in the Amazon.

*The God of Small Things* by Arundhati Roy (India). Roy invents a peculiar and dazzling poetry to tell a story of twins in southern India.

*The Orphan Master's Son* by Adam Johnson (North Korea). In a feat of imagination, research, and empathy, Adam Johnson takes the reader into the dark heart of the North Korean ruling class.

*We Need New Names* by NoViolet Bulawayo (Zimbabwe). Bulawayo tells the story of a Zimbabwean childhood in language that sizzles with energy.

*Brief Encounters with Che Guevara* by Ben Fountain (Haiti, Colombia, Myanmar, Sierra Leone). A collection of short stories, each of which packs the punch of a four-hundred-page novel. By turns comic and tragic, these stories are every bit as wonderful as Fountain's brilliant novel *Billy Lynn's Long Halftime Walk*.

*The Vagrants* by Yiyun Li (China). Li's novel presents a bleak portrait of life in provincial China through a wide range of characters.

*The Feast of the Goat* by Mario Vargas Llosa (Dominican Republic). A harrowing and meticulously orchestrated look at the assassination of Dominican dictator Rafael Trujillo and its aftermath.

*The Sound of the Mountain* by Yasunari Kawabata (Japan). In spare, evocative language, Kawabata captures the rhythms of family life in postwar Tokyo.

*To the End of the Land* by David Grossman (Israel). A mother begins walking when her son goes to war, resulting in a novel that is glacier-like in size, pace, and ultimate power.

*I Served the King of England* by Bohumil Hrabal (Czechoslovakia). Hrabal, an unjustly under-read novelist, takes the reader on a trip through twentieth-century Czech history with the often hilarious story of a hotel waiter.

For additional
Extra Libris content and more
on your favorite authors and books, visit

**ReadItForward.com.**

Discover fabulous book giveaways,
sneak peeks at great reads, downloadable
reader's guides, and behind-the-scenes
insights from authors, editors,
booksellers & more.